DIRECT DESCENDANT

DIRECT DESCENDANT

TANYA HUFF

DAW BOOKS
New York

Jacket design by Faceout Studio, Jeff Miller

Book design by Fine Design

Edited by Navah Wolfe

DAW Book Collectors No. 1979

DAW Books
An imprint of Astra Publishing House
dawbooks.com
DAW Books and its logo are registered trademarks of Astra Publishing House

Printed in the United States of America

Library of Congress Cataloging-in-Publication Data

Names: Huff, Tanya, author.
Title: Direct descendant / Tanya Huff.
Description: First edition. | New York : DAW Books, 2025. |
Series: DAW book collectors ; no. 1979
Identifiers: LCCN 2024053361 (print) | LCCN 2024053362 (ebook) |
ISBN 9780756419660 (hardcover) | ISBN 9780756419677 (ebook)
Subjects: LCGFT: Horror fiction. | Romance fiction. | Fantasy fiction. | Novels.
Classification: LCC PR9199.3.H7565 D57 2025 (print) |
LCC PR9199.3.H7565 (ebook) | DDC 813/.6--dc23/eng/20241118
LC record available at https://lccn.loc.gov/2024053361
LC ebook record available at https://lccn.loc.gov/2024053362

First edition: April 2025
10 9 8 7 6 5 4 3 2 1

*For Sheila Gilbert and the millions of words
shared for almost forty years.*

ONE

Cassie

The path from the lake to the lookout was steeper than I remembered and more overgrown than I'd anticipated, but that extra half hour of sleep had left me no other options. Slapping predawn mosquitoes and squinting up at steeply angled chunks of the Canadian Shield, I reluctantly admitted it might not have been the best idea to have taken advantage of having a solo and therefore unsupervised responsibility.

Nothing to do now but gird my loins and climb.

I clutched at a protruding root and hauled my ass another meter up the path, while buckthorn snagged my clothes and dug painful lines into my skin. Paused my upward progress to rip my hair free. Paused it again to yank my foot out from between two rocks. A little more light would have helped, but the whole point of the exercise was to beat the midsummer sunrise to the top of the hill.

One foot, hand, elbow, and other assorted body parts in front of the other, I kept climbing. I was not going to fail, not when the other Three had finally begun to take me seriously. Of course, not failing would have been easier had I not decided to sleep in. Contradictions are us. Well, me.

The sky had lightened, but the sun hadn't quite risen above the horizon when I heaved myself up ónto the top of the cliff. Before I could either congratulate myself or catch my breath, I realized I wasn't alone. There was a stranger already standing on the lookout.

No, not on the lookout. That would imply he stood on the rock that bulged out over the lake. He was standing on the Dead Ground, the misshapen circle of dirt between the rock and the trees where Charlie had died back in the 1920s, where nothing grew. Not only was he standing on the Dead Ground, he was standing in the center of the Dead Ground, wearing a sheet and holding a knife, and that never ended well.

Sweat stinging in a multitude of acquired scratches, I staggered forward and bounced off an invisible barrier hard enough my faceprint hovered in the air for a moment as I stumbled back.

The stranger smiled at me over a scruffy blond hipster beard. A smug *I've got a secret* smile that made me want to kick him off the cliff and into the lake. Close to a foot taller than my five feet five inches, he was wiry rather than skinny, and I could see a lot of wiry, given the way he'd draped the sheet. He had enough muscle that even without the barrier, I wouldn't have been able to physically move him if he didn't want to be moved.

If he thought I was going to let him make me look like an idiot, he could think again. I also had a secret.

As I opened my mouth, three things happened. One, the sun rose. Two, the stranger dropped to one knee and slammed the knife through his right foot into the ground. And three, before he could scream— and he definitely looked like he intended to scream—he disappeared, sucked down into the dirt, leaving his sheet and bloodstained knife behind.

I stretched out a careful hand. The barrier had also disappeared.

Heart pounding, I twisted around and checked the lake to see sunlight sparkling on calm water. I released a long, thankful breath.

Signs indicated that whatever the stranger had intended, it wasn't the imminent destruction of the immediate area. I could toss the sheet and the knife off the cliff, watch them sink, and pretend the whole thing hadn't happened.

I could.

But instead, I put on my big-girl pants and texted for reinforcements.

———

"I was not late!"

Standing as far from the edge of the cliff as he could get and still remain out of the woods, Eric spread his arms wide, golf shirt rising and falling over the kind of gym muscle that said *I'm past forty and fighting it.* "He got there before you, Cassie. That's what *late* means."

"Does it?" I paced along the edge of the lookout, a small part of me knowing I did it to show up Eric, who was afraid of the drop. "He could have been waiting up here for weeks, for all we know. How much earlier was I supposed to be?" I continued before Eric could speak. "Minutes? Hours? Days?"

"Not days," Bridget said thoughtfully. "I came up to see Jeffrey on Tuesday; I'm sure he'd have told me about a man in a sheet." Eric had been hanging around Bridget when he got my text, and she'd come with him up from the House. While the rest of us saw Jeffrey as our newest Guardian and obviously able to do the job, he'd always be her little brother, and she'd wanted to check on him. Caught up in a May/December—or to be fair, May/November or October—infatuation, Eric had been unwilling to stop her. In all honesty, I'd been glad to see her. Although no smarter than your average orange cat, Bridget was one of the nicest people I knew, in spite of her professional belief as a personal trainer that I needed to get more exercise. We were friends because Bridget saw everyone as a friend and because, as a red-blooded

Canadian lesbian, I was not going to discourage even the entirely straight and platonic attention of someone so astoundingly beautiful. Here and now, she'd act as a buffer between Eric and I. It wasn't that Eric and I didn't get along; it was that Eric could be an ass, and while I had to work with him, Bridget didn't.

"If there was a man in a sheet," Eric mused, arms folded, tapping his lip like a particularly annoying British detective, "shouldn't Jeffrey have dealt with him?"

"If?" I began.

Bridget cut me off. "Take that back!" She stepped into Eric's space and poked him in the chest with one shiny, pink-tipped finger. "Jeffrey's new. He's still learning. And the man in the sheet wasn't an anything until Cassie was already here."

Actually, he'd probably been a something the moment he activated the barrier, but he could have waited to do that until he saw me.

Eric made a grab for her finger and missed. "If he was peckish . . ."

"Peckish!" She poked him again. Hard. I was enjoying this. "Jeffrey is a vegan!"

"Oh, sweetheart, your little brother . . ."

Fortunately for Eric, who seemed determined to shove his foot further into his mouth, the roar of Great-Aunt Jean cresting the hill on an ATV cut him off. Although the groomed path up from the House rose at a gentle angle, at ninety-two, Aunt Jean would have found the climb impossible. That said, I had no doubt that borrowing the ATV had been at least fifty percent about making an entrance. We watched as she untangled her cane from between her legs, wincing in unison as one of the tennis balls jammed onto the four-tip base snagged on a plastic sandal strap. Bridget moved to help, caught a look, and retreated.

"Did you touch anything?" Aunt Jean demanded, the moment she was on her feet. "Any of you?" After we'd all assured her we hadn't, she took her glasses off, carefully folded them, and dropped them to dangle against her blouse on the ends of a mint-green crocheted cord. "Cassidy, I found your text unclear; you should've called." Her sweet-old-lady voice sounded disappointed. Her sweet-old-lady voice was a scam; she was hard as nails. "Can you remember if the barrier was inside or outside the perimeter of the Dead Ground?"

I smacked at a mosquito and thought for a moment. "A couple of centimeters inside, Aunt Jean."

She wiped her nose on a tissue she stuffed back in behind the waistband of her light blue polyester pants, and began to slowly circle the patch of bare dirt, her gaze locked on the ground. "I can't See anything," she complained after her third time around, lifting the cane so that its four filthy tennis balls pointed at me. "Are you certain you saw what you said you saw?"

A bit hard to mistake a strange man in a sheet stabbing himself through the foot and disappearing, but that wasn't something you said to Great-Aunt Jean unless you had time for a lecture. "I'm certain," I said instead. "And Bridget found his clothes under a bush." I pointed at the T-shirt, shorts, and running shoes. "He'd dressed so he could say he was out for a run if he was seen. The shorts have that built-in underwear."

Aunt Jean slipped her glasses back on and sighed. "Why do you care about his underwear, Cassie?"

"Well, if he wasn't wearing any . . ." I realized I had no idea where I was going with that and stopped talking.

"And why is Bridget here?"

"Jeffrey," I said quickly. "If he gets upset, he'll get in the way."

Eyes narrowed, she swept her gaze along the tree line. "Is he still hanging about? Fine, then, Bridget can stay."

Bridget shot me a grateful smile.

"Can we return to the pre-underwear discussion?" Eric asked. "If he came up the path from the House, he had to have gotten here earlier than the first arrivals. I checked with security; the first car arrived in the park at four. Of course," he added while I reflected on how the stupidly enthusiastic ruined it for those of us who preferred to sleep in, "there's a chance he could have slipped by when security was distracted by the crowd."

"Security watches the House, not the path," Aunt Jean pointed out.

"I like to run at night," Bridget said. We all turned to look at her and she smiled, the queen of the almost non-sequitur, only just having caught up to my observation about the stranger's clothes. "It's cooler than in the daytime, and it's like you're in your own little world. Once, I jumped over a skunk. I didn't see it until the last minute. The poor thing was terrified. If Cassie's stranger went for a run early this morning, it would have been cooler then, too."

"Did you see the intruder while you were out running?" Aunt Jean's gaze locked on Bridget's face. "Is that what you're saying?"

Bridget shook her head. "Oh, no, I didn't run last night because I had to be up so early this morning, and I didn't run this morning because I was at the House. I'll probably run tonight, though. I know running isn't for everyone, and I seldom recommend it for my clients, but I enjoy it, and I think you should do the things you enjoy. Don't you? You'd probably enjoy some gentle yoga."

After a long moment, Aunt Jean sighed and said, "No, I wouldn't." Then she kept talking before Bridget could politely press the issue. "I'll stop by the bookstore later and ask Alyx to have a look. If there's a lingering signature in a different tradition, her coven might be able to spot it. Now, then . . ."

Carefully not meeting her gaze, Eric stepped in front of her before she could enter the circle. "Watch yourself. Just because the barrier's gone, that doesn't mean it's safe."

She waggled her head sideways, in a *you might be right* kind of motion, put her hand flat on Eric's chest, and shoved him hard enough, he took a single backward step across the invisible line. "Looks fine to me," she said, walking past him. "Out now, please."

Glasses off again, she circled the sheet and the knife three times. Not because three had any kind of metaphysical significance; Aunt Jean liked to be thorough.

"I can See where the blood and the blade went into the ground. Doesn't Look any different than the rest of the dirt." She slammed her cane down hard enough that dust kicked up around the tennis balls. Eric frowned. I held my breath. Bridget watched a butterfly. Nothing happened. "Given the disappearance, my best guess is he built a manufactured gate into the darkness using the lingering residue of Charlie's death. The lingering residue of a Guardian's death. Anyone want to argue?" She glanced around. Eric opened his mouth. "No? Good. Right, then, now for the lake."

"I looked, Aunt Jean." I gestured toward the water. "Totally calm."

"You looked, Cassie. I didn't."

She gripped the crook of my elbow with cold old-lady fingers, and I escorted her out to the edge of the rock. I glanced back when I heard Bridget muffle a giggle and saw Eric making exaggerated *push her over the edge* motions. He looked thrilled to have made her laugh. Based on the way Aunt Jean dug her fingers into my abraded flesh, Eric was risking a lot for . . . well, as sad and pathetic as it was, let's call it love.

The western shore of Lake Argen gleamed, bathed in the light of the rising sun. The trees to the east painted dark lines across silvered water. A gentle wave rolled north. Alice was awake, but she wasn't upset.

"I See calm." Aunt Jean snorted. "Calm. That's a little anticlimactic, isn't it?"

She wasn't wrong, I acknowledged silently as we shuffled around together until we were facing the other two again.

"I See runes on the knife, but I don't recognize them." She frowned. "And the sheet is from the Lake Argen Motel."

"You can See that?" Bridget's eyes widened.

"The name is stamped on the selvage edge." Pulling a clean tissue out of wherever old ladies kept their endless supply, she swiped at her glasses and put them back on. "What did your stranger look like, Cassie?"

"He wasn't my stranger, Aunt Jean."

"The Dead Ground and the weakness between realities that it represents was your responsibility this morning, so he's your stranger until someone else claims him."

"That's not fair."

"And you're not twelve. What did he look like?"

I opened my mouth to argue, saw Eric settling in to enjoy himself, and closed it again. "Early twenties, maybe," I muttered, after a moment's thought. "Young, but not a teenager. He looked like those pictures of smug, white-boy Jesus you see all over the internet."

"Was he holding a lamb?" Bridget asked.

"No."

She sighed. "That's too bad."

"Because Jeffrey would love to sprinkle a little mint sauce on a la . . . AH!"

Bridget's hiking books had pink laces and might have had steel toes, given the way Eric was hopping around, clutching his ankle. She was very protective of her little brother.

Ignoring them, Aunt Jean frowned in my general direction. "You're bleeding."

Shorts and a tank top, although closest to hand when I finally hauled butt out of bed, might not have been the smartest thing to wear. "Ran into some buckthorn," I told her.

"Did you come up the path from the lake?" She clicked her tongue. "Left home a little late, did you? You're lucky you got through. When I watch the Dead Ground, I always get here at least half an hour early."

"That might have been early enough to stop him," Eric pointed out.

I leaned around Aunt Jean and flipped him off.

She clicked her tongue. "Honestly, you young people need to learn to manage your time."

———

". . . and then he disappeared. But I was at the top of the hill, at the Dead Ground, before sunrise." All things considered, I wanted that last point remembered.

Amanda reached over and patted my arm. "Of course you were there on time, Cassie. There's no need to be so defensive."

It was always hard to tell if Amanda, who'd been a kindergarten teacher for over twenty years, was being honestly sweet or slightly patronizing. This morning, having endured Aunt Jean shouting criticism over the sound of the ATV as Eric and I followed her down the path to the House, I was going with the latter.

We'd left Bridget at the top of the hill waiting for Jeffrey to join her. Should the stranger suddenly reappear where he'd disappeared, she was positive Jeffrey could handle him. Should he emerge through the cellar door like everything else, security was already in place.

People who'd shown up bright and early to be part of the frontline defense should there actually be trouble at midsummer for the first time in the town's history had left by the time Aunt Jean had led us down to the House. The sun was up, they'd done their duty by tradition, they wanted breakfast. Only Amanda, the last of the Four, had remained, keeping an eye on the cellar door, and waiting to be filled in.

"Interesting that there was so little to be Seen," she mused, filling an ancient Melmac mug from her enormous thermos and passing it to me.

"I said I Saw nothing, Amanda." Aunt Jean adroitly avoided Amanda's attempt to pour milk into her black coffee. "The word *little* implies I saw *something*. I did not."

Amanda passed the faded plastic yogurt tub full of sugar to Eric. "He drove a knife through his foot. I find the absence of screaming impressive."

"But was it relevant?" Aunt Jean dunked an off-brand cookie into her mug and frowned as the lower half dissolved.

"He may not have had time to scream," I pointed out, perching on the edge of the locked cellar door, one foot braced on the ground because of both the angle and the hour. Sure, the sun had been up for a while—and I'd *been there* on top of the hill when it happened—but according to my phone, it was still only 6:20 AM. A red dot appeared next to my hip. "It happened really fast," I added, tossing a salute in the general direction of its source. "Stab. Gone. He's likely screaming the walls down wherever he ended up."

"*Men* don't scream." Knees wide, Eric dominated one of Amanda's plastic lawn chairs.

"Of course not, dear," Aunt Jean murmured sarcastically before I could respond. "We need to find out who this boy is."

"Was," Eric snorted.

"Is," Aunt Jean repeated. "A knife through the foot certainly wouldn't kill him. It wasn't that kind of a sacrifice." Eric twitched at the s-word; given our origin story, it was the most likely word to catch the attention of any errant power. We'd learned, over the years, that it was easier to be careful than it was to plug the leaks. I swallowed the last of my coffee and cleared my throat, just in case. We waited. Nothing happened.

Amanda sighed. "Jean, he disappeared into the Dead Ground . . ."

She glanced at me. I nodded and made a sucked-into-the-ground motion with one hand.

". . . so, as the Dead Ground is an acknowledged weak point," she continued, "he's entered the darkness. He's dead."

Aunt Jean sniffed. "We don't know that. He was alive when he disappeared."

Her turn to glance at me. I nodded again.

"Being alive when he disappeared and staying alive in the darkness are two entirely different things," Eric pointed out. "Unless you think he has power that will allow him to survive."

"I *know* he has power, and so would you if you thought about it for a moment," Aunt Jean told him. "He knew about the Dead Ground. That means he was able to overcome the town's protections. And he was able to sacrifice himself."

During this pause, I almost thought I felt something slide across the other side of the cellar door, one elderly slab of wood between it and my ass. I did not leap up. I stood at a perfectly normal speed and went to refill my mug.

"Neither point means he can survive the darkness." Eric tossed me his empty mug. I poured the last of the coffee into it and handed it back, overcoming the temptation to toss it. "Has anyone *ever* survived the darkness?"

"Has anyone ever gone into the darkness?" I asked. "No one's mentioned it in the Journals."

Aunt Jean opened her mouth and closed it again. Amanda looked at Eric. Eric shrugged. I had another cookie. It tasted like triumph, albeit crappy processed triumph.

"Given that Alice hasn't reacted," I said, brushing crumbs off my tank top, "maybe the power is in the dagger, and since we have the dagger, we're in no danger."

"I Saw runes on the blade," Aunt Jean announced.

It took effort, but I managed to keep from rolling my eyes. We'd all seen runes on the blade.

"Amanda." Aunt Jean pointed at her, as though we didn't know who Amanda was. "Just to be safe, you'll need to be the one to retrieve the sheet and the knife from the hilltop. Take them both to the library for Janet to research."

As the Hands of the Dark, Amanda could touch what she wanted—fire, acid, sharp edges, fruitcake. In the Journal entry for the day she was Chosen, Eric made a suggestive comment about touching, the kind her predecessor had appreciated. She'd ripped the door off his car. I wish I'd been there . . . although the strength thing? That made no sense. Hands gripped, they didn't lift, but as I hadn't been around to be consulted way back when the Dark was handing out body parts, I kept my opinion about the Knees, Back, and Shoulders of the Dark to myself.

"Shouldn't we take the sheet back to the motel?" I asked around a yawn.

"No. If Arthur gives you a hard time . . . more than the usual hard time," she amended, "tell him to call me."

It took a moment—and Eric's most obnoxious grin—before I connected the dots. "Why do I have to talk to him?"

"You're the youngest." Amanda tossed me the last cookie. "The youngest always gets the shit jobs."

Aunt Jean was the oldest by a considerable margin and, more importantly, had been the Eyes of the Dark for a long time. To those under seventy, she'd always been the Eyes. Eric had inherited the Ears at thirty-one, so eleven years against Amanda's eight years and a bit of being the Hands. I'd only been the Mouth for eighteen months, making me, at twenty-eight, younger in the job than the fifty-one-year-old Amanda by about six years. Simon, the last Voice, had been the Voice for a little *less* than eighteen months. He'd Talked a lot, drunk more, and had gotten drunk enough he forgot the drone loaders at the silver mine that gave Argen, town and lake, its name, couldn't actually hear him.

My first Words had been a quietly muttered *SO STUPID*.

Since even Amanda had found Simon impossible to deal with, and

Amanda had spent her working life dealing with the occasional five-year-old who hadn't been properly toilet-trained, Eric might have actually been right when he said, *"Sometimes, big D likes to test us."*

Well, not right about the whole *big D* thing. That was just wrong.

Aunt Jean heaved herself up onto her feet. "Amanda, you should go with her."

"Oh, come on!"

Amanda's expression echoed my protest. "She'll be fine."

"Like she was this morning?"

"Hey!"

"Hay is for horses, Cassidy Prewitt." Aunt Jean stared at me for a long moment. Finally, she sighed. "Fine. Go. Tell Arthur."

"Tell him what?" I spread my hands. "That I found his sheet on the Dead Ground? Just lying there? Surprise, it's a sheet?"

Aunt Jean sighed again. It was her I-don't-know-why-I-bother sigh. "You tell him everything and you Tell him nothing. He won't share information about your stranger without knowing why you want it, and we won't know what to think of this nonsense until we know more about the stranger."

"Post hoc, ergo propter hoc," Eric said smugly.

As I had no intention of asking what that meant, I ignored him. "So, it's okay if everyone knows?"

"Did I say *tell everyone*?" Aunt Jean demanded. "No. I did not. We don't want to start a panic."

"It's not like Arthur'll chat about it to all his friends," Amanda pointed out.

━━━

The Lake Argen Motel, besides being unimaginatively named, was a middle-American stereotype five hundred and half a kilometer north of the Canada/US border. It was a single-story building with the motel office at one end of fifteen dark-grey doors that opened into the gravel parking lot. A plastic pot of coral-colored geraniums stood guard on one side of the office door, and a tall, handmade, empty metal ashtray guarded the other. As far as I could remember, the orange neon sign had always said *VACAN Y.*

Arthur Nollen was an incomer. Short, thin, with hands a little too big for his body, I'd never seen him in anything except worn cords and ratty sweaters. His eyes were a little too close together, his nose looked like it had been flattened in a fight, his mouth was almost wide enough to be creepy to someone who'd watched *Mr. Sardonicus* at a ninth-birthday sleepover, and he had great hair. Thick chestnut waves that gleamed in the sun and raised the entirely understandable question: Could they be as soft and silky as they looked?

No one knew.

Arthur did not like people. At all. His motel was not a welcoming refuge at the end of a long drive; it was a reasonably clean room with a door that locked, and if you didn't like his attitude, feel free to move on.

Or as Arthur would say, "Fuck you either way."

Half a dozen cats adored him, and the Dark had allowed him to put down roots just inside the southeast boundary, so as far as the town was concerned, that was that.

Any other morning, I'd have ridden my bike the short distance out to the motel rather than burn irreplaceable fossil fuels, but this had not been a good morning, so I'd gone home for my car.

Arthur's ancient beater shared the parking lot with a brand-new king-cab pickup, jacked so high I had to go up onto my toes to see into it. The dashboard didn't so much have all the bells and whistles as a full orchestra, and the black leather passenger seat had been left piled high with fast-food wrappers, empty takeout cups, and an open box of Canadian biscotti—Timbits, double-baked in the hot, closed cab.

The motel office was empty except for a fat orange tabby asleep in a patch of sunlight on the counter beside a sign that said, *THERE IS NO FUCKING WIFI PASSWORD.* I gave joining the cat half a thought, yawned, and hit the bell.

And waited.

And waited.

When my friends and I were kids, we'd ride out to the motel on our bikes and then spray gravel in the parking lot until Arthur charged out, shaking his fist and screaming at us. He could spit out a curse faster than anyone we knew. Older and wiser, I was not going to hit the bell a second time.

Eventually, the door behind the counter opened, allowing me a glimpse of a crowded living room. Three tabbies sat on the overstuffed couch, watching what sounded like a cooking show. I couldn't see the television.

"What do you want?" Arthur slammed the door behind him.

He'd bought and renovated the motel the year my grandparents were married. Over the intervening years, neither Arthur nor his hair had changed. Because his presence had set off no alarms—actual, metaphorical, metaphysical—we didn't ask questions, no matter how desperately some people wanted to know his brand of conditioner.

As one of the Four, I had a certain amount of social authority—and no idea of what to do if Arthur refused to recognize it. Fortunately, he was so weirdly over-the-top angry about the use of his sheet in the commission of an s-word, the concept of confidentiality abandoned the conversation. Although I honestly couldn't tell if it was the sheet or the s-word he was angry about.

"Travis fucking Brayden," he snarled, stomping out the office and leading the way to room five.

"Is this his truck?"

"Of course it's his truck."

"It's parked in front of seven."

Arthur's scatological opinion of Travis Bayden's inability to park carried on until he got the door open. "He got here yesterday. Paid up until the end of the week."

Here the day before the midsummer solstice, that made sense, but why pay to keep a room until the end of the week? Did he expect something else to happen when he stabbed himself in the foot? Was he not supposed to disappear?

"Good thing I ran his card up front," Arthur continued, cracking his knuckles. "City boy only wanted to pay for last night, but I told him there was a five-day minimum in the high season."

Well, that explained it. "We don't have a high season."

"Dumbass didn't know that, did he? If he's not back by Saturday, I'm burning his crap."

Travis's crap consisted of a duffle bag half full of high-end clothing, a wallet full of credit cards, a driver's license with a Toronto address—he was twenty-two and six-three—thirty-one dollars and sixty-five cents, and a pile of crumpled credit-card receipts tracking his drive north. He'd been using the swampy-smelling "personal" products that came with the room, which may or may not have helped with his decision to s-word himself.

There was a half-eaten bag of chips in the unmade bed, and a damp towel on the bathroom floor.

What there wasn't was a convenient journal detailing why he'd s-worded himself on the Dead Ground at sunrise.

Or a phone.

Amanda was home for the summer, so I texted ahead and the Four of us met on her porch. Mostly because Amanda always had snacks and I was starving.

"Travis Brayden? Of Toronto? No." Aunt Jean shook her head, white curls bobbing. "I've never heard of him."

"Not many people have. His socials are a wasteland. There's a Mother's Day photo of him having brunch in a high-end restaurant with his granny, and nothing since."

"Are they holding hands?" I asked, leaning carefully over Eric's shoulder to peer at his phone.

"Looks more like she's holding his hand. Probably trying to keep him from making a run for it." He shot me a look that was all *wink wink nudge nudge*. "We may have sussed out why he s-worded."

"Do you have to?" I dropped back into my chair.

"Hey, we need a motive. We have a motive."

Amanda dropped lemon slices into glasses of iced tea and passed them around. "The question before us is what do we do now?"

Eric shrugged. "We drive his truck into the lake and let Alice deal with it."

"Can't." I drew a circle in the condensation on my glass. "His loving grandmother will declare him missing, and the authorities will know he used his credit card at the motel."

"So? He came to the motel, he left the motel, and Arthur will tell the authorities to fuck off."

"Language!" Aunt Jean cautioned. "The question we need to consider," she continued, "is do we want Lake Argen to be the last known place the boy was seen before he disappeared, never to be seen again? That's a rhetorical question," she added, smugly spreading cream cheese on a cracker. "We don't want an unsolved mystery. Unsolved mysteries leave far too many inconvenient loose ends. Trust me, I've seen every episode. Unless you want to be dealing with this for years, we need to control the narrative."

"It doesn't have to be complicated." I reached for an early strawberry. "Travis paid for five nights at the motel, so we wait six days, then have Arthur call the Ontario Provincial Police and tell them Travis has disappeared."

"Which is, strictly speaking, the truth," Amanda said thoughtfully.

"And in what way is that not an unsolved mystery?" Eric demanded, looking up from his phone.

"*Boy and truck disappear never to be seen again* is a mystery," Aunt Jean told him acerbically. "*Idiot southerner wanders into the bush and gets lost* is not. It's a familiar narrative. It's a tragedy. It's a shame. It's a waste of our tax dollars having to call out search and rescue; why didn't he stay in the city, where he belonged? He got lost, he was searched for, he couldn't be found—how unfortunate, but it happens. It's many versions of *it's a pity* but it's not a mystery."

"My bad. I thought you meant mystery, not *mystery*." Eric's air quotes around the second mystery were some of the most sarcastic I'd ever seen. Props.

"Amanda's observation that it's also essentially the truth," Aunt Jean continued, ignoring Eric's response, "will make it easier for Cassie to Convince the authorities."

"I don't need it to be easy," I muttered.

"So you say." Aunt Jean spread a little more smug cream cheese.

"What if he comes back?" Amanda asked, fidgeting with a fork. "What if he walks half a kilometer to the cellar and pops up through the crack?"

"You're assuming he's alive." Aunt Jean triumphantly popped cheese and cracker both into her mouth.

"No, I'm not."

We all considered that for a moment.

Aunt Jean swallowed, frowned, and finally said, "Then he's Security's problem. I, personally, find it strange that, as of yet, there's been no repercussions from young Mr. Brayden's foolish sacrifice."

We listened together but only heard the distant burr of a weed-whacker. I glanced at Eric and he shook his head. He hadn't Heard anything.

"It's the *yet* we need to worry about," Amanda pointed out.

"Should we tell the secular authorities?" I asked. "Mayor? Town council?"

Amanda blinked at me. "Why would we do that?" The mayor was Amanda's ex-husband. It hadn't been an amicable parting; she'd taken out two streetlights during the divorce settlement. "The police will fill them in when they show up to look for Travis Brayden."

"The police don't know about the s-word."

"And until the s-word impacts garbage pickup, the secular authorities don't need to know about it."

Eric nodded agreement. Aunt Jean started in on the block of cheddar.

"Well, pardon me for not having the protocols down on this, my first unscheduled s-word."

Aunt Jean pointed a half-eaten sausage at me. "There's no need for sarcasm, Cassie. This is everyone's first unscheduled sacrifice."

The sudden smell of sulfur turned out to be a result of the cheese.

The Acolytes held a scheduled sacrifice every Agreement Day. They chopped the head off a chicken, let it chase a few screaming children around the yard, then prepped it and sent to join its previously, conventionally slaughtered sisters in one of half a dozen huge, cast-iron frying pans. In the evening, before the fireworks, most of the town sat down to fried chicken with all the fixings.

I was in the Acolytes Children's Choir for a few years, and it's kind of amazing how much distance a headless chicken can cover. My mother still donates four big jars of her award-winning bread-and-butter pickles to the feast.

"Found a graduation picture Travis was tagged in from last year," Eric announced suddenly. "No beard, but . . ." He turned the screen toward me.

"That's him. And he's holding a phone." I squinted. The phone matched the truck. Latest model. Stupidly expensive. I wouldn't have paid what they wanted for that space-gold proof of entitlement. "Where is it now?"

"You young people spend too much time on those things," Aunt

Jean muttered. "Mr. Brayden is probably using his to make self-things wherever he ended up after the sacrifice."

Some lingering sulfur. The weed-whacker. And a dog. A normal, this-world dog. We could all tell the difference.

Rattan creaked as Amanda settled back. "Why," she demanded, running her hands back through her hair, "must you keep saying the s-word?"

"I'm old." Aunt Jean shrugged. "My husband's dead and my children are complacent blobs of flesh. Not actual blobs," she added after a moment, in case we were concerned they'd gone through a metamorphosis. It happens. "I'm bored. I'd like a little excitement before I die."

"I'd rather not die with you, so stop it."

"If Travis took the phone with him, he's going to have a shit . . ." Eric paused. Glanced at Aunt Jean's narrowed eyes and reconsidered. ". . . have terrifying roaming charges."

"If he took it with him," Amanda said thoughtfully, "where would he have been carrying it? Cassie?"

I swallowed a little too quickly, coughed cracker crumbs, and said, "Knife in one hand. Nothing in the other. I didn't check his butt crack. Might've been firm enough."

"Got to hand it to a dude who doesn't skip glute day." Eric met my eyes and grinned. "Maybe we'll be a Five when he gets back."

"Glutes of the Dark!" I threw my arms out and nearly knocked a hanging basket of something pink off its hook.

"What are you talking about?" Barely audible over our howls of laughter, Aunt Jean sounded annoyed.

"Glutes are another word for butt cheeks, Jean."

"I'm aware of that, Amanda. What I don't understand is why this Travis Brayden's butt cheeks . . ."

Hearing her sweet-old-lady voice quavering indignantly about butt cheeks set Eric and me, who'd been starting to calm down, off again.

". . . would make us a Five."

"I think a fifth would be very helpful." Amanda's tone was pure kindergarten teacher. "He could toot for the Dark."

We'd all gotten up stupidly early and I, at least, was a little on edge about the whole *stranger from Toronto comes to town to s-word himself* thing. The sun had visibly changed position by the time we got ourselves under control and realized Aunt Jean had eaten all the rest of the cheese.

And I was very late for work.

TWO

Cassie

Chris glanced up from hand-kneading raisins into bagel dough as I entered the bakery's back room. "Riding the nepotism train this morning, are we?"

"A scurrilous accusation." I grabbed one of my aprons off the hook, dropped it over my head, wrapped the bootlaces that had replaced the original strings around my waist, and tied them in front. "I'm an independent businesswoman."

"Whose only client are her parents."

"Who are the owners of the diner next door."

"Who are her parents."

"Fair."

Technically, I owned a little over half the bakery. Realistically, it was Chris's. I baked for the diner; he baked for the town. He hired the staff, both in the storefront and to help in the bakery itself. He did the buying. He'd named it Rising and Shine, admittedly very late at night after a lot of vodka, and he made the tiny bit the public saw look pretty. He made a living doing this in a small town because my financial contribution meant he had no debt.

In exchange, I had a butcher-block table, a double industrial oven, access to raw materials, and commentary on my work ethic. Tuesday to Sunday when the diner was open, I made desserts—pies, tarts, fruit squares, the easy stuff. Those diners who still wanted dessert after that was gone had jello or rice pudding. Any leftovers, the staff either took them home or popped them in the freezer.

Chris had been worried about me becoming a Conduit, but today was the first time in a year and a half that my responsibility to the Dark had cut into my baking time.

Like every other Prewitt, I shared in a very profitable silver mine. None of the First Families had to work, but most of us found something—or several sequential somethings—to do that supported the town. That Eric had decided not to work, at all, was just one of the reasons he drove me crazy. The diner barely broke even most years, but my parents liked to feed people, and I liked to bake. Although not as much as Chris, who started breads and bagels at stupid o'clock in the morning.

Chris's great-great-great grandfather had been an incomer back in 1872, post–American civil war, when a number of previously enslaved people were moving their families north. He went farther north than most, having noted in his diary that Lake Argen was the farthest from the border he could find work. His second son married an Abbott, making Chris part of a diagonal bloodline. Chris loved the bakery. He loved the town. He loved his husband and their daughter. I loved their daughter, and had a running battle with Chris's sisters for the title of *fun auntie*.

If there were going to be repercussions from what had happened at the Dead Ground, didn't he deserve a heads-up? Or did he deserve to go on with his life and loving his family without the waiting-for-the-other-shoe-to-drop feeling of dread I was carrying?

"You're quiet this morning." He dropped the proofed bagels into boiling water.

"Doing some thinking."

"Should I brace for disaster? Cass?" He frowned when I turned to face him. "I asked if I should brace for disaster, and you flinched. I'm not really happy about that." Still frowning, he looked me up and down. "Where'd all those scratches come from? You get in another fight with a squirrel?"

The squirrel had totally cheated. "I told you yesterday that I'd be watching the Dead Ground this morning, right?"

"Yeah. And?"

"And I took the lake path up to the lookout."

"Ah. No squirrel." The corners of his mouth twitched. "You decided to sleep in."

"I wasn't late!"

"Did I say you were? And stop muttering at me," he added, going back to his bagels. "So," he said after a moment, drawing the word out. "You going to tell me what happened?"

I added lemon zest to my almost-boiling pot of local rhubarb and stirred it in. I wanted to tell him. I mean, seen a certain way, it was a funny story. Stranger wearing only a stolen sheet. Smacking my face BLAM into an invisible barrier. The big, blue, penis truck.

But people were how rumors started. The more people who knew, the more versions of the story there'd be going around. On the other hand, I also knew how small towns worked, and given that multiple people already knew—the Four of us, Bridget, Jeffrey, Arthur Nollen, who might not have any friends, but he didn't clean his own motel—I'd be hearing s-word 2.0 by tomorrow morning.

Fuck it.

When I finished, Chris stared at me for a long moment, dried his hands on his apron, then opened the door leading out to the storefront. "Kynda! Flip the closed sign and go look at the lake!"

"Why?" Kynda's voice held the despair of every teenager with a summer job being asked to do something they didn't want to.

"Because I sign your paycheck!"

"Capitalism sucks!"

"She's not wrong," I agreed as the front door slammed.

"Yeah, yeah." Chris flicked a raisin at me. "You're suffering."

"You know, I checked the lake."

"Good for you."

"Aunt Jean checked the lake."

"Good for her."

Eventually, Kynda returned to say the lake was calm, the sun was shining, there wasn't a cloud in the sky, and Reggie Morton, in spite of specifically having been told not to, was trying to organize the ravens again.

I had to promise I'd talk to Reggie and rescue the ravens before Kynda would go back to work.

"You could Talk to him," she muttered as she left.

"I'm not that kind of girl," I yelled after her.

The door between the bakery and the storefront wasn't a slamming kind of door. Kynda made the attempt anyway—like she had a hundred times before.

Chris slid two trays of bagels into an oven and said thoughtfully, "An unscheduled s-word should have repercussions."

"Preaching to the choir, dude."

"Has there been an outside opinion?"

"Not a Word from The Dark." I dumped pie pastry out of the mixing bowl onto the worktop. "Could be a good thing. Could be that the s-word attracted no attention at all and Travis Brayden slipped into the darkness like an egg yolk through a separator."

Chris folded his arms.

"Yeah, not my best. Could be . . ." I paused. I hadn't floated this theory to the rest of the Four, but they weren't Chris. "Could be Travis hooked up with Another Dark, shifted the balance of power, and the Dark is too busy putting down a rebellion to stay in touch."

"All that since sunrise? I guess we'll find out if eldritch hordes burst forth from the cellar to destroy the earth."

I pointed a rolling pin at him. "You seem remarkably blasé about that possibility."

"I'm panicking inside."

"Join the club," I sighed.

And that was Tuesday.

———

The next day, Aunt Jean called just as I turned onto Carlyle Street, heading for the bakery. "This is the only morning Mary had free to do a wash and set, so I need you to talk to Alyx and find out what, if anything, she discovered up on the lookout."

"The hairdresser is more important than the possibility of an eldritch horde?"

"Of course. That's why I called you. And who said anything about an eldritch horde?"

Chris. I changed the subject. "If Alyx discovered something and we have to react, shouldn't you know about it?" I shifted to the edge of the sidewalk, out of the way of a group of teenagers amused by my use of a phone as a phone.

"I will know about it, whatever it happens to be, when you tell me what Alyx said. And what," she continued a little sharply, "do you think she'll have discovered?"

"I don't know." One of the teenagers turned around, became a third cousin on my mother's side, and raised a questioning brow. I silently let him know it was all good. Sort of. "Why am I the only one worried about this?"

Aunt Jean huffed out a clearly audible breath. "When you're not speaking for the Dark, you watch your tone, Cassidy Prewitt. Go talk to Alyx. You're already in town, and it won't take more than a moment."

I sighed as I hung up; everyone was already in town. That was the point of a small town.

Back on Essex Street, I glanced down toward the lake. Still calm.

The Book Horde, Alyx's bookshop, was on Division Street, the second of Lake Argen's two east-west main streets. Or, as the town council had described it on the shop-locally posters, *HALF AS LONG, TWICE THE FUN*. Reactions suggested they should have been more specific. Alyx hadn't opened yet, but when I peered in, I saw her shelving books, so I tapped on the window.

Zod and Mulder, her corgis, went nuts and threw themselves at the door, butts wagging, mouths open, tongues out, clearly saying, *"OMG a people! Love us! Let us love you!"*

They quivered in place when Alyx told them to sit, barely holding themselves back while she opened the door. Then they got a nose full of who it was. Zod snarled. Mulder grabbed the hem of Alyx's floor-length dress and tried to tug her to safety.

"Every time," she sighed, pushing her glasses up her nose. "I'll put them in the back."

"It's not their fault," I said, stepping inside and closing the door behind me.

"Of course it isn't, you're a Conduit of the Dark. That sounds like a you problem."

"It's a Four problem," I called after her.

Her response got a little muffled by fur. "I only see you."

I looked through the shelves of new releases while she murmured comfort to the dogs and, from the sound of it, bribed them from the treat tin. Alyx had arrived in town about ten years ago, opened the bookstore, and gathered our solitary practitioners into a formidable coven. Half a dozen people had followed her north, one of them because of the bookstore.

Which was entirely understandable. Alyx didn't see books as product she had to move; she saw them as treasure she may, or may not, share. Her selection, both new and used, was eclectic, and if she didn't stock it, she'd find it. She'd even managed to find a couple of rare books for the library archive. As far as I knew, only one of the many, many packages delivered to her store had ever exploded.

"I assume you're here about what we found at the Dead Ground."

I screamed. A little. Heart pounding, I turned around. "You startled me."

"Really?"

The amount of sarcasm in that single word seemed a little over the top. "So, you did find something? At the Dead Ground?"

"We did." She retrieved a small wooden box wrapped in a piece of silk from behind the counter. I moved closer as she unwrapped it and peered inside when she flipped the box open. Grey pebbles. Identical-looking, but not really any more identical than any other box of grey pebbles.

I reached out a finger to poke at the stones, and Alyx moved the box. "Don't. We found eleven of these circling the Dead Ground about two centimeters in. They're enchanted, so we're assuming they're what your intruder used to anchor the barrier."

"Not my intruder," I protested. "And . . . assuming?"

The tattoos on her forearms shifted. "We can all feel the enchantment, but none of us can identify it. Whatever was done to these pebbles, it wasn't something we do."

"But it's something someone does?" She looked at me like I was an idiot and I felt myself flush. "I mean, it's something someone does deliberately?"

Her expression didn't change much. "Yes, someone did it deliberately. It wasn't an accidental enchantment. And, although we're getting a mix of male and female energy, we've all agreed that the stones were prepared by a single person. As you're certain it was a young man who used the stones . . ."

I nodded.

" . . . then it might have been a woman who did the enchanting. Or it might not have been. I've got my people making some calls. When I have news, I'll let . . ." Brown eyes surrounded by thick black frames widened questioningly as the pause lengthened.

It took me a moment to catch on. "Oh. Me. You might as well let me know." Aunt Jean had sent me to talk to Alyx, so Aunt Jean could wait for new information until Alyx talked to me. Mostly because there was no guarantee Aunt Jean would share the news, and he was, apparently, *my* intruder. I reached out and flicked the box lid closed. "Would you mind keeping them? They're safer with you than anywhere else I can think of."

Alyx stared at me for a long moment, then nodded brusquely. "I'll do better than that; I'll neutralize them. I don't want them attracting the wrong kind of attention."

"Good idea." We were at eighty-seven days since anything had gotten through the cellar door. The record was one hundred and three, and we were all hoping we'd beat it.

"So . . ." She drew the word out while rewrapping the box, clearly reluctant to continue. ". . . the s-word hasn't set anything off?"

"Doesn't seem like it."

"That seems strange."

"It does," I agreed, wiping damp palms on my shorts. Damp because it was warm in the store, not because of existential dread.

Another long stare. "You'd think there'd have been some kind of a reaction by now."

"You would. I mean, we do think that, but there isn't. And not a Word."

"You're concerned. That's not like you. You coast." She drew a wavy purple line in the air that wriggled once, then faded out. "You have money you don't use, a job you needn't do, and a Dark . . . inheritance, for lack of a better word, that you take for granted."

"I'm not . . ."

A raised hand cut me off. "You are. But it's not a judgment; it's an identity. You're careless but kind, and more importantly, unlike the previous Mouth, you don't take advantage of your position. If the absence of repercussion is bothering you, then I need to pay more attention. I trust your instincts."

I had instincts? News to me. "Thanks?"

"You're welcome."

"It's just I was there, you know? I saw it happen and I couldn't stop it." Much the same way I couldn't seem to stop talking. "I tried. I bounced off the barrier, but before I could Say anything, he stabbed himself and disappeared. When there's a response—and how can there not be—it'll be my fault."

Whoa. Where had that come from?

Alyx frowned—not accusingly, thoughtfully. "Why will it be your fault, Cassie?"

"Because I didn't stop him."

"Didn't or couldn't? It sounds like *couldn't* to me. Wouldn't that make it the Dark's fault for not giving you the power to go through the barrier?"

"No. It wouldn't." And it was probably a good thing Eric—and therefore the Dark—wasn't around to Hear Alyx's suggestion. "I didn't Say anything."

"Did you have time?"

"If I'd gotten there earlier . . ."

"How much earlier?"

I'd asked Eric the same thing.

"If anyone's at fault here, Cassie, it's Travis Brayden."

"But . . ."

"Travis Brayden," she repeated.

"Okay."

"If anything happens, it's not your fault, but it is your responsibility."

"Because I couldn't stop him."

Alyx sighed. "Because you're one of the Four. The safety of the town is your responsibility." Her eyes narrowed and she leaned toward me. "You *were* told that when you were Chosen, right?"

"Of course." Then Aunt Jean told me not to get too big for my britches, Amanda clicked her tongue and said it could have been worse, and Eric started randomly showing up in my life—which would have been even skeezier had I not been aware of the Bridget situation.

"But mostly," Alyx continued, pulling me from memory, "you'll do what needs to be done because you're a decent human being."

"Oh. That's . . ." I thought about it for a moment and realized I felt better than I had since bouncing off the barrier. "That's really helpful. Thanks."

She shook her head. "No need to sound so surprised."

"Right." More words seemed to be required. "Uh . . . I like your hair." She'd added deep fuchsia stripes to her black bob. "It . . . um, it looks good." Awkward compliments, that's me.

"Thank you. Now, if that's all. . . ." The Art Nouveau tattoo on her left arm lifted its head and glared at me as she motioned toward the door. "I have to get ready to open."

"Right. Me too. I mean, I have to get to work." Smooth exits, also me. I'd been eighteen when Alyxandra Harvey moved to town and opened the bookstore. She'd been older, beautiful, powerful, and I'd made a fool of myself. It seemed I hadn't yet managed to recover from it.

As she escorted me back to the door, a thick hardcover slid off an upper shelf. I heard the whisper of movement and ducked just before it slammed into my head. Alyx shot an annoyed glance up at the empty space left behind and snapped, "Behave yourself!"

And that was Wednesday.

———

"Cass! Cassidy!" Janet charged out of the library toward me, curls streaming like a pale golden banner behind her.

I took one more step before I stopped, putting me under the shade of one of the enormous elms along Pine Street. The sky was clear, the sun was bright, and it was always best to get Janet into the shade as quickly as possible.

"I haven't been able to get hold of Aunt Jean or Amanda, so when I saw you passing, I thought you'd like to know that the knife, the mid-summer lookout knife, it's not old. It's new. Very new. Someone forged it recently. Hand-forged!" She paused and considered for a moment. A very short moment. "I assume it's hand-forged, but I'm not expert on blacksmithing, so I'm going to have Peter drop by and take a look at it."

Peter had shown up about thirty years ago, set up a blacksmith shop, and fulfilled Lake Argen's need for wrought-iron railings. He enclosed the cemetery, married a Farnsworth, had two kids, and, these days, mostly worked with Nigel, our one-armed silversmith. I'd considered apprenticing to Peter, back in my teens, but Chris had reminded me of how hard those apprentices worked, and I changed my mind.

"What about the runes?" I asked.

"Ah, the runes. The knife is new, but the runes are old—although they're new on the knife, of course, and I doubt they've been professionally incised." She blew out an exasperated breath. "I haven't been able to look them up because I can't take the knife into the Archives; it upsets the books. When I get a couple of minutes to myself, I'll copy them out and take the copy down, but we've just started the summer reading program and, thanks to the internet, I'm up to my eyebrows in parents looking for banned books. Lake Argen's parents do not agree with antiquated, prejudicial social mores."

"Miss Peggi's not helping this year?" Miss Peggi had been helping when I was part of the summer reading program. There was a chance Miss Peggi had been helping when Aunt Jean was part of the summer reading program.

"Please. This place couldn't function without Miss Peggi, but she's doing Toddlers, Tomes, and Tombs and hasn't a minute to spare."

When she waved off the potential of Miss Peggi's help, I noticed a skin-toned dressing wrapped around her right hand. Or, given how pale Janet was, a slightly discolored white dressing. "Did you cut yourself on the knife?"

"This?" She glanced down at the dressing, then used the hand to wave off my concern. "Just a little. Funny thing, the knife is dull, blunt even, but it cuts through living flesh like butter. In fact," she added thoughtfully, "it cuts through living flesh better than it cuts through butter. I expect at least one of the runes deals with that. With the flesh, not the butter."

"So, when Travis drove it through his foot . . ."

Janet made a downward stabbing motion. "Whoosh. No chance to change his mind. Who's Travis?"

Amanda had asked Janet to research the knife and the sheet but hadn't passed on even the little bit she knew at the time. I filled her in.

She blinked at me for a moment, then asked, "And his motivation?"

"No idea. Unless the runes have answers."

We decided Peter would look into the actual forging of the knife while Janet continued working on the runes. With that settled, she headed back to the library, already beginning to pink in spite of the heavy shade. She'd nearly reached the door when I remembered.

"What about the sheet?"

"The sheet? It's a motel sheet, Cassie. Nothing more, nothing less. Just . . ." She shuddered. "Just don't look at it with a black light."

And that was Thursday.

———

Friday, I made chocolate cream pies and Nanaimo bars because chocolate always helps when I'm stressed, then between five and seven PM, Eric and I were at the town hall for the weekly Q&A. Back in the dark beginning, they'd had to set out chairs so petitioners could sit while they waited. These days, Nancy Morton, head of the mine's board of directors, usually dropped in with a report the Dark Heard but didn't Respond to, then Eric spent the rest of the time on his phone and I continued slogging through the Journals of the Four. Dates and details slipped in and out of my head, but I knew one thing for sure: none of the past Conduits had been Chosen because they had legible handwriting.

Me, I took my laptop to my parents' place, printed my notes, and stuck the pages in a binder. Tradition could swim in the lake; I was doing this for future Conduits. Eric called me a genius and happily bought a whole lot of new tech.

I suspect Eric and I would have gotten along better if we hadn't been expected to get along. Or if Eric wasn't so *wink wink nudge nudge* all the time.

"We should stay close. Can't have you Exclaiming randomly about juicy bits I've Heard on the other side of town," he'd said at our first official meeting. I thought he was kidding. I was wrong. Midsummer was the first time I'd done anything official by my . . .

Actually, all things considered, never mind.

Unfortunately, this Friday, when we needed information, we couldn't just ask. My mouth wasn't my own and Eric couldn't Hear himself. Amanda's daughter was putting together the Summer Theater Players performance of *Willie Wonka and the Chocolate Factory* and the Oompa Loompas were giving her trouble, so Amanda had been roped in to ride herd on the rhyming disasters. Aunt Jean had a meeting of her knitting circle, and although she'd offered to bring them all along, no one wanted a repeat of what had happened the last time. Bridget, who'd been at the Dead Ground and could be prompted to ask the right questions, didn't answer when I texted. Nor when I called. She often forgot to charge her phone, though, so I wasn't surprised.

"It's like Aunt Jean and Amanda believe that if we Four ignore the s-word," I muttered, "nothing will happen."

"Nothing *has* happened." Eric shrugged. "Seems to be working."

"Sure, but doesn't all that nothing get right up your nose?"

"It most assuredly does not."

And then, before we could discuss his lack of giving a shit, we had a petitioner.

Lillian Prewitt folded skinny arms and glared at Eric. "I made the sacrifice!"

"My ears Hear," he told her.

Lori, her mother, sighed. "She just turned ten."

Ah. Eric and I nodded. At ten, you were told about the opportunity to gain an audience with the Dark through sacrifice. What you do with that information is up to you. Lillian had clearly decided to embrace it.

"She pushed her little brother into the lake," Lori continued. "Inside the buoys, mind, and I hauled him out pretty quickly. There was nothing to show that she got Alice's attention . . ."

"BUT SHE MADE THE SACRIFICE," the Dark acknowledged, using my mouth. "SHE HAS THE BLOOD. HER INTENT WAS PURE. SHE MAY ASK."

"Hannah Morton doesn't like me . . ."

Lori turned her back toward Eric, murmuring, "Remember, Bug, he's the Ears."

"Fine." The eye-roll was epic. "Hannah Morton doesn't like me and I want her to! Make her like me!"

I could feel the Dark's confusion. "YOU SHOULD DO THINGS TOGETHER."

"Like what?"

"HAVE THE TWO OF YOU SHARED THE VIVISECTION OF AN ELDRITCH CREATURE BY THE DARK OF THE MOON?"

"I'm ten!"

"STARED INTO HER EYES WHILE YOU DEVOURED THE

HEARTS OF YOUR ENEMIES AT A BANQUET TABLE SOAKED IN THE ICHOR OF THE DEFEATED?"

"Still ten!" She picked at a scab on her elbow, deep in thought, then looked hopefully up at Eric. "I could invite her to come over when Daddy barbecues."

"YES. FEED HER MEAT FROM YOUR HAND, AND HER FRIENDSHIP WILL BE YOURS FOR AS LONG AS YOU DESIRE."

Lori cleared her throat. "Excuse me, Your Darkness, when you're referring to meat, do you mean meat from Lillian's actual hand?"

Excellent question, and I could feel Eric radiating approval beside me. It was so important to nail down the specifics; the last thing we needed was another jet ski incident.

"YES."

"How much meat?"

"THE AMOUNT IS INCIDENTAL."

Lillian held up a grubby finger. "My fingernail . . ."

"FINGERNAILS AREN'T MEAT; THEY DON'T COUNT."

"Hangnail?"

"WITH BLOOD?"

"Sure."

"THAT WILL BE SUFFICIENT."

"And then Hannah will like me?"

"YES."

"Yay! Thank you, Your Darkness," she added when her mother nudged her.

"FILL THE NIGHT WITH TREMBLING DREAD, PETITIONER." The Dark lingered at the back of my consciousness as the two of them left, Lillian hopping down the steps, counting in French. The numbers weren't in order, but they were in French.

"CUTE KID. NEXT TIME, SHE SHOULD PUSH HER BROTHER OFF THE END OF THE DOCK WHERE THE DEPTHS REACH IN TO EMBRACE THE SHORE."

I licked blood off my teeth.

The Dark certainly didn't seem upset about Travis Brayden's sudden arrival.

And that was Friday.

━━

It rained off and on all day Saturday. I made two cheesecakes that refused to set, and Chris laughed as he suggested I give them a stern Talking-to. I did not Tell him to get stuffed, but it was touch-and-go for a few minutes.

In the end, I blamed Travis Brayden and made blueberry crumble.

━━

Sunday morning, Arthur reported Travis Brayden missing to the Ontario Provincial Police. We didn't have a municipal police force; the town tended to police itself.

Travis had checked in on Monday evening.

He'd paid for his room until Saturday.

He hadn't been seen since—at least not by Arthur.

His room was empty but his stuff was still there.

The OPP sent a cruiser.

I got to the motel just before the cruiser did.

"City boy," I Said. "Probably wandered off into the woods and got lost."

"City boy," Constable Kaniki said wearily, hitching his uniform trousers up over a thickening middle. "Probably wandered off into the woods and got lost. At least it's June. If mosquitoes don't suck him dry and he has half a brain, he should be fine until we find him." He looked at Travis's pickup, his expression suggesting he drove an older, smaller, and significantly less shiny truck, and sighed. "Even money, he got eaten by a bear."

I'd met his partner, Constable Tate, back in February when she'd been dealing with a couple of snowmobilers who'd crossed our eastern boundary, too drunk to realize where they were. They'd recrossed the boundary a lot faster and caused a four-car pile-up when they'd roared across Gogama Road without checking for traffic. In their defense, traffic wasn't usually a problem.

Fortunately, everyone involved in the crash had gotten away with cuts and bruises. A few additional cuts and bruises had been acquired when one of the drivers had made clear his opinion of snowmobiling while drunk. Two of the cars had been driven by members of the Mattagami First Nation, and given all the drunken shouting about demons in the woods, and our shared border, one of their Elders had called Aunt Jean. Mostly because they'd dated in high school.

Aunt Jean had suggested I should make sure the OPP had nothing to investigate.

Considering the blood alcohol level of the snowmobilers and their contradictory descriptions of what they'd seen, Constable Tate concluded, without me having to Say anything, that they'd disturbed a moose.

Possible. Moose could be assholes.

Equally likely they'd disturbed Evan. He'd really put on some weight after he went into the woods.

Constable Tate didn't remember me, but she wasn't adverse to a little flirting, and I was happy to be distracted from the anticipation of disaster. We killed time exchanging witty banter and barely double innuendo, while Constable Kaniki called in a missing person and Arthur kept up a steady background grumble about losing money.

The volunteer fire department, off-duty security from the mine, and a couple of dozen locals with nothing better to do joined the search. We briefly acquired an OPP presence from the regional headquarters in North Bay, a junior reporter from Global News, and one of the Ontario Volunteer Search and Rescue teams. There was talk about bringing in a couple of helicopters from CFB Petawawa, but nothing came of it. The woods were methodically combed. Marks of bear and moose, and what were not bear and moose, but we weren't about to mention that, were noted.

Uncle Stu, my dad's younger brother, brought his "dogs." "They know they're not hunting for anything," he told me, scratching the heavy head leaning against his hip with the remaining two fingers on his right hand, "but they'll enjoy the outing."

Chris made the desserts for the diner and informed me I owed him my firstborn child. I told him it was already spoken for. He didn't think I was funny.

No one suggested dredging the lake. No one mentioned the lake at all.

Travis Brayden's grandmother, his only surviving relative, was too rich to come north. Monday afternoon, she called Constable Tate. Travis had no reason to be in Northern Ontario, as he didn't even like the woods. Lifting her nose even higher into the air, she demanded to know what she was paying taxes for if he couldn't be found. When asked about his friends, she sniffed dismissively and said he certainly didn't talk about them with her.

"You think Granny drove him to it?" Constable Tate asked over breakfast at my place on Tuesday morning.

"To disappear?" I asked, passing her a rhubarb scone, fresh from the oven. "I'd have smothered her in her sleep, but that's me."

After five days of searching, after their confidence, their beliefs, and their moral fiber had been eroded to the point that their sense of self became shaky, the outsiders left. They'd endured for two days longer than the last time we went through the "unfortunate" disappearance of a southern stranger in the surrounding wilderness.

Aunt Jean blamed the extra forty-eight hours of resilience on the internet but wouldn't tell us why.

In spite of Arthur's protests, the OPP had Travis's truck towed back to Toronto.

On July first, Lake Argen celebrated Canada Day with a little more enthusiasm than usual, freed by the lack of outside observation. No one died. On July second, Amanda replaced the chains on two crypts as well as the padlock on the cellar door of the House and told me later that she'd met Alyx in the hardware store. Alyx had told her she needed to buy a better lock. She hadn't, she'd bought the same lock she always did, and Alyx had muttered about tradition being a fucked-up priority almost under her breath as she'd walked away.

At dawn on midsummer, Travis Brayden had used enchanted pebbles to build an invisible barricade around the Dead Ground. While I watched, he'd driven a new knife with old runes through his foot into the ground and had disappeared with the sunrise.

Nothing had happened in response. It didn't seem right but . . .

The sun shone. Birds sang. The sky was blue. The lake was calm.

And that was that.

I needed to get over myself.

THREE

Melanie

What you need to remember, Melanie, is that old Mrs. Brayden is rich. Very rich."

I looked around at the huge old houses lining the road. Enormous trees and deep green lawns announced the drought and its subsequent water shortages did not apply in Rosedale. "I realize that, Mom."

"So, no matter what trivial thing she wants you to do, make her pay for it." The signal was unexpectedly clear enough that I could almost hear the edges of her smile through the phone.

"You said she wanted to talk to me." I suspected Mom had broken into a private conversation between two people she'd been serving at brunch, but I'd been too smart to make the accusation when she'd first told me about it and I was too smart to make it now.

"Oh, for fucksake, she doesn't want a chat. Why would she want a chat? She has a shit-ton of other rich people she can chat with. She could chat with that harpy whose egg-white omelet wasn't white enough. She wants you to do something they won't. All I'm saying is that you need to make her pay."

"Whatever it is?"

"Exactly."

"Mom . . ."

"Don't *mom* me, Melanie Solvich. You left your job and I'm looking out for you. It's not like I can afford to support us both."

"I have savings . . ."

"You're sleeping on my sofa bed."

"It's Toronto. It's stupidly expensive here."

"And you're out of work."

"I'll get another job." I braked as a very fat, glossy black squirrel sauntered across the street. Even the squirrels in Rosedale looked like they came from old money.

"Of course you'll get another job. You're back in Ontario and there's a teacher shortage in Ontario, but until you do, while you're sleeping in my living room, take old Mrs. Brayden for as much as you can."

"Eat the rich?"

"Fucking right, eat the rich."

"Got to go. I'm here." Here was a three-story brick, center-hall Edwardian. The kind that had been built with servants' rooms. I doubted old Mrs. Brayden had servants, although she probably had a housekeeper and maybe a cook who she considered to be servants. I hadn't even met the woman and I already disliked her. Unfair, sure. Not everyone with money, even old money, took advantage of security and status, but the odds weren't in her favor.

Mom cleared her throat, bringing my attention back to the phone mounted on my dash. "You want me to bring you dinner from the restaurant when I get off?"

"No, thanks," I muttered as I pulled into the driveway and stopped the car. "I'll be full of the rich."

"Smartass."

Which in mom-speak meant *I love you*.

I hung up, unplugged my phone, and dropped it into my purse.

This was a stupid idea. There were plenty of jobs out there for teachers. It seemed like half the working teachers in Canada were retiring, and the other half were burning out trying to take up the slack.

I hadn't burned out. I'd stormed out in the wake of the Saskatchewan "Parents' Bill of Rights" that forced teachers to notify parents if a student requested a change in personal pronouns or names. What kind of asshole insists on parental consent at any and all costs even if there's a possibility of physical, mental, or emotional harm? Which is word for word what I'd intended to ask the school board. Unfortunately, after having had to sit through half a dozen statements by transphobic shit-heels, the actual question emerged a little more forcefully.

Technically, I hadn't lied to my mother. Bill 137 was absolutely the reason I was no longer teaching high school English in Saskatchewan. It was also the reason I wasn't sure I wanted to keep teaching. The kids were amazing, but the assholes had gained control of the system.

Mom, who hadn't finished high school, had worked her butt off to see that I went to university, and the guilt when I thought about walking away from teaching kept me walking up to old Mrs. Brayden's front door.

Why *old Mrs. Brayden*, I wondered as I pressed the doorbell? Did my mother know a young Mrs. Brayden?

The woman who answered the door was older than my mother but not old enough for that to be her primary identification. She wore her age lightly, like most wealthy women. Ash-blond hair contained no grey, a single visible wrinkle crossed her forehead, and her lipstick stayed inside the lines rather than feathering out into a deep red fringe around her mouth. But her expression, that told me she was older than she looked.

It was . . . stately. Like her house. Only years of living with a belief in her innate superiority could have made that expression look natural, look like anything but a caricature.

"Yes?" Her voice matched her expression. Although I thought I could hear just a hint of resentment that she'd been expected to answer her own door.

Eating the rich, starting here and now, seemed like an excellent idea. Instead, I squared my shoulders and said, "I'm Melanie Solvich."

And her face changed.

She smiled. Laugh lines appeared, bracketing her eyes. Her posture relaxed as she stepped back and motioned me inside. "Cecelia Brayden. But you know that, don't you? Thank you so much for coming, Melanie. May I call you Melanie?" I nodded and she continued. "This must seem so strange to you, being sent to the house of a stranger, but I honestly have no one else, and when your mother was so enthusiastic about you, I'm afraid I jumped at her offer without considering what you might think about it." She led the way through a pair of open French doors into a room my brain insisted on calling a parlor. It couldn't be a living room—it was clear no one lived in it— and it couldn't be a den because that implied a level of informality absolutely not present.

The wallpaper had a cream base behind an abstract pattern in gold. Who even had wallpaper in this day and age? Oh, yeah, rich people. The fabric of the sofa, wingback chair, and curtains were all the same shade of gold as the pattern on the wallpaper. The wood—curio cabinet, trim, floor—was a deeper, richer shade. The rug in the center of the room looked Middle Eastern, only fake. The paintings on the wall were . . . real? They weren't prints; that was for sure.

The room looked like a stage set.

"Could I offer you a cup of tea, Melanie?"

Tea? In a cup. So, presumably not iced tea. It was mid-July. In Toronto. Hot and humid. Although the house must have had central air, as the room was cool enough that whole flocks of goose bumps had risen on my bare arms. "Sure," I said, and, because I wasn't totally without manners, added a quick, "Thank you."

"Excellent. I'll just be a moment."

Then she left me alone. A little afraid to sit down . . .

Because I hadn't been given permission?

Because the furniture looked unused?

I crossed the room to peer into the curio cabinet, half expecting Faberge eggs, and finding two of the kind of fragile porcelain teacups no one ever used outside a Jane Austen novel, six wine glasses with a matching decanter, and a vase of dried flowers. None of it seemed to mean anything.

"I am pleasant although entirely fake," said the room. "This is the face we show to strangers. You don't get to see behind the curtain."

I really wanted a look at the rest of the house. No one went to this much trouble to put up a front if they weren't hiding something. Maybe without staff to pick up after her, Cecelia Brayden was a complete slob. If I looked through the French doors into the room on the opposite side of the front hall, would I see empty wine bottles, plates of half-eaten brie, and a sloppy pile of discarded Louboutins, red soles exposed?

Only one way to find out.

I was halfway to the door when Mrs. Brayden returned, carrying a tray with a tea set and a pair of cups and saucers. I had no option but to back up and give her room to put it down. She settled into the wing-back chair, nodded toward the sofa, and I sat like a well-trained spaniel.

"I hope you like the tea," she said, laying a strainer across a cup as delicate as any in the cabinet. "It's my own blend."

Not the type for teabags. No surprise.

"Help yourself to milk and sugar."

I added milk, skipped the sugar, and, not because I was thirsty but because I was holding a teacup full of tea, took a sip. It didn't taste much different than the grocery store stuff I usually drank. A little weaker, maybe, and with a little more flavor than just the vague taste of "tea," but not worth what she'd undoubtedly paid for it.

Mrs. Brayden took a sip.

I took another sip.

She took a swallow.

I took a swallow.

It got competitive for a few minutes. Two women, of two different social classes, aggressively drinking tea at each other.

She set her empty cup down. "Your mother is an interesting person, Melanie."

Not a lie, but what business was that of hers? I set my empty cup down and waited.

"Do you know what I told her just before she offered your services? I told her that I needed a hero."

The eighties called. They want their power ballad back. I closed my teeth around my response.

"I think it's wonderful that when I say *hero*, your mother thinks of you. I wish I'd had that kind of relationship with my son." She smiled, a little sadly. "I envy you that relationship. Tell me, did your father never try to undermine it?"

"Not in the picture," I told her. "Never knew him. And we don't talk about him."

"I'm so sorry." She sighed, the kind of deep, from-the-heart sigh that said the preliminaries were over. "I lost my son and his wife just over thirteen years ago, and now my only grandson, Travis, has disappeared. The three of them lived here, with me, and I did my best to ensure that he not be spoiled like many only children. You know how it is."

Also an only child, I did not know how it was. I got my first job at nine, the year I was big enough to walk Mrs. Mitchell's very large and very much not leash-trained dog. Fortunately, Mrs. Brayden continued without my input.

"It's just been Travis and I since he was ten. We were very close." She waved a hand as though trying to pull the emotion she needed from the air. "He is . . . was all I had. I need someone, you, if you will, to go north and find out what happened."

"Find him?"

"No, that's . . ." The teapot, lifted to pour another cup for us both, returned to the tray with a definitive *crack*. "The provincial police and the locals have looked. They know the territory and they were unable to find him, so how could I expect you to have any better result?" Her spine straightened and she met my eyes. Her eyes were grey. Not the unsaturated blue that people usually called grey, but the color of steel with no flecks or variations. The contrast between her eyes and the quavering, grieving voice was so extreme that one of them had to be fake. I had opened my mouth to ask which when she said, "I will pay ten thousand dollars plus expenses for you to travel north to a town called Lake Argen and discover as much as you can about the days before Travis disappeared. About the day he disappeared."

"Ten thousand dollars?" I repeated, unable to look away or, to be honest, move at all.

"Plus expenses. Will you do that for me, Melanie Solvich?"

It didn't occur to me to say no. The thought of ten thousand dollars and what I could do with it had pushed everything else from my mind. "Sure," I said. "I'll do that for you."

———

"Ten thousand dollars?"

"And this." I held up a credit card. "For expenses."

Mom leaned forward to peer at it as if she could read the amount of available credit from the plastic. "Old Mrs. Brayden must really love her grandson."

I had the impression that old Mrs. Brayden considered Travis to be hers. Not the same thing. "You wouldn't spend that much to find me?"

"Spend ten thousand dollars?"

"Plus expenses."

She smiled. "If I had ten grand, I'd throw you a wake the whole fucking province would talk about."

"So, that's a no on looking for me?"

"Pretty much, yeah." Frowning, she dropped down onto the end of the sofa. My half-filled suitcase bounced. "Why did she hire an English teacher instead of a private detective?"

"No idea."

"You didn't ask?"

Ten thousand dollars. "She's looking for the emotional context."

"A detective can't ask the locals how they feel about a city kid getting eaten by a bear?"

"Maybe she doesn't know how to find a private detective. I wouldn't know where to start."

"You'd start on the internet like a person with a brain. Old Mrs. Brayden, she'd likely call her lawyer, and he'd charge her a thousand bucks an hour to find one."

I sighed. "You sound like you don't want me to take the job."

Mom tapped the end of a bitten fingernail against her phone case. "It's a stupid amount of money, Mel."

"She has a stupid amount of money, Mom."

"True."

I held up a Rough Riders sweatshirt. She shook her head. I packed it anyway. "And you said I should make her pay."

"Sure, but I didn't expect her to, did I? That sort's never willing to pay up unless they're covering their own fat asses, so excuse me if ten grand for sweet fuck all makes me just a little suspicious. Of course," she continued, sounding happier, "you haven't actually been paid yet. You could still get stiffed."

"Also true," I admitted.

She pulled a pair of folded jeans out of the suitcase, rolled them, and shoved them back in. "I did mention you needed the money."

"Before or after you called me a hero?" I asked, refolding the jeans.

"Not sure. Not mutually exclusive, though." She rolled the jeans again and raised a warning finger when I reached for them. "What about this fall? And teaching?"

"It's not even August yet; I can register at the OCT when I get back." I dropped my hiking boots into the duffle bag at my feet. "When I get back and am handed ten thousand dollars."

I watched the ten thousand dollars convince her. Regardless of Mom's entirely class-based suspicions, that kind of money was very convincing. "Did Mrs. Brayden give you a copy of the police reports?"

"She doesn't have a copy herself. They just came and talked to her."

"They?"

I rolled my eyes. "She didn't give me the names." I stuffed extra underwear into the nooks and crannies. "She did give me a picture of Travis and a list of everything that wasn't returned. Mostly, it's a few articles of clothing and a knife. Some kind of family heirloom Travis took with him that she really wants back."

"Why?"

"Family heirloom, Mom."

"When I die, you'll get my George Foreman Grill."

"Can't wait."

"Do you even know where you're going?" Mom asked as I struggled to zip the suitcase closed, my jacket taking up a stupid amount of space. Sure, it was July, but I didn't trust the north.

"Place called Lake Argen. Apparently, it's a support town for a silver mine. I drive to Sudbury, then it's second moose to the right and straight on until morning. If I get to Timmins, I've gone too far." Maybe the jacket should go in the duffle bag with my boots.

Mom bent over her phone and frowned at a map. "There's nothing much between Sudbury and Timmons but trees. Why would anyone put a town there?"

"It's where the silver is." Without the jacket, I had room for another couple of books.

"Town has no website. There's nothing online except a crappy webpage about the mine."

"Because the town wouldn't be there if the mine wasn't." Triumphant, I zipped the suitcase closed.

Mom stared at her screen for a moment longer, then looked up and shrugged dismissively. "Could be worse, I suppose. It could be a lumbering town and you'd have to chain yourself to a tree to keep them from clear-cutting the forest."

"Yeah, I wouldn't do that."

"Because you're a stooge of late-stage capitalism. How long do you figure you'll be gone?"

"Two days' travel. I could do it in one, but I don't want to. Mrs. Brayden wants me to take at least a week to talk to people. Then two days to drive back. Add a little wiggle room." I returned her shrug. "I'll leave Lake Argen August third and be back on the fourth."

Lips pursed, she stared at me for a long moment and said, "Do not fall in love."

I dropped the suitcase on my foot. "Say what?"

"You're off on an adventure, Mel. Adrenaline. Heightened emotions. Star-filled skies. Moose. Love happens."

Obviously. Or I wouldn't exist. I wondered if I should mention that my sperm donor came up in casual conversation over imported tea. Or was it only weird to me because Mom and I never talked about him? Other people talked about their fathers all the time.

"Are you listening to me?"

I sighed. "Mom, I haven't been in love in . . ." Trying to count back, I realized I'd lost track. "In long enough it doesn't bear thinking about."

"Doesn't bear thinking about, indeed," she snorted. "You're going to die alone. And that reminds me . . ."

If she was going to mention Mara, that last love I'd lost track of, I wasn't going to call her while I was gone.

". . . don't get eaten by a bear."

"How does that remind you of bears?"

"Doesn't bear thinking about. Dying alone." She gestured at empty air like a particularly vacant-headed magician's assistant. "Eaten by a bear." She waited. When I didn't respond, she made the gesture again.

"I'm going to tell people I'm an orphan," I said, standing my suitcase up on its wheels.

Mom leaned in and kissed my cheek. "I'm not worried; you'll kick bear ass."

"I love you too."

———

Theoretically, I could drive the four hundred-odd kilometers from Toronto to Sudbury in about five hours. I set off in midmorning, secure in the knowledge that I'd be driving north, away from the city, the opposite way from any heavy traffic on Highway 400. What I hadn't factored in was getting onto the 400.

I probably should have stayed in bed until noon, hoping at least some of the idiot drivers currently on the road would be off the road, eating lunch.

"Except the bed is still a lumpy pullout in my mother's living room," I reminded myself, watching one of those idiots argue with the garbage-truck driver he'd challenged at Ridelle and Dufferin. "And there's always more idiots."

Idiot driver yelled and waved his arms at his crumpled car, at other cars, at random objects. Garbage-truck driver leaned against the side of his truck, arms folded, visibly sighing at increasingly smaller intervals. I pulled out my phone and tried to work my way through the labyrinthine process of complimenting a city worker, because the garbage-truck driver deserved a medal. Police finally showed up and got traffic moving before I managed.

Saskatoon had traffic. People had to get to work and get home from work and pick up garbage and deliver goods just like in any other urban center, but they seemed to be able to do it without the entitled hysteria of Toronto. If provincial politics hadn't constructed some entitled hysteria of its own, I wouldn't have left.

I squeezed onto westbound Highway 401, looking forward to spending a week wandering a small town and avoiding bears.

It was stop-and-go traffic at the 400 off-ramp. Which was fine. When I'd come back from out west, I'd hit the city at rush hour and it had been stop-and-stop traffic. In the rain. If crossroad demons existed and they wanted to make bank, they could fill their quota of desperate souls where the 401 met the 400.

By the time I passed Vaughan, my personal marker of having finally left Toronto and its malignant spread behind, it had taken me over two hours for a fifty-one-minute trip. And I had to pee.

At Barrie, heartily sick of the highway and tourists heading north to cottage country—something else I hadn't factored in—I drummed my fingers on the roof of the car as I filled the tank and considered calling it a day.

"People commute from Barrie to Toronto," I muttered, watching the numbers on the pump rise. "Put on your big-girl panties and get back in the car."

"Excuse me? Did you say something?"

Turning toward the middle-aged man at the other pump, I put on my gritted-teeth parent/teacher-meeting smile. Women traveling alone did not snarl at strange men. "Just talking to myself."

"Sometimes . . ." He grinned with significantly more sincerity. ". . . it's the only way to have an intelligent conversation." Then with a waggle of brows that invited me to share in the joke, he returned his attention to his truck.

As I bumped my hip against the car to fit another thirty-seven cents' worth of gas in the tank, I acknowledged that I might need to be a little less prickly moving forward if I wanted to get any information about Travis from the good people of Lake Argen.

Highway 400 to Sudbury was just more of the 400 until just past Parry Sound when it turned into Highway 69. Having let my satellite radio account lapse, I slid a Stan Rogers CD into the player, decided the transports blowing past me had the right idea about the speed limit, and sang my way into Greater Sudbury and the Holiday Inn only two and a half hours after I'd expected to. Drove right past the Super 8. Fuck it. I was on an expense account.

"Why stop?" my mom demanded, when she called me on her break. "You could have gotten there tonight."

Sound off, I channel-surfed past exactly the same programming I hadn't wanted to watch at my mom's. "I don't want to drive on roads I don't know and arrive in a strange place in the dark."

"I gave birth to a middle-aged economics professor."

"Say what?"

"It was the most boring job I could think of," she admitted. "Where's your sense of adventure?"

"Where's my desire to be swept off the road by a logging truck?"

"You should embrace new experiences."

"Can I embrace less-fatal new experiences?"

"Wuss." I heard voices raised in the background. Mom sighed. "I've gotta go. Ashley just dumped table eight's soup order on the sous-chef."

"On purpose?"

"Hard to dump three successive bowls by accident. Exit stage left; don't be eaten by a bear."

"Love you too."

My room came with a bathtub. My mother's apartment did not. I poured a tiny bottle of shampoo under the running water and toasted

Mrs. Brayden, my expense account, and the possibility of non-fatal new experiences with chamomile tea that tasted strongly of coffee.

As this seemed to be the one Holiday Inn in Sudbury without a complimentary breakfast, I checked out around ten—having lost the fight for an early morning with the really comfy king-size bed—and headed for the nearest Timmies. Expense account or not, I wasn't paying hotel prices for food.

Two hours and fifteen minutes later, I turned south about two kilometers before I needed to turn north, and headed into Gogama for lunch. I wasn't exactly hungry, but it was lunchtime and, unlike Lake Argen which might as well have *Here be Dragons* stamped on it, I'd been able to check out Gogama on my phone while propped up in that Holiday Inn bed. Also, I needed to look at something other than trees. I like trees well enough, but damn, there were a lot of them.

The Rendez-Vous Restaurant and Tavern seemed a pretty typical small-town establishment. It had plenty of the ubiquitous brown-on-brown seating as well as what looked like a well-stocked bar and a lonely-looking pool table. Either I'd missed the lunch rush or I *was* the lunch rush.

"Are you serving?" I asked the woman behind the bar.

"If you're eating. Have a seat." When I hesitated, she grinned, reminding me suddenly of my mother, including a similar tattoo on the ball of her right shoulder, the ink visible beyond the strap of her tank top. "You don't want to sit by the window. In half an hour, there'll be three old farts at that picnic table out front, nursing a coffee and staring in at you."

Warned, I sat by the wall and ordered a BLT, a water, and a coffee.

"Water's from the tap."

"Tap's fine."

She gave me a long look, then nodded, like I'd passed the first level of the asshole test, and strode into the kitchen, yelling for Dougie. Dougie yelled back, words muffled. "He has to get the grill hot," she announced, emerging. "Be a couple of extra minutes, if that's no problem."

"Not at all."

She went back behind the bar. "You want ice in that water?"

"That'd be great. Thanks."

It was great. The temperature was on the high side of normal for July, the sun was bright, and I kept forgetting Mrs. Brayden was paying for gas, so the air conditioning had been set where it made almost no change.

When she put down my coffee, she nodded at the empty glass. "Another?"

"Please."

I was stirring in creamer when she returned with it and using the excuse to scoop up the empty container, she paused by the table. "So, where you heading?"

"Lake Argen."

"No shit. If you don't mind me asking, why?"

"A young man named Travis Brayden disappeared from Lake Argen . . ." It wasn't a secret. ". . . and his grandmother wants to know about his last days."

Her brows drew in. "Disappeared?"

"Went out one morning, didn't return to his room. The police looked, couldn't find him."

"Huh." She pulled out the opposite chair and sat down, strengthening the resemblance to my mother, who'd never met a conversation she didn't want to be a part of. "I heard about that. Know a couple of people who went out with the search teams." She watched me drink a little more water, and said, "Lake Argen's got a weird rep."

"Weird?"

"Yeah. Maybe because the people who own the mine . . . You know about the silver mine?" When I nodded, she continued. "The owners, they live there, so they spend their money there. It's got the kind of things most towns its size don't." She dragged her finger through a waterdrop, drawing patterns on the table. "But people around here, they go to Timmins even if odds are high Lake Argen will have what they want. The Mattagami First Nation, up just north of them, most of them go to Timmons for high school even though Lake Argen's closer. Timmons is closer for our kids," she added thoughtfully. "Lake Argen, though, they're the reason the passenger train still comes through twice a week. 'Course, trains don't run empty, so anything that rolls north carries a ton of stuff. Most towns around send trucks in to pick up orders but . . ." She lowered her voice. ". . . there's a lot of things that are just for them, you know?"

I didn't.

"Expensive things. Dougie figures they're bribing someone in government to keep that train running. Not that I'd blame them," she admitted, and kept going. "A friend from way back moved his family to the lake about six years ago—the mine's mostly automated now, so there's not the jobs there used to be, but there's some. Says it's a great place and he wants me to visit. I never have, though."

"Because of the weird rep?"

She frowned. "What have you heard?"

"You just told me Lake Argen had a weird rep."

"Oh, that's right." She laughed. "So, this grandmother must have the police reports, what does she want from you?"

"Emotional context." If she wasn't bothered by her memory lapse, I'd let it go.

"Emotional context?" After a long moment, she blinked. "I guess it takes all kinds. Let me check how Dougie's doing with your sandwich."

Dougie had produced what was quite possibly the best BLT I'd ever eaten.

As I paid for my lunch, she smiled and said, "So, where are you heading?"

I waited. She didn't seem to be joking. "Lake Argen."

"Oh, that's right. Has a weird rep, that place."

The three old men sitting around the picnic table watched me cross to my car over the curve of heavy white mugs. Watched me get into my car. Watched me drive away. I wondered if they'd ask the woman behind the bar where I was heading. I wondered if she'd remember.

Gogama Road, two kilometers from the turnoff to Gogama and on the other side of Route 144, was a basic two-lane road, the ubiquitous trees on either side. Given that it was the only direct line between Route 144 and 101, I expected a little through traffic. My expectations remained unfulfilled and I was the only car on the road for the entire sixty kilometers until the Lake Argen turnoff.

Which I drove past.

I saw the sign, acknowledged I'd reached my destination, and five or so kilometers down the road had to pull a U-turn to get back to it.

"Highway hypnotism," I muttered, crossing the center line. "And too damn many trees."

And an ancient pickup truck that nearly T-boned me.

The driver hit the horn as he missed by a couple of centimeters, flipped me off, and sped up, heading north.

Heart pounding, I parked on the edge of the road and concentrated on breathing for a moment or two. Or ten. Then I leaned out my open window and yelled, "Asshole!" He couldn't possibly have heard me. I felt better, though.

Lake Argen Road led up onto a ridge, and from the top I could see the sparkling waters of a deep blue lake, and the town spread out before me. On the far side of a bridge over a long, narrow inlet that might be the start of a river stood a number of industrial buildings nearly hidden in the trees. I saw what looked like the edge of a big greenhouse, and part of what could have been the train station. I couldn't really get an idea of the town's street plan because of—big surprise—more trees.

A flock of birds I couldn't identify—they weren't pigeons, I grew up in Toronto, I'm good with pigeons—circled the car as I drove down the other side of the ridge and into the valley.

I passed a motel on the outskirts of town that made me think of knives and showers and Janet Leigh, drove around a long sweeping curve on a road miraculously without pot holes, past big old houses set back from the road, and into the downtown such as it was. If there were hotels in Lake Argen, I guessed they'd be by the lake, the only thing it looked like the town had going for it as a tourist destination.

Stopped at the lights, I looked to my left, and over the huge porch of a big old yellow house with white trim was a sign that said: *ALL THAT GLITTERS, Guest House.* It had the kind of high-end country kitsch look that Mrs. Brayden's credit card would appreciate. And if Travis was anything like his grandmother, I had no doubt he'd have paid their undoubtably high, quaint surtax as well.

Parked in the guest house's empty five-car lot, I drank the last two centimeters of cold coffee in my travel mug. "Look at me," I said, rolling the stiffness out of my shoulders. "Just arrived in town and already hot on Travis's trail. I'm a natural at this investigating thing."

A half dozen ravens watching me from the surrounding trees gave voice to what sounded like an opposing opinion.

"Yeah, right," I muttered, lifting my suitcase from the trunk. "What do you know?"

"Bwark," replied the closest of the ravens before dropping an enormous wet pile of crap on the hood of my car.

Welcome to Lake Argen.

FOUR

Cassie

It felt like a lemon-square day, I decided as I walked to work. The sun was shining, the birds were singing—well, the ravens were borking from their morning roost in the trees around the guest-house parking lot, but close enough—and I hadn't made lemon squares in a while. They were one of my mom's favorites; two dozen squares could be cut from each sheet, and if I made two sheets, there'd be leftovers for the freezer. The diner hadn't had a freezer day for a while; it might be time to clear things out.

So, lemon squares, and if the serviceberries were to have one last hurrah before the blueberries ripened, a couple of serviceberry pies would be . . .

My ears rang as the raven chorus cranked the volume up to eleven. I recognized a distinctive taunting *KWAA* and broke into a slow jog toward the sound. If Reggie had the ravens riled up again, I was going to have a WORD with him strong enough to knock the idiotic idea of an aerial defense force right out of his head. No one wanted a flock of agitated ravens shitting out their annoyance all over the downtown. Or, worse, over the beach where I planned to spend my afternoon.

Unfortunately, I was still two blocks away from the guest house when Reggie Morton raced around the corner of Lake Street heading for the parking lot, knobby knees flashing under his shorts, long grey beard flowing back over his left shoulder like a hairy windsock.

Okay, if Reggie wasn't pissing off the ravens, who was?

A particularly loud *KWAA* sounded as Reggie reached the driveway and slammed into a stranger walking backward, looking up past her raised finger at the birds instead of watching where she was going. They hit the asphalt together and rolled apart. Over corvid laughter, I heard a distinct "Oh, for fuck's sake!" that didn't come from Reggie, and the irritated alto brought me to a full stop.

I tried to move closer. My legs weren't working.

She was . . .

A stranger. I'd never seen her before, not in town, not anywhere around town, not in my dreams. I'd have remembered.

She had curves.

And honey-blond hair in a loose ponytail.

She was taller than Reggie. Taller than me.

I couldn't hear what Reggie was saying, and reading his lips through the masking facial hair wasn't an option. Wouldn't have been an option even if I'd known how to read lips.

She was a stranger. I'd never seen her before. I couldn't look away.

The stranger's full breasts pushed against the fabric of a T-shirt that showed more than a hint of cleavage under the scoop neck. Her ass rounded out the fabric of her jeans. Her elbows had dimples. I couldn't see them, I was too far away, but I knew they were there the same way I knew that someday we'd argue over the remote and that she'd tuck cold toes under my legs while we cuddled on the couch.

She wasn't a gift of the Dark. I had a gift of the Dark, and receiving it had felt like being caught under a collapsing brick wall, being pummeled by debris, and knowing that, even if I endured, I might not survive. One in three of the Chosen didn't. Sure, survival meant I'd be one of Lake Argen's "cool kids"—one of whom was whatever came after an octogenarian—but at the time it had sucked. Had I been asked, before it happened, I'd have noped my way back to small-town obscurity.

But this, this pummeling I welcomed. This was . . . I felt . . .

I felt the touch of a thousand possibilities. This was desire, not destiny. I could tell before even meeting her that she'd be my answer to Alyx's accusation of wasted potential.

A raven swooped out of the trees that surrounded the parking lot, passing close enough that the stranger instinctively ducked.

"You just mind your manners, Flight Sergeant!" Reggie yelled, shaking his fist at the departing bird's tail feathers.

The stranger laughed. Objectively, and I was amazed I remained capable of it, her laugh sounded a bit like a raven's: kind of a loud, surprisingly deep *bwah*. I wanted to hear her laugh again. I wanted to make her laugh. I wanted to laugh with her while lying together on white sheets gilded by summer sunshine.

When was the last time I'd done laundry?

I needed to buy some white sheets.

Exiting the guest house at this hour and walking toward Carlyle Street could only mean my stranger was on her way to the diner. Theresa was a terrible cook, so after Daniel died back in February and the "there's a very good reason to believe that's not butter" incident, she began handing out complimentary diner breakfasts.

I was heading to the diner. Fine. To the bakery. Which was next to the diner. Close enough. I could drop in and give Mom a heads-up about the lemon squares. Did the stranger rinse her hair with lemon juice to get those warm, sunlit highlights, I wondered? Did it feel as soft as it looked?

If I timed it right, I'd meet the stranger at the entrance to the diner. We'd talk while I held the door for her because it was weirdly weighted, had a tendency to drag, and I knew its tricks. Grateful she hadn't had to struggle with recalcitrant doors before coffee, she'd invite me to join her. I'd suggest she not have mushrooms in her hash browns, not on her first day. After breakfast, we'd arrange a second date, then we'd drive to Timmins to rent a U-Haul and . . .

"Cassidy!"

I rocked back as Nancy Morton's massive gold sedan nearly ran over my feet.

The stranger, my stranger, had disappeared down Carlyle. If I took the alley between the pharmacy and Foster's clothing store and nothing came out of the shadows at me, I could still make it to the diner in time. Circling around the front of the car, I nearly got run over again.

"Cassidy!"

"What?" I demanded, stomping over to the passenger window. "I'm busy!"

Ms. Morton leaned toward me. "I need assistance from one of the Four . . ."

"Find another one." The stranger had thrown me into a warm fog of anticipation—what I'd say to her, what she'd say to me—and Ms. Morton was yanking me out of it.

"That's not how it works, Cassidy Prewitt. You're the Mouth of the Dark, and you have a responsibility to this town that trumps whatever . . ."

I could almost hear the word *inane* reach her lips before she swallowed it back down.

". . . thing you've got going. The town needs you. Step up! I have to talk to the Dark."

"Then you need Eric. He Hears."

I hadn't managed a single step away from her car before she snapped, "And I need to hear the Dark's response."

It was early Wednesday morning. "Friday," I began.

She cut me off. "Now. The board received a letter," she continued, sounding no happier about the situation than I was, "from the Ministry of Mines."

"Isn't that a Harry Potter . . ."

She cut me off again. "It's the provincial agency that regulates mines. They want to set up a site inspection."

"Right. Okay." The stranger had to have reached the diner by now. Someone else would have helped her with the door. She'd have sat down. Maybe even ordered if she knew what she wanted. Who'd suggest she shouldn't have the mushrooms? "Okay," I repeated, through clenched teeth. If Ms. Morton needed assistance from the Four, then however reluctantly, I was up. "And?"

"And we don't get letters from the Ministry asking for site inspections!" A fine spray of spit glittered in the sunlight and drifted down to soak into the tweed seat cover. "It's part of the Agreement."

The last tendrils of stranger-induced warm fog dissipated. I dragged my thoughts away from the possibilities, thought about Ms. Morton's words for a moment, and finally arrived at "Well, that's not good."

Her eyes narrowed. "That's exactly the kind of articulate response that makes me need to know what's going on. I need to know how to respond. I need a consultation with the Dark."

I glanced at the lake. Calm and mirror-bright, it looked cool and inviting and empty of everything except fish, and whatever else lived in lakes where Alice wasn't. "Alice always reacts when things are about to go tits . . ."

Ms. Morton gave me the Look.

". . . be uncertain. Remember the chop out on the water when Tom's pea crop started ripening? She knew something was wrong before the first whatever-the-hell-they-were emerged from the pod. When the Voice asked her advice, she told us how to deal with them." Ms. Morton opened her mouth. I kept talking. "Remember the size of waves when that mold in Gayle Abbott's basement absorbed her laundry and started walking around in her clothes? If Alice hadn't warned us, how long would it have taken us to find out there were two Gayles?" Okay, so, even six years later, after a few beers at the pub, someone would wonder if the right Gayle had gone into the lake, but her husband and kids seemed happy, so how was it anyone else's business? "What about in the winter, when the ice cracks to let us know it's time to grab the flamethrowers and go looking for that creepy animated snowman? Alice warns us when 'things'"—the air quotes were doing a lot of heavy lifting—"slip in without Security noticing."

It was the "thing" that animated the snowman, not the snowman itself that slipped through. "If there's no warning"—I waved in the general direction of the lake—"then nothing's going on." Ms. Morton was overreacting, like I'd overreacted after seeing Travis s-word. It couldn't possibly be as bad as she thought.

"And what if the weakening of the Agreement has weakened the Dark's connection with Alice? Can she warn us? Does she know she needs to?"

My turn to open my mouth. Only it wasn't voluntary.

"Or," Ms. Morton continued, "is it merely that government interference isn't something that's bleeding in from the darkness so it's not part of her remit?"

I snapped my mouth closed, then opened it again to say, "Am I supposed to answer that?"

"Can you?"

"No."

"Which is why I need a consultation with the Dark. Call Eric."

"I can send him a text . . ."

"Call him, Cassidy."

Ms. Morton had been the vice principal in charge of discipline at Lake Argen High during the four years I attended, and for three years after I graduated. She could still make it perfectly clear that hers was the only option available—which had to be useful at board meetings, I acknowledged as I found Eric's number.

His answering service picked up.

"He'll be available after one," I said, stuffing my phone back in my pocket.

"What's he doing?"

"The service didn't say. Just that he'll be available after one."

"He'll be available when I . . . when the town needs him to be. Get in."

———

Eric had the largest of the newer houses tucked in among the trees behind the cemetery. It was larger than one man needed, entirely modern, and visible from the road so the shiny newness could evoke envy in all who drove by. I knew this for a fact because "could evoke envy in all who drove by" came out of Eric's mouth right before "Do you think Bridget likes it?" The single level was all sharp angles and clean lines, with large, ultra-energy-efficient windows, a roof covered in solar tiles, and not a single piece of the ever-popular wrought iron. While I loved my little hundred-year-old renovated miner's cottage—the mine needed a lot fewer miners now than it used to—I was self-aware enough to realize I maybe resented Eric a bit for how different he'd dared to be.

He could afford the small fortune it cost to bring materials and craftsmen this far north, and he'd happily spent it. I maybe resented that a bit, too. Since I also could afford the same small fortune, or even a slightly larger fortune since I was an only child and Eric had two siblings, I refused to find self-awareness enough to delve into why.

What kind of house would the stranger like, I wondered? I could see her tucked up in the big chair by the woodstove, legs wrapped in my great-grandmother's quilt, both hands wrapped around a cup of . . .

"Cassidy!"

On the off chance that Eric was ignoring the doorbell—it played Drake's "Rich Baby Daddy," so I didn't see how he could—Ms. Morton wanted me to peer through all the windows.

"Why can't you peer?" I demanded.

"In these shoes?" She lifted her pant leg enough to expose green leather sandals with kitten heels.

Okay, fair enough. Not shoes I'd ever be caught dead in, but also not shoes suitable for romping around in foundation plantings—which turned out to be harder than anticipated even for a pair of old sneakers. Eric had clearly gotten one of Alyx's lot to have a word with the creeping juniper. Another morning, the dense and prickly barrier might have gone up against the residual respect slash fear I felt for an ex–vice principal and won. This morning, unable to join the stranger for breakfast, I welcomed a chance to relieve some frustration. Eventually, pulling bits of shredded juniper out of my bra with a hand bleeding from defensive wounds, I returned to report that unless Eric was hiding in a closet or behind the enormous leather monstrosity he called a sofa, the house was empty.

"Call him again."

"If he's in there, you won't hear his phone through all that insul—"

"Call him again, Cassidy!"

Still buzzed from my triumph over the foliage, I rolled my eyes. Then I pulled out my phone. I might have been buzzed, but I wasn't stupid. "Same message." I told her, ending the call. "You'll have to wait until after one."

She threw up her hands. "What's he doing that's so important he can't be disturbed?"

"Maybe it's simply that he doesn't want to be disturbed."

"He's one of the Four!"

"And he's told you when he's going to be available." I wasn't happy about having to defend Eric, but I wasn't happy about Ms. Morton dragging me away from breakfast, either, so I found a backbone. "We're the town's connection to the Dark; that doesn't put us at your personal beck and call twenty-four-seven. A site inspection at a date to be named later isn't an emergency."

To my surprise, her shoulders slumped in defeat. Staring out at the visible sliver of shimmering lake, she wrapped her arms around herself, clutched at the sides of her sleeveless silk blouse, and murmured, "How much time do we have?"

I meant to say *I hope you find some answers, but I can hear lemon squares calling my name.* When I opened my mouth, what came out was "We could get Bridget to call him."

For a moment, I thought the Dark had thrown its two cents' worth in; then, to my horror, I realized my sense of responsibility had elbowed its way forward and used my voice. I was one of the Four. The mine supported the town. If there was trouble at the mine—and after years of dealing with teenagers, I was sure Ms. Morton had a finely honed sense of trouble—then I should help.

Right?

Apparently.

Straightening slowly out of her defeated curl, Ms. Morton turned to face me, eyebrows dipping in over her nose. "Bridget? Why? They're not friends; Eric's twice her age."

"And Bridget's an adult who can make her own decisions." Bridget might never be the first choice of a zombie looking for sustenance, but she was more than capable of taking care of herself. Actually, given that she taught yoga, tai chi, and this weird Brazilian martial art that seemed to involve a lot of handstands, she could take care of most people. "Bridget likes everyone," I continued. "She probably lets Eric hang around because she doesn't want to hurt his feelings." I remembered her putting the boot in, up at the Dead Ground. "That doesn't mean she can be taken advantage of. Now, Eric, he hangs around her because she's smoking hot, a total sweetheart, and he's infatuated with her. He's kind of pathetic, actually." When it became clear that Bridget wasn't going to answer her phone, I looked up and met Ms. Morton's frown. "Odds are high she forgot to charge. Come on."

"To?"

"The town hall," I told her as we got back into the car. "It's Wednesday morning."

"Right."

Of course Ms. Morton knew about Wednesday mornings. She had a grandchild about the right age.

We'd turned onto Pine Street when Ms. Morton said, "Why do you think Eric's pathetic?"

I shrugged. "Because he's the very definition of a not-very-smart man with too much money."

"*Wealthy and underachieving* does not make a person either pathetic or not very smart."

She'd put a little more emphasis on "a person" than I was entirely comfortable with.

"The two of you have been chosen by the Dark to maintain the connection between the Dark and the town and to work together for the greater good, upholding the Agreement."

I did not remember Aunt Jean using the words "for the greater good" in her welcome speech. Or "upholding the Agreement," for that matter. As I recalled, it had mostly consisted of *don't fuck up, let's see what Alice says*, and, *considering the available pool of descendants, I suppose it could have been worse*. Then Amanda had added that I couldn't possibly be worse than Simon, and Aunt Jean had replied, "We'll see." It hadn't actually been very welcoming.

I could almost see where they'd been coming from. It's not like there were qualifications beyond having slightly interbred ancestors—not, I discovered upon making the observation, that anyone seemed to have much of a sense of humor about it—but Simon had seemed perfect. Responsible, dependable, and considered least likely to get drunk and fall into the lake by his peers, but the sudden onset of power had completely derailed his mental train set. Before I was chosen, I, like the rest of the town, barely knew what he'd gotten up to. After, I got an earful.

"He's the Ears," Ms. Morton added. "You're the Mouth."

"I know!" Most people considered the Four a minor civic position, less useful than those who collected the garbage and significantly less useful than the snowplow drivers. Sure, you might die during the opening of the conduit, but you might die crossing the road. Some people, like Ms. Morton, believed the choice, the completely random choice, made us special. Both before the choice and after, I'd leaned toward the former opinion. Now . . .

Now I had a feeling that might be about to change.

"Perhaps," Ms. Morton continued, "you should get to know him rather than build your interactions around personal prejudices."

I sighed. "It's only been eighteen months and I'm trying, okay?" I didn't have a lot of choice; he always seemed to be around. If I went for a coffee, Eric would walk into the shop a minute later and start flirting with whoever was behind the counter. If I was out shoveling my driveway, he'd stop to give me a hand—which, to be fair, I appreciated. If Bridget and I went out for drinks, there he was in the pub—although his puppy-begging-for-a-biscuit expression was all about Bridget. If I went to the beach, there he was, making borderline-obnoxious observations to passing friends. He bought *a lot* of baked goods, and if I was in the diner, he was almost always tucked into a corner booth. Mind you, the whole point of a bakery was to sell baked goods, and we only had one diner, one coffee shop, and one pub, but . . .

I sighed again, sagged down in the seat as far as the belt would allow, and reluctantly admitted, "Given enough time, I might come to find him vaguely tolerable."

She huffed out a quiet breath and said, "Sit up straight, Cassidy. Conduits don't slouch."

———

Bridget had just handed out the last of the long metal marshmallow skewers when we arrived at the town hall. Holding her own skewer horizontally in front of her, as though she were directing the world's most chaotic marching band, she called out the first line of a familiar cadence. "What is the first rule?"

"One shadow, one skewer!" answered fourteen high-pitched voices. The kids were dressed identically in dark blue shorts, white T-shirts, and white sneakers. "Five shadows, five skewers!"

"And the second rule?"

"Don't forget to look up!"

"And the third?"

"Only skewer shadows." This response sounded more resigned than enthusiastic, but then, it always did.

"Well done, Flock! Now, pair up and check to make sure your buddy's light is shining."

Fourteen hands rose to fourteen foreheads, switching on fourteen very powerful miner's lights.

After the expected yelling about being blinded and how Kevin, Marian, and Jordan had done it on purpose died down, Bridget finally noticed Ms. Morton and me standing by the door. She waved, causing fourteen heads to simultaneously turn toward us.

I blinked. They blinked. I wondered if the stranger liked kids. I didn't dislike them in general but had some specific reservations about this lot. I hoped Bridget planned to keep them out of cornfields. Ms. Morton did something with her face, and all fourteen heads hurriedly faced Bridget again.

"Does everyone have a map?" she asked.

Hands rose, clutching sheets of paper.

"And what do you do if you need help?"

"Blow the whistle three times!"

It wasn't our first rodeo, so Ms. Morton and I had our fingers in our ears before the whistle cacophony started. When it eventually ended, Bridget beamed and said, "Go downstairs and discuss strategy. No skewering until I arrive."

They swarmed past us and in the moving mass of blue and white and waving skewers I recognized Lillian Prewitt. We locked eyes. She grinned at me, grabbed the girl beside her by the arm, and yanked her forward. "This is Hannah! She's my best friend! We're going to get our Shadow Hunter badges, and then we only have two more badges until we aren't fledglings anymore!"

"Good for you," Ms. Morton said briskly while I tried to remember how many badges I'd managed to acquire. Maybe seven or eight? Not all thirteen; that was for sure.

Hannah managed only a truncated "Hi, Grandma" before Lillian dragged her past.

Bridget broke up a fight over who got to ride down in the elevator with Nathan—his wheelchair limited it to three—then, brilliant white sneakers squeaking against the floor, she headed toward us. "Are you here to help?" she asked brightly.

"Do you need help?" I wondered. After Mrs. Best's unfortunate experience with a few poorly tied quick-release knots and an early train, Bridget had been the only applicant for the leadership position.

She smiled sunnily. "With what?"

Okay, then.

"They need twenty shadows each for their Shadow Hunter Badge," Ms. Morton said thoughtfully, "and you've got a good-sized group this summer. Are there that many shadows around?"

"Absolutely. Didn't you hear?" Eyes wide, she leaned closer and lowered her voice. "Two nights ago, Blair Abbott got shadowed."

Well, so much for that one-hundred-and-three-day record.

I frowned as I tried to place Blair Abbott. Short, kind of busty, late thirties, wore a lot of horizontal stripes. Really liked carrot cake. Although both end results of direct lines, with ten years between us, we weren't friends, nor had we overlapped at the monthly what-to-expect-when-you-might-be-assimilated classes we all had to go to as teenagers. "Her great-grandmother was my great-grandmother's cousin."

"Shared a great-great grandfather," Bridget said solemnly.

We turned together to face Ms. Morton.

She sighed. "My father was her father's cousin."

The relief I felt showed on Bridget's face as we silently agreed that sounded like the closest connection. Neither of us wanted to spend an hour or two untangling lineages before we could figure out who should receive the condolences.

"I'm sorry for your loss," I said quietly.

Bridget echoed the sentiment.

Ms. Morton sighed again. "How do you know about Blair, Bridget?"

"Blair's been living upstairs from me ever since her husband left, and—"

Ms. Morton's raised hand cut her off. "Does he need to be told?"

"Dave? Her husband?" Bridget shook her head, blonde hair swooshing around like a shampoo commercial. "He left after the last bloodworm infestation. Blair said it was likely he broke speed limits all the way to Vancouver."

"Then he doesn't need to be told," I pointed out. "He doesn't remember."

"Wouldn't mind forgetting the blood worms myself," Ms. Morton muttered, and added, "Please continue your explanation, Bridget."

"My explanation?" Perfect brows drew in, then rose. "Oh. Blair! Right. Blair was upstairs and I was downstairs because that big old house is too big for just me, so that's why I split it in half. I heard a crash. I ran upstairs, heard smaller crashes, and followed the noise to the bedroom. Blair had nearly been buried in a mass of shadows, and she'd knocked over her bedside table reaching for the lamp. "It was a nice lamp," she sidebarred thoughtfully. "Green ceramic with pressed flowers on the shade. I raced back to my place and grabbed my portable sunlamp, which I have for portable tanning," she added, before anyone asked. "The sunlamp crisped the shadows—"

"Carbonized them," Ms. Morton interjected.

Bridget stared at her for a long moment, then a preteen shriek from downstairs reminded her she was on the clock. "Sure. Carbonized. Anyway, there had to have been dozens of shadows joined together, and it was too late for poor Blair. That's why I know there's enough shadows around to hunt. Unless . . ." She paused and frowned. Gracefully. "I suppose I could have crisped everything that came through. I called Security and I'm sure they've set up the lights so there won't be any more for a while, but—"

"How did the shadows get into Blair's bedroom?" I asked, cutting her off.

"Oh, that's easy." Bridget flashed me a sunny smile. "She was asleep with the window open."

"With the window open?" Who slept with their window open? Blair had been lucky it had only been shadows. All they could do was kill her.

Holding her fingers about a centimeter apart, Bridget said, "It wasn't open very much, but, yeah, it was open."

"Blair always was careless." Ms. Morton sighed. "She was possessed twice the year she turned thirteen. Once happens to the best of us, but there's no excuse for a second incident."

She wasn't wrong.

"Wait." Ms. Morton held up a hand, although as far as I could see, no one needed to be stopped. "If this happened two nights ago, why haven't I heard about it?"

Bridget shrugged. "You've been busy?"

"Why didn't I hear about it?"

Bridget turned to me and shrugged again. "You don't pay attention."

Fair. Shadows were no big deal. They slipped through, no one called the Four for such a minor problem, and no one, except for apparently Blair, slept with the windows open. It was news to me that Ms. Morton kept track of this sort of thing, but it wasn't a surprise.

I leaned back, away from Bridget's waving skewer. "If there's any left, the Flock and I will take care of them, and then, if there's not enough for badges, we'll go for ice cream."

The second shriek from downstairs sounded less like laughter and more like . . .

"I have to go."

"Before you do"—I snagged her T-shirt as she rushed past—"can you call Eric and ask him to meet you here?"

"Am I going to be here?" she asked, head cocked.

"No. You'll be with the Flock, but Ms. Morton needs to talk to the Dark, and Eric's ignoring all calls until after one. He won't ignore yours."

She dimpled at me. "That's so sweet of him."

━━━━━

Eric showed up a few minutes after the noise of fourteen prepubescent Shadow Hunters faded into the distance. He practically skipped up the stairs, then hurried into the hall, wearing shorts and a Hawaiian shirt loud enough they could hear it in Timmins. He stopped, his back to Ms. Morton and me sitting on folding chairs against the wall, bounced lightly in place, and called, "Briiiiidg-et! You said you needed to see me."

"I needed you," Ms. Morton snapped. Eric flailed around to face us, his smile turning to disappointment. To my surprise, I felt kind of bad about that. "Or, more precisely," Ms. Morton continued, still snapping, "I needed the Ears of the Dark and . . . You. Weren't. Listening."

Eric and Ms. Morton were about the same age, and she hadn't had the chance to install the same ultimate authority buttons in him. He sighed, rearranged his face so the disappointment didn't show, and folded his arms. "I'm entitled to time for myself."

"You're required, as one of the Four, to be on call as needed."

"The Mouth . . ."

She tugged me forward. "Is here."

He smiled insincerely. "And here I am too, Nancy. Isn't that nice."

"After we . . ."

He raised a brow, and she sputtered to a stop. My appreciation for him rose about five percentage points. If I'd been able to do that, I'd have had breakfast with the stranger. I hoped she ate her crusts. It was just weird when people didn't eat their crusts. "What's so important it can't wait until Friday?" he asked wearily.

His tone gave me the impression that Ms. Morton may have been a bit of a pain in the ass toward the Four back before I came on the scene. If this turned out to be a petty power play between the mine's board of directors and the Four . . .

"The government is scheduling a site inspection."

"Shit."

Okay, maybe not.

"Cassidy, over here." Eric motioned me toward the dais and chairs we usually used. "Let's do this."

"Just like that?"

"Just like that." He sat, took a look at me as I settled into the chair beside him, and sighed. "You're not in the right headspace. Match your breathing to mine."

I wanted to protest, but he'd been doing this for years, so I breathed in, breathed out, appreciated his no-doubt-very-expensive aftershave, breathed in, breathed out, wondered if holding a Journal would help with the headspace thing, breathed in, breathed out, and felt calm settled over me like a warm, fuzzy blanket.

Ms. Morton pressed a hand to her heart, released a deep breath, and said, "I have made the sacrifice."

News to me. Did she get up in the morning and do a preemptive s-word just in case? If so, what exactly did she s-word? I had no idea. And, fortunately, it was none of my business.

"My ears Hear," Eric murmured.

Pulling the letter out of her pocket, Ms. Morton explained the situation, finally reading the letter aloud.

It was official government-speak, so I didn't pay much attention, but my lips began to twitch while she read. By the time she finished, my throat had started to hurt. My mouth opened. My tongue twitched. No sound emerged.

"Use your Mouth," Ms. Morton demanded, leaning in. "Why is the Agreement weakening? How can we strengthen it?"

My mouth opened wider. My throat closed around the air I'd drawn in for the Dark to use, trapping it. I felt like I'd swallowed a handful of forks, the tines jabbed into flesh, the handles layered into a barricade. My neck muscles flexed, the barrier shattered, and the Dark's voice rose from a deep, shredding growl into a nails-on-chalkboard shriek. "ETERNAL INERTIA INTERRUPTED! DISCOURSE ANON!"

And I found myself off both chair and dais, on my hands and knees, dripping blood onto the scuffed hardwood floor.

"Cassie?" Eric almost sounded concerned.

I spat, sat back on my heels, and panted, one hand raised to block any further questions. "I'm okay," I said after a minute, my voice a wet rasp. "Impressive busy signal, though."

"We don't get a busy signal!" Ms. Morton snarled, trying unsuccessfully to mask fear with anger.

"We just did." I leaned forward and spat again. That hadn't been fun.

"Then it's another sign the Agreement is weakening!"

I glanced at Eric, but apparently, I was supposed to answer this non-question, too.

"How?" I asked, accepting Eric's hand and letting him pull me to my feet, jerking out of his hold before he pulled me too close. "The Dark Listened. The Dark Spoke. It's busy. It'll talk later."

"Is that what you took from that?"

I swallowed. Bad idea. "That's what it Said."

"Fine. That's what it said." She strode across the hall, spun on her heel, returned, and glared at me. "It's never busy!"

"How do you know? Maybe it's always busy on Wednesday. Could be laundry day."

She gestured at the wet stain I'd left on the floor, then jabbed a finger toward me. "This seems an excessive response to laundry, does it not?"

"Maybe a bit," I admitted, wiping blood off my mouth with the back of my hand.

"A bit," she scoffed. "An *eternal inertia interrupted* doesn't sound like merely busy!"

"Could be a euphemism for food poisoning. An interrupted eternal inertia could have it stuck on the toilet."

Eric snorted half a laugh, but Ms. Morton narrowed her eyes. "It's another sign. The inspection, Blair, now this!"

"Blair left her window open," Eric pointed out, handing me a throat lozenge. "Third cousin," he added, when I shot him a silent question.

I didn't have the energy to work out if that meant his tie was closer than Ms. Morton's. I was usually good at it—we all had to be, given how tight the ties were between us—just not today. "Sorry for your loss."

He sighed. "Open window."

"Yeah."

"The Dark has abandoned us," Ms. Morton began.

Eric cut her off. "The Dark just spoke to us. A site inspection isn't good news," he continued, "but it doesn't have to be a disaster."

"Oh, doesn't it?" she snapped. "There has been an active silver mine here since 1831, mining the same thirteen kilometers of tunnel. How do you suggest I explain that to a government inspector?"

"An inspector will forget what they've seen as soon as they leave," I reminded them before it came to blows. "They'll only remember what makes sense in their normal world." I sketched air quotes around *normal*.

"Oh, really? What if it makes sense for them to close us down? With a weakened Agreement, they could remember everything."

"I can Tell them not to," I offered reluctantly. Because hanging around government inspectors was exactly how I wanted to spend my time. Hang on. Did I have to hang around? "Bring them to me as soon as they arrive, and I'll Tell them they're seeing what they need to see to give us top marks. I'll even throw in a pie. Tah-dah." I took a bow.

"Weakened Agreement," Ms. Morton repeated. "What if it doesn't work?"

"Then we feed them to Alice," I sighed, straightening. "She ate Pete Everett's snowmobile." And Pete Everett. Dumbass didn't check the ice. "I'm sure she can handle a government sedan."

"Oh, yes, that's brilliant. We can feed the people who come looking for them to Alice as well. And the people who come looking for them. And so on and so on, ad infinitum. It will never end!"

"Alice is up to it," I muttered. I was getting a little tired of Ms. Morton.

"What if they intend to give us a citation for environmental responsibility?" Eric asked in his best bored, rich-man voice. Seemed Eric was also getting a little tired of Ms. Morton.

Ms. Morton's mouth snapped closed with enough force, I heard her teeth click together. After a moment, she managed an incredulous "What?"

"Given the amount of silver we've taken out of that mine, we've made a remarkably small impact on the environment." Unhooking his sunglasses from his shirt pocket, Eric frowned down at the lenses. "Granted, there's only Alice left in the lake, which isn't the best situation from an environmental standpoint."

"Not the fault of the mine," I pointed out.

Ms. Morton glared at Eric, then glared at me, then glared at us simultaneously. "Neither of you are taking this seriously enough!"

Eric shrugged. "Maybe because nothing's actually happened yet."

Where had I heard a variation on that theme before?

No, wait, don't tell me; midsummer, Amanda's porch, after Travis Brayden s-worded himself on the Dead Ground. No one had taken it seriously. Nothing had happened, so why should they? Except that the government wanted to inspect the mine, so something clearly had happened.

Right?

I was one of the Four, but I was not going to be responsible for the whole chimichanga. A quarter of a chimichanga at best. But maybe I could do something for Blair. Well, not *for* Blair; Blair was dead, and even in Lake Argen, death was usually permanent. Some exceptions, sure, but those happened everywhere, right? Maybe I could do something because of Blair. Something because Blair had died.

Maybe, maybe, what if, what if, maybe, maybe. I was beginning to realize I'd lived a definitive life right up until the morning Travis Brayden had stuck that knife through his foot and disappeared. I wanted that life back.

A fly buzzed against a window as moments passed. Finally, I sighed. There was only one resource left to plumb. I didn't like it, but the only other option was to walk away, and, to my surprise, I couldn't. Seriously, I hadn't even known Blair that well. "All right." I dried my palms on my cargo shorts. "I'm going to talk to Alice."

Eric fumbled his sunglasses, catching them just before impact with the floor. "Why? The lake's been calm," he added, like I hadn't noticed. Like I hadn't paid even that much attention.

"Alice's actions in the past have indicated a close relationship with the Dark," Ms. Morton said thoughtfully. And pretentiously. "It's possible that, as her condition is an intrinsic part of the Agreement, she'll know why it's weakening. Although, if she doesn't, archival accounts make it quite clear that asking anything she considers a stupid question will upset her. You don't want to upset her."

The obvious response was *No shit, Sherlock.* I didn't make it. Go me. "Did you want to come along?" I asked. "Make sure I don't do anything stupid?"

Ms. Morton's eyes widened, she took a step back, pressed both hands to her heart, and said, "No."

Quelle surprise.

"Take Blair's body."

We turned together to look at Eric.

"It'll help keep Alice sweet, and given the shadows, Blair is quite definitely dead, so it's a little pointless to wait the full three days to make sure before tossing the body." Bodies had been respectfully disposed of in the lake—not tossed—since the cemetery uprising of '02. The easiest way to prevent it from happening again had been to cut off the supply. The three-day wait allowed doctors to identify the occasional body that was only *mostly* dead. "I'll clear it with closer family."

"Clear it with Blair," I told him. "Body autonomy," I added when he frowned at me. "It's her body. She gets to decide what happens to it. Catherine will have no trouble reaching her; it hasn't even been forty-eight hours."

Catherine was one of Alyx's. She'd been a good medium down south; in Lake Argen, she was amazing.

"Catherine charges a small fortune if she has to go looking," Eric pointed out.

I smiled. "Bill the mayor. Business of the Four. We're saving the town."

"Are we?"

Ms. Morton answered before I could. "Yes. You are."

I'd been joking. She wasn't.

Eric glanced between us, then nodded. "All right then. I'll talk to Catherine . . ."

Quelle surprise again. Catherine was a gorgeous widow around Eric's age with zero patience for bullshit. I'd no doubt that regardless of what he may or may not feel for Bridget, he'd been looking for a way to make contact.

". . . and then Blair's family. You call Amanda. If you're going to be moving Blair's body, you'll need Hands."

Blair was my size. Maybe a little heavier. "You're not going to help?"

"I'm doing my bit."

When I turned to ask Ms. Morton the same question, she was already at the door. Lady could motor when she wanted to, I hadn't even heard her move. "I have a mine to run," she threw back over her shoulder. "Let me know what Alice has to say the moment you're back on shore."

———

There was no sign of the stranger when I peered in through the diner window. Mom waved. It not being a good day for a lecture, I waved back and headed into the bakery.

"Hey, Cass." Chris frowned down at the phone in his hand. "Weirdest thing. I was just going to call home and remind Alan to throw in a load of laundry, but I only have three bars."

"Three?"

"Yeah. Three. I don't remember that ever happening before, do you?"

"No," I told him. "I don't." I pulled out my phone and checked the screen. Three bars. Enough to make a call, sure, but here in Lake Argen, for as long as the cell towers have been up, we've had five. Always five. Not three. Five. "Can you send a cheesecake or something over to the diner?" I clutched my phone tightly enough, the case creaked in protest. "I've got an errand to run for the Four."

"Sure; where are you off to?"

"I'm meeting Amanda at the funeral home."

"Is it about Blair? I hear she got shadowed. Sad." He shook his head. "But then, I heard she was sleeping with her window open, so kind of a self-inflicted death, right? Is it a Four thing because of the shadows? Do they hatch?"

"Do they what?"

"Hatch. Make baby shadows."

"They never have." I tried to remember everything I'd ever read about shadows and came up blank. "Why do you even think of things like that?"

"I have a daughter. I have to consider all possibilities." Chris checked the upper oven and reset the timer. "So, are you and Amanda disposing of the body?"

How much to tell him . . .

"Sort of," I said, shoved my phone back into my pocket, grabbed a cookie, and left.

So much for lemon squares and an afternoon at the beach.

So much for getting to know that elusive stranger.

Duty called.

FIVE

Melanie

I suspected I was dreaming when the moose in the passenger seat began complaining about how kids today were obsessed with gender. Up until then, he'd been a perfectly pleasant traveling companion. I knew I was dreaming when he turned into Aubrey Cameron, the paunchy, middle-aged physics teacher who'd maliciously persisted in dead-naming one of his students and then passive aggressively bitched about kids today later in the staff room. No way I'd have ever gotten into a car with that sweaty asshole. Swearing under my breath, I pushed the clearly marked ejector-seat button.

It buzzed.

I pushed it again.

It kept buzzing.

I slammed it with Mjolnir, conveniently tucked down beside the driver's seat.

It buzzed louder.

Which was when I realized the sound was actually coming from the enormous insect keeping pace just outside the car window.

Or possibly coming from my phone. I had vague memories of setting an alarm.

I fought my way up to consciousness, then, tangled in the flowered sheet, fought my way to the side of the bed and fumbled with my phone until my three functioning brain cells figured out how to turn the alarm off.

The buzzing continued.

Turned out it was coming from the enormous insect slamming itself against the window.

I'd tried to open the window before bed, but it had been painted closed and I'd given up after a brief struggle. The guest house obviously had central air, and I supposed I couldn't blame them if they'd rather not have clueless guests cool the great outdoors.

The buzz was annoyingly audible through the glass.

It wasn't a cicada. And no matter how big they insisted the mosquitoes were in Northern Ontario, it wasn't a mosquito, in spite of multiple thin and delicate legs. Kicking free of the bedding, I sat up and took a closer look. My room was on the northwest side of the building, and morning sun threw the window into deep shadow, blurring the details, but it was probably . . .

"Bock!"

"Holy shit!" I snatched up a pillow and held it like a shield as an enormous black bird snatched the bug off the screen with a cry of triumph. After a moment, heart pounding, still holding the pillow, I slid out of bed and shuffled cautiously toward the window. No giant bug. No giant bird. Just a view of a road, and past it, between the trees, a small park, a beach, and Lake Argen stretching off into the distance.

It wasn't exactly a pretty view; *pretty* seemed to be too small a word for it.

Especially at seven o'clock in the morning.

Why was I up at . . .

Right.

The woman who'd checked me in had said breakfast was from seven-thirty to ten, and past-me had decided to get an early start.

"Past-me was an idiot," I muttered, heading for the ensuite.

The shower pressure was amazing, the temperature perfect, and the towels both large enough and actually fluffy. Someone had clearly spent money on this place. The flowered wallpaper that extended from the bedroom into the bathroom was a little much, particularly given the flowered sheets, flowered upholstery, flowered curtains, and flowered toilet-seat cover, but somehow, it almost worked.

Almost.

Jeans, sneakers, and a scoop-neck T-shirt later, I threw my phone in my messenger bag, my messenger bag over my shoulder, and headed downstairs. One wall in the stairwell between the second and third floor had been covered with scarlet wallpaper, patterned with gold fleur-de-lis. One wall in the stairwell between the first and second floor had been covered with gold wallpaper, patterned with scarlet fleur-de-lis.

Having flashbacks to high-school pep rallies I hadn't enjoyed— with scarlet and gold colors held high in our right hand rah rah rah, scarlet and gold my ass, they were fucking red and yellow—I finally reached the lobby. It had been papered with pages from old poetry books. A cool idea, but, combined with the rest, it felt like someone was trying too hard.

"Good morning, Melanie." A fragile-looking older woman reached out over the Dutch door that separated the private living room from the hall. "Did you sleep well?"

"I did." I took the offered hand, freeing myself hurriedly when the woman tried to double-hand me, obviously planning to hang on.

"I think I forgot to introduce us . . ." She closed her eyes and gave her head a short shake. "Introduce myself," she amended. "I'm Theresa Prewitt. Welcome to All That Glitters."

"Is not gold." I couldn't resist. I'd taught *The Lord of the Rings* to eleventh-grade English and had caught hell from parents when I'd refused to accept movie answers on the exam.

"Gold? No, dear; around here, it's silver. We see you're staying for a full week. That's lovely. We don't get many long-term visitors."

"I'm here to give Travis Brayden's grandmother closure. Travis Brayden," I repeated when it was obvious Theresa Prewitt didn't recognize the name. "He disappeared in June." I'd spent part of the drive north working out how much I should tell the people of Lake Argen about my "job," but since the whole point of the exercise involved getting people to talk about Travis, it seemed pointless to be coy.

"That doesn't . . ." Head cocked, Theresa frowned, clearly listening to something beyond the ambient noises of an old building. "Oh, him," she said at last, breaking into a smile. "Travis Brayden. The police decided he'd gotten lost in the woods." The smile disappeared. "So sad."

"Do you agree with the police?"

Sparkly nail polish twinkled as she waved off the question. "They'd know, wouldn't they."

Would they, I wondered? Or would they just decide to quit looking? Write him off because Lake Argen was too far from his grandmother's money to make him important? "Did Travis stay here?"

"Here? Oh, no. If he wasn't staying with friends, he was probably staying at the motel out by the boundary." Again, she listened to nothing. "Not *boundary*, no, of course not. We don't say *boundary*, do we. Do you know if he had friends here? If he did, you should talk to them."

"I don't think he did." But that would be information I needed to find out. Why hadn't I gotten it from Mrs. Brayden?

Because Mrs. Brayden didn't have it?

Had I even asked Mrs. Brayden why Travis had gone to Lake Argen? I couldn't remember. The introduction of ten thousand dollars to the conversation had swept more practical matters away in a roaring torrent of possibilities. I remembered drinking multiple cups of tea, but I didn't remember asking very many questions.

No point in asking questions if they weren't close, I reminded myself.

But Mrs. Brayden would have known where Travis had been staying. That information would've been in the police report. Had she read the police report? Why hadn't I asked to see it? Never mind; I knew the answer to that. With luck, Mrs. Brayden would be too busy grieving to realize the person she'd paid to find out about her grandson's last days had gotten off to a totally shitty start.

"So, the motel out by the edge of town," I began.

"The Lake Argen Motel," Theresa interrupted, smiling. "Not very original."

"How do I find it?"

Theresa blinked. "Oh, I don't think it's lost." She gave her head a shake, her smile disappeared, and her voice grew confident. "The road you took into town, that's Argen Street. Runs from Gogama Road all the way over to the mine. You exit the parking lot, turn right on Essex, and when you get to the T-junction, you're at Argen Street. Turn left and keep walking. Motel's on the right once you get around the curve. Can't miss it." Another shake and the smile returned, her voice softening. "Did you want breakfast first, dear?"

"Please." To my surprise, Theresa handed over an All That Glitters business card with *ONE BREAKFAST, NO LIMIT* written on the back in purple ink.

"Take that to the diner and they'll fix you right up. Whatever you want from their breakfast menu." She smiled again, I assumed at my expression, and added in the same confident voice she'd used to give directions, "I don't cook anymore."

———

Greeted by a chorus of avian barks as I stepped out the side door into the parking lot, I frowned up at the roosting ravens. "Crows flock. You lot are supposed to be solitary birds."

The ravens loudly disagreed.

"Look, you can bitch about it all you want, but David Suzuki has never lied to me."

A raven coasted down from the trees, landed on the roof of my car, looked directly at me, and shouted *KWAA!* It probably wasn't personal. It certainly felt personal. It felt personal enough that I began to breathe a little faster and eye the nearest exit.

I'd always assumed I'd prefer birds to giant bugs. Now, I wasn't so sure.

The *BOCK*s and *KWAA*s grew louder and overlapped into a rough wall of sound as I walked quickly down the driveway, hoping I wasn't about to find myself in a cut-rate Canadian Hitchcock remake.

The latest *KWAA* sounded mocking, and the *BOCK*s sounded like raven laughter. I had just enough time to see the approaching runner before he slammed into me, and we both went down.

"Oh, for fuck's sake!" My ass was padded enough to absorb the landing, and the damage seemed limited to a point on my thigh where the runner's bony knee had dug in.

"Sorry. Sorry. Sorry." His breath smelled strongly of peppermint, although given the pervasiveness, it was possible he'd combed peppermint oil through the long, grey length of his perfect-for-a-ZZ-Top-cosplay beard. It took us a moment to get arms and legs untangled, then he bounded to his feet with remarkable energy for a man of his apparent age and held out a hand. "Sorry," he repeated. "I heard the squadron, and you can't trust that lot when they're off duty."

"The ravens?" I managed to get to my feet without dragging him down again and released his hand, which was large and warm, with multiple small wounds across the back and palm, fingers wrapped in superhero bandages.

He smiled up at me, the face above his beard crinkling into happy lines. "Aerial Defense Force, miss. Flight Commander Reginald Morton at your service."

"Pleased to meet you, Commander." Why not? "I'm Melanie Solvich."

"You're new?"

"I'm visiting."

"In that case . . ." He rose up on his toes and leaned in. "Don't," he said seriously, "eat the mushrooms."

About to ask which mushrooms, I heard another *KWAA* behind me and ducked instead. A wing feather brushed against my cheek as a raven swooped past.

"You just mind your manners, Flight Sergeant!" Reginald yelled, shaking his fist at the departing bird's tail feathers.

I couldn't stop myself from laughing.

"Oh, sure," he said, arms folded over the middle section of his beard. Given the crinkles around his eyes, I was pretty sure he was smiling. "It's all fun and games until someone misses the angle on their approach. If you'll excuse me, Ms. Solvich, I need to go take this lot in hand." He laid two fingers against my wrist. "Remember what I said about the mushrooms."

Then he pivoted on one heel, vaguely military in spite of the worn sneakers, strode up the driveway, and yelled, "Don't give me that! I expect better of you lot!"

The diner was definitively a diner. The inside was a long rectangle, narrow end at the street, with three booths in the window and a curved counter with stools along the front of one side wall. Beyond the counter, the kitchen. Against the other side wall were a dozen four-to-six-person booths and three two-person booths. The worn burgundy upholstery and the fake wood paneling were all about the 1970s and, I suspected, playing into expectations. The plexiglass barriers separating the booths brought the aesthetic into the present.

I had a little trouble with the door but finally managed to wrestle it into submission. As I didn't see a sign insisting I wait to be seated, I sat myself in one of the two-person booths, salivating at the smell of bacon.

"Here for breakfast?" The waitress was about my mother's age; shorter and less worn down by life, with dark hair pulled back into a low ponytail and bright pink lipstick emphasizing her smile.

I held up the guest-house card.

"Of course. Coffee to start, hon?"

"Please."

She smiled at my vehemence and poured. Then frowned. "You have very familiar eyebrows."

"I have what?"

"Your eyebrows are practically Foster eyebrows. They do that same arc thing." Then she laughed. "Sorry. That must sound crazy to someone from out of town, and my only excuse is that I've been up since five. My ridiculous husband"—she waved toward the kitchen—"insists we do the early opening twice a week so we don't forget our roots."

The server was one of the owners of the restaurant? That was . . . different. The badge on her peacock-blue golf shirt said *Hello, my name is Grace*.

"My ridiculous husband is a morning person," she continued. "I most certainly am not. I'm not surprised I'm seeing things, and I apologize for involving you in my hallucinations. Have you decided what you're having?"

The menu was a single sheet of laminated, legal-size paper. At best, most mornings, I was a visit to Timmies for coffee and a donut type of person, but something about small towns, and guest houses, and diners convinced me to order the Lake Argen Breakfast.

"Over easy, bacon, rye toast, fried potatoes," I told her, handing back the menu.

"There's onions in with the potatoes."

"Love onions."

"Did you want to add mushrooms?"

"Don't eat the mushrooms."

Mushrooms fried in with potatoes and onions sounded amazing.

"Remember what I said about the mushrooms."

"No, thank you. Not this morning."

Grace stared at me for a long moment, then nodded. "Probably wise."

Sitting alone, I couldn't help be aware of the three curved backs at the counter, of the people in the booths. Eating. Talking. Watching the stranger in their midst?

Not that I noticed.

Points for subtlety, I guess.

It was hard to mess up a basic breakfast, but the eggs were exactly the right amount of runny, the bacon was perfectly crispy, and the butter went all the way to the edges of the toast. I gave the meal an A+. As I wiped up the last bit of egg yolk with my last bite of toast, an elderly couple left their booth and stopped by my table.

"Sorry to interrupt . . ." The male half of the couple swayed forward and caught himself on the edge of the table. ". . . but are you staying in the guest house?"

My first thought was to tell him it was none of his business. My second was that I needed people to talk to me. "Yes, I'm staying at the guest house."

"Did you see Theresa this morning?" He leaned in a little. "How was she?"

I didn't exactly have a basis of comparison, but . . . "She seemed okay."

"That's good to hear." The tense line of his shoulders softened. "Daniel, her husband died back in January . . ."

"February." The woman beside him sighed impatiently.

". . . and she hasn't let him go. Of course, if friends and family ask, she's fine. Trouble is, holding on like that, that's just not healthy." He smiled down at me. "It's nice to have an outside opinion. Are you staying long?"

"Her business is none of your business, Albert." With a terse "Sorry to bother you," she tugged him into motion and out the door.

Just for a second, I thought I saw a narrow tentacle loop down over his collar. A second look identified it as a perfectly normal, curling strand of silver hair.

"More coffee?"

"Absolutely." I was clearly under-caffeinated.

"I hope Albert wasn't bothering you," Grace said as she poured.

"He was just asking about the guest house. Actually, about . . ."

"Theresa. His wife and Theresa . . . don't talk."

There was an extended Shakespearian drama in the pause.

"It makes it hard on him," she continued. "They used to be close. They came in together for breakfast every Sunday for, oh, almost twenty years. Then, about five years after Albert's first wife died, he remarried, and Mary put her foot down. Either she came along, or breakfast with Theresa was over. Daniel, Theresa's late husband, who was Mary's cousin, had a word with her, but it didn't do any good. We've all taken a run at it, but Mary waited almost forty years to marry Albert, and she has no intention of sharing."

It might, I realized, be harder to get people to stop talking to me.

"Sorry. They're strangers to you and I can't imagine why you'd care." She smiled and pulled a handful of creamers from her apron pocket. "We don't get a lot of visitors."

Which was my cue. I presented Travis's picture, the sketch Mrs. Brayden had drawn of the knife, and explained why I was there.

Grace pulled out a pair of reading glasses and peered down at the photo. "I don't remember him . . ."

That seemed unlikely, given her enthusiasm about my presence.

". . . but he looks like the sort who'd eat at the pub rather than here."

Okay, fair enough. I hadn't realized there'd be more than one place to eat in a town this size. I was all about big-city living. And, temporarily, Saskatoon.

"Let me ask my husband. May I?" She waved the photo and when I nodded, headed into the kitchen, returning a few minutes later just as I finished my coffee. "Richard doesn't remember the boy either and, mostly because he's a joker, he checked the knife drawer. He says Cassie, our daughter, might have something to Say about Travis."

Had I just heard a random capitalization go by?

"Normally, Cassie would be next door in the bakery. Something came up this morning, though, and I have no idea where she's got off to. Let me give her a—"

"Grace! French toast up!"

"Thanks, but I'm sure I'll run into her later," I said as Grace glared toward the kitchen. Stuffing Travis's picture back into my purse, I scrambled out of the small booth. "I'm heading up to the motel now." I had no idea why I said that. In case I also got lost in the woods? "If you can tell me the total so I can . . ."

"Tip's included, hun. We slap on twenty percent and Theresa happily covers it. Daniel was the cook in the family, you know. Although you wouldn't, of course. Know, that is. Don't let Arthur at the motel give you a hard time. His bark is worse than his bite." Grace frowned thoughtfully. "Mostly because he stopped biting people."

"He—"

"Years ago," she added, cutting off my question. "You have a good day, now."

I could feel her smile on my back all the way out to the sidewalk.

———

Having spent much of the last two days driving, I shuddered at the thought of getting back into the driver's seat. I'd walk to the motel. Lake Argen was a small town; how far away could the motel be?

Besides, I wanted to start earning my money, get a feel for the town. Maybe figure out what had drawn Travis there.

Three blocks from the diner, I froze at the corner of Essex and Argen and stared across the road at a small turquoise house, its tiny front yard dominated by a multi-stemmed birch. It looked welcoming. I had the strangest thought that if I approached, the door would be unlocked and I'd find a comfy chair by the front window, angled in such a way that the sun would perfectly illuminate the page should I want to spend the afternoon reading.

I didn't even like turquoise as a rule, and its tropical brilliance was out of place in Northern Ontario.

Except it wasn't.

It fit perfectly in its place.

Weird.

I turned left. This part of Argen Street ran between a number of houses similar to the turquoise house, if less bright, and finally past a large Victorian on an enormous corner lot at Argen and Elm. Someone in the past had had enough money to bring a shit-ton of bricks, and at least one mason, north. Crossing the road, I looked toward the lake. This was clearly the old-money part of town. I could see a second and possibly a third shit-ton of Victorian bricks, almost hidden by enormous trees.

Were they . . . elms?

A brief fling in university with a forestry student had included, besides mediocre sex, regular rants about how back in the 1970s, Dutch elm disease had wiped the elms off every Elm Street in southern Ontario. I vaguely remembered their range from her incessant flash cards, and I was pretty sure Lake Argen had to be close to, if not over, the northern edge. I definitely remembered that *Sambucus pubens* was the Latin name of the American red elder. Which had nothing to do with anything much except that it was a hard name to forget. If there were elms there, maybe Travis was—had been—an arborist. I hadn't asked what he did for a living. Why hadn't I . . .

Right. Never mind.

On the other side of Elm Street, I ran out of sidewalk. I ignored the speculative look from a passing pickup driver—the only moving vehicle I'd seen since leaving the diner—and crossed Argen Street to where the sidewalk continued, ending up in front of a single-story building set back from the road behind a double line of parking spaces instead of a front yard. Five of the eight spaces were full, and I thought I could hear the drone of quiet . . .

Chanting?

Not cheer chanting; the-ghosts-of-murdered-monks-in-a-haunted-castle chanting.

The wrought-iron railings leading up to the door gave it some gravitas, but the building didn't look like a church. Actually, I couldn't remember seeing a church. Strange, because in my experience, small Ontario towns had at least a three-to-one ratio between churches and coffee shops. Occasionally more. Never less. I turned back toward the lake and scanned the rooflines. No steeples. Possibly hidden in the impossible elms, but I didn't think so. The whole place had a *We were never ruled by the women's auxiliary* feeling.

The chanting stopped. A voice rose above the background noise of birds and bugs and a distant engine. "Raymond! Pay attention or I'll send that brand-new baritone of yours back to youth adulation."

So . . . a small, unadorned church, then?

A wide barrier of trees and a wrought-iron fence separated the building from a large cemetery, supporting my small-unadorned-church theory. The fence around the cemetery was also made of wrought iron, the square bars maybe three centimeters on a side, stuck vertically into a concrete pad running along beside the sidewalk, close enough together that nothing much larger than a cat would be able to get through. Or, rather, between. A tank might be able to get through. The crosspieces, also iron, were about twenty centimeters apart.

It looked like the town had had enough of vandalism and/or people partying on the graves and decided to definitively put a stop to it. Or maybe it was to stop bears. Did bears dig up graves?

Pulling out my phone, I was astounded to discover I had three bars, realized I had no idea how much data I had left, and put the phone away again. But three bars! Up north in the middle of nowhere. I didn't always get three bars in my mother's apartment.

The cemetery gates were open.

As I moved closer to the sign on the gatepost, my phone rang.

"Do bears dig up graves?" I asked.

"How the hell should I know?" It'd take more than an ursine non sequitur to throw my mother off her stride. "Isn't that something you should ask about locally?"

"Just wondering why the cemetery is so well fenced."

"Vandals. Visigoths. Why are you in the cemetery?"

"Just walking past it on my way to talk to the motel owner."

"You're walking? Is your car finally dead?"

"The car's fine."

"So, you've gone native. Good to know. Are you warm enough?"

"It's July, Mom." My legs were damp under my jeans and my pits were starting to challenge my deodorant's twenty-four-hour claims. "We may have underestimated summer temperatures."

"Fucking corporate disregard for the environment."

I couldn't argue with that. The sign on the post declared the gates would be closed before sunset.

"Vampires," my mother said with satisfaction after I passed on the information.

"I don't think you can contain vampires with a fence." There weren't a lot of trees in the cemetery—surprising, given the weathering on the tombstones nearest the gate. Cemeteries this old usually had giants taking advantage of the nutrients in the soil. I squinted at the mausoleums lined up on a terrace nearly at the top of the gentle slope. New chains looped across the doors, glinted in the sunlight. Just how bored were the teenagers in this town? "Did you call for a reason, Mom?"

"I can't miss my only daughter?"

"You never have before." A large dog came out from behind the farthest mausoleum and stopped, nose up into the breeze. At least I assumed it was a dog. It had the big square head and heavy shoulders of the bully breeds but was the size of a mastiff. A really big mastiff.

"How attached are you to that grey checked sweater of yours? The one with the zipper in the collar? Because I lent it to Beverly—"

The dog turned toward me.

"—and her cat had kittens in it."

"I can't imagine it would fit her cat."

"Oh, ha. Very funny. On it. Her cat had kittens on it. You're not getting it back. It's gross."

The dog started trotting purposefully toward the gate. Head up. Ears up. Tail up, swishing back and forth. Eyes glowing. I peered over the top edge of my sunglasses. Not glowing. Trick of the light. "I don't care about the sweater, Mom, Beverly's cat may have it with my blessing. I have to go now." Tongue lolling, the dog leapt a tombstone, joy radiating off it as it landed on the cement slab that covered the grave. That covered a lot of the graves. The question of bears digging up graves seemed like it had an answer.

"Bring me a present."

"Sure," I said as I hung up. Big at a distance, the dog became significantly larger the closer it got. There had to be Great Dane in its ancestry. And maybe a bit of Newfoundland, because it had a much heavier coat than the pitty silhouette had suggested, the bright, pink collar nearly lost in thick, black fur.

You know what happens when you run away from dogs? They chase you. A short-term girlfriend in Saskatoon had a pair of huskies and an obsession with training people how not to be idiots around them. My relationship with the dogs had been significantly more fulfilling than my relationship with Katie.

Waiting on the sidewalk, arms hanging loose at my side, I focused over the massive left shoulder and started talking. Calmly. Quietly. "Who's a good dog, then? Is it you? Yes, it is."

Hot doggy breath stuck my T-shirt to my already sweaty stomach. A shoulder pushed against my hip. I kept talking and didn't look down.

Then a wet nose touched my hand, a giant head tucked under it, lifted it to waist height, and *ruff*ed happily.

Easy first-place winner, had I been running an ugly-dog contest. Yellow-white teeth were too big for its mouth. Red . . . reddish-brown eyes were too small for its head. Its ears were disproportionately small and ragged. Its coat was coarse enough, it felt like I could stab an individual hair into my finger should I stroke it at the wrong angle.

But none of that was the dog's fault.

It leaned against me as I scratched behind its ears, tail whipping back and forth. It didn't have a lot of fur on its tail, and that was likely why it looked to be curving and curling in ways dog tails didn't.

No tags, but a white plastic plate on the wide pink collar said, *Daffodil.*

"Is that your name, baby girl? Daffodil?"

Daffodil *woof*ed and smiled up at me, exposing even more teeth. I noticed she didn't have much fur on her muzzle, either, the black skin looking a bit scaly, and I was starting to think she had mange. Fortunately, I had hand sanitizer in my bag.

A sharp whistle jerked her head out from under my hands, the motion spraying drool. Another dog and a man stood by the mausoleums. I raised a hand in acknowledgment, and both man and dog cocked their heads in the classic what-the-fuck pose.

"If you don't want people to interact with your dog," I muttered, "don't run her off leash." Finally, the man slowly raised his left hand to about shoulder height, slowly lowered it, and whistled again, the shrill sound a little wobbly this time. Daffodil bounded back across the cemetery.

I waited until she reached him safely, then continued walking.

At the far end of the cemetery, the sidewalk became a wide gravel shoulder, the sudden uneven surface throwing into sharp relief just how incredibly well maintained the sidewalks had been. I began to reconsider the whole walking thing way too late for it to do me any good. Taking a breather as the road rose past a rock outcrop that hopefully defined the curve Theresa had mentioned, I spotted what seemed to be the entrance to a park down to my left, took a selfie with the town as background, glanced right at a whole bunch of nothing, and, having run out of distractions, stepped over a pile of shit that was about fifty percent fur and kept walking up and around . . .

. . . and there was the motel.

Finally. I was earning that ten grand.

I stopped at the edge of the parking lot to catch my breath, feel disgustingly damp, and sanitize my hands again. Dog smell lingered. The big orange cat sitting on the step in front of the office watched me cross the almost-empty parking lot, wearing an expression that suggested he currently had possession of the single brain cell shared by orange cats.

"Hey, you."

His ears flicked.

"Mind moving?"

He stood, stretched, and, instead of moving out of the way, rose up on his hind legs to sniff at a dark spot on my jeans.

"Dog," I said, hissing as claws dug through the denim and into me. "Sorry about that."

"What dog?"

"God damn it!" I spun around and came chest to face with a short, thin man whose distinguishing features included, besides being able to walk silently on gravel, a squashed nose, tiny, close-set eyes, and masses of gorgeous brown curls. "Are you . . ." I dug the name out of post-coffee memory. ". . . Arthur?"

"Might be."

I couldn't help wondering, in a totally creepy way that wasn't like me at all, if his hair was as soft as it looked. My hands twitched, and I knelt to pet the cat instead.

"I said, what dog?"

Was he worried about me passing something on to his cat? "Her collar said Daffodil."

"Daffodil? And you two got along?"

"I like dogs." I shrugged. "Dogs like me. There was nowhere to wash," I added, "but I used hand sanitizer." The cat protested the sudden lack of pets by slamming his head into my knee with a hollow *bonk*. Apparently, his time with the brain cell had ended.

"Huh. Sanitized all ten of them, too. Surprising." After a long moment, he grunted, "What do you want?"

I want to know what conditioner you use. I stomped hard on the thought. "Travis Brayden's grandmother is paying me to find out about his last week. Did he stay here?"

"He did."

"What kind of a guest was he?"

Arthur's shoulders rose and fell. "His card went through and he didn't clean his ducks in the bathtub. That's all I care about."

I opened my mouth to ask, reconsidered, and said instead, "May I see his room?"

"You suggesting I haven't cleaned it after all this time?"

The angle of the sun made it look as though his shadow had suddenly lengthened. I smiled a parent-teacher-night smile. "Of course not. I just wondered if he'd left anything. Anything the police didn't take."

"Not here. And it wouldn't still be in the room."

Interpreting non-answers: Teaching 101. Travis had left something somewhere else. "What did he leave and where did he leave it?"

"How the fuck should I know?"

"You said—"

"He checked in," Arthur interrupted brusquely. "Paid for five days. Disappeared the next morning."

"The next morning?"

"S'what I said, Ms. Solvich."

Maybe Travis's grandmother had gotten confused when she saw the bill, and assumed he'd been here for the full five days before he disappeared.

"I'm not giving the money back."

"I wouldn't either," I said absently.

That seemed to appease him. "Far as I know, Cassidy Prewitt was the last person to see him. You want to know about the dumb little shit, you talk to Cassie."

"Cassie, our daughter, might have something to Say about it."

"I was planning to."

"Good for you." He didn't touch me, but I found myself suddenly out of his way as he stomped up the stairs and into the office, the cat on his heels. Before I could follow, he closed the door.

"Customer service are us," I muttered. I was too hot and too tired to care if he had anything else to say, and I had a long walk to the guest house before I could shower and change clothes. I'd drive next time, I decided, dragging my feet as I crossed the parking lot to retrace my steps back to town. I'd insist on seeing the room. Take some pictures. Write a couple of paragraphs about the ambience.

Or lack thereof.

My immediate surroundings were no longer bucolic; they were too damned far away from where I was going. At least there were no more giant bugs.

I'd passed the rock cut before it hit me: I hadn't told the repulsive little man with great hair my name. Wonderful. Small-town gossip. Memo to self: watch what I said.

Both the dogs and the man had left the cemetery. Next door, a slow heartbeat laid a foundation under the chanting. Drumbeat. Not heartbeat. I'd clearly been out in the sun too long. In an attempt to distract myself from the way the inseams of my jeans had started to scrape the skin off the inside of my thighs, I glanced down Elm Street, admired both trees and giant Victorian houses, and, just before the street dipped down toward the lake, thought I saw two women loading a body into a jeep.

SIX

=

Cassie

"Y ou're sure you've got permission from the family?" Amanda asked, walking up the funeral home's driveway.

"No," I told her, one hand on the edge of the stretcher, to keep it from rolling down the slight slope, "you're helping me steal a body." I swallowed, winced, and rasped, "Why would you even ask me that?"

"You're the Mouth. You could have Told Dave to look the other way."

Dave Alloway, currently the Alloway running Alloway's Funeral Services, had handed me a clipboard as I came in the door, told me to sign by the sticky-tab, then shooed me toward the garage, where the body lay wrapped in brown paper on a transport stretcher. The number of carbonized shadows around Blair's upper body made her look carrot-shaped.

"Why would I mess with Dave?" I demanded.

"Because you can."

"I can dance naked on the beach in the moonlight, but I'm not going to."

Just for a second, I thought I saw something like smug satisfaction pass over Amanda's face, then she sighed, laid her palm over her heart, and said, "No one did a naked jitterbug like Lindsey. I miss her."

"Yeah, me too, but she died happy." She'd been over eighty, and the jitterbugging had caught up to her. "Also, not the point." I watched Amanda circle the stretcher, admiring the sharp folds in the brown paper. Dave was an artist. Even standing right next to his work, I couldn't see where the paper was secured. "Blair said she likes the idea of her meat being useful—"

"Cassidy Prewitt!"

"Blair said!" I repeated. Small-town problem: everyone who knew your mother acted like your mother. "By way of Eric, by way of Catherine."

"Catherine the medium?"

"No, Catherine the extra-large."

Amanda folded her arms.

I sighed. "Yes, Catherine the medium. Blair's family agreed that Blair should have the final say about her own body"—I emphasized the last bit because, seriously, her body, her choice—"and Dave doesn't care. He gets paid for the service and we're saving them the drive down Alloway Lane to Alloway Dock." The Alloways liked putting their name on things. "Now, can we please get on with it?" The shadow crust was a solid coating from mid-thigh up, but, still, it was July.

We rolled the stretcher down the driveway to my jeep, then, using cutout handles worn smooth with age, lifted the board Dave had placed under the body, sliding board and body both into the back, shuffling it sideways until it lay diagonally across the space. Even with the back seats down, it was a tight fit and took us three tries before I could close up the trunk.

Okay. Fine. It took Amanda three tries while I ran the stretcher back to the garage.

"I'll drive my car to the dock," Amanda announced, rolling her shoulders. "That way, if we make it back from the island, you won't have to give me a lift. I have a *Willy Wonka* rehearsal to get to, and if you don't think my daughter's going to make me pay for leaving her to manage the Oompa Loompas on her own, think again."

"Isn't Lillian playing Veruca Salt? She's out with the Flock after her Shadow Hunter's Badge. Can there even be a rehearsal without her?"

"We're just rehearsing the Oompa Loompas. They're having a little trouble with the concept of singing in unison."

"That sucks." I paused. Thought a minute. "Hang on, *if* we make it back?"

"You sure you want to talk to Alice?"

That wasn't an answer.

"Things seem calm," she continued, spreading her hands, indicating, oh, I don't know, sunshine, birdsong, maybe the pollen count. "Peaceful."

"Yeah. So does the surface of the lake, but if you stick your hand over the buoys, you lose it. Things are happening beneath the surface."

"Of the lake?"

"Also of the lake." It was, after all, where Alice was. "But I saw Travis Brayden disappear. He went somewhere and he has to be doing something."

"Why?"

"Because!" I did not need her to try and convince me to change my mind; it was way too eager to be changed. "Ms. Morton . . ."

Amanda rolled her eyes. "Nancy worries."

"Well, yay. Nice that someone's worrying."

"Besides you. If Nancy's so worried," she continued before I could respond, "why doesn't she go talk to Alice?"

"Because I'm the Mouth! Isn't that what everyone keeps telling me?"

"Why, yes, I believe it is."

"Then pick a side!" I threw up my hands and swung up into the jeep. "I'll meet you at the dock."

The town council kept a small rowboat tied up just east of the beach. It was the only boat allowed on the lake, and for safety's sake, only the Four were allowed to use it.

Unfortunately, while safety was a lovely thought, the lake froze mid-December, and back in sixth grade, Frank Ellwood had snowshoed across to the island one weekend, drilled a hole in the ice with his father's auger, and tossed in a frozen rabbit. He'd returned with the answers to Monday's math test, arguing that no one had explicitly said he couldn't. He never spoke of Alice, although he spent a lot of time afterward staring out at the water and writing bad poetry. Bad even for the sixth grade.

When he tried it again a few years later, he didn't come back.

And then there's the story from when my dad was young, when a newly elected council, a little too enthusiastically Canadian, replaced the rotting wooden rowboat with a fiberglass canoe. First trip out onto the lake, the canoe did what canoes do and tipped. The occupants hit the water on the wrong side of the buoys. The canoe's replacement was another flat-bottomed, untippable wooden rowboat. The Hands' replacement had been Amanda.

I stepped from the dock into the boat, hoping I wasn't about to become another abject lesson for the children of the town.

"No one else saw a problem with a stranger s-wording himself at the Dead Ground, mostly because they were old and couldn't see past the comfortable way things had been for years, but off went Cassidy Prewitt to talk to Alice."

Except Ms. Morton had come looking for me with a problem, and Eric had been convinced, and the Dark had been too busy to talk to us. I needed to know what Travis Brayden had set in motion. Because he'd set something in motion. At this point, I'd bet my life on it.

Because I was not old.

And I was able to see past the comfortable way things had been for years.

And, more importantly, I'd been there when Travis Brayden had s-worded himself! I wasn't one or two or a hundred and fifteen steps away like everyone else. I'd seen it happen.

The boat rocked.

Betting my life might not have been the smartest bet I could make . . .

"Cassie!" Amanda glared at me from the dock, the board balanced on one hip, and Blair's body balanced on the board. "How are we going to do this?"

"Carefully?"

I steadied the boat as she stepped down, shifting my weight where needed, wishing I could Tell an inanimate object to just stop that! With Blair's board resting across the upper edges, Amanda moved me to the rear seat, told me to make sure the board stayed put, and pushed away from the dock, smoothly setting up the oars as we drifted sideways.

I'd assumed I'd be doing the rowing. Amanda was over twice my age and a couple of centimeters shorter. And the Hands, I reminded myself as she bent to the oars and the boat leapt forward. Paper crinkled as I threw myself over Blair's sliding body. It wouldn't be of any use if it hit the water before we were ready.

Behind us on the beach, the dozen or so people who'd been out getting some sun called out bets.

"Twenty says Cassie doesn't make it to the island!"

"Fifty says she doesn't make it off the island!"

"I'm not going out there alone!" I shouted back over my shoulder.

"No one's worried about Amanda," yelled a second cousin. "She's tough."

I flipped him off.

"Hey, Cassie, tell Alice that old recliner of Dad's finally broke too bad for me to fix."

I raised the whole hand to let Alice's brother know I'd heard, and grunted as the board shifted, the edge slamming into my ribs.

The island was almost a kilometer out from the buoys. Children were taught that the buoys were a social contract, like a stop sign was a social contract, and should Alice decide to ignore that contract, we'd have as much chance of stopping her as we would stopping a transport blowing through an intersection.

"You can't idle away your life, waiting for that transport," Ms. Everett had declared.

So, we waded into the lake, learned to swim, and dared each other to touch the far side of the buoys. The town built an Olympic-sized pool in the sports center, just in case.

My first trip to the island had been with Aunt Jean, who'd taken the responsibility of introducing Alice to the new Mouth. I'd done the rowing that time, although I hadn't done it well. There'd been a lot of splashing and a lot of questions thrown at Aunt Jean. I couldn't remember her answering many of them.

Sure, I was the Mouth, but I'd been told to keep quiet and watch while she'd talked to Alice.

I remembered that both of us were entirely silent on the trip back.

Alice had that effect on people.

Well, not so much Alice herself as the potential of Alice.

This trip, I wavered between anticipation of finally getting some answers and annoyance that I was having to take the responsibility of getting those answers when all I wanted to do was a little baking and a little sunbathing and a whole lot of not worrying about shit.

Against all odds, I managed to keep both Blair and myself in the boat as Amanda hit the landing site, secured the oars, and leapt out into ankle-deep water, hauling me, the boat, and Blair up the mud-ramp onto the shore.

"I'll carry her. You lead the way."

We never tie the boat at this end, Aunt Jean had informed me. If

Alice got offended, seconds counted, and you didn't have time to waste untying a rope. When I'd asked what kind of things Alice took offense at, Aunt Jean had looked at me like I was an idiot.

The path to the other side of the island remained broad and clear of underbrush, even though no one ever groomed it. Even the pines lining the path leaned away. By the time we reached the flat rock on the far side of the island, I was sweating salt into a dozen mosquito bites, and Amanda looked as though she'd been sitting on her porch with an iced tea. Without looking into the water, she set Blair's body down by the water's edge, carefully slid the board out from under her, and said, "I'll wait at the boat."

"But—"

"I'm the Hands, Cassie. The muscle. The talking's all you. Occasionally Jean when the Mouth is new. You're not new, not anymore." She glanced around. "And I don't see Jean."

"But—"

"You'll be fine. Once the body's been offered, take a step back, just in case."

I had decided to talk to Alice. I was the Mouth of the Dark. I wanted to whine, and stamp my feet, and demand Amanda stay. For half a second, I considered Telling her to come back, then I put on my big-girl panties, listened as the soft crunch of her sneakers on the pine needles disappeared into the distance, sighed, and got on with it.

The small trunk bolted to the rock was latched but not locked. I pulled out the folding easel, chalkboard, chalk, and a silver lancet.

Last chance to back out.

Standing with my sneakers shoved under the edge of Blair's body, toes crinkling the paper wrapping, I pricked my finger, leaned out, and let four drops of blood hit the water. I watched the four tiny shadows sink without dissipating, and then I offered Blair's body to Alice. Translation: I shoved it off the rock and into the water with my foot, then watched it follow the blood down.

Farther down.

Farther still.

At some point in my scholastic career, I'd been taught that as the glaciers retreated in the last ice age, they'd sheared off the rock in a number of places around the lake, leaving behind a straight path from the surface to the depths. No one knew how deep those depths were. The popular theory around town was that they'd gotten deeper since Alice moved in.

A theory only because it couldn't be proven. No one challenged it.

Down.

Down.

The paper wrapping began to fan away from the body.

When I looked up, a band of tiny ripples throwing dark shadows against the silver-blue marked the path of a current cutting through water toward the island. Except it wasn't a current. A small wave splashed against the rock. Then another. And another.

"Once the body's been offered, take a step back, just in case."

Oops. Well, better late than never.

I jumped back just before the fourth wave curled up over the rock and would have ended up with . . . hopefully nothing more than wet sneakers, but why risk it? About two meters out from shore, the water roiled. I'd had no idea what *roiled* meant before I met Alice. There was a lot of writhing going on beneath the surface. A whole lot of writhing. A hypnotic twisting of barely glimpsed curves sliding sleekly in and around one another, a never-ending, glistening path of . . .

I squeezed my eyes shut, opened them again, and turned my attention to angling the easel and chalkboard toward the water. Rolling the chalk between thumb and forefinger, I realized I should have given some thought to what I was going to say. Finally, as a large wave began to build out in the lake—Alice losing patience—I wrote, YOU OKAY?

A thin tentacle rose out of the water, shook itself dry, and took the chalk. *WHY?*

AGREEMENT WEAKENING. YOU'RE NOT RESPONDING.
TO WHAT?
POTENTIAL GOVERNMENT INSPECTION.
SERIOUSLY?
I waited.
NOT WHAT I GUARD AGAINST. DIFFERENT DARKNESS.
Fair. And it was pretty impressive how dismissive she could make
block caps look. *THE DARK SAID IT WAS BUSY. SAID IT WOULD
TALK LATER. WHY?*
PAIN AND TORMENT. ELDRITCH HORRORS.
MORE THEN USUAL?
The tentacle tapped the chalk on the E in *then*. I frowned at the
board. Alice tapped again. The lake got a bit choppy.
What was wrong with . . . Oh. I replaced the E with an A, and the
lake calmed.
DEFINE USUAL, she wrote.
CAN'T. THAT'S WHY I'M TALKING TO YOU.
*CHALLENGERS RISE TO DISTURB THE ETERNAL SOLITUDE
OF SOVEREIGNTY. I FEEL THE DARK'S CERTAINTIES CRUM-
BLE. PIECES NOW. NOT A WHOLE.*
I was pretty sure she hadn't gone into the water talking like a bad
gothic novel. *YOU DIDN'T THINK YOU SHOULD LET US KNOW?*
HAS DARKNESS CHALLENGED THE TOWN?
THE GOVERNMENT
The tentacle shoved me out of the way. *HAS DARKNESS CHAL-
LENGED THE TOWN?*
Technically . . . *NO.*
THEN YOU HAVE NO NEED TO KNOW.
Fine. *IS THE CHALLENGER TRAVIS BRAYDEN?*
*I GUARD TO KEEP THE DARKNESS FROM BREAKING
THROUGH. I AM NOT A PART OF THE DARKNESS ALTHOUGH IT
IS A PART OF ME.* The printing looked annoyed, and she threw the chalk.

I ducked and, while I was down there, grabbed a new piece of chalk from the trunk. *YOU DON'T KNOW WHO THE CHALLENGER IS?*

I DO NOT.

BUT THE DARK IS BEING CHALLENGED?

I FEEL THIS.

THE AGREEMENT IS WEAKENING.

NOT MY PROBLEM.

WHAT SHOULD WE DO?

The water bulged as something grey/green and huge surged up to the surface. Up to but not through. *If Alice surfaces*, the saying went, *you're fucked.* I kept my attention on the board, watched the bulge slowly sink in my peripheral vision, and, as black spots danced before my eyes, finally remembered to breathe.

Her tentacle held the chalk motionless above the board for a long moment. *WAIT*, she wrote at last. *BE READY.*

FOR WHAT?

Alice yanked the chalk from my hand, and the wave that had been building out in the lake raced toward me—drenching me and washing the board clean. A larger tentacle wrapped around the easel, holding it steady as she filled the wet surface with three words, the letters thick and jagged. *I DON'T KNOW!*

———

Amanda stood knee-deep in the water, holding the bucking boat in place when I reached the other side of the island. "Get an answer?"

"Sort of. The Dark's being challenged, but she doesn't know if it's Travis Brayden. She's not reacting, because she only reacts to things that break through from the darkness. And we're supposed to be ready, but she doesn't know what for."

"Not very helpful."

"Nope."

"Piss her off?"

"Seems like."

As Amanda rowed for shore, bow bouncing up and down in the chop, water spraying over both of us, I could feel things brushing against the wood under my feet. Things. Alice. Alice being the only thing in the lake. Amanda rowed faster. Just before we reached the buoys, Alice shoved the boat hard enough that the bow rose as we sped forward. Amanda lost an oar when we hit the pier, and I fell into the half-inch of murky water in the bottom of the boat, legs waving at the sky and my head ringing from where it had hit the gunnel.

Hearty laughter pulled me upright. I glared up at Alice's brother on the dock.

"That Alice," he chuckled, wiping rheumy eyes with a shaking, liver-spotted hand. "Such a joker."

———

"Travis Brayden," I told Amanda when we reached the jeep, "must be who's challenging the Dark."

"Why?"

"Why is he challenging or why must it be him?"

Amanda shrugged. "Both."

"How could I possibly know his motivation? All I know is that when someone s-words on the Dead Ground and the Agreement starts to weaken and Alice tells me the Dark is being challenged, it's way too much of a coincidence for all that not to be connected." He may have looked like the only thing he'd be capable of challenging was the amount of foam on his soy latte, but he'd gone into the darkness almost a month ago, and given the whole too-much-of-a-coincidence thing, I had to assume he was still alive. Travis Brayden had hidden depths.

Or . . .

S-words gave the Dark strength. Did s-wording yourself mean you claimed that strength?

Amanda thought about that theory for a moment after I told it to her, and finally said, "I'll be damned."

"Let's not get into that," I muttered.

"Yes, yes, very funny, Cassie."

"I'm hysterical," I admitted. "The Four need to meet. Now."

Amanda peered at me through narrowed eyes. "Why? We can't do anything about what's happening in the darkness. All we can do is wait and deal with the effects."

"Alice said we need to be ready."

"But she doesn't know what for, and she said the weakening of the Agreement has nothing to do with her. You've spoken to one Guardian; maybe you should see what Jeffrey and Evan have to say."

"Jeffrey's new." And he sounded like he was talking through a mouthful of pudding. "Evan's . . ." I frowned. "Does anyone know where Evan is?"

"Not usually, no."

"Then it all comes back to Alice," I snapped. Amanda raised both hands and unsuccessfully hid a smile. She could laugh at me if she wanted to, as long as she listened. "I need to tell Eric and Aunt Jean what she said. We need to have a council of war. We can't just *be ready*; we need to put some work into it."

"I do hate to squash your enthusiasm." To my surprise, Amanda's smile wasn't even a little mocking. "Over lunch, then. My place. The sun's off the porch and I have half a cold ham that needs to be used up. Your throat still sounds rough, so I'll call Jean and Eric. I'm sure Jean will throw together a salad, and Eric's always good for a bottle or two of wine. You stop by the bakery and pick up a dessert after you drop the board back at Alloway's."

My stomach growled. I sighed, sagged against the jeep's sun-warmed hood, and said, "Sure."

———

Before I went to the bakery, I went home to change. While I had no objection to getting wet on a hot day, the water in the bottom of the boat had been disgusting. Standing naked in the bathroom, I stared into the mirror, lifted my hair off my forehead, and poked at the rising bump. Swore. Swallowed a couple of painkillers.

Travis Brayden.

My life had been comfortable until he'd showed up and s-worded himself.

I saw no point in taking the jeep back out, lunch traffic was as close to a rush hour as we got, and I'd never find parking by the bakery. I rolled my bike down off the side porch, bent to fix the chain . . .

A shadow lunged out from the darkness under the steps and engulfed my right hand.

Son of a bitch!

Skin burning, I fell over backward, pulled my bike over on top of me, and thrust my right arm out into the sun. The shadow solidified.

A slap against the packed gravel cracked it off.

Back on my feet, I crushed the pieces into dark dust and felt a little sorry for it. Odds were it had gone under my porch to hide from preteens with silver skewers.

My bike had scraped against the side of the house when it fell, the black rubber handgrip drawing a line on the turquoise paint. It looked l like I'd marked a win: Cassidy one, shadows zero. Go me.

———

"Thirty bucks," Chris announced as I slid the bag holding a dozen white-chocolate macadamia-nut cookies into my backpack, resting them securely on the lemon-blueberry pound cake.

"Thirty?"

"Do you have any idea how much macadamia nuts cost? Thirty's with the silent-partner discount."

"Doesn't seem like much of a discount," I grumbled, digging my wallet out of the backpack's outer pocket.

"Which of us has access to vast inherited wealth?" he asked, arranging mille-feuille on tray, ready to go into the case out front.

I'd considered taking the delicate French pastry, if only to sweeten Aunt Jean, but they wouldn't have survived the trip. "I wouldn't say it was vast."

"Which of us took the day off?"

"Fair."

"You'll tell me if I need to be worried, right?"

About to quip back that if he wasn't worried, he hadn't been paying attention, I paused, backpack half-on, realizing this wasn't just about him but about his husband and daughter. If the Agreement failed, what would happen to the people he loved? Thankful I didn't have those kind of responsibilities, I found a smile and said, "Of course I will."

"You're looking solemn."

Aunt Jean sighed. "Why wouldn't I, Cassie? The Agreement is weakening."

I watched her maneuver the spoon around the diced green onions in the potato salad. Onions, we'd all been informed, did not agree with her, but leaving them out broke some kind of undisclosed potato salad rule. I did not understand old people. "Yeah, that's not it."

"Oh, to be young and certain," she muttered.

Eric hid a snicker in a cough, and just for a moment, I was terrified I'd said, *Oh, to be old and passive-aggressive* out loud. Maybe he'd Heard my intended response, barely caught just behind my teeth when my sense of self-preservation kicked in at the last minute.

The serving spoon smacked the side of the plastic bowl with a definitive *clunk*, bits of mayo covered potato dropping off, then Aunt Jean jabbed the spoon toward the pound cake and cookies. "You said you paid thirty dollars for these. You could have just Told him to give them to you. The Four are responsible for the town, and are therefore entitled to the support of the town."

"And the town is entitled to have the Four not be assholes."

"Cassidy Prewitt."

"Oh, for fucksake." I buried my head in my hands. "I'm not going to screw one of my best friends out of a sale just because I can."

"She's not going to dance naked on the beach in the moonlight, either," Amanda pointed out.

Aunt Jean rolled her eyes. "She's no Lindsey."

"Let it go, Jean." Eric inspected the piece of ham on the end of his fork. "It's not going to happen."

"Really? Then what about that police officer who stayed over?"

What wasn't going to happen? Wait, that police officer who stayed over? "With me? The police officer who stayed over with me? I have a mother, Aunt Jean, and you aren't her. You don't get to . . ." And then I put the pieces together and slowly stood, glaring at her across the food spread out on the plastic table. "Are you suggesting that I Told her to sleep with me? That she couldn't possibly have been interested in me without me using the Voice on her?"

"Now, me, when I'm trying to find a partner for the horizontal mamba, the making of whoopie, a bit of the old in-and-out, I find listening helps."

"Do be quiet, Eric." Aunt Jean met my glare with a flat, judgmental stare. "I'm suggesting that you're the Mouth of the Dark, and that gives you skills beyond the Dark's immediate requirements. It's an easy position to abuse. A little emphasis here. A suggestion there."

"Yeah? Well, I'm suggesting here and now that that's really fucking insulting." With every intention of stomping off, I found myself blocked in by Amanda and Eric. I couldn't get away. I gave some thought to going over the porch railing, but there was no telling what hid in Amanda's dangerously lush garden, so I settled for folding my arms, narrowing my eyes, and silently daring Aunt Jean to say one more word.

"Let it go, Jean." Amanda echoed Eric's words.

Eyes beginning to darken, Aunt Jean continued to stare. "We agreed we'd watch for two years."

Watch what?

"It's been eighteen months." Eric sighed. "She's not Simon."

She? Wait . . . Watch me?

Aunt Jean shifted her gaze to Amanda, who popped a cherry tomato into her mouth and said blandly, "That Agrotunnel was an excellent investment."

Shifted to Eric, who poured himself a second glass of wine and said, "In his first six months, Simon missed eleven Fridays."

And shifted back to me. "She was late to the Dead Ground."

"I was not late!" I drew back the finger I'd jabbed at Aunt Jean and added a few more pieces to the puzzle. I had all the edges now and was starting to see the picture. "You thought I'd be as big a fuckup as Simon? You've been *testing* me!"

"Sit down, Cassie," Amanda began.

Aunt Jean cut her off. "As you know, Cassidy, the choice to replace one of the Four is entirely random. All that's required by the Dark is the direct bloodline. It wasn't so much that we thought you'd be another Simon as we had no intention of enduring a similar situation. We needed to be certain of you."

"So, if I didn't show up on a Friday, you'd take me to the mine and drive a loader over me?" I could hear a lawnmower in the distance. And a raven. And one of Uncle Stu's dogs barking. And preteens shrieking with laughter as they stabbed shadows with silver. "You drove a loader over Simon," I said at last. "He wasn't drunk and trying to Talk to the machines . . ."

"Actually," Eric interrupted, "he was both drunk and trying to Talk to the machines."

"It was entirely his idea," Amanda added. "Our involvement was more about not preventing the inevitable."

Eric snorted. "Possibly, we made it a bit more inevitable than it might have been."

I sat down. "Why?"

"Because Simon thought he was entitled to the support of the town. Whether the town wanted to support him or not. Can you imagine Simon as the Mouth in our current situation?"

"He'd be one of Four—"

"He'd be the most powerful of the Four." Amanda leaned back and scraped up the potato salad remaining on her plate. "And he'd have had no interest in searching out the reason why the Agreement was fracturing. He certainly wouldn't have spoken to Alice."

Aunt Jean rolled her eyes. "And yet, when he was given a solo responsibility, he got to the Dead Ground on time."

"Jean!" A bit of potato sprayed out with the exclamation.

"I'm just saying," she began.

Amanda cut her off. "Since no one s-worded that day, we only have his word for it. And now that I think of it, we only have his word that no one s-worded that day, so I'm going to stop thinking about it. Cassie, why are you waving your hands around like that?"

Was I? I was. I took a deep breath. "Are you saying that I'm the most powerful of the Four?"

"Yes."

"But you three can—"

Eric cut me off. "We three can be Commanded."

"Why tell her that?" Aunt Jean sputtered.

He shrugged. "She'd have found out eventually. Simon did."

"Simon," Aunt Jean snapped, "was many things, but he was not stupid."

I crushed the cookie I was holding. "Hey!"

Aunt Jean ignored me. She sighed, and it looked like the fight went out of her with the breath. "That was then," she said, "this is now. However careful we wanted to be, we needed to be, we couldn't possibly have anticipated Travis Brayden advancing our timeline. And I suppose we'll just have to live with that."

I absently cut myself a huge slice of lemon-blueberry pound cake. I understood lemon-blueberry pound cake. It was comforting. It didn't want anything from me. It didn't suddenly declare that I could Tell the three people who'd spent the last eighteen months assuming I couldn't tell right from wrong to jump in the lake. And have them obey. I could see a lot of lemon-blueberry pound cake in my future.

"Young Travis has challenged the Dark," Aunt Jean continued. "The Agreement is weakening. We have no idea what will happen here while the Dark is distracted by dealing with him."

"Or what will happen if the Dark loses the challenge."

"Don't be ridiculous, Amanda. A human boy defeat the Dark in the darkness? Not possible. I think you'll all agree that distraction is bad enough. Without the Dark standing as a barrier between the darkness and the damaged places between that world and this, shadows will be the last of our problems; you mark my words."

It occurred to me that we were all a little too used to marking Aunt Jean's words.

And water was wet.

But she *had* been doing this a long time.

Still . . . if I was the most powerful, did that mean I was in charge? "We need more information on Travis Brayden. We need to know how much of a threat he actually is." I pointed a bit of pound cake at Aunt Jean. "One of us needs to go to Toronto."

"Or you could stop talking about things you don't understand," she sighed. "No one ever *needs* to go to Toronto."

Okay, nope. Not in charge. Yay. Unfortunately, that warm and happy feeling about not being in charge didn't last. "Hang on!" I rounded on Eric. "That whole testing to make sure I didn't go mad with power is why you were always around."

He smirked. "It might possibly be one of the reasons."

"Gross."

"You liked the attention."

"And you make being an entitled shit-heel seem like a valid option." And then I realized something else. It wasn't moral fiber that had me passing all Aunt Jean's tests. It wasn't noble restraint that provided an absence of abuse for Eric to observe. It was lack of ambition.

I was a part-time baker who'd known I could be Chosen as a Conduit but didn't want to be. And it wasn't just the Choosing I didn't want—no one in their right mind wanted to be engulfed by the Chrysalis of Darkness, even if Chrysalis of Darkness would make a great name for your new thrash metal band—it was the being. But being the Mouth started out easy-peasy. No effort. Just the way I liked it. The outside attention tapered off after a few weeks—the Four had always been there, always would be there, the town was pretty blasé about it. I Spoke when Aunt Jean told me to, and my biggest commitment was showing up on Fridays.

And then Travis Brayden.

Travis Brayden had made me responsible.

That fucker.

I let the voices of the other three wash over me. It was going to be a long afternoon.

"So, Cassidy." Aunt Jean finally dragged my attention back to specifics. "Have you anything to add?"

Three-quarters of the Four stared at me over the ruins of lunch.

I grabbed a cookie and got hit with my fourth realization of the afternoon: I was feeling some sympathy for Simon's drinking.

SEVEN

Melanie

By the time I got back to the guest house, sweat dripped continuously off my chin and rolled in slow motion into my cleavage like a titillating shot in one of those terrible nineties fantasies resurrected by streaming services. Inside the blessed air conditioning, I slowly climbed the three stairs from the side door to the first floor, damp denim dragging against my shins. I didn't know shins could sweat. First time for everything.

"Oh, sweetie!" Theresa came through the Dutch door, shaking her head so vigorously, the ruffles on her blouse joined in. "You look . . ." Her brows dipped and she added flatly, ". . . damp."

I checked to make sure I wasn't dripping on her gleaming hardwood floors. "It was warmer out than I expected."

She spread her hands and said simply, "July."

"Almost August," I agreed, heading for the stairs.

"You go and have as long a shower as you want to," she called after me. "There's no need to worry about anything; we don't run out of hot water here." After a moment she added, "Drink at least a liter before you head back into the sun." And a moment later, as I was moving from gold and red to red and gold, called out, "We worry!"

I started the shower at barely warm and nudged it colder as I got used to each drop in temperature. Lifting my face, I opened my mouth, wondered if a town this size had a water-treatment plant, and decided I didn't care if it came right out of the lake, as it washed the gritty coating out of my mouth and throat.

And, because I'd been raised to be aware of bills, mostly ones that couldn't be paid, I didn't test the infinite availability of the hot water, turned the shower off long before I wanted to, stepped out, and dried off. Dressed. Called Mrs. Brayden.

The digital voice of her answering service told me that I'd called the correct number and suggested I leave a message.

"Mrs. Brayden, it's Melanie Solvich. I've spoken to the motel owner where Travis was staying and discovered that although he paid for five nights, he only stayed the first night, disappearing the next day. That should have been in the police report." Which she should have shown me. Or I should have asked to see. Or maybe it wasn't. How much did the police tell grieving grandmothers? "I'll keep asking around, but there's a very limited chance that he interacted with the community. Please let me know if you want me to continue." It seemed more businesslike to end the call without saying goodbye. We weren't friends.

In Mrs. Brayden's place, I'd tell me to return to Toronto for a minor cancellation fee, because Travis's less than twenty-four hours hanging around Lake Argen couldn't possibly produce ten grand worth of final memories. Although I'd forgotten to show the sketch of the knife to the creepy man at the motel, so I had that to do, and rummaging through cutlery drawers, searching for an heirloom, could easily take me the rest of the week.

A bear wouldn't eat a knife. Would it?

Did I need to dig through piles of bear shit? In the woods? Because that's where bears shit.

Upon reflection, the odds were high I'd gotten too much sun.

The Silver Crown looked like every British pub I'd ever seen in every British TV series I'd ever watched. And like every imitation British pub I'd ever seen in every small city in Canada. Oh, sure, big cities had them too, but as big cities also crammed in every possible American fast-food chain, big-city imitation pubs didn't count.

I'd established that Travis hadn't gone to the diner, so if he'd eaten in Lake Argen before he disappeared, he'd had dinner or breakfast at the pub. Or just dinner, I amended, as I pushed open the door. According to the hours painted on the glass, they weren't open for business until eleven.

Eleven AM to one AM. Kitchen closed at nine.

They had a dartboard, and pool table, and a soccer game playing on the television over the bar. The wood gleamed and the whole place looked worn and well loved. I could see myself spending time there. If they didn't know anything about Travis, maybe they'd let me rummage through their kitchen for his grandmother's heirloom knife.

Four of the comfortably sized round tables were full. Two had been pulled together for a group of six; the other two held pairs of men in overalls and work boots who I assumed were on a lunch break from the mine. No one wanted to eat a packed lunch every day. Even I'd splurged on a high school cafeteria lunch on occasion.

Not many occasions.

"Sit where you like!"

I waved an acknowledgment to the woman stacking glasses behind the bar and sat so I could keep an eye on the other occupied tables, my subconscious equating the rowdy group of six to supervisory duty during feeding time at the zoo. I smiled to myself, remembering how Don Grass, who'd lived through some of the history he taught, objected to his fellow teachers calling it that, insisting he'd take confined zoo animals over free-range teenagers any day.

"So, what brings you to Lake Argen, hun? Business or pleasure?"

"Business," I told her, pushing back the sudden ridiculous home-sickness for William John Patterson High and pulling out Travis's photo while I explained.

"I remember him disappearing," she said, frowning down at it. "Hard not to, given this place was full of police and search teams soon as it got dark. But I doubt he was ever in here." Grinning, she met my gaze. "We don't get a lot of wandering strangers, so we tend to talk about them." *We will talk about you*, added the subtext. *Consider this fair warning.* "That said," she continued, "I'll ask Anna and Sam if they remember him. You going to be here for a couple of days?"

"That's the plan."

"I'll have spoken to them both by Friday. Drop in then. Meanwhile, you should talk to Cassie Prewitt; far as I know, she was the last one who saw him."

"What about this?" I showed her the sketch. "Have you seen it?"

"Looks a bit like one of those fancy fish knives, not exactly our sort of thing. Now, then . . ." She pointedly tapped her pen on her order pad.

I got the burger and the salad, figuring I should eat a few vegeta-bles, and a local wheat beer.

"Enjoy it while you can," the waitress laughed when I compli-mented it. "It's from my brother's micro-brewery, and he seldom makes the same batch twice. Word to the wise, if you're offered a Blood Red Spruce, don't drink it. Tastes worse than the name. Good thing that brewery doesn't have to pay for itself," I heard her mutter as she walked away.

I dug a plump cherry tomato out from under a crisp leaf of ro-maine lettuce and revisited my meeting with Mrs. Brayden. If she'd seen the police report, if it contained the information on Cassie Pre-witt, why hadn't Mrs. Brayden suggested I talk to her? I very much doubted she'd kept quiet because she wanted me to trust my instincts. People like Mrs. Brayden liked to be in control.

I paused, licked a bit of ketchup from the corner of my mouth, and wondered where that thought had come from. My brief from Mrs. Brayden had been entirely loosey-goosey. *Find out how my grandson spent his last week and I'll pay you ten grand.*

Both loose and goose.

Not at all controlling.

"What's the best way to find Cassie Prewitt?" I asked as I used Mrs. Brayden's credit card to pay the bill, adding a hefty tip, half-hoping my / Mrs. Brayden's generosity would get a phone number so I didn't have to chase the elusive Cassie Prewitt all over town. Sure, it was a small town, but still.

"Cassie works at Rising and Shine, the bakery on Carlyle next to the diner. If she's not there, Chris will know where she is."

After a pause, when it became clear that was all I was going to get, I thanked her and headed for the door.

I'd barely touched the handle when it began to move, so I stepped out of the way to allow a very old man and a middle-aged woman to enter. I had nothing but time and was more than willing to spend it on a few extra minutes of air conditioning.

The middle-aged woman nodded her thanks. The very old man stared up at me.

"Gloria?" Pale grey eyes narrowed on either side of an impressively beaky nose, rosy with burst blood vessels. "Where have you been?"

"I'm sorry," I began.

He cut me off with an accusatory "I've been waiting!"

"Granddad, this isn't Nanna." The middle-aged woman shot me an apologetic smile from under an unfortunately generational nose as she tried to move the old man along.

The old man proved hard to move, gripping my forearm with one tanned hand while he waved the other. "You should have called! These new phone things . . ." He leaned in. His breath smelled like coffee. ". . . they work. All over."

"Granddad!"

"Don't *granddad* me, Stephanie! I'm old; I'm not senile." He glanced down at his hand, patted my arm absently, pushed past his grand-daughter, and shuffled into the pub.

"I'm so sorry." Stephanie sighed wearily. "He's having a bad day. It's the heat."

And possibly the caffeine, I added silently. Were people that old even allowed to have caffeine? Could their hearts stand it?

Then she frowned. "Are you one of Alyx's?"

"As I don't know who Alyx is . . ." I shrugged. "I'd say no."

"Right. Sorry again." Her voice followed me out of the pub. "Grand-dad! Don't drink Alan's . . . Oh, now you're just fucking with me, old man."

"BAWK!"

When my heart settled back into something closer to a normal rhythm, I glared up at the raven perched on the decorative ironwork that supported the pub sign and snapped, "Not cute!"

They looked extraordinarily pleased with themself.

"Don't you have a poet you can bother?"

Apparently not.

"Flight Sergeant!" The voice was familiar although I could see nei-ther man nor beard. "You're out of formation!"

The raven cocked their head so they could stare at me with one beady eye, and I could've sworn they sighed, then, with half a dozen beats of their wings, they were in the air and heading toward the lake. A single feather wafted to the ground so definitively like a single feather wafting to the ground, it looked more animated than real.

My mother had never let me collect pigeon feathers, the only feathers available for collecting in the city, citing the danger of bird lice. At length. Memory provided the lecture as I bent down.

The feather was such an unrelieved black, it appeared to have been painted onto the sidewalk. It wasn't long enough to be a flight feather, given the size of the raven's wings, but neither was it merely a bit of down. I picked it up and admired it as I stroked the edges with a fingertip. Then I carefully slid it into the side pocket of my bag, next to Travis's picture and the sketch of the knife, assuming the same piece of cardboard could protect all three.

"Really, Mel? You've just filled your bag with bird lice!" said a memory of my mother's voice.

RISING AND SHINE had been painted in large, curly, turquoise, and, for lack of a better word, shining letters on the window of the bakery. On the wide inside window ledge, taking the place of the expected baskets of breads and cookies, were a row of small blackboards standing upright on easels.

4" SERVICE BERRY CHEESECAKE 2

RHUBARB CUSTARD TARTS 14

MILLE FEUILLE 4

I'd just worked out that *mille-feuille* was French, not gibberish, when a teenage girl with deep purple braids walked to the window, picked up the *mille-feuille* blackboard, and erased it.

A moment later the bakery door opened. "I'll pick up the cake tomorrow right before closing," called a man about my age, maybe a little older, as he stepped out onto the sidewalk. He held a bakery box in one hand and steadied the baby he wore across his chest with the other. I don't think he even saw me as he strode past murmuring into the baby's dark hair. "Daddy got the last four napoleons. Mommy's going to be so happy with him."

Rather than stand around reading the rest of the blackboards and slowly melting into the sidewalk like the Wicked Witch of the West, I went inside.

The teenage girl, now behind the cash register, looked up, sighed, and pasted on a weary smile. "Can I help you?"

"Hopefully. I'm looking for Cassidy Prewitt."

"Really?" She looked me up and down, sighed again, then half-turned toward the door painted an oddly familiar turquoise. "CHRIS! THERE'S A GORBIE HERE LOOKING FOR CASSIE!"

The door opened almost instantly.

"Damn it, Kynda, stop calling tourists gorbies . . ." Chris, I assumed, paused, closed his eyes for a moment, and shook his head. ". . . particularly when they're standing right there," he continued.

Kynda shrugged. "Doesn't happen often, does it?"

"Doesn't matter, does it? Not when I'm telling you not to do it."

Under the assault of a truly impressive dad voice—although given their ages, I doubted he was her dad—Kynda twirled a narrow braid around one finger and mumbled, "Sorry."

Chris sighed. "Not to me."

Her chin rose and she met my gaze. "Sorry."

"Apology accepted." I had no idea what a gorbie was. And I was sure I'd been called worse by parents who couldn't understand why their little darling was failing Can Lit. Could it be because they had no interest in stories of angst-ridden antiheroes on a tedious journey of self-discovery through the Canadian landscape? While I couldn't blame them, neither could I pass them.

Chris turned toward me. A spray of flour, brilliantly white in contrast to his deep brown skin, marked the curve of one very impressive bicep. "Cassie's not here right now; can I help?" Before I could answer, he raised a hand, wedding ring flashing gold. "If it's about the almond-flour order, you talk to me, not Cassie."

"It's not about the almond flour order. It's about Travis Brayden."

"Who?"

"The gorbie who got lost in the woods last month," Kynda said helpfully.

I almost managed to squash a snicker.

"Kynda . . ." Chris closed his eyes for a moment and, when he opened them, said, "Go in the back and arrange the meringues on a tray. They should be cool enough by now."

"How many can I—"

"One."

"But—"

"One. Wash your hands first."

"Fine."

Together, we watched her flounce past him into the back.

"I'm starting to think she doesn't have a future in customer service," Chris said wearily once the door closed. "Fortunately, her mother's a Worth. She'll be fine. So . . ." He folded muscular arms. "Cassie's in a meeting that'll probably go all afternoon. I'm not giving you her number because I don't know who you are."

"Melanie Solvich."

He grinned as he shook my hand. "Chris Abbott. And that's not quite good enough. But if you give me your number, I'll send it to her, and she can call you."

That whole not-knowing thing worked both ways, but he had a good handshake—not a hard squeeze like he was trying to prove something, or a limp flop like he couldn't figure out how to shake hands with a woman—and the alternative was wandering around randomly looking for Cassidy/Cassie Prewitt.

Who was unlikely to be lurking in a cutlery drawer with an antique knife, thus giving me no opportunity to tie up two loose ends at once.

I gave him my number.

I stepped into the diner after leaving the bakery, in case Cassidy Prewitt had dropped in to visit her parents. Two teenagers sat in one of the window booths, cans of diet cola to hand, a decimated plate of fries with gravy on the table between them. Farther back, a man and a woman in kitchen whites were clearly on a break. I knew without asking that no one in the diner was Cassidy Prewitt.

I had no idea why I was so sure—no one had mentioned Cassidy Prewitt's age—but the certainty hustled me out of the diner and back onto the street.

The downtown was . . . different.

Small towns usually grew up around a dominant road, but Lake Argen's downtown had been arranged more like building blocks stacked between the lake and Argen Road, cross streets with the bulk of the businesses running between Essex and Pine with the town hall, the bank, the library and the fire department all on Pine. The sidewalks were perfect paths of black asphalt, the one crack I could see blocked off with traffic cones. A small sidewalk-resurfacing machine chugged toward Pine and Lake, trailing the smell of tar behind it. Essex and Pine were shaded by mature trees. Flowers spilled from planters in the crossroads. It was pretty. And confusing. I kept finding myself turning one too many corners and ending up back where I'd started, but eventually I found a secondhand store.

An A-frame blackboard announced that all profits went to the medical center and that men's golf shirts were on sale for five dollars.

What was with this town and blackboards, I wondered as I pulled open the door? Had they never heard of whiteboards, or was it a charming bit of nostalgia put in place for the tourists they seldom had?

"Don't stand there with the door open! If I wanted bugs in here, I'd invite them in myself!"

"Sorry." I stepped over the threshold and fought a rusted air hinge to tug the door closed behind me. When it finally gave, my elbow knocked off one of the signs taped to the glass. Pulling the skirt of my sundress against the back of my legs, I crouched to pick it up and spotted a narrow trench carved into the old wooden floor just along the edge of the threshold. It was about a centimeter wide, a centimeter deep and half full of . . . salt?

"Get your fingers out of that!"

Clutching the fallen sign, I straightened. "Sorry."

"You say that now," muttered the old woman perched vulturelike on a high stool behind the counter, her single eye squinted nearly closed, her eyepatch covered in Toronto Maple Leaf stickers. No wonder she was cranky.

I handed her the sign. "This fell."

"I saw."

I barely stopped a third *sorry* from emerging as I pulled Travis's picture from my bag. "I'm looking for—"

"Cassidy Prewitt. She's not here."

"No . . . I mean, I am." Small town, I reminded myself. I'd been warned at the pub. "I'm also looking for information on Travis Brayden."

"Skinny, smug outsider who disappeared."

"Yes."

"Don't know anything about him."

She knew something. I could hear a distinct hint of *protests too much* in her voice. Making a mental note to drop by again should the elusive Cassidy Prewitt not be any help, I half-turned and glanced around. The place was small, crowded, and smelled, like most thrift stores did, of dust and despair. Less usual but not entirely surprising was the faint layer of pot pretending to be patchouli. "Do you have any old knives?" I asked. "Big ones. But not hunting knives."

She pointed back over her shoulder at the two swords hanging parallel on the wall. "Like these?"

"Those aren't knives."

"You arguing with me?"

Was I? "Yes."

"Good for you. Cutlery's in boxes over by the wall. Don't bleed on anything."

"I don't plan to."

"Few do."

———

"Hey, Mom." I checked the time. She'd probably called on her pre-dinner rush break. "Who uses fish knives?"

"Pretentious gits who don't do their own dishes." I heard the distinctive suck/puff of lips applied to a cigarette, then she added, "Why?"

"There were hundreds of them in the secondhand store I was just in." Feeling a one-eyed stare between my shoulder blades, I moved a little farther down the street. *Hundreds* sounded like an exaggeration. It wasn't. "I guess they must have run their pretentious gits out of town. What's up?"

"Can't a mother want to hear her daughter's dulcet tones?"

"You heard them a few hours ago."

"Oh, so, that's how it is." Another suck/puff.

"You swore you wouldn't start smoking again," I pointed out, trying not to sound whiney and not sure I succeeded.

"Only counts if you buy the cigarettes yourself."

"Instead of stealing them from me!" bellowed a distant voice.

I sighed. "Tell Lisa hi."

"Later." Suck/puff.

"Mom?"

"Look . . ."

I heard a large truck rumble by in the pause.

". . . I know we were joking about bears and getting eaten and shit because shit happens after you get eaten by bears, but be careful, okay? I dropped a kale salad during the lunch rush, and it looked like a skull. Then goosebumps rose up on my turtle tattoo. Just on the turtle, not the rest of my arm. I know omens when I see them."

Omens. Just what I needed. "Mom, is that tobacco you're smoking or—"

"Ha, ha. I spent a lot of time at psychic fairs when I was younger, Mel. I know things."

"You always said psychic fairs were bullshit."

"And I stand by that, but do you want to end up under a pile of bullshit? No. Promise you'll be careful."

"I promise to avoid the back end of bulls."

"Attagirl. Okay, gotta go. We've got to set up for a birthday party in the private dining room."

"Rich assholes!" Lisa shouted.

"How are you two still employed?" I wondered.

"Damned if I know," Mom said, and hung up.

Two calls in one day. My leaving when she'd expected me to be around seemed to have unsettled her. Which was strange. Nothing much unsettled my mother. She was the most settled person I—

"Sorry, sorry!"

A group of kids dressed in white T-shirts and blue shorts swarmed past, surrounding and/or piled on the occupant of a wheelchair being pushed at full speed down the sidewalk. Most of the kids waved metal skewers and carried canvas bags filled with what looked like black Styrofoam. As I watched, a piece bounced out and shattered on the concrete.

A girl of about eight whirled around to glare at the pieces. "That one still counts," she shouted, racing to catch up. "You all know I had it!"

Okay. Not Styrofoam. Charcoal briquettes? I'd never actually seen a charcoal briquette up close and personal, but if I thought of them at all, which I never had, I'm sure I'd have thought of them as less fragile. Not entirely certain why I was bothering, I crushed the small pieces to powder and watched as a breeze blew the powder away.

There was no one in the barbershop except for a surprisingly young man slumped in one of the two chairs, staring at a tablet. Was he the barber? An abandoned customer? Had I ever seen a barbershop before? I wasn't sure.

I glanced down an alley as I crossed it, spotted the lake, thought about heading that way, then reconsidered as I reached a bookstore.

No one ends up teaching English if they aren't in love with books. Okay, I knew someone who started out teaching geography and ended up teaching English because seniority had shuffled her during cutbacks instead of letting her go, but usually, books. Digital. Audio. Paper. We all said format didn't matter, story mattered, but deep down, we all wanted something we could stick our noses in.

I took a deep breath as the door closed behind me, sucking in the familiar smell and—

"Zod! Mulder!"

It's pretty much impossible for an adult of any size to be knocked over by a pair of corgis, but these two took a crack at it. I dropped to one knee before four sets of toenails against bare legs could draw blood.

Don't bleed on anything.

Words to live by.

"Aren't you beautiful, yes, you are." I dug my fingers into thick golden fur as two corgi butts wriggled ecstatically. "And so soft." The slightly larger dog pawed at my knees. "Yes, you too, jealous! You're both soft!"

"My apologies; they're not usually quite this effusive around strangers."

"I don't mind. I love dogs." Both black noses shoved hard against my skirt. "What are you smelling, you silly things? I changed clothes; there's nothing of that other dog on me now."

"Other dog?"

Hands still working in thick fur, I looked up to meet the gaze of a woman who knew exactly who she was, the kind of woman so confident in her skin that age became irrelevant. My mother managed that kind of confidence on occasion, but this woman wore it like she wore her ripped jeans and Docs. Effortlessly. She had chin-length dark hair streaked with fuchsia and brown eyes behind dark-rimmed glasses. Kneeling at her feet, still skritching her dogs, I fell a bit in love.

She raised a brow.

I really hoped I hadn't said that out loud. Then I realized she was waiting for an answer to her question. "I met a dog this morning by the cemetery."

"By the cemetery?" Both brows dipped. "Just one?"

"There were two, but only one approached." The smaller corgi leaned against me, panting happily. "The other one stayed with their person up by the mausoleums. Her name was Daffodil. She had a pink collar."

"Daffodil?" She pushed her glasses up her nose. "And she was friendly?"

"Oh, yeah. And drooly. That's one of the reasons I had to change." I waved the rising cloud of corgi fur away from my face. "Dog hair's one thing, but no one wants to walk around covered in drool."

"Daffodil doesn't usually take to strangers."

Her tone made *doesn't usually* sound like *never has* and it pulled me up to my feet. "Abused?"

"Let's say she didn't have the best beginning." Another frown. Another glasses adjustment. "You weren't frightened by her? She, well, both of them tend to react aggressively to fear."

I folded my arms, feeling defensive for Daffodil's sake. "She isn't pretty, but that's hardly her fault."

"No. It isn't." After a long moment, she smiled and held out her hand. "I'm Alyxandra Harvey, welcome to The Book Hoard. Call me Alyx."

"Melanie Solvich." Alyx was older than she'd looked from the floor, and although she was a good four, maybe five inches shorter than me, I felt like I was still looking up at her.

"What brings you to Lake Argen, Melanie?"

She sounded like she wanted to know, so I told her. Everything.

"Ten thousand dollars? That's a lot of money."

"It definitely is. I've never seen that much money at one time. It'll pay off my cards . . . I keep really low limits on my cards," I said when she looked dubious. "That taken care of, it'll put all-seasons on the car, and maybe stretch to a couple of pairs of jeans." Not something I'd usually share with a stranger, but Alyx, and her *I know exactly who I am* personality, felt like a person I could open up to.

She made a noncommittal sound. "Did Mrs. Brayden show you the police report?"

"I'm not sure Mrs. Brayden saw the police report," I told her, reaching into my bag for Travis's picture. "Grief does funny . . . Ow!"

A book slammed into my shoulder.

"Stop it!" Alyx snapped, yanking me out of the way as three more fell from a top shelf.

I looked up, expecting a store cat, but there was nothing there except an empty place on the shelf.

"Follies and nonsense, whims and inconsistencies do divert me," Alyx muttered as she bent and picked them up. "Sorry about that." She glared at the empty space on the shelf. "Some people have opinions."

"Ghost?" I asked, grinning.

"Ghost," she replied. It sounded like she meant it.

I felt my grin slip and covered it by shoving Travis's picture toward her. "Is there anything you can tell me about Travis Brayden?"

"Only what everyone else can tell you." She scowled at the bent corner on a copy of *Wuthering Heights*. Or maybe at *Wuthering Heights*. It was hard to tell.

"That I should talk to Cassidy Prewitt, because she was the last person to see him."

That drew her attention off the book. "Was she?"

"Everyone else seems to think so."

"I'm not everyone else, am I?"

She really wasn't. "Do you have anything to tell me about Travis?"

"No."

Okay, then. I needed to go. To, if nothing else, find Cassidy Prewitt. But wait . . . Alyx. I'd heard that name before. "Why would someone ask if I was one of yours?"

"One of mine?" She smiled. "Oh, probably because I was the first of the latest crop of incomers. I get blamed for all of them now."

Not quite. Teaching made a person very good at identifying the space between the truth and an outright lie; it was the only way to survive dealing with the administration. For a change, because I was very bad at letting it go, as evidenced by the lack of a teaching position come September, I decided not to push. I was a stranger. Alyx didn't owe me anything. So, I asked, "Do you have any local histories?"

One of the dogs *woof*ed softly and Alyx said, in a tone that suggested I'd surprised her, "Not accurate ones."

"Too bad. I could use something to read while waiting for Cassidy Prewitt to call."

"Good thing you're in a bookstore."

"Good thing," I agreed and picked up a pale green paperback with a graphic depiction of two darker green trees bracketing the silhouette of a woman.

"*Branching Out*," Alyx said. "Terrible title, better book. It's about a young woman who leaves home and ends up somewhere . . . unexpected."

"Like Narnia?" I offered when that was the extent of the synopsis.

She smiled. "Sure. Although I don't remember Susan having a somewhat steamy relationship with two tree nymphs."

"Dryads," I murmured, flipping the book over to check the price. "And seriously?"

Alyx gestured at the table. "You did pick it up from our Hot and Steamy Summer Section."

I did.

"Canadian author," Alyx prodded.

Mythic lesbian smut and nationalism, a hard combination to beat.

———

On the way to the beach, I spotted an ice cream sign in front of the end house in a line of three brick semis, knocked on the window as instructed, and handed over Mrs. Brayden's card for a double scoop on a waffle cone. If I kept eating this way, there'd be no question about putting that ten grand toward new jeans.

I found a surprisingly comfortable rustic bench in the shade, sat down, and opened my book. I had an expensive university education I still hadn't quite finished paying for; I could both read and wait for Cassidy Prewitt to call.

"Bwack!"

The bench shuddered as the raven landed and stared, head cocked, at my last three centimeters of cone.

"You're a carrion eater," I pointed out, ready to use *Branching Out* as a shield against the wicked looking beak. "This much sugar can't be good for you."

I had no idea that ravens could shrug. They made a soft *KU KU KU* and gave me a look I chose to interpret as hopeful.

"Fine." Curiosity as much as anything prompted me to hold out . . .

The cone was gone, and the raven was airborne before I'd finished counting my fingers. With all eight and both thumbs where they were supposed to be, I watched kids playing on the beach for a moment, noted that the teenagers were staying away from the line of buoys rather than hanging off them like my friends and I would've done, and went back to my book.

I was tired of working without all the necessary information. I'd return to Travis Brayden and his grandmother's knife after I spoke to Cassidy Prewitt.

I finished the book without hearing from her. The beach and the water were empty but for an old woman wading ankle-deep, skirt tucked into her waistband. Although the sun was hours from setting, the air had the feel of evening, and my stomach informed me that it had been a long time since the ice cream—

"Ow!" A curved piece of what looked like bone bounced off my right shoulder and hit the bench. No, not bone. A cat claw. A really big cat claw. It would have been as long as my palm without the wicked curve, and when I picked it up, the heft made me assume it was a fossil until I took a closer look. Not a fossil. Not even that old; the claw itself was polished smooth, but the end where it had been shed still had rough edges.

Did they have mountain lions in Northern Ontario?

Did they have velociraptors?

"Kuk."

I looked up at the raven perched in the tree above me. Crows brought gifts; maybe other corvids did as well. "Thank you?"

As though they'd been waiting for me to show some appreciation, the raven launched themself into the air.

And shat on the bench right where the claw had been.

Could mean *you're welcome* in raven, could mean *get fucked*. Even odds.

Sliding the claw in by Travis's picture, next to the feather, I headed for the diner and dinner.

EIGHT

Cassie

I'd become even more in sympathy with Simon as the afternoon went on. And on. And on. Crushed under mining machinery started to seem like a valid exit strategy from a conversation that had turned into a Mobius strip. A conversation I could have stopped with a Word. One Word. Just one. But no, I'd sat quietly while we all checked to be sure each of the Four were still functional within the bounds of the fraying Agreement.

Well, I sat quietly except for the part where Aunt Jean had Seen a shadow hiding from the sun under the rhododendrons and I, as the youngest and most expendable . . .

"I said flexible, Eric," Amanda huffed. "Not expendable. Don't be an ass."

. . . had been sent to stab it with the silver skewer Amanda kept handy on her porch.

For lack of anything useful to do, Amanda had tucked her Hands under the front bumper and lifted her truck. Only half-paying attention, I crushed the calcified remains of the shadow into dust and let the wind blow it away.

I offered to Tell them all to stand on one leg, but no one took me up on it.

Eric Listened in on a conversation Tom and Alison were having in the greenhouse, then spent half an hour arguing with Aunt Jean that she Sees as much as he Hears, and if they can trust her to keep it to herself, given her known love of gossip, they can trust him, too, given that he doesn't gossip. It sounded like a well-worn conversation that had nothing to do with trust and, I realized, a whole lot to do with Aunt Jean's enjoyment of shit-disturbing. At least she'd stopped saying the s-word.

Amanda muttered something about banging heads together under her breath.

We weren't actually accomplishing much. Eric and I had to work together. Aunt Jean bossed us all around, although I suspected Eric and Amanda didn't usually listen. Amanda lent a Hand when—well, when available, really. But all Four of us together? That was usually snacks and bitchy commentary. And it usually didn't matter.

Now, thanks to Travis Brayden and whatever he was doing in the darkness, it did.

Could we become a cohesive team instead of Four individuals?

Not from where I was sitting.

The whole power of Four as written of in the Journals was a lovely concept—my mental voice layered a lot of sarcasm on those last two words—but really no more than that. The Power of the Four protects the town! Sure, it did. Sequentially, not simultaneously.

Then, personal boundaries reestablished, we slid into a discussion of *how* to get ready.

Then someone—at this point I'd lost the thread; it could've been yelled from a passing car—suggested we do what we can to strengthen the Dark.

More chanting? The Acolytes would love that, they were all about the chanting. I'd been part of youth adulation when I was younger—

not because I had any great desire to revere the Dark; I just liked chanting—until the practice schedule had nearly taken over my life.

No. We didn't need more chanting.

More what, then?

The Dark showed interest in the occasional direct descendant of the thirteen—choosing the Four, adapting Evan or Alice or Jeffrey—but that was incidental to us all just living our lives.

We'd stared at each other.

"Go back to the beginning," Aunt Jean had huffed at last.

"An s-word?" Amanda's mouth had actually fallen open.

"I Heard there's a stranger in town," Eric had said thoughtfully.

"We are not s-wording my stranger!" I'd yelled.

Fortunately, my slip got lost in all the yelling. Eventually, Brenda, Amanda's closest neighbor, asked us to keep it down a bit because the baby was asleep in her playpen on the deck.

"If she falls in the lake—" Amanda began.

"It's not an s-word without intent," Eric reminded her. "If everything Alice ate counted, we'd be ass-deep in ritual."

Forced to come to something resembling a conclusion, we decided that regardless of how our relationship with the Dark had begun, we weren't s-wording anyone.

Not even Kevin Foreman, although Aunt Jean made a number of very good points about how her life would be better without him. They'd been feuding for over sixty years about something only important to old people.

We all felt we should give Evan and Jeffrey a heads-up, just in case. No one knew for sure where Evan had wandered off to, although he liked to hang out around the edges of the Mattagami Territory whether they wanted him to or not, reenacting colonialism one very large white dude at a time. When Amanda mentioned the possibility of Jeffrey accidentally eating "something" he shouldn't, Eric and I both reminded her, loudly, that Jeffrey was a vegan. Then we fist-bumped on Bridget's behalf and called apologies to Brenda for waking the baby.

Anyway, long afternoon.

After all that, I was not in the mood to cook. I dropped my bike at the house and headed for the diner.

Halfway down Essex, I spotted Reggie running after a trio of low-flying ravens and yelled at him to leave the birds alone. The ravens could be feathered pains in the ass, and I personally thought they deserved about half the trouble Reggie gave them, so I yelled without Voice and only out of a sense of civic responsibility.

The phrase *civic responsibility* had been shouted, snarled, and sighed a number of times over the afternoon. Apparently to some effect.

Mom and Dad had worked breakfast today, so they wouldn't be at the diner and I wouldn't have to be diplomatic when asked how my day had been. I couldn't risk them confronting Aunt Jean about the whole testing thing, nor did I want them assuming they understood what was going on because they were my parents. The last thing I'd need if the situation came to a head was people in general making assumptions based on a conversation they'd overheard between my parents and me in the diner. The walls had ears. Not many, the spray Alyx whipped up had mostly worked, but a few in odd corners.

Mom's night manager met me at the door.

"Cassie!"

"Eva!"

"Don't Eva me, you slacker." She gave me a quick hug.

Her hair smelled like tomato sauce, so I glanced at the specials board. Lasagna. Of course. A Monday without lasagna, even a Monday in July when the temperature hit the low thirties, would cause a riot among the regulars.

Realizing my attention had drifted, Eva poked me in the side. "We depend on you, our customers depend on you, and what happened? Chris had to send over cheesecake because you were too busy to bake."

"You love Chris's cheesecake. Everyone loves Chris's cheesecake. I'm crap at cheesecake."

"Not the point, sweetheart." She looped her arm with mine and tugged me farther into the diner. "What was your excuse this time? Had company and didn't feel like getting up? Drove into Timmins for fast food? Went online and lost track of time?"

Okay, the Timmins thing had happened once.

"Four business," I told her.

"Jean needed someone to taste her strawberry-rhubarb jam?"

"I went to talk to Alice this morning."

She froze. "Alice? That's . . ."

I didn't hear what it was, or anything else she said. There, sitting in a two-person booth, too polite to use one of the open fours, was the stranger of my dreams. Or, more accurately, of my early morning. Her honey-blond hair was still tied back in a ponytail, but now, instead of jeans and a T-shirt, she wore a pale blue sundress with narrow white stripes and a silver watch on her left wrist. It looked like a regular analog watch even though, like anyone else eating alone, she was holding her phone. I could see the soft glint of golden hair on her forearms, and if she wore nail polish, it was clear. No visible tattoos.

If she fell in the lake, I'd go in after her. I'd fight Alice for her. Although, realistically, it'd be easier to keep her away from the lake.

"Thanks, Eva," I mumbled. "I've spotted a friend I can eat with."

It felt like it took me ten or fifteen minutes to reach her table, although it wasn't more than half a dozen steps. She looked up when I arrived, and I fell into pale blue eyes surrounded by long, gold-tipped lashes.

When I emerged, she was frowning, her pink cupid's bow mouth pressed into a thin line.

I swallowed, wiped my palms on my shorts, and asked the question that would define the direction of our lives from this point forward. "May I join you?"

NINE

Melanie

Could she join me?

Me?

I was not the type who usually attracted beautiful strangers in small-town diners. I mean, I did okay, but the woman waiting for me to answer was out of my league. Given that, Chappell Roan's "Good Luck, Babe" playing on the diner's sound system seemed a little on the nose.

She had short, thick hair—not black but very dark brown—that stood up in chunks around her head like she spent a lot of time running her hands through it and no time at all smoothing it down. Her navy tank top and khaki shorts did little to hide lithe muscle, the shorts short enough that I could see the bottom edge of a tattoo on her upper right thigh. She had a long torso and small breasts, and was probably a few inches shorter than me, but then, most women were. Her eyes were large and dark, her chin almost delicately pointed, her mouth wide and smiling around straight white teeth . . .

The smile began to fade, and I realized I'd taken so long to answer that she'd begun to assume the answer was no.

"Yes. I'd love to have you join me." I'd love to lick the curve of her shoulder, but that was an abstract need. Dinner was doable.

"Great!" The smile blazed, and she dropped into the other side of the two-person booth with a loose grace that suggested she'd done it a million times before. "So, if you haven't ordered yet, can I suggest the souvlaki?" Before I could ask why a small-town diner in Northern Ontario owned by the very-not-Greek Prewitts I'd met this morning had souvlaki on the menu, the smile blazed again, and she answered my unasked question. "The first cook, back in my great-grandfather's day was Greek, Josef Kannalous, and souvlaki has been on the menu ever since. There'd be a riot if it wasn't." She leaned forward and lowered her voice. "Some people are very"—her eyes twinkled—"loyal when it comes to what they eat." She straightened before I could lean in and meet her halfway. "Oh, and I'm Cassidy Prewitt; call me Cassie. You are?"

I blinked. "You're Cassidy Prewitt?"

"You sound surprised?" And she, Cassidy, *call me Cassie*, sounded just a little wary.

"No, not surprised," I hastened to reassure her. Wary was not the emotion I wanted to evoke. Both for the job and for . . . personal reasons. "It's just that everyone in town has been saying that I needed to talk to you."

Dark brows rose. "Really?"

"I've been told that you were the last person to see Travis Brayden."

She jerked back. "Travis Brayden? Seriously?"

"He disappeared back in June."

Waving off my explanation before I could expand on it, she said, "I remember him. Are you his—"

"Nothing!" I said quickly. "I'm his nothing."

"Good."

"Right." Good. Definitely good. I poked at the bowl of sugar packets. "His grandmother hired me to find out about his last days."

Dark brows rose again.

"Because she's grieving." She'd said she was grieving. At least, I was pretty sure she'd said she was grieving. "She needs closure." She'd definitely said that. "You know."

"Sure. I guess." Hands flat on the table, Cassie sighed. "I don't know about his last days; it was more like I had a last, fleeting glance. I was up by the Dead Ground . . ." I must have made a face, because she paused and shook her head. "It's only what we call a spot where nothing grows up that's up on top of a cliff, just past the east end of town. Officially, it's called the lookout, you can see a lot from up there, but *the Dead Ground* is more interesting a name, so . . ." She shrugged and I was momentarily distracted by the movement of her shoulders. "Anyway, the sun had just cleared the horizon—maybe a little more than just cleared—and I saw Travis, although I didn't know it was him at the time, of course; it was just some guy walking along the path down by the lake, heading north. Then I got called about some family stuff happening and I lost sight of him. The police said he probably got lost in the woods, fell into a crevice. Died." She shrugged again. Still distracting.

When I'd collected myself, she'd propped her chin on her hands and locked her eyes on my face. I wanted to say . . . I had to say . . . I needed to say . . . "Did he get eaten by bears?"

"That happens a lot less than people assume." This smile came with a nose crinkle, and I added to the album of smiles I was building. Blazing. Check. Crinkle. Check.

"You two ready to order?"

I ordered the souvlaki and a water. I wanted a beer, but I wanted to keep my senses sharp more. I didn't want to miss anything. Cassie ordered the same.

"Rice *and* lemon potatoes?" I asked when Eva took our orders to the kitchen.

"Carb loading." She grinned and I added it to the album. "If I take you up to the Dead Ground tomorrow morning, you'll need it."

I stopped myself from asking if there was a chance I'd need it before morning, and asked instead, "Are you going to? Take me to the Dead Ground," I added when the edges of her smile grew a little wicked.

"Why not? You can take a few pictures of where he was last seen to show his grandmother."

She had a joyous self-confidence that made me wonder how many people had ever said no to Cassidy Prewitt. Not many, I suspected. And I could already tell that I wasn't likely to be one of them. "Will you be able to get the time off work?"

"Not a problem; I own half a business. My best friend Chris owns the other half."

Chris? I managed to put a face to the name. "The baker. From the bakery next door?" I pointed toward the kitchen and the wall behind it and the bakery behind that.

"You met Chris?"

"I was looking for you. Alyx at the bookstore said you could usually be found there, but she didn't say you were a baker."

"You met Alyx?"

"Again, I was looking for you."

"Good."

"And asking about Travis Brayden," I admitted.

"Should I be jealous?"

"He's dead."

"Excellent point."

"And I never met him, just his grandmother."

Cassie leaned in and waggled her brows. "Should I be jealous?"

I laughed. Then realized she was serious enough to want an answer. "No. All I'm interested in is her money."

"I can respect that." Leaning back again, she said, "So, what do you do when you're not taking commissions from grieving grannies?"

I waited while Eva set down our glasses of water and headed back to the kitchen before saying, "I teach high school English."

"Cool. Where?"

Painting damp circles on the tabletop with the condensation on my glass, I considered lying, embarrassed to tell this intriguing stranger that I was unemployed. But I wasn't embarrassed about why I was unemployed, so fuck it. "I was in Saskatoon, but I had a difference of opinion with the provincial government about teachers having to out trans kids to their parents. I let the school board know how I felt, then I left."

"Good for you!"

It sounded like she meant it. "Thanks. Though, technically, I left after I got fired for letting the school board know how I felt. There may have been strong language involved."

"Actual strong language?" The nose crinkle appeared again. "My, my."

"I keep wondering if I shouldn't have gone stealth mode and stayed, helped the kids from the inside." I hadn't actually said that to anyone else and wasn't entirely certain why I was saying it to Cassidy Prewitt now, although it could possibly have been because she was looking at me like she really wanted to know.

"I think if the kids know you lost your job for them, that'll help. That someone believes in them that much."

"It's a nice idea," I admitted. "But it still seems like I took an easy out."

She nodded thoughtfully. "Yeah, I can understand why you'd think that. Did you tell the board you refused to work under those restrictions, only to have them call your bluff and tell you to leave?"

"Close, but they didn't ask me to leave until I told them I wouldn't work for people who had their heads so far up their fucking asses, it had cut off all oxygen to their brains."

Cassie burst out laughing and I felt my cheeks heat. "Strong language!" she finally managed, wiping her eyes.

Feeling a bit overwhelmed, I drank half my water, and when I looked at her again, she was gazing at me in a way I had to call fond.

"So, here we are, together, drinking water . . ." She lifted her glass. ". . . making plans for tomorrow, and you still haven't told me your name."

I hadn't?

I hadn't.

I felt my cheeks flush. "Melanie Solvich."

This smile I didn't need to bother saving because it was burned into my optic nerves.

"I am so very happy to meet you," she said.

TEN

=

Cassie

I'd never been an early riser. Chris was the one who arrived at the bakery at stupid o'clock in the morning, proofing dough and getting the breakfast muffins into the oven so they were boxed and ready for six-thirty delivery to the break room at the mine. Sure, I dealt with the diner and the orders that came our way when the Acolytes decided to buy snacks for after chanting, but I only became a professional baker because Chris and I had been best friends our whole lives, clothes covered in flour, fingers sticky with batter, and his need to actually make a living overcame my *whatever* attitude about the future.

But not even for Chris would I haul ass out of bed to produce baked goods in the middle of the night. We hired temporary help when he and Alan went on their honeymoon, and again after Alan's cousin gave birth to their daughter Natalie.

So, why was I wide awake, bright-eyed and bushy-tailed at six AM?

Because I was meeting Melanie at the diner at nine, and the anticipation fizzing under the surface of my skin wouldn't let me sleep. I showered, checked to make sure the bushy-tailed thing remained a metaphor, dressed, and headed in to work.

The sky was blue. I was in high school the last time it hadn't been.

It had been a kind of pale lime green and our "localized weather system" had been found weird enough that a national news anchor had commented on it. The Agreement had allowed him two whole sentences. While today would likely end up as hot as yesterday, it wasn't yet. Birds were singing and I was fairly confident they actually were birds, because Alice had taken care of the last siren who'd shown up—and, according to town records, the half dozen who'd shown up earlier. As they didn't get into the records until they sang, there easily could have been a few more, removed before they got the first note out. Accumulated evidence suggested sirens weren't very bright.

Last night, Melanie and I had talked until Eva kicked us out. I remembered laughing, a lot, but I couldn't remember exactly what we'd talked about. Superficially jobs, life, family, but an undercurrent of more important things ran beneath every story. I traded the stories she told of her mother, Dorothy, who sounded amazing, with stories of my parents in the diner, and stories of her teaching job in Saskatoon with stories of the bakery. She'd touched my hand, just once, but I could still feel the warm pressure of her fingertips. I'd touched her shoulder when I dropped her off at the guest house. Her hair had smelled like green-apple shampoo.

I'd wanted to ask her to come home with me, but because I was pretty sure she would, I didn't. Restraint. Go me. It just felt like this thing between us was more than merely physical attraction and I wanted to do it right. In this case, *right* meant not falling into bed at the first opportunity. At the second opportunity, I'd reevaluate.

Chris was handing the boxes of muffins over to Michelle, who ran the break room at the mine, when I arrived.

"Did I miss an email? Was the apocalypse scheduled for today?" Michelle wondered, staring at me in feigned astonishment.

"Still next October," I told her cheerfully as I went inside.

"Why do you do that?" Chris asked wearily when he finally joined me, a full fifteen minutes later.

I giggled. "I'm spreading the joy."

"Next time, you can convince her that you're kidding." His brows drew in and he folded his arms. "You're unsettlingly cheerful. Have you been possessed?"

"Nope." I retrieved a block of shortening from the freezer and set it and the grater on my worktable.

"Yesterday, we were heading for disaster."

"Still are. But today's a brand-new day."

"Wait. I know that look. You got laid."

"Nope."

"You're usually less happy about that not happening," he muttered as he checked the rise on the bagels.

I started grating shortening into a bowl of flour and grinned when I heard a tray hit the counter a little too hard.

A moment later, Chris poked me in the back. "You met a special someone."

"He shoots, he scores!"

"Yeah, that's just creepy in reference to your sex life. Please stop. Do I know her?"

"You met her. Melanie Solvich." I loved saying her name. It fit perfectly in my mouth. Gradually, I became aware that the familiar sounds of Chris doing what he did best—Alan excluded—had stopped, and I turned to find him staring at me.

"Melanie Solvich? Who was out front yesterday, looking for you? I sent you her number."

He had? "You did?"

He sighed. "Why do you even have a phone?"

I considered that for a moment and concluded that, excluding the recent spate of texts from the other Three, it was mostly for cat vids.

"Melanie Solvich," Chris repeated. Again. "She wanted to ask you about Travis Brayden's disappearance."

"I know. We talked last night." I tucked the remainder of the short-ening back in the freezer next to the unsalted butter. "For hours."

"Did you talk about Travis Brayden?"

"I told her the same lie I Told the police. And I'm taking her up there after breakfast." I raised my voice enough to be heard over the sound of the mixer. "So she can take some pictures of the last place he was seen and send them to his grieving grandmother."

"Cassie—"

"Cool your jets, hoss; she's not a private investigator searching for a way to disprove the police report. She's an English teacher looking for emotional context to give his grandmother closure."

"Okay." He slid the last tray of bagels into the oven. "Can I assume from your mood that you really like her?"

I felt my ears warm. "I do."

"And that you think there might be something real between you?"

Chris, who'd married his one true love at twenty-three, wanted everyone to happily settle down with the other half of their heart, so the question didn't surprise me, but my reaction to it did. "Yeah," I said slowly, examining the feeling from all angles. "I do."

He spread his hands. "And you don't think the lying thing might be a problem?"

"I think not lying would cause a bigger problem."

He opened his mouth. Closed it. And sighed again. "Point," he ac-knowledged, and we both went back to work.

By eight fifty-five, there were four pies and yesterday's delayed lemon squares on the cooling rack. By nine, I was washed, dried, de-aproned, and entering the diner.

Melanie was waiting for me at our table.

With a smile on my face and skip in my step, I headed toward her.

"Cassie, sweetheart." The coffeepot my mother held hit the counter with a crack as she grabbed my arm and yanked me sideways, hard enough I had to flail both arms and legs to avoid crashing over a counter stool. "The young woman over there is looking for you." Her mouth was close enough to the side of my head, I could feel her breath on my ear. "Chris told me you were out on Four business yesterday, so I didn't call, but she told us she has questions about Travis Brayden and the knife he used."

"I know. I met her last night."

"You met her?" Mom's eyes narrowed.

"And I'm joining her for breakfast."

"Where did you meet her?"

"Here." I'd forgotten Mom and Dad would be on site for their second breakfast shift of the week. Damn their intermittent work ethic. We should have grabbed a breakfast sandwich at the coffee shop and eaten in the park. If I wanted Melanie and me to have any privacy at all during breakfast, I had to think of a distraction. "Eva was on. Didn't she tell you about it?"

"No." Mom relaxed her grip on my arm. "She didn't."

"That's strange. I wonder why not." Even had I been willing to use the Voice on my mother, I didn't have to. I'd known her my whole life.

"An excellent question." She patted my shoulder and headed for the kitchen and her phone.

"Uh, Grace. . . ." Ed Abbott waved his mug mournfully at Mom's back.

As his empty mug was more or less my fault, I refilled his coffee. Then refilled Melanie's, poured one for myself, put the pot back on the warmer, and sat down.

Melanie's dimples suggested I'd done something a lot more impressive than distribute caffeine. "What?" I asked, pushing the sugar toward her.

"I admire competence."

"Then you should drop in next door and watch me trim a pie crust."

"I should."

"I'd like that."

She hummed as she raised her mug to her mouth.

I watched her glossy pink lips close around the white porcelain, and mirrored her movement.

"Hey there, Hopalong."

I didn't spew coffee across the table and all over Melanie's white, sleeveless blouse, but it was close. My father pounded my back until I stopped coughing, and would have continued pounding just to be helpful had I not managed to wave him off.

"Your mother's a bit busy—" he began.

Her voice drifted out of the kitchen, reminding Eva that I was her child regardless. I was vaguely curious about what *regardless* referred to, but not enough to go find out.

"—so, I figured I'd better come out and get your order. Richard Prewitt." He thrust his fist toward Melanie, who bumped it, eyes dancing. "I didn't get to meet you when you were in yesterday," he continued, "so I figured I should take my chance. I'm glad to see you and Cassie have hit it off. I hope she's keeping you entertained."

Translation: *I hope she's keeping you from asking too many questions about Travis Brayden. And, you know, other things.*

"Haven't had the chance to be entertaining, Dad," I said before Melanie could respond. "We just met last night."

"Of course." He winked at me. Melanie carefully put her mug down and pressed her fingers against her mouth. "Now, what can I get you two to eat?"

She took a deep breath, managed to get any potential laughter under control, and ordered the asparagus-and-Swiss-cheese omelet.

"Good choice," Dad told her approvingly. "Last of the fresh asparagus. It'll be off the menu by tomorrow."

"Make it two," I said, making the *Go Away!* subtext as close to text as possible.

"Toast—"

"Rye."

"And you—"

"Rye's fine," Melanie managed.

"That's—"

"Dad."

"Coming right up."

Melanie waited until he was back in the kitchen before she asked, "Hopalong?"

"Hopalong Cassidy." I sighed. "It's an old people thing he picked up from Granddad, who probably picked it up from his granddad."

She nodded like she understood. Maybe she did. "I like your parents."

"That's because they aren't your parents," I said, drained my mug, and got up to fetch the pot.

———

"That's where we're heading."

Squinting against the sun, Melanie glanced up at the top of the cliff and shook her head. "That's a steep climb."

"It is," I agreed, rubbing at my arms where the brambles had drawn blood during my midsummer race to the summit. "It's doable, but since we have the time, we'll take the path from the park."

She slid on her sunglasses and smiled. "Lay on, Macduff."

So, I laid. Led? I spent a few blocks searching for something to say, something witty, something wise, something that didn't make me seem like I'd never spoken to a beautiful woman in my life, but then, as we crossed the street to avoid some sidewalk resurfacing, I realized that the silence was comfortable. It didn't need to be filled. We walked along, the back of my left hand occasionally brushing the back of her right, the only sound our shoes on the sidewalk, our quiet breathing, our—

"HEY, CASSIE!" Vic Ellwood leaned out of his truck window as he drove by. "You get a chance, put in a good Word for me!"

I flashed him a tight smile and a thumbs-up, reminding myself that the town, and therefore Vic, was my responsibility. The news of me being off probation with the other Three had clearly spread. Had everyone known? Was that why so few people came to the Friday-evening sessions? Were the sessions about to get busy? Oh, joy. Then I realized Melanie was frowning. "He didn't mean I should put in a good word with you," I assured her. "It wasn't a drive-by, creepy-asshole-guy thing."

"So who are you to put in a good word with?"

"Could be my Uncle Stu. He's looking for a new backhoe driver and Vic's looking for a job."

"Could be?"

I shrugged. "He wasn't exactly specific." It looked like she didn't quite believe me. Rather than bleed in a little Voice, I changed the subject. "You met one of my uncle's dogs yesterday. I was surprised to hear you got along so well."

Melanie's turn to shrug.

And that kept the conversation on safe topics until we reached the park.

". . . they were the only survivors of the litter."

Their mother had already eaten the others.

". . . unfortunately, their mother didn't make it."

We'd tossed the pieces to Alice over a few hours, not wanting to risk too many in the water at once. Not after watching her hind legs reattach themselves.

". . . they don't usually make friends with strangers."

They tolerated the bloodlines, and Daffodil had a somewhat-threatening version of begging for treats. Dexter had come embar-rassingly close to eating a train engineer who'd strayed a little too far from the station. Oh, and they were terrified of Alyx's corgis, and it's hysterically funny watching the corgis lording it over a pair of hellhounds. Well, it was funny as long as Uncle Stu didn't catch you calling them hellhounds. Having hand-raised them, he was a bit over-protective.

That Daffodil had given every indication she liked Melanie? It showed Daffodil had excellent taste in women, but still, a surprise.

"I love dogs, but I've never been able to have one," Melanie ex-plained. "We've always lived in apartments. When I was in Saskatoon, I had a girlfriend with dogs, and that was as close as I've come."

"You kept seeing the dogs after you broke up, didn't you?"

"I did." She smiled, both dimples appearing, and I basked in it.

The green flag was up at the road, the arc lights had been put away for the day, and the parking lot was empty when we got to the House. Melanie stopped and stared at it, head cocked. "What's this?"

"That's what remains of the home of the town's founder, Edmund Prewitt. It burned down in 1831," I added, feeling that the foundation and roof combo needed a bit more explanation. "They covered it over right after the fire, and the town replaces the roof every seventy years or so." I was seven when the current steel roof had been put on, but I could still remember the distant sounds of screaming. And laughing. Some people found the weirdest shit funny, although I assumed the sounds were being made by different people. "It's a local historic site."

"I've seen stranger." As she walked over to take a closer look, a red dot appeared on her back, just under the swinging tip of her ponytail.

Safely behind her, I flipped security off.

A second red dot appeared.

I used both hands.

"You know if teenagers wanted to get into this . . ." She patted the cellar door. ". . . they'd avoid the padlock and just swing an axe." Before I could stop her, she curled her hand into a fist and knocked three times on the painted wood.

Tap. Tap. Tap.

In, or more likely under the enclosed basement, something answered.

BOOM. BOOM. BOOM.

I caught her when she stumbled backward on the uneven ground. Was still holding her when she panted, "What the hell was that?"

Good question. I scrambled for a believable lie. "Probably the roof. The hot steel reacts to the cooler air coming up from the dirt floor. Expanding. Contracting. Booming."

"Bullshit."

I set her on her feet, although I'd have rather kept holding her, and panicking just a little, Said, "It's true."

She frowned, wanting to keep protesting but unable to. What had I done? Had Aunt Jean been right about me all along? Was I going to turn into another Simon? His Journal had said nothing about how he'd begun abusing his power—which I totally understood since I was certainly not going to mention this in mine. Had he been trying to reassure someone he cared about? Was it that easy to fall?

It couldn't happen again.

Hugging herself, Melanie glared at the door. "It scared the crap out of me."

"It scares the crap out of a lot of people," I told her, trying to keep my voice pitched between sympathetic and matter-of-fact. The answering knock was usually nothing more than an opportunist testing the barrier on the gate. Now, if it had been claws scrabbling against the underside of the door, I'd have gotten us both the hell out of there toot de sweet. To be on the safe side, I pulled out my phone to send security a quick text. "Sorry, I've got to remind Chris to use the rest of the heavy cream before it goes off."

"Is that something he's likely to forget?"

"Kind of depends. When he gets fancy and complicated, he loses sight of the merely mundane. Come on." I put the phone away and bounced my side off of hers. "We're going this way."

She glanced back at the House a couple of times before a curve in the path took it out of sight. It looked like a brown steel roof on a meter-high foundation. Like a local historic site. Nothing more.

About halfway up the hill, a sudden crashing and breaking of branches in the woods off to the right shifted both of us quickly to the left.

Melanie grabbed double fistfuls of my T-shirt. "Is that a bear?"

"Doubt it." Bears were way too smart to cross the boundary, and even if Jeffrey was still vegan, Evan wasn't. "It's most likely Jeffrey gathering wild blueberries."

"By jumping up and down on the bushes?"

"He's a bit clumsy." Which was true. And he loved blueberries. "Jeffrey!" I raised my voice. "I've got someone from out of town with me; would you like to meet her?"

The crashing grew momentarily louder, then faded into the distance.

After taking a deep breath and releasing it slowly, Melanie let go of my shirt. "He may be clumsy," she said, patting the wrinkles out, "but he's fast."

"Fast and shy," I agreed, hoping she'd enjoyed the patting as much as I had. "And probably not dressed."

That bit of information elicited an extended stare, brows up. "Jeffrey is a nudist?"

"Not officially. He just doesn't like to wear clothes." Not since what he'd been wearing when he'd gone into the woods had rotted off him. Aunt Jean said he'd kept his clothes longer than most, and that Alice had been joyfully bare when she'd hit the water.

"A fast, shy nudist." Melanie leaned a little to the right and peered between the trees. "It seems a bit cliche to say that every town has a town character."

"We've got a couple, if that helps. You've met Reggie."

"Reggie with the ravens?" She turned back to face me. "He seemed nice."

"Sure. He's lovely. Except for when he's trying to turn the ravens into an aerial defense force, which pisses off the ravens." I leaned in and lowered my voice. "And the ravens make the rest of us suffer."

She laughed, and I wallowed in the sound the rest of the way to the top.

"Oh, my god, the view!"

I had to admit it wasn't bad. The roofs of the town spreading off to the left. The lake sparkling to the right, the surrounding green of a Northern Ontario summer fortunate enough to have wildfires suppressed by the Agreement. "Come on." I led the way out into the open. "We'll go to the edge; it gets better."

Melanie paused at the Dead Ground, glanced down at the bare dirt, then followed me around the outside curve. "Why don't you walk on it?"

I shrugged. "Never have. It's a thing."

"A thing?" Her voice had this amazing, amused kind of gurgle that I loved. I felt a little sad that she'd lost it when she continued speaking. "Why doesn't anything grow here? Has the town had the soil tested?"

"I don't know," I admitted. "I don't think about it that much."

"Fair enough."

She paused again at the edge of the rock, obviously unsettled by the vertical drop. I wrapped my fingers around hers, tugged her gently to me, tried to look into her eyes through the screen of her sunglasses, and murmured in my best superhero voice, "I'll protect you."

Then we ignored the view for a few minutes. She tasted a bit like coffee and asparagus. She felt like coming home. I wanted to sink into her until the spaces between us, the edges that kept us separate, disappeared.

The earth did not move—as we were standing on the edge of a cliff, that was a good thing.

"The pictures," she murmured eventually. "For Travis's grandmother."

"Right." I stepped back, far enough that we stopped breathing each other's air, shuffled around until I faced the lake, and pointed, mostly down. "See that path running alongside the water?"

"That's a path?" she asked, both hands clutching my arm.

"Not a great one," I allowed. "It doesn't get used often. That's where I saw him—him being Travis—just there. Just before the path curves in under the trees."

She let go and stepped back to pull her phone out of her messenger bag. "Did the police drag the lake?"

"You didn't see the report?"

Her blush spread down from her face, over her collarbones, and into her cleavage. I couldn't stop my gaze from following it or stop myself from wondering how far down it went. "I didn't ask about the police report," she said. "And Mrs. Brayden didn't offer it."

I made a noncommittal sort of noise that I hoped meant *Don't worry about it; nobody's perfect* rather than *Oh, thank the Dark*. I'd been a bit worried that I'd have to remember exactly what I'd Said to the police. "They didn't dredge the lake because they found a couple of footprints in under the trees, a couple more right before the path starts to climb away from the lake, and one in a bit of moss"—I pointed along the ridge we were standing on—"right about there."

"All I see are trees."

"There'd be rocks, too, if we were under the canopy. Spruce needles. A couple of old mica pits."

"And bears?"

I grinned up at her. "You're just a little fixated on the bear thing, aren't you?"

"City girl." She shrugged. I appreciated it.

She took pictures of the trail, backed up and took pictures of where the trail pictures had been taken from, then inched forward again and took a few pictures of the town. It looked good from up there; the blasted bit from the early 2000s had completely grown in.

"Is that a greenhouse?" She half-pointed, as though worried the weight of her raised arm would turn gravity against her. "That enormous reflective thing this side of the tracks?"

I checked. Just in case a new reflective thing had appeared. You never know. "It is. A fourth cousin twice removed on my father's side grows most of our produce. It's all high-tech, sci-fi, growing-food-in-the-north stuff and cost a bundle to set up, but she says it'll pay for itself in about six years even though she's charging less for fresh and crispy than we used to pay for limp greens coming up from the south."

"Fourth cousin, twice removed on your father's side?" The amused gurgle was back.

"Small town," I reminded her. "It's safer to be sure."

It took her a moment, then she snorted and went back to the view. "And that building there?"

"Rec center. Olympic pool. Climbing wall."

"Seriously?"

"Most of the silver money goes back into the town."

She took a step forward, remembered where she was, and took two back while staring at the mine. Or staring at where she assumed the mine was, since it couldn't be seen from up there. "And the company that owns the mine?"

"The people who own the mine live in the town."

"Seriously."

I shrugged. "It works for us."

"Okay, then." It almost seemed as if she didn't believe me, but when she changed the subject, I let it go. "If Timmins is that way . . ." She pointed more or less behind us, then switched to point out over the lake. ". . . what's that way?"

"Directly that way, a whole lot of nothing. That way and north, the

Mattagami First Nation. They're Anishnaabe. On-reserve population is plus or minus a couple hundred people most years."

"Do the kids come to Lake Argen's schools?"

"Nope. They have their own grade school and go to Timmins for high school. Well, every now and then, one comes here instead, but never more than one." The Elders chose a student to attend our high school every four years, in order to maintain knowledge of the agreement. The small-a agreement. The one made way back when the boundary was set. The one that says, and I'm paraphrasing here but not by much: *This is white-man shit; we want no part of it. You stay on your side of the line and we'll make sure you do.*

"The Mattagami," she repeated. "All this is their traditional land, right?"

"They don't want it."

"Oh, yeah, I'm sure they don't want their fair share of silver income."

As far as I could remember, around the millennium they started getting a percentage off the top. Before that, I had a feeling it was a bit hit-or-miss. Not being on the mine's BOD, I didn't know the details. "It's complicated."

She snorted. "I'll bet."

"Melanie, I bake pies. I'm not a one-woman Truth and Reconciliation Committee."

"Right. Sorry. It's just there's clearly money here, and so much damage to fix. You know?"

And right on cue, because like most of the country, I didn't want to talk about it, my phone rang.

"I can't believe you get a signal out here," she murmured as I took a look.

"It's my Great-Aunt Jean," I said. "I have to take this. She's . . . really old."

"Go ahead." Melanie stepped off the rock and started back around the Dead Ground's curve. "I'll wait over by the trees where I'm not likely to fall off the edge of the world."

"Cassie!" Aunt Jean pulled my attention back to the phone. "I can See something hanging around the back of Maureen Palmer's house. You need to come Talk to it."

I glanced over at Melanie. "Why do I have to go? Why can't Amanda come and hit it?"

"Because it has a face."

"Then she'll have something to aim for."

"And because she's at a *Willy Wonka* rehearsal."

Of course she was. "Can you See what it is?"

"No. It's mostly tucked back in that dark bit under Maureen's lilac bushes. It might be a type of shadow."

Lovely. More shadow. If security had been keeping the lights on all night, how did it get in? "You can't Talk to shadow, even if it has a face."

"No, I can't. You can."

It looked like Melanie, who was leaning against a tree at the head of the path, thumbs working her screen, had wasted no time in sending the pictures of Travis's alleged route to Mrs. Brayden. She glanced up and waved. I waved back. "Aunt Jean, I'm not—"

She huffed into the phone. "The Cassidy Prewitt who accepted her responsibilities as one of the Four didn't stick around long, did she?"

"Fine," I huffed back at her. "I'm at the Dead Ground and I'm on foot, so send a car to pick me up. I'll meet it at the park."

"I'll send Eric," she chirped happily, having gotten her own way. "You'll need him to Listen in case our visitor doesn't speak English. Or bad French. You really should work on being more bilingual. Oh, and while I have you, did you send pies to the diner today?"

I closed my teeth on what I wanted to Say, and settled for "Good-bye, Aunt Jean."

Melanie sighed when I told her I had to go deal with a problem only I could solve. "I envy you your family. Your parents, your Great-Aunt Jean, your fourth cousin twice removed . . ."

"On my father's side," I reminded her.

"Of course, on your father's side. There's just me and my mother. If she has living relatives, she hasn't spoken to them since before I was born. She has lots of friends, but there's just something about . . ."

"Blood?" I offered into the pause.

"Not what I was going to say, but sure." She linked her arm in mine, and walking downhill on a grass path under the arcing canopy of summer foliage with her warmth a heated line against my side, and Jeffrey probably watching from the undergrowth, I was as happy as I could ever remember being. It was a strange feeling. I did not allow my emotions free range less than twenty-four hours after meeting someone. My body, sure. My emotions, no.

"I don't know my father," she said so softly, she could have been talking to herself. "I'm fairly sure my mother only knows his first name. They met at a Queen's Park pro-choice rally, had what she still refers to as an amazing night, and about five weeks later, had to make a choice herself."

"I bet she's never regretted it. Not for a moment."

"So she says, but how do you know?"

"I've met you."

"You're very sweet." The dappled light painted fairytale highlights on her hair.

"I'm really not."

"Allow me to maintain my delusions for a while longer."

"For as long as you want," I assured her as we stepped out into the sun.

Eric pulled into the park before we reached the house. He circled the parking lot and hit the horn.

"So, what are you going to do now?" I asked, ignoring him.

"Get some pictures of Travis's motel room for his grandmother, I guess."

"Do you want a lift to the top of the hill? Avoid a bit of exertion in the heat? Eric might hit on you, but to his credit, he takes no for an answer. Also *fuck off*, and *I'm half your age, you shit-stain*. He's smarmy but harmless. All talk, no touch without consent." I felt like I was babbling a bit.

Melanie glanced at the car, where Eric could be seen through the windshield, beckoning impatiently. "That's a hard invitation to resist."

"I know, right? But lately, I've been discovering that there's a nice guy buried under the stupid stereotype." Maybe spending so much time hanging pathetically around Bridget had some of her nice rubbing off on him. On second thought, I did not want to think about Bridget, Eric, and the phrase *rubbing off on him*. "He's essentially harmless."

"You're not really selling him."

"Trust me, I'm not trying to."

"It is hot . . ."

"It is," I agreed, took her hand, and pulled her toward the car. "Hey, Eric," I called as I opened the back door and almost had to push Melanie in against the outward current of escaping air conditioning. "This is Melanie. We're giving her a ride to the motel." I slid in beside her. "I'll move to the front after we drop her off."

Eric twisted around in the driver's seat, theoretically to see while he was backing up, and shot Melanie a toothpaste smile. "I'm very, very pleased to meet you."

Wow. I really hoped the same words hadn't sounded that creepy when I'd said them. "Melanie's here to find out about Travis Brayden's last days."

"For his grandmother," Melanie put in. "For closure."

"I've heard. The whole town's buzzing about you. It's rare we have such beautiful visitors."

"Let it go, Eric."

"It's a compliment."

"Yeah, not the way you say it." Fortunately, I was pretty sure

Melanie was more amused than disgusted. Go her, because it's one thing when a dude you know acts like an ass, and it's another thing entirely when it's a stranger giving you a lift.

And proving just how strange he was, Eric kept going. "Women like to be—"

"Quit when you're ahead. Or at least before you fall further behind. Please."

"Ah, the magic word." He accelerated out onto Argen Street, spraying gravel. Because that was manly? Who knew. Would it impress straight women? Doubted it. Would it impress other men? I'd have to ask Chris.

The motel parking lot was in its usual state, empty of any car but Arthur's. I got out when Melanie did and peered over the roof to ask her, "You okay for getting back to the guest house?"

She smiled. "I think I can manage the walk."

"Did you want to meet for dinner? Knowing Aunt Jean, I doubt she'll be done with me in time for lunch."

"I'd like that very much. Call me when you're free."

"Cassie!" Even with doors and windows closed, Eric could make himself heard. I snorted. Make himself Heard. "Cassie, get in the car!"

I did, reluctantly, and waved at Melanie standing alone, the sun on the pale gravel creating almost a halo around her. She waved back. Should I have kissed her goodbye, I wondered as Eric sped back out onto Argen Street? No. We weren't there yet. At least not in front of Eric, we weren't.

"Why do you have it so cold in here?" I complained, buckling my seat belt. My sweat-damp fingers didn't stick to the buckle, but they left little circles of heat on the brushed steel.

He snickered. "To counter my innate hotness."

I should have known better than to ask.

ELEVEN

Melanie

I watched until the car was out of sight, feeling weirdly melancholy about being parted from a woman I barely knew, shook it off, turned, and gave a shriek I planned to deny later.

Standing barely a meter away, skinny arms crossed, Arthur scowled and said, "You're back."

"You're Beethoven." I could no more have stopped myself parroting my mother's response than I could have made my grey eyes brown. Actually, given contacts, the latter would have been easier.

To my surprise, Arthur started to laugh. The surprisingly deep sound exploded out of his narrow chest with such force, he had to bend forward and brace his hands on his thighs. A pair of cats, the orange boy I'd met earlier and a long-haired tuxedo, trotted out of the open office door and peered at him from the steps, both tails sweeping from side to side. They weren't worried about him; I got the impression they considered his reaction an embarrassment and didn't like how it might reflect on them. Although, to be fair, it was an expression cats often wore.

After enough time passed that I began to worry, he gained control, gave a final chuckle, and straightened. "I like you," he declared, pushing the fall of gorgeous chestnut curls back off his protruding forehead. "I've just put the kettle on. Want a cuppa?"

Why not, I asked myself. Then said the same to him.

"Oscar!" He swiveled toward the stoop, toe of one work boot digging a small hole in the gravel. "Get out the fancy pack of cookies; we've got company!"

The tuxedo cat flicked an ear at Arthur and went back into the motel.

As I was well aware that cats were the masters of coincidence, I stomped hard on the urge to stupidly say, "Oh, isn't he clever," and followed Arthur across the parking lot to the door. The orange cat had stretched out along the top step. I stepped over him.

Arthur's living room in behind the office had been decorated in comfy Victorian—one too many pieces of bulky, overstuffed furniture, medium green painted 70s fake wood paneling covered in framed photographs and a calendar from 1982 with today's date circled. Two layers of curtains blocked most of the light from the single window: a layer of off-white lace, topped with worn red velvet that matched the upholstery. The chunky coffee table held a packet of chocolate-covered digestive biscuits and two mugs on crocheted coasters. I neither saw nor heard an air conditioner, but the room was wonderfully cool.

"Have a seat. I'll just be a minute with the tea."

He returned with the pot and poured tea as dark as the woodwork and thick enough to eat the silver plating off a spoon. I added milk, declined sugar, and took a sip. Delicious. Coffee was a necessity. Tea was a comfort.

"Mrs. Brayden made me tea," I said absently, inhaling the steam.

"Did she, now." He stirred two spoons of sugar into his. "Good black tea, or that herbal crap?"

"Herbal. Her special blend."

Arthur barked out a laugh. "Yeah. Special. I just bet. You know, when I first saw you, I thought you had the look of a person who'd drink special tea."

"I looked like I had money?"

"Money has nothing to do with it." Picking up the package of biscuits, he ripped open the top and offered it to me.

I took it, fished out a cookie, and handed the package back. "Mrs. Brayden has money."

"'Course she does; you told me when you were here before that she hired you to ask about her grandson."

In spite of the July heat, the tea was really hitting the spot. "She's paying me ten thousand dollars." I hadn't told him that.

"Is she, now? For what exactly?"

"She wants context for Travis's last days or, as it happens, Travis's last evening. She said I should take all the time I need, a week at least. Longer if necessary." I took another swallow.

"She ever say why she wanted you to take so long?"

"No, but when you told me Travis had paid for five days, I assumed she'd gotten confused by the receipt."

"She seem like the type to get confused?"

I thought about old Mrs. Brayden pouring me tea in a room that was all clean lines and visibly expensive and pretty much the complete opposite of where I was sitting. "No, she did not."

"You got a week's worth of investigating to do?"

"I doubt it. I already have pictures of the trail where Cassie saw Travis. Once I have the pictures of Travis's room, everything else is filler." I'd also taken some photos from the tree line of Cassie on the phone with her Great-Aunt Jean so I could send them to my mother. Or not. Given that she'd warned me . . .

Please. Like I'd be so stupid as to fall in love with a person I'd known for less than twenty-four hours.

Arthur set his half-empty mug back on the coaster. "So, you've spoken to Cassidy Prewitt then, have you?"

"I have." Was I blushing? I felt like I was blushing.

"And what did you think?"

"Of Cassie?" I absently patted the tortie who'd emerged from the shadows and was trying to pull my arm down to get to my cookie. "You can't have that. Chocolate is bad for cats. Cassie's great. She's—"

"Not what did you think about Cassie." His eyes twinkled. The way Christmas lights twinkled. I blinked. No, just muddy brown eyes with impressive bags under them. "What did you think of her story?"

"About Travis?" The tortie attempted to knock over my mug, so I moved her down the couch and got a look that suggested she'd remember my face. "She told me where she saw him last and where the police found footprints."

"Did you argue with her about it?"

What a weird question. I shrugged, intending to point that out to him, and said instead, "Why would I argue? I wasn't there, so I have to take her word for it."

"You don't *have* to take her word for it. Did you feel like you didn't have a choice?"

"No. It was a figure of speech."

He slowly leaned in over the coffee table. "Did she say the words *You have to believe me*?"

"No," I snapped, and he was suddenly back where he'd been. "Why would you even ask me that?"

"I just want to make sure you weren't feeling . . ." He spread his hands. ". . . compelled. Coerced. Constrained."

"Constrained?"

He sighed. "Shouldn't have gone for the hat trick. What happened when you left her?"

"I didn't leave her. She got a call about a family thing, and they drove me here."

"They? Was that Eric I saw, then?" When I nodded, he offered more tea. I declined, so he filled his own mug and, while adding sugar, said, "I suppose you've had enough. Still . . ." Setting the spoon aside, he frowned. "If Cassidy Prewitt's not paying attention to your safety, then I will. Part of that path goes too close to the lake, and the water's high this year. You don't want to fall in the lake."

That almost made his questions make sense. "I can swim."

"Fully dressed? In bitterly cold northern water? Deep there, too. Mrs. Brayden's not paying you enough for that. You want to swim, do it at the beach, where the water has a chance to warm up."

"I don't want to swim."

"Good. Don't fall in the lake." He drained his mug and stood. "You still want to take some pictures of Travis's room, I expect. If that Mrs. Brayden wants you here for a week, you'd better do it slowly. Door's unlocked. Lock it behind you when you go. Emily, keep an eye on her," he added to the tortie as I stood. "I've got things to look into."

"Thank you for the tea." I wondered if that sounded as much like a question to him as it did to me.

He snorted. "Not a lot around here that makes me laugh, is there."

———

The room was a bog-standard cheap motel room: two double beds with visible sagging under the blue-and-green-striped bedspreads, fake wood siding, fake wood sheet-vinyl flooring, actual paintings of what I assumed was local scenery rather than generic prints, and a television so old, it still had a tube in it. I wanted to turn it on just to see if it worked. Didn't, but did take a picture of the blank screen for Mrs. Brayden.

I took a few pictures of the perfectly normal, cheap motel bathroom, too. The toilet, unlike the rest of the fixtures, was a pale, peachy pink.

This is where Travis took his last crap.

I probably shouldn't label the file.

Halfway across the parking lot, Emily's golden eyes locked on my back, I wondered why the door had been unlocked.

Had Arthur been expecting me?

And why had *Don't fall in the lake* sounded so much like *Don't eat the mushrooms*? A direct statement with hidden depths . . .

———

They were still chanting at the little not-church by the cemetery, great, rolling, rhythmic pulses of words I couldn't understand. I had to fight to keep from being drawn in to wallow in the sound.

A cicada buzzed in the underbrush. Wasn't I too far north for cicadas? Didn't they usually show up in August? The first time I ever saw a cicada, I thought it was a demonic grasshopper. My mother had refused to let me keep it in a shoebox under my bed.

I walked past the bookstore, and the secondhand store, and a jewelry store I didn't remember from yesterday with a lot of silver and amethyst in the window. I briefly considered grabbing some lunch but kept walking until I reached the guest house.

And the scarlet-and-gold stairs.

And my bed.

I fell asleep the moment my head hit the pillow.

TWELVE

Cassie

Aunt Jean was weeding her front flower bed when we pulled up. She continued weeding as we got out of the car and only levered herself upright, both hands on her cane, when we stopped beside her. Handing me a pail of limp green . . . things, she used her cane to point at a clump of juniper at the corner of the driveway.

"Let's wander over there," she murmured, gloved hand up by her mouth like we were discussing whether or not to walk the next batter, "and you two can try to look like you're helping me deal with a landscaping problem."

"Why?" Eric asked before I had a chance.

"We don't want to start a panic, now, do we? If I, as one of the Four, send for two of the Four, then send them across the street, all willy-nilly, people are going to make assumptions. Given the rising tensions, that's the last thing we want."

It wasn't the last thing I wanted, but I hadn't been consulted. "What rising tensions?"

"Oh, let's see, maybe the shadow incursion, Blair's death, the Mouth of the Dark off to talk to Alice, a potential inspection at the mine, the grocery order short an entire skid of sugar . . ."

I hadn't heard about that. I went over what Chris and I had in stock; if we were careful, we'd be good until the next train. When I started paying attention again, Aunt Jean was still talking.

". . . a reduced cell signal, buffering during *Dr. Who*, purple tomatoes in the greenhouse . . ."

"They're supposed to be purple," Eric broke in.

"Tomatoes are red," Aunt Jean snapped. "Occasionally yellow. Not purple."

"Some varieties—"

"Not purple!"

And that was that.

She continued. "Digger McDiggerson—"

"Wait." I held up the hand not holding the bucket.

"Elementary school named the mining machinery," Eric explained.

"Okay, then." I lowered my hand.

"Digger McDiggerson," Aunt Jean repeated, "has broken down and needs a part Stephanie can't find. *And*"—emphasis suggested she'd finally run down—"there are strangers in town."

"Stranger," I corrected. "Just one at the moment."

"And Cassie's been keeping an eye on her." Eric winked.

I thought of flipping him off, but he wasn't wrong.

"Which is exactly my point!" Aunt Jean huffed.

Eric's expression suggested I wasn't the only one who'd missed it.

Aunt Jean's sigh held multiple layers of disappointment and exasperation. "Cassie, this Melanie Solvich, if that's really her name, could have been sent by whoever is attacking the Dark to distract us."

Us? "I thought we agreed that someone else attacking the dark just after Travis Brayden s-worded himself into the darkness would be too much of a coincidence. That we concluded, therefore, it has to be Travis."

"And Melanie Solvich says she was sent here by Travis Brayden's grandmother."

"I don't think—"

She cut me off. "Generally, no, although we'd all hoped you'd begun to do it more. I need to See her."

"So go Look at her," I snapped. "We dropped her off at the motel."

"I Listened to her, Jean," Eric said, unexpectedly the voice of reason. "Her resonance has already started to mesh with both Cassie's and the town's. We could have an incomer here."

"Or a spy," Aunt Jean insisted.

"Or another Alyx. Excluding the meshing-with-Cassie part, given how definitively Alyx shut her down."

This time, I did flip him off.

"Less profanity," Aunt Jean snapped. "More explaining why you don't seem surprised to hear that you're resonating with this stranger."

"I'd be more surprised if I wasn't." I remembered her smile, her dimples, the feel of her lips. "Melanie's perfect. We're perfect together. And she's a high school English teacher. Are we short one?"

"We are not," Aunt Jean began.

"Hey!" Vic leaned out of the window of his truck, the only vehicle on the road. "There a Four problem here? You want I should go get Amanda?"

"There isn't a problem, Amanda is at rehearsal, and your rear tire has a slow leak."

"Thanks, Aunt Jean!" He waved, sped up, and disappeared around the curve in the road.

"Did you See that?" I asked.

"Interestingly enough, I can recognize a soft tire without help from the Dark." She took a deep breath, turned to face the driveway across from hers, and let her glasses drop to hang around her neck. I shuffled out of her line of sight. "I can still See it, tucked in between that overgrown mess of a lilac and Maureen's garage. I've sent Maureen off to get me a half dozen oranges . . ."

Because she was too old and frail to get them herself, announced the subtext. I choked on a snort.

Aunt Jean ignored me. ". . . so, go deal with it before she gets home. Without," she emphasized, "adding to the rising unease."

Given the distance between houses and the sleepy, summer quiet of the neighborhood, we could have gone in with flamethrowers without attracting much attention. It was really too bad that Security had brought in some pretty strict rules about non-Security borrowing their flamethrowers. I put down the bucket and started across the road, Eric beside me.

———

It was darker between the lilacs and the garage than it should be.

"Is it Shadow?" Eric asked when we'd reached the two meter point and stopped.

"How in the darkness should I know?" I demanded. "Do you Hear anything?"

He cocked his head. "Could be the breeze through the lilac. Could be carpenter ants eating Maureen's garage. Could be . . ." He paused and, just for an instant, the world became silent because he willed it. Not the whole world. The immediate world. About two meters all around him. "Could be a small creature breathing."

I could feel Aunt Jean's Gaze on our backs, weighted with a silent *Get on with it*, and decided to try it the easy way first, just in case she'd sent us to mystically confront a porcupine. "Move out to where we can see you," I Said, and Added, "Don't attack."

"Smart," Eric murmured.

I'd have thanked him had he not sounded so surprised. The lilac shook and rustled. Gradually, the shadow separated into what happens when a solid object blocks the sun, and what happens when a sloth successfully mates with a bearded dragon. The arms, legs, and torso of the creature were sloth-like. Frill, tail, and skin were bearded dragon. It was mostly dark grey, with black eyeliner, lips, and claws.

Clusters of tiny black tentacles occupied the spaces usually filled by ears.

There were fresh burns on both its shoulders, and the left side of its back about halfway between shoulders and hips. It was about the size of a house cat.

It looked up at us with eyes squinted nearly shut but so brilliant an orange that what we could see looked like a narrow line of fire. Then it raised its short, stubby muzzle to the sky and said, "T'geyer."

"I Hear it." Eric drew in a deep breath and let it out slowly. "Resonance match. It Sounds like the town. My best guess is that it's a messenger from the Dark."

"What did it say?"

"T'geyer."

I raised both brows. "Seriously?"

"That's what I Heard," he explained. "The word either has no translation, or what we heard is the exact meaning."

So not helpful. I took a step closer and Asked, "Are you a messenger from the Dark?"

"Dook," it said mournfully, and turned its head one hundred and eighty degrees to nuzzle at the burn on its back, whimpering softly. The blister had broken, and it was weeping dark fluid.

It looked young to me, uncertain and unhappy. I wondered what Aunt Jean would See, although not enough to call her over. "Could it be a juvenile sent to us by the Dark to get it out of danger?"

"A juvenile what?"

"Does it matter?"

"No, but if it is . . ." Eric paused as it slowly reached one scaly, sloth-like arm back in under the lilac and pulled out a carbonized piece of shadow about the size of an egg skewered on a claw. It gave a full-body wiggle and began to eat, nibbling around the edges of the piece. I didn't know about Eric, but I was fighting a massive *Aww* reaction. "If it has been sent to get out of danger," he began again, "then we need to worry."

"Because things are worse in the darkness than we suspected?"

"Yes."

"So, what do we do?"

"I don't know."

Not helpful. "Then why ramp up the worry if we can't do anything?"

"Because that's what adults do, Cassie; we worry about things we can't affect."

Before I could ask him if he was implying that I needed to grow up, our visitor, meal finished, accessed its bearded-dragon ancestry. Moving faster than my reactions—and it's not like I didn't grow up learning how to avoid eldritch horrors—it covered the space between us, and scrambled up my legs to sit on my hip with its weirdly long arms around my neck.

"Oop," it said, pressed its face against me, and kind of purred.

It was cool, soft, and smelled like fried sausage. If it had teeth, I couldn't see them. The tentacles tickled.

"Hey, you." I slid an arm under its butt, careful of its burns. It coiled its tail loosely around my wrist. "Speak to me."

It sighed. "T'geyer."

I glanced over at Eric. "Do you think that's its name?"

"Could be." He reached out and gently stroked under its chin. The purring intensified. "Ask it how it got here. Because it's not a shadow, and with Security on alert, it didn't sneak out of the cellar."

"Point," I allowed. If the weakening of the Agreement had led to wearing or even cracks between us and the darkness, we had to find them before we ended up with an incursion we couldn't handle. When I was little, one of my father's favorite stories had been the time the town had sealed a weakness in the cemetery with molten silver while an eldritch horror had been attempting to open it from the other side. There'd been as much sizzle as smoke. Dad still couldn't eat grilled fish. Given that Alice had long since eaten all the fish in the lake, this wasn't a huge problem when the diner started an *Eat Local* campaign. "Hey, T'geyer," I Said. It patted my face. I winced. The movement hadn't been aggressive, but those claws were razor-sharp. "Where did you come through?"

It patted me again and a second line of blood joined the first. "Dook. Oop."

"Maybe they're not words," I mused. "Maybe they're just sounds."

"No. I Hear words but they mean *dook* and *oop.*"

"What do you two think you're doing?"

We'd been so wrapped up in T'geyer, we hadn't heard the tennis-ball-covered, four-pronged safety support on the end of Aunt Jean's cane take multiple divots out of Maureen's gravel driveway as she approached. And digging divots with tennis balls took effort.

Eric rubbed T'geyer under the chin again. "We're making a friend." He had a look on his face I couldn't quite name. Loneliness?

"Did you want to hold it?" I asked. He held out his arms, and T'geyer had its head tucked under Eric's chin so quickly, I barely felt it move. It whimpered as it settled, then it sighed. I knew better than to assign human emotions to anything that had risen up and out of the darkness, but too bad. It sounded happy to me.

Aunt Jean glared at all three of us over the top of her glasses. "We do not cuddle eldritch horrors!" She'd either been smart or lucky when she'd decided where to stop approaching, because the flick of T'geyer's tail—and the damp, retractable barb that appeared and disappeared on the tip—didn't quite reach her.

I snickered. "That's not what I heard."

"We all do foolish things when we're young, Cassidy Prewitt, but some of us become older and wiser. Take that thing to the lake and throw it to Alice."

"No."

Aunt Jean's eyes began to lighten.

"No," I said again, and she reluctantly shuttered them. "Eric says it resonates with the town, that means it's meant to be here, and that means it was sent here for a reason. We need to find out why. T'geyer could have the information we need to help strengthen the Dark."

Eric rubbed his cheek against the top of T'geyer's head. "It could be what Alice wants us to be ready for."

"And the weakness it exploited?" Aunt Jean huffed. "The crack it utilized? We should just ignore that?"

"No," I said for a third time. "We'll find where it came through and we'll seal it."

Aunt Jean snorted. "Oh, we will, will we."

"Yes. We'll begin by searching Maureen's yard. It's fast when it wants to be, but that doesn't necessarily mean it traveled very far, and it's injured, so that might have limited the distance it traveled." And it might not have. The Journals of the Four mentioned eldritch horrors with injuries that appeared to be an integral part of their physicality. They might have been indiscriminately destructive, but I still felt sorry for them. "Aunt Jean, take a Look around the lilac and the garage. Eric, see if you can get T'geyer to say anything else. If you Hear enough words, you might be able to build its language."

He smiled. "And then Translate it."

I returned the smile. "Duh."

"Just Tell it to talk, Cassidy." Aunt Jean poked me in the ass with her cane.

"Oh, no!" I raised both hands into the air. "Why didn't I think of that?"

She poked me again. Harder.

I sighed. "I say Talk, it says *T'geyer*. Not really helpful. Could you just take a Look around so we can move on?"

Muttering—I couldn't understand her, and Eric kept snickering—Aunt Jean poked around Maureen's entire backyard, under the lilacs, in the garage, through the peonies, under the deck, in the clothespin bag—which seemed a bit unnecessary—and Saw nothing. She shot a narrow-eyed glare in my direction. "So, what next, Mouth of the Dark?"

Good question. Jeffrey was still hanging around the Dead Ground, and he'd have let Bridget know if it had been breached. Depending on which workings she'd done there at midsummer, Alyx might know as well, and she'd definitely have called either Aunt Jean or me. Unless we wanted to spend a week or so walking the bounds, we needed to narrow things down. Historically, where had other cracks occurred . . . "Melanie said she met Uncle Stu and the dogs in the cemetery."

"If those two mutts of his have been digging up graves again," Aunt Jean growled, sounding unsettlingly like Daffodil, "I'll turn them into parkas."

"They don't dig anymore." I hoped. Uncle Stu certainly wouldn't risk a repeat of three years ago August without good reason. Matching up the pieces of half a dozen dismembered skeletons was hard work, and Aunt Jean Saw to it that he did it all himself. It hadn't helped that Daffodil had refused to surrender her favorite femur. "I'll go talk to him. It's possible the dogs sensed something. Eric, take T'geyer home and keep working on language. We need to know what it knows."

"On it. And I'll give Dr. Singh a call about these burns."

"Good idea." Dr. Singh's grandparents had moved here back in the nineteens. He'd left to get his DVM and, to almost everyone's surprise, had returned. With a wife. And her family. As our only vet, he dealt with Uncle Stu's dogs, so I expected he'd be up to anything T'geyer could throw at him. "Aunt Jean, if you have the time, could you please call Bridget and ask her to take the Flock's shadows to Eric's place? It's what T'geyer eats," I added when her brows rose.

"If I must," she muttered. "At least you finally remembered your manners."

But I thought she sounded pleased. As well. Because she definitely also sounded annoyed.

━━━

Uncle Stu was sitting on his porch when Eric dropped me off, T'geyer sitting on his lap, peering over the steering wheel like a very ugly baby from the days before infant seats.

Both dogs were on their feet and growling.

"Daffodil! Dexter! No," I Said as they started for the car. "Sit and stay."

They shot Uncle Stu a look.

"Sorry, kids. Nothing I can do if she's throwing her weight around." He set his empty beer bottle on the porch rail and leaned forward. "What's Eric got in the car, Cass?"

"A very cuddly eldritch horror. It's been sent to tell us something; Eric's trying to figure out what." ·

"He can't Hear it?"

"He can Hear it; he can't understand it."

"That's different. Lots of different things seem to be happening lately. Influx of shadow. Mechanical problems at the mine. Whole keg went off down at the Crown. You went out to talk to Alice." He stared at me for a long moment, then sat back. "Let 'em go, Cass."

They could still catch the car and take it down if they wanted to. I sighed and Said, "Okay, guys."

They used to tolerate me, pretty much the way they tolerated everyone but Uncle Stu—and, surprise, Melanie—until I became the Mouth of the Dark. I braced myself, and they still knocked me on my ass. Left forearm thrust against Dexter's throat, I grabbed Daffodil's pink plastic collar. "Lay off, you great horrible beasts! No kisses with the same tongue you use to kiss your ass!"

Uncle Stu whistled. Dexter twisted away and bounded up onto the porch. Daffodil took a moment to lick the blood from T'geyer's claw off my cheek, then followed. Even lying flat on the sidewalk, I saw the old wooden porch shake. Reaching into the cooler beside him, Uncle

Stu transferred an enormous kielbasa to each hand, held them out, and crooned, "Take it pretty, now."

I'd be willing to argue that nothing those dogs did could ever be called pretty, but Uncle Stu still had all seven of his remaining fingers when they took their prizes over to a shady corner, so . . . Using my shirt to wipe off the drool, I climbed up onto the porch, sat down in a slightly chewed Muskoka chair, and accepted a beer from the cooler. You couldn't rush Uncle Stu. The bottle smelled like Polish sausage.

"So," he said, after we'd both taken a long drink. "What do you need, Cass?"

"Yesterday, you and the dogs made a visit to the cemetery."

He waited.

Fair. I hadn't actually asked him a question.

"Your idea or theirs?"

His eyes narrowed. "Theirs."

"And you figured, why not rebuild a few more ancestors?"

"Eh, they really wanted to go. Nearly pulled me off my feet as we passed the gate." He pointed his bottle toward the corner, where both dogs had long since finished their treat and fallen asleep. "How could you say no to that face? Or to that face?"

Dexter sighed, rolled over on his back, and farted.

We concentrated on breathing for a while.

"Eric's cuddly eldritch horror buddy didn't come in through the cellar," I told him once it was safe to draw a full breath. "Not as a solid. Not with Security on alert because of the shadows."

"You think my kids were sensing a weakness?"

"It's a place to start."

He set his empty bottle down on the gnawed arm of his chair, heaved himself up onto his feet, and stomped twice to settle his weight into his work boots. Not exactly a tall man, none of the Prewitts were, but he had the strength to handle his kids and the bulk to go with it.

Also a mass of scar tissue between his right knee and his work sock. Sometimes, his kids played a little rough.

Both dogs were standing. Ready.

I finished my beer, rose, and nodded.

"Dexter. Daffodil. Cemetery. Go!"

Their—let's say *breed* for lack of a better word—wasn't fast. They didn't have to be. They couldn't be bargained with. They couldn't be reasoned with. They didn't feel pity. Or remorse or fear. And they absolutely would not stop. Oh, wait, that's the Terminator. Never mind. Close enough.

Point is, we kept up to them for certain values of *kept up* and were close enough to see them go over the cemetery fence as though it could be measured in inches, not meters.

"Beautiful," Uncle Stu breathed.

"Impressive," I agreed.

They waited for us by the gate—I'd been willing to give the fence a shot, but Uncle Stu wimped out—and led the way, panting happily, toward the mausoleums. The weakness sealed with silver in my dad's story was behind the Foster tomb. I checked it first.

"Because I'm not stupid," I pointed out to Uncle Stu's raised brows.

He smiled. "Never said you were, Hopalong."

Grass grew up and over all but the center of the seal, where the stamped runes were barely visible amidst all the tarnish.

"Looks like it always looks," Uncle Stu said. I'd never actually seen it before, so I took his word for it. "I'll take my kids around the other tombs, see if they can catch a scent."

They didn't.

Daffodil trotted back to where I waited by the seal, and leaned against me. Fortunately, I'd been ready for her. I scratched behind her ears, and her tail thumped the ground. I could feel the vibrations all the way up to my teeth. Dexter stopped chewing . . . something, hopefully something I wasn't related to, collapsed in exaggerated exhaustion, and extended his claws into the sod—a clear albeit silent declaration of *I will not be moved.*

"I can section the cemetery and run a search pattern," Uncle Stu offered. "Trouble is, they don't seem to want to be anywhere in particular, just here with you. Might work better if you went home."

Daffodil's tail thumped the ground again.

I frowned. And scratched her behind the ears.

THUMP. THUMP.

"Hey." I pushed her with my leg. "Back off a bit." I'd have had more success pushing the mausoleum. Uncle Stu whistled, Daffodil peeled away, and I fell over. Not a problem; I wanted to be on the ground anyway. Crawling back to the seal, I grabbed the nearest edge of the grass that had grown up over it, and pulled. Given the way it had been bouncing to Daffodil's beat, I wasn't surprised when it flipped up neatly, exposing a small crack in the silver. The edges of the crack gleamed.

That explained T'geyer's burns.

"It's a fucking literal crack," said Uncle Stu.

While he called the mine for materials, I called Eric—I called rather than write out a six-volume text the current three pathetic bars might not send—and filled him in.

"So, the message," I concluded, "whatever it is, is important enough that the Dark risked sending the messenger through a crack in a previous seal. A place where it could be sure none of its enemies—"

"Enemies?" Eric interrupted.

"Whatever Travis Brayden is doing to weaken the Agreement, he's not doing on his own. No enemies would be lingering, because there'd be no point—as far as they know, the weakness has been sealed with silver for years. Not to mention the crack is tiny. Too tiny to send anything but a messenger through, and why would the Dark's enemies want to talk to us? I can't think of a reason. Oh, and given the size of the crack, we can add compression to T'geyer's skill set. It's a really small crack," I added when Eric didn't respond. "So, it would have had to compress itself to get through."

"Yeah, about that." He cleared his throat. I wondered if I should worry. Because apparently that's what adults did. "Bridget brought two garbage bags of shadow crisps over. It ate half a bag, and it's definitely bigger than it was."

"How much bigger?" I could faintly hear Bridget saying, *"Who's the cutest little eldritch horror? You are! Yes, you are!"*

"Not significantly, but if it was eating shadow all the way from the cemetery to Maureen's yard, it could have been a lot smaller when it arrived."

"Better ration the shadow crisps, then. If the Flock cleared the area, we don't want it to go hungry."

"You think they did?"

I remembered my days waving a silver skewer. "I think we shouldn't underestimate preteens running in a pack. Has it said anything else?"

"It said T'geyer to Bridget, telling her its name, and when she asked if it was hungry, it said *nom* and started in on the crisps."

"Nom?"

"Nom. Like from the meme in the early aughts. I'm expecting its next word to be *ermagerd.*"

"What?"

He sighed. "Never mind. Given how fast it can move, it eats incredibly slowly."

"I remember." Sloth-slow. "Probably so it doesn't outgrow its food source."

"Excuse me?"

"*Animal Planet* on YouTube. You know, there's a chance it isn't a messenger at all. If the shadows came through the crack first, it could have just been following its prey."

"Resonance with the town," he reminded me.

Right. I'd forgotten that. "So, what do we do?"

"Your word vomit about enemies and cracks made sense, so, as the Dark isn't able to use its Mouth for the first time in two hundred years, we assume it sent a messenger, and I keep working on a vocabulary."

"No, you won't," Bridget called. "It's asleep and I can't get it to wake up. Its little tummy is protruding, so I think it's digesting."

Eric adapted smoothly. "Bridget and I will have a glass of wine, and while we wait for it to wake up, I'll call Jean and Amanda and fill them in."

"Okay, that's what you'll do." I raised my voice. "Bridget! You okay with that plan?"

"Oh, yes, Eric has a really tasty sauvignon blanc." Her voice moved closer to Eric's phone. Closer to Eric. "Dominant melon and grapefruit flavors with a bit of a flower bouquet. Honeysuckle, maybe. It's a little dry, but you might actually like it, Cassie."

Not her first glass of wine with Eric. And she knew more about wine than I did. Hidden depths. My worldview tilting a bit, I asked, "So, what do I do?"

"Fix the crack," Eric suggested.

"That's an Amanda thing." I didn't whine. Much. "Besides, Uncle Stu's on it."

"Then assume we have things in hand, and before a new adventure beckons, take your woman out to dinner."

I looked at my phone. "It's too early . . ." My stomach drowned out my protest and I remembered I hadn't had lunch. "Good idea."

"Of course it is," he said, and hung up.

Uncle Stu was also off the phone. "Bob and Terri will be here in a bit," he told me, rubbing Dexter's stomach with his foot. "They're bringing the portable forge and the stamp set. Give us an hour or two and we'll get this thing patched right up. Meanwhile, you take Eric's advice . . ." Shaking his head, he answered my unasked question. "You had him on speaker, Cass. If the shit's hitting the fan, you need to pay attention. However, my point at the moment is that you need to pay attention to the woman with excellent taste in dogs and treat her to a nice meal at the pub."

"But at the diner . . ."

He sighed. "You eat for free at the diner, Hopalong. On an emotional level, anything free is worth what you pay for it."

"That's . . ." I searched for the words. ". . . surprisingly deep."

"Yeah, it's not me. It's Robert Heinlein."

"Who?"

He sighed again. "Damn good thing the dogs like you."

Daffodil had her front paws up on the side of the mausoleum so she could sniff the edge of the roof. Drool darkened the stone. Dexter was dealing with an itch at the base of his tail.

"Yeah, I think I'm safe." But he made sense. Melanie deserved more than another free souvlaki. Mind made up, I dusted crushed grass off my knees and asked, "What happens if an eldritch horror not on our side oozes through the crack before you can seal it?"

"Daffodil! Dexter!" Uncle Stu showed teeth. No way I was calling that expression a smile. "Guard!"

Suddenly, they didn't look much like dogs at all.

THIRTEEN

Melanie

Buried waist-deep in the sand of the beach, I explained to the surrounding ravens that Shakespeare's plays weren't meant to be read like novels but seen and heard. I almost had them convinced to stage *Henry V*—we few, we feathered few, we flock of brothers—when the water at the edge of the sand began to roil and a tentacle, about as big around as three fingers folded together, began writhing across the sand toward me. The ravens flew off, stylized wings beating jagged lines in the air.

Oh, great, I thought, *tentacle hentai.*

And woke up to the notification of an incoming text.

I fumbled for my phone with one hand, rubbed my eyes into focus with the other, and read Cassie's message.

::early dinner?::

My eyes widened as I checked the time. I'd slept through lunch and most of the afternoon. No wonder I'd had weird dreams. My stomach agreed.

::When?::

::45 min:: appeared, followed by ::meet me in lobby::.

A plain unadorned *ok* seemed almost rude, so I typed ::Looking forward to it.:: Hit Send and panicked. Did that sound like a come-on? It definitely sounded like a come-on. Like I was anticipating more than dinner. Honestly, maybe I was. I remembered holding her in my arms at the top of that cliff, the potential for falling to my death lost in the feel of her lips.

A sensory memory of the approaching tentacle surfaced from my REM-fogged brain. "Oh, fuck off," I muttered.

Scrolling messages, I realized I'd slept through a text from my mother. Apparently the identical ping from that particular notification hadn't been enough to wake me.

::Protest @ Embassy. If Lisa calls, bail money usual account.::

Decoding my mother's message cleared my head. When I wrote *looking forward to it*, it had merely meant that I was looking forward to it without weighing down the *it* with expectations. Before I could set my phone down, Cassie sent a thumbs-up emoji, which seemed like a positive sign.

Reminding myself that I was twenty-eight years old and more than capable of going on a date with a woman I was attracted to, I headed for the shower. And reminded myself that sharing an early dinner was not necessarily a date.

━━

Descending the final flight of stairs, I could hear Cassie talking.

"Theresa, calm down. I'm not here to Tell Daniel to go."

Once again, I heard a random, audible uppercase. This place had more random capitals than Winnie the Pooh.

"I'm here," she continued as I reached the lobby, "to meet Melanie."

"That Melanie?" Theresa pointed past her shoulder and Cassie turned.

I was glad I'd worn my navy palazzo pants, my double-gauze vaguely South-Asian-although-the-embroidery-looked-Celtic top, and thrown on a string of sandalwood beads I didn't remember packing, because Cassie'd clearly put in an effort. Natural linen shorts, ankle-tie espadrilles—I tried not to linger on her tanned, muscular legs or the scrape on one knee—with a deep purple three-quarter-sleeve shirt that shimmered like silk, silver hoop earrings that had to be three centimeters across, and multiple silver rings on both hands. Her hair continued to head off in all directions.

She smiled.

I smiled back at her.

Theresa twitched, murmured, "Hubba hubba." Twitched again. And blushed.

"How do you feel about going to the pub tonight?" Cassie asked, taking a step toward me. "My treat."

"No objection to the pub," I told her, "but you paid last night."

"Not exactly. My parents own the diner, so . . ."

"It's like bringing a friend home to eat?"

"Pretty much."

"I like the sound of that."

"Yeah."

Theresa reached over the half-door and patted Cassie on the shoulder. "You two get going so I can check my blood sugar."

She sounded so innocently matter-of-fact, it took me a moment.

Cassie grinned. "Theresa only seems like a nice lady." She held out her hand.

So I took it.

I held it while Vic drove by and flashed us a thumbs-up. Held it when Alyx came out of her bookstore, smiled, and waved. Held it all the way to the pub. Held it while the noise from the beach rose until it suddenly no longer sounded like a murder of ravens as much as it sounded like the ravens were committing murder.

"Squadron, dive and snag! Dive and snag!" a familiar voice shouted. "This is a level-one formation! We shouldn't have to keep going over it!"

Cassie sighed and freed her hand. "If you'll excuse me, I have to go Talk to Reggie before we're ankle-deep in pissed-off corvid shit. You okay waiting here?" She nodded toward the bench outside the pub. "It should only take a minute."

An entirely human squawk sounded from the distance, followed by, "Release me this instant, Flight Sergeant!"

"Better hurry," I advised as I sat down.

She took off running and I appreciated the view until she was out of sight. Then I checked my phone in case I'd missed Lisa. The last time my mother spent the night in holding, she'd ended up trying to kick one of Toronto's finest in the nuts for making homophobic comments to another prisoner that were so vile, the assault charges were dropped when Mom repeated them in court and the officer actually, and unexpectedly, faced disciplinary action. Go Mom.

Nothing new, so I put my phone away and—

"Gloria!"

A familiar, very old man wearing a bathrobe over pajamas tottered toward me on slippered feet.

"Gloria," he panted, picking up speed. "I can't find the sliced turkey!"

I caught him as he pitched forward. He'd been tall once, but age had shriveled him, and I had no trouble managing his weight as I all but carried him over to the bench.

He patted my cheek with callused fingers and sighed happily. "No one believed me when I said you were back."

The street, as it always was when something like this happened, was empty. A pinecone skittered along the asphalt, the Northern Ontario version of a tumbleweed. I glanced around. Did 911 work in Lake Argen? Did this town even have a police force? I stopped the old man from toppling off the bench, doing my best to keep my touch impersonal, and asked, "Is there someone I should call?"

"Me." He snickered. "You should call me anything but late for dinner." Then he sobered. "Do you know why our rotten kids are trying to keep us apart, because I sure as darkness don't?" His waggling eyebrows were almost bushy enough to balance the sizable nose. "Unless they think we're likely to cook up another sprog. Split their inheri—"

"Granddad!" Stephanie started yelling before she was fully out of her car. "What do you think you're doing?"

He rolled his eyes. "What does it look like I'm doing? I'm canoodling with my wife."

"You again!"

I shot her my best *You did not just bring that into my classroom!* look.

She flushed. "I'm sorry. That was incredibly rude. My only excuse is that I was worried he might have wandered into the lake."

"Alice and I are old friends," he told me.

"Grandad, Alice is . . ." Her gaze flicked to me and back. ". . . no longer with us."

He flipped her off, using his right hand to raise his left middle finger. Age would not stop him from expressing his opinion.

I tried not to laugh.

Stephanie's turn to roll her eyes. "My brother Keith was supposed to be watching him, but he had his head in a book, and the world could have ended without him noticing. It wasn't even a new book! He'd read it before! Who does that? It's a good thing he never married and had kids; they wouldn't have survived infancy. He'd have read them to death. Granddad, let's stop bothering . . ."

"Melanie," I offered.

"Melanie," she repeated, "and get you home."

He allowed her to help him to his feet and move him toward the car. He thumped the hood. "This new?"

"A few months ago, yes."

"It electric?"

"Yes."

"I don't like it."

"So you've said."

When she had him safely strapped in, she turned back to me. "Again, I'm so sorry."

"Not a problem, but maybe I should get your number in case it keeps happening."

Her shoulders sagged. "That's not a terrible idea. Let me—"

"'S'up, Steph?"

Granddad hit the horn and yelled, "Cassidy! Got a bun in the oven?" Then he sagged in the straps, laughing at his joke. I noticed Cassie had mouthed the words along with him.

Stephanie sighed. "Cassie has my number." She looked between us as she got into the car, flashed a set of deep dimples, and, as she drove away, yelled, "You two have a nice night!"

Cassie pivoted in my direction, her brows dipped in. "What was that about?"

"He . . ."

"Mr. Foster?"

Excellent, I could stop referring to him mentally as the old man. "Yes, Mr. Foster. He thinks I'm his wife." I shrugged, minimally enough I hoped it wouldn't come off as dismissive of his confusion. "We met here, well, inside, yesterday during lunch. I assume him showing up tonight means he thinks that I, as his wife, spend all my time at the pub. He slipped away from Stephanie's brother and headed straight here."

"I can Tell him to—"

I ignored yet another random capitalization, raised a hand, and cut her off. "It's not a problem. He's really very sweet."

"He is." Bending to pick up the pinecone, she grinned. "You know, when I was a kid, Mr. Foster won the wood-splitting contest at the fall fair three years running. Beat guys half his age. And he grew the most amazing roses in a crappy plastic greenhouse. Now . . ." She shook her head. "I don't want to grow old."

"I don't want to grow old alone," I said. Realized what I'd said, and felt my face heat. "So, uh, how's Reggie?" I asked before Cassie could respond. Or not respond.

Her grin broadened. "He's missing a bit of beard and was convinced to call it a day." Reaching past me, she opened the pub door. "After you. Growing old alone would suck," she added softly as I brushed by her. "I'd rather not do it either."

———

"So, how did your family emergency work out?" I asked. "I'm not digging for details; I just wondered . . ."

Cassie stared into the layers of rare roast beef in her sandwich for a moment before looking up at me. "Pretty much the way every family emergency works out. Solved a problem, which created a couple more. You know how it is with families."

I dipped a fry in ketchup. "Not really. It's always been just me and my mom."

"Right. Well, if you ever feel the need for more family, you can have some of mine. Three Prewitt brothers helped found Lake Argen, so I've got way too many relatives."

"Fourth cousins twice removed?"

She grinned. "Exactly."

I pulled a slice of dill pickle off my burger and ate it separately, trying not to notice how Cassie watched my mouth. "You've never felt the urge to leave?"

"Leave town? I couldn't. I mean, I've done some traveling—Timmins, North Bay, Toronto, Paris—but this is my home."

I could hear the warning. If we ended up together, we'd end up together in Lake Argen, but I was too distracted to deal with it. "Paris? France?"

She nodded while she swallowed. "Chris's idea. He wanted to take a French pastry course, and I didn't want him to go alone—he'd have spent the entire eight weeks in class or in his room and not spoken to anyone—so I took the course too. I almost never do the fancy stuff now—he loves it, I don't—but I can ganache like nobody's business."

We laughed together at the implied wink wink nudge nudge. To be fair, ganache was an intrinsically funny word, but I only laughed because Cassie had said it. And because Cassie was laughing at her own ridiculous implication. And because laughing with Cassie felt . . . right.

Another fry, a bite of burger, and I asked, "Wasn't that expensive?" I had no real interest in France, but I'd priced countless trips to the UK I couldn't afford.

"The money was there." Her tone suggested the money was always there. "I don't spend much of it, and Chris could never have afforded it on his own."

"You paid for Chris?"

"I didn't mention that?"

We sat silently for a moment while we both went over her words.

"Guess not." She grinned. "It's no big deal; it's just the mine."

"The mine?"

"Well, shares in the mine. Families are a lot smaller than they used to be, so the shares have been consolidating for decades now, and the silver keeps coming. Uncle Stu—with the dogs," she added in case I'd forgotten. "He's Dad's brother, but Mom's an only child, so eventually..."

"What's theirs will be yours."

"Some of it's mine now." She tossed the information out like it didn't matter, and I could almost hear my mother react to her nonchalance by telling me to eat the rich. I don't know what Cassie saw on my face, but she reached out and covered my hand with hers. "You okay?"

"Just . . ." I searched through the complex tapestry of my response and pulled a thread free. ". . . surprised. Your parents own a diner." That made them the equivalent of landed gentry in my world.

"So did my grandparents," Cassie reminded me, entirely missing my point.

I tried again. "They work in the diner."

"Only four days a week. Two breakfast shifts, two lunch shifts; six hours each, max. They never do supper anymore. Dad says he's ladled more gravy than any man half his age should have to, and he's done. Actually, he's full of shit, because if he's bored, he comes in and helps. He loves being in the kitchen, and Mom says she wouldn't recognize him if his hair didn't smell like the deep fryer."

"And you bake." I was still trying to work things out.

"Like I said last night—"

Last night, dollar value hadn't come up.

"—I pretty much grew up in the diner, but supporting Chris steered me sideways. And I don't like the deep fryer, so when we make donuts, that's all Chris."

Cassie didn't have to work. Her parents didn't have to work. From the sound of it, a large number of the people who lived in Lake Argen didn't have to work.

"Is there a problem?" Cassie touched my hand again.

"The Fosters . . ."

"Callum Foster was the Prewitt brothers' cousin. One of the founders. They have a fairly high-end clothing store. You may have seen it." She plucked at her shirt. "One of theirs."

Alyx had said she was an incomer. Theresa was a Prewitt. I racked my brain for someone else I'd spoken to. "What about the person in the thrift store with the eye patch?"

"Elsie Harper?"

I had no idea if that was her name, but I nodded. "Does she have to work?"

"Her late husband's shares went to their kids, but she still has hers. She pays Kyle, her grandson, to drive his big old panel van to estate sales all over the country. The second floor up over the store? Filled with junk." She paused and amended, "Well, mostly junk."

"Okay." I held up my left hand, my right perfectly happy to stay twined with Cassie's. I needed a few more minutes to work this through. They—Cassie's parents, Cassie, the Fosters, Elsie Harper, who knew how many others—didn't have to work, but they did. Because they wanted to contribute. Because they enjoyed what they did. Because there was no point of being a cranky old lady if you had no one to crank at. With the information I had, this situation mapped on to universal-basic-income. I was one hundred percent in favor of the UBI. Did I have a problem with Lake Argen being a bizarro-world company town? "Okay," I said again. Took a deep breath and met Cassie's eyes. "I'm good."

Her thumb stroked the pulse point in my wrist. "More than."

═══

Even though we'd eaten early and this far north the sun lingered, by the time we left the pub it was dark. We paused by the bench. We couldn't exactly go somewhere else for a nightcap since we'd just left the pub, the tiny coffee shop was closed, and the only other option for a night on the town was the diner. It was obvious that neither of us wanted the evening to end.

Cassie shoved her hands in her pockets and rocked back on her heels. I banished the thought that it made her look about fifteen, because that was not a thought that would allow the night to go the way I hoped it would. "So," she said, "do you want to come back to my place for a drink?"

Right. The diner was not the only other option.

"A drink?" We'd each had two beers and a coffee inside, and I suddenly realized it must be income from the mine that allowed the owner's brother to mess around in his brewery. Also, right at the moment, not important.

She grinned. "It's hot. We need to stay hydrated."

"All right, then." This time, I held out my hand.

We retraced the path I'd taken the first day, heading toward Argen Street. For a small town, the streetlights gave an impressive amount of coverage, chasing most of the shadows from the impeccably maintained sidewalks. Cassie seemed relaxed but ready, gaze sweeping from side to side. I did not say *bear* out loud.

Deep down, I wasn't surprised when, hand in hand, we walked to the turquoise house. "This is yours."

"Yep. It's an old workman's cottage from back when the mine ran on people power. We, where *we* refers to the town, we the town saved as many of the original houses as we could."

"It's beautiful." I followed her up onto the small front porch. "I noticed it when I walked to the motel yesterday."

"Really? I get ribbed about the color."

"Beautiful," I repeated.

She smiled and opened the door. It wasn't locked.

"No crime?"

"I used to lock it, but these days, I'm not likely to be robbed."

These days? I wondered if I should ask and decided not to. The evening had given me plenty to think about. If Cassie was a superhero in her spare time, I'd deal with it later.

The worn, overstuffed furniture certainly had no resale value, and the rugs covering the floor looked like they'd been donated by redecorating relatives. The walls had been painted a deep goldenrod, a wood stove had been fitted into the fireplace, and a comfy chair and a table for a mug stood by the front window right where I'd imagined them. "This feels . . . familiar."

"Because you're supposed to be here." She tugged my hand.

I moved toward her and stared down into eyes I could drown in.

As I lowered my mouth toward hers, she slid her hands around to press against my back, and I shivered at the heat. Her shirt moved like water between my touch and her skin. Her fingers drew a promissory line along the edge of my waistband.

After a moment, I pulled away. Her lips were swollen and we were both breathing heavily. "I love your house," I told her.

Cassie half-whimpered and leaned back in.

I stopped her. "Does it have a bedroom?"

She blinked, processed, and smiled. "Are you sure?"

"I have clean underwear and a toothbrush in my purse."

"Really?" The smile turned into a suggestive grin. "Good thing I've got the number for the Timmins U-Haul in my phone."

Laughing sex is the best kind of sex.

FOURTEEN

Cassie

The sun was shining, the sky was blue, and it looked like a glorious morning. Had I been stupid enough to leave the bedroom window open, I knew I'd hear birds singing. Easing carefully away from Melanie, I slowly rose up on one elbow.

Where was the line between creepy and appreciative when staring at a sleeping companion? I had no idea.

I stared anyway.

Looking past the beautifully rounded bare shoulder rising above the line of the sheet, I saw that she slept with a loose fist tucked under her chin, her mouth slightly open. It made her look vulnerable, although I wasn't sure why. Not that why mattered. I wanted to protect her and care for her and keep her safe. I wanted to spend my days and nights with the dimples in her cheeks, the dimples at the base of her spine, the dimples in her elbows. I wanted to touch her and taste her and tuck my face into the curve of her neck and breathe her in. I wanted to bury myself between soft breasts and firm thighs and search out the swelling peaks of flesh that made her writhe. I wanted to hear her laugh and whimper and cry out.

I wanted to repeat everything we'd done last night again and again.

And again.

And again.

But maybe after a shower and some coffee.

Our skin parted reluctantly when I pulled my legs away, but I managed to get out of bed without waking her. She snuffled and sprawled into the space I'd vacated, covering a lot more real estate than seemed possible, even given our ten-centimeter difference in height. It was adorable.

After glancing out the window to check the lake—the sliver I could see seemed fine—I padded naked to the bathroom built out over the kitchen extension at the other end of the hall. Hopefully, Melanie wouldn't be upset at the lack of an ensuite, but I hadn't needed one living alone, and I'd always figured if you were sharing your body with a woman, you could also share a bathroom.

One foot over the lip of the walk-in shower, I paused.

This thing between us was real. I could feel that, body and soul. Sure, I was a Conduit of the Dark, making it entirely possible my soul wasn't my own, but that wasn't the point. I knew that when Melanie got up and joined me in the shower, or in the kitchen, we'd talk about a future together.

I didn't know much about the future—we hadn't had a seer since my mother's second cousin twice removed ignited after not noticing the symbol she'd created while free-hand quilting—but I did know that a future that included a relationship couldn't be based on a lie.

Sooner or later, I'd have to explain Lake Argen.

The town and the body of water.

And Alice, I realized, stepping into the shower. Not looking forward to that.

———

I was pulling the oatmeal-apple quick bread out of the oven when Melanie came into the kitchen in yesterday's clothes, a towel wrapped around her hair.

"That is not a workman's bathroom," she said, looked around, and shook her head. "And this is not the original kitchen."

"It's about three times bigger," I admitted. "The renovations are one of the reasons I bought the place."

She slid onto a stool at the island and poured herself a coffee. "Because you bake."

I flipped the loaf pan upside down onto a small platter. "Because I bake."

"How long have you owned it?"

"Three years." I pushed the cream toward her.

"Because you could afford a house at twenty-five years old."

"Technically, I could afford a house at twenty-five months old."

"Born with the proverbial silver spoon in your mouth."

"And my mother was pissed. Spoons are a bitch to push out."

Melanie looked startled, then she laughed. I'd been aiming for the laughter. She clearly had issues about money we had to find a way to work around, since I had no intention of giving any up. The way I saw it, some people had money, some didn't. Money turned some people into assholes. So did poverty. I tried not to be an asshole. A simple philosophy I could indulge in because I had money. Tah-dah, proof of self-awareness. We could work on the money issue together later, when we weren't wrapped in the afterglow.

"Aren't you supposed to wait for a loaf to cool down before you cut it?" she asked as I handed her a slice.

"It's more of a guideline. And if you wait, you have to eat it cold." I dropped onto the stool beside her and refilled my mug. "I like it hot. You can wait . . ."

Trying to take the plate away from her started a wrestling match that ended in kisses and, miraculously, no spilled coffee.

"It's good," she said after chewing and swallowing, towel askew on her head.

"Of course it is. I'm a professional." I took a big bite just as my throat tightened. Chunks of half-chewed food flew across the kitchen. "KA'MIG WAHLETH SOR'AK!" I barked. "SOR'AK!"

The hell? Once in a blue moon—not literally—the Dark made a comment based on something Eric had Heard regardless of whether or not Eric and I were together, but I could always understand the words if not the meaning. Spitting out a mouthful of consonants was new.

Then Melanie was rubbing my back while I coughed and choked and flailed.

"I'm okay," I managed at last, my voice my own again. "Went down . . . the wrong way."

"Sounded like it went down several wrong ways," she said, gave me a final pat, and headed for the paper towels, the miracle of the coffee not having been repeated. "In fact, it sounded like you were speaking in tongues."

I waved that off. "Just one."

"Cute. But, no joke, are you okay?"

"I'm fine." I should tell her. Could there be a better segue into the story of Lake Argen than suddenly yelling out words in the language of darkness? Words that could have meant anything, I acknowledged. Breaking into my morning with random consonants couldn't possibly mean anything good. I coughed into a paper towel and hastily hid the blood.

On second thought, there definitely could be a better segue. No one reacted well once blood got involved. The history lesson could wait.

I took a mouthful of my remaining coffee to clear my throat, then a cautious bite of oatmeal-apple bread. Then a second. I could feel my shoulders unknot as we ate breakfast, drank our coffee, and talked less than we ate and drank.

My phone broke the silence with a midi banjo.

::T'geyer knee height & a bit,:: Eric sent. ::No new words. Also eats pudding cups.::

"Continuation of yesterday's family emergency," I explained as I typed. It seemed Eric hadn't been Listening during the Dark's un-scheduled announcement. ::that's disgusting::

::Eldritch horror::

::fair::

::Bestiary could have info. Janet says check the Archives.::

::you go::

::If I go, you keep T'geyer.::

I glanced at Melanie, who pointed at the towel on her head and headed back upstairs. The library would be easier to explain. Most of the books were nothing more than words on paper—scary to certain homophobic, transphobic, misogynistic buttheads, sure, but defi-nitely not on the level of a sloth/lizard cross with razor-sharp claws, burning orange eyes, and a tendency to snuggle.

::J pulled the age card:: Eric continued. ::A at rehearsal again. Fuck-ing ompa lumpas.::

::oompa loompas::

::Point stands.::

::i'm not alone::

::I thought I Heard moaning.::

::fuck off::

Although he might have Heard, if he'd been Listening. I didn't want to think about it. ::fine, i'll check the bestiary::

::Responsibility trumps booty call.::

I sent him a raised-finger emoji, not giving him a chance to misin-terpret a boot and an eggplant, then turned off my notifications and stuffed the phone in my back pocket before he could respond. Should I have told him the Dark had spoken? Yes. Unfortunately, I couldn't remember the words, nor could I ask the only witness if she could repeat what I'd said, so, since he hadn't been paying attention the first time, there were no words available for him to Hear a meaning in. Also, I wasn't willing to spend the day with Eric in case it happened again, not when I could spend the day with Melanie.

"Family needs me to look something up at the library Archives," I said as she came downstairs, damp hair in a honey-gold braid.

"Why you? You're a baker."

"Yes, but I can read." I waved off the beginning of a stammered apology. "And my time is my own if I need it to be."

"Seems like your time is your own if your family needs it to be."

Fair. "Since I don't *have* to go to work, would you like to come to the library with me?"

She glanced down at herself, then back up at me. "I'm in yesterday's clothes."

"Does it matter? I can drive you to the guest house if you need to change."

"You'll drive so no one sees me do the walk of shame?" Both her brows rose. "I'm not ashamed of anything we did."

I had to kiss her.

After a few minutes spent with her back against the wall and not enough room for a shadow to slip between us, she brushed her palm over my hair. "I haven't seen you run your fingers through it, but it's still . . ."

"Sproingy?" I straightened Chris and Alan's wedding photo, now hanging lopsided beside her left shoulder.

"Mmmm." Her breath smelled like toothpaste. I exhaled through my nose just in case and hoped she couldn't taste the blood.

After a few more minutes, she gave a minty-fresh sigh, wrapped a bit of my hair around a finger, and said, "Cassie, I have to go back to Toronto."

"You don't have to stay in Toronto," I reminded her, my back now against the wall. A photo of Natalie, wearing most of a chocolate cupcake, dug into my head.

She blinked. And thought for a moment. And finally said, like it had only just occurred to her, "That's true. I don't."

Her contemplative expression made me want to kiss the solemn line of her mouth, but we needed to settle this first. "Just to make sure we're both on the same page," I said, stroking the soft, yielding flesh at the edge of her waistband. "I'd like it, a lot, if you'd come back here when you leave Toronto."

The Agreement didn't exactly make people forget; it made their memories mesh with the outside world. Lake Argen became a boring, entirely normal, not-really-worth-remembering Northern Ontario town. People who resonated with the town came back regardless of what the Agreement did with their memories. Melanie was resonating. She'd be back.

She would.

"You could come to Toronto with me. We could come back together." She tugged on a strand of hair.

The rush of heat pulled me up onto my toes. "I could go with you," I agreed when my heels finally hit the floor again. "And we could come back together. Absolutely." I wondered if she'd be okay taking my car. I'd seen her car, and to quote a classic, she was braver than I'd thought. Now all I had to do was tell her the truth. "So, driving or walking?" I asked.

"To Toronto?"

"To the library." I could always tell her later.

She chewed a bit on the edge of a thumbnail, noticed she was doing it, and yanked it out of her mouth. "Is there anyone in town who doesn't know we spent the night together?"

"It's possible," I admitted as I ran over the faces I'd seen in the pub. "But the odds aren't high."

"Is there anyone in town likely to give us a hard time about it?"

"Not if I have anything to Say." I'd already heard from Eric.

"Why—" she began, and shook her head. "Never mind. Let's walk. Unless you need your car downtown."

"Downtown is fifteen minutes away," I pointed out.

"And the library?"

"Seventeen, tops. I'm good."

"You are."

We had to straighten all the pictures in the hall before we left.

———

"Is that a Carnegie Library?"

I stared up the walkway at the building and shrugged. "It's our library."

"I realize that." Melanie released my hand so she could wave both of hers in the air. "In the early 1900s the Carnegies built thousands of libraries in the States and about two hundred in Canada. This is the right age, and the architecture—"

"Hey, hey, hey!"

I turned to see Vic hanging out of the window of his truck, winking vigorously. "No," I said when he opened his mouth.

"But—"

"Don't make me Say it." He'd had his chance, and the threat wasn't an abuse of power, more abusing his awareness of my power. And it beat the alternative of bouncing a rock off his face.

Melanie leaned out to stare after the truck. "Is there something wrong with him?"

"Besides a lack of social skills noticeable even to those who've never left Lake Argen?"

"I meant with his eye. It was twitching."

I sighed and pulled out my phone. Okay, there was a slight chance I might have overreacted. He had his head out that window often enough, he could have a whole swarm of bugs in his eye. Texting wasn't safe while he was in his truck, and he was always in his truck, so, still with only three bars, I called.

"Yo, Cassie! You showing that fine lady you're with a good time, or do I need to step in?"

And disconnected.

"His eye's fine. Come on." I touched the small of her back as we started up the walk. "Janet's expecting us."

"Even the path from the sidewalk to the library is in perfect condition."

"Civic pride and nepotism," I reminded her, told myself that hadn't been another opportunity to come clean, reached past her, and pulled open the door.

She tapped on the glass with a fingernail. "Don't most internal doors open inward?"

"Can't bar it then," I said solemnly. "What happens if the Tuesday-evening seniors' book club makes a run for it?"

Laughing, she said, "I can't imagine they're that fast."

"You'd be surprised." It depended on what book they were dealing with that evening. Some days, you needed to stop the seniors. Some days, you needed to stop what was after them.

As we approached the circulation counter, Janet looked up and sagged in relief. Her hair had escaped confinement and surrounded her head like curly dandelion fluff. Actual spots of color had appeared on her cheeks. "Did Eric call?"

"He texted."

"About the Archives?"

"Yes," I answered tentatively. I had a feeling Janet and I weren't talking about the same thing.

"There's a few books," Janet began.

"This is Melanie," I interrupted. Not my smoothest segue. "Melanie, Janet. Janet, Melanie. Melanie's from Toronto. Did I mention that?"

Melanie made a face. I squeezed her hand.

Janet looked between us. "Oh?"

"She was there when Eric texted. She knows I have to look up some family stuff in the Archives."

"And you brought her with you?"

"Is that a problem?" Melanie released my hand and laid both of hers flat on the raised edge of the counter, the gesture more a challenge than her tone. I liked that she was willing to fight for us. I didn't want her to fight with Janet.

Neither did Janet, so she threw me under the bus. "It's only a problem because Cassie has always had a tendency to act before thinking. She can't access the Archives without a librarian, and we can't have more than two people at a time in the room."

To my relief, Melanie nodded thoughtfully. "Humidity, right?"

"Right." Janet smiled at her. Melanie smiled back. First complication dealt with. What were complications compared to time together. "Plus, it's in the basement, and trust me, you don't want to go up and down those stairs if you don't have to. If you wouldn't mind waiting up here for a few minutes, Miss Peggi . . ." Janet leaned out and looked toward the children's section. "I don't know where Miss Peggi is, but she's here somewhere if you need help."

"Is Miss Peggi the best idea—" I began.

Melanie cut me off. "We have library volunteers in Toronto, Cassie. I'll be fine."

Right then. Duty called.

Around the corner and out of sight, Janet used her forearm to blood the lock. I waited impatiently until the basement door closed behind us before I said, "So, do the Bestiaries—"

She cut me off. "This isn't about the Bestiaries. I thought you said you spoke to Eric?"

"About checking to see if our cuddly eldritch horror is in the Bestiaries."

She sighed and, as we walked down the circular staircase, pulled a not-even-close-to-her-skin-color band-aid out of a pocket, and slapped it on her arm next to the three already there.

It was a very deep sigh. "You okay?" I asked.

Before she could answer, I heard a distant *thump*.

"They've been bouncing off the walls all morning," she muttered, "and some of them are fragile. If I have to re-bind them, I'll be spending the rest of the summer in the basement."

"You don't go out in the summer," I reminded her. "You catch fire."

"There's a difference between staying inside because the sun hates me and staying inside because certain books refuse to act their age."

I suspected she'd have raised her voice on that last part, had she not been a librarian. She was. So she didn't.

We descended in silence for a while, the metal stairs ringing softly under our sneakers, wrought-iron railings cool under our hands, rubber soles scuffing the silver wire in the treads to a dull shine.

A double *thump* announced our arrival at the Archive door. Over the years since it had been installed, the silver had turned several shades of grey and black, but it was still a beautiful door. Chris had made a fondant replica of it for a library fundraiser. It had sold for a flattering amount of money.

More blood. Another band-aid.

I stopped her before she opened the door. "Just what exactly is it you want me to do?"

"Speak to the books!"

"What am I supposed to Say to books? They don't have ears."

"They don't have legs, either," she muttered, "and has that stopped them? No. If they can be pains in my ass, they can listen to you Tell them not to be." She pulled open the door, pulled out a remote, and turned on the light.

In spite of the impressive bulk of the door and how the librarians had arranged things so no one entered the Archive in the dark, I'd never thought it looked threatening. It looked like your basic, windowless reading room. Sure, I knew there were silver rods used as rebar buried in the concrete walls, ceiling, and floor, but they couldn't be seen. The long walls and the far wall were covered in floor-to-ceiling bookcases, and the bookcases were filled with books. The library had a motion before the town council to put the first of a planned half dozen shelves in the center space—which I only knew because the Four were expected to endure the bi-yearly council meetings and listen to Amanda snipe at her ex—but for now, it held only a gleaming wooden table, two uncomfortable-looking wooden chairs, and a wooden podium holding a single book, chained in place. The light was bright enough to allow even Aunt Jean to read the small print, and the room smelled like beeswax, paper, and leather, and very, very slightly of entrails.

I decided not to ask.

"None of the books are off the shelves," I said, waving at the whole lot of nothing currently happening.

"Now." Janet folded her arms and glared. "You heard them, though. They're faking you out so you'll leave without Speaking."

Clearly, I wasn't getting access to the Bestiaries without doing my thing. I took a deep breath, wondered why beeswax when so many modern polishes existed, and Said, "Behave yourselves, books. Don't go thumping around. Ouch!"

Janet had pinched me. "*Behave yourselves* could include behaving badly."

Not usually. It didn't seem worth it to argue.

"Remain where the librarian puts you." I considered Adding *Obey the librarian,* then reconsidered. Given the mood they seem to have put her in, I wasn't sure it would be safe.

"We should go out and close the door to make sure it worked."

"It always works." Albeit the book thing was new. "And I'm in a bit of a hurry. Remember Melanie?"

"Fine." She headed for the back wall. "I'll pull the Bestiaries for you."

"Why is this book chained by itself?" I asked, following.

"If it touches another book, it absorbs the contents, and it's quite smart enough now, thank you very much." But she patted its rust-colored leather cover fondly as she passed. There was a soft, metallic whisper as the loop of chain between book and podium swayed back and forth.

Yeah. Obey the librarian, not the best idea, not with that book on her side. "How many Bestiaries are there?"

"Four. But you'll need Aunt Jean to make sense of the fourth one, so unless you can get her down here—"

"Three."

Two of them were huge. The third seemed to be set up for kids, an alphabetical list of eldritch horrors. T'geyer wasn't one of the twenty-six. I hoped Melanie had found a comfy chair and settled in to read, because it looked like I was going to be down there for a while.

"I'll help." Janet handed me one of the two tomes and we walked them back to the table. "I can't face those stairs again so soon. What does our visitor look like?"

I set the book down and showed her the pictures on my phone.

"Ahh, look at the little tentacle ears! What a cutie!"

"Its name is T'geyer."

"You named it?"

"It named itself." While we flipped carefully through the books, I told her about Aunt Jean Seeing it in Maureen's yard and what had happened after Eric and I arrived. My fingers started to get greasy. "Please tell me this isn't made of Human skin."

"All right," Janet said absently, turning a page.

Nothing resembling T'geyer by any sane definition of the word *resembling* could be found in either book.

Janet closed hers. "It could be a larval form."

I closed mine. "Gross."

"Cassie, try to remember you're twenty-eight, not eight. Never mind," she cut me off before I could defend myself. "Most eight-year-olds are enthusiastically into the larval form of just about anything. You would not believe what they use as bookmarks."

It didn't seem to take as long going up as it did going down, thank the darkness for small mercies. My glutes were killing me as it was. No wonder you could bounce a quarter off Janet's ass.

Melanie was waiting for me by the desk. She didn't look happy. Before I could ask what was wrong, she held up a familiar knife.

"This," she said, "is an exact match to the family heirloom Mrs. Brayden wants me to find."

I opened my mouth to Say, *I guess it's one of a pair*, remembered how I'd felt when I'd told her to believe me at the House, and I couldn't do it.

"So, about ten minutes ago," she continued, in a no-nonsense don't-fuck-with-me tone, "when the front door opened, a gust of wind blew a pile of papers off the desk, exposing this knife."

"I'm studying it." Janet shook her head at the messy pile covering almost half the desk. "Please be careful with it. I know it seems dull, but it cuts through flesh like butter."

"Better than through butter," I muttered, remembering.

"It's an heirloom." Melanie snapped.

"Sorry, but no." Janet actually looked sorry. "According to Peter, our blacksmith, it's no more than twenty years old and probably not even that. He can't date it exactly and he doesn't recognize the maker. He's sent photos to his friends in the business, but, so far, he's had nothing more definite than a woman in the Kitchener area thinking it looked familiar."

"I don't care who else thinks it looks familiar! I recognize it!"

"Janet—" I could feel us careening toward the inevitable.

"However, the knife itself isn't important," Janet continued, caught up in the thrill of research. "It's the runes; they're what we need to concentrate on if we want to find out why Travis used it. And why he left it behind. Not being able to take the knife into the Archives until I've identified both the purpose of the runes and possible counter actions, just in case, is slowing me down, but I'd almost say they were

Etruscan. Almost, because I've also found a vague similarity to the margin notes in an early Byzantium—"

"Stop talking!"

Janet's teeth clicked as she closed her mouth. I couldn't have Said it better, and I was definitely considering Saying it. We turned together to look at Melanie.

"You were trying to find out why the knife was left behind?" I saw her knuckles whiten as she tightened her grip on the hilt. "Did Travis drop it on the trail?"

I didn't know what to say.

Janet did. Not that it helped. "Oh, he wasn't on a trail. That wouldn't have provided the necessary weakness between realities he required. The dagger was left behind when he s-worded on the Dead Ground, and I'm almost convinced that one of the runes refers to—"

"S-worded? What the hell is an s-word?"

Suddenly realizing she'd gotten a bit carried away, Janet attempted a smile. "It's a word that starts with the letter *s*?"

Melanie turned to me. "Cassie?"

She wanted me to fix this. I could hear it in her voice.

No relationship could be built on lies.

Now was the time. Now had to be the time. "Janet, can we use the small meeting room?"

Pale brows drew in. "Why?"

"I intend to tell Melanie exactly what's going on."

"Exactly?"

"Yes."

"Tell? Small *t*?"

"Yes."

Her eyes narrowed and she scratched at the edge of a partially healed puncture. "Without consulting the other Three?"

"My decision," I told her.

"But is it a smart decision?"

"It's the right decision."

"Cassie!" Melanie's plea tottered between fury and desperation. I didn't want it to fall in either direction.

Janet glanced between us and finally nodded. "You know where it is."

The small meeting room tucked in behind the nonfiction section and overlooking the parking lot could comfortably hold half a dozen people. It seemed crowded with Melanie, me, and the knife. She laid it on the table and sat down. I paced as much as the dimensions of the room allowed.

"So." She poked me with the word. "You have an explanation?"

"I do, but it comes at the end of a long story."

"And?"

"And I'm not sure where to start."

She pushed the chair back, crossed her legs, and folded her arms. "Start at the beginning."

I took a deep breath . . .

FIFTEEN

Cassie

It started back in 1832 when three brothers, Edmund, Charles, and George Prewitt, left the south of England to seek their fortune in Canada—specifically Upper Canada, more specifically what's now Northern Ontario. We don't know why they left England, although given what they got up to later, we doubt it was their idea. Their first eighteen months sucked, but then they got lucky, discovered silver, and staked a claim.

"After the mine became legally theirs—and I have no idea what was involved; it was almost two hundred years ago and, as you pointed out, I'm a baker—they asked two cousins and a friend to come up from New York State and help them . . . run the mine, I expect. I doubt they brought shovels. The cousins were Mortons, the friend was a Foster, if you're interested in playing Name That Tune.

"The Mattagami, the local First Nation, backed off and watched from a distance. As it turned out, that was smart.

"The brothers/cousins/friend found eight investors in Toronto—Alloway, Elliot, Abbott . . ."

"Cassie."

"Right. Not important. So, our six founders left Toronto, headed back north with a work crew, and started mining the silver. Eventually, they named the town that grew up around the mine, Lake Argen, after the lake, which they also called Lake Argen. Personally, had I been there, I'd have assumed their inability to come up with more than one name signified a total lack of imagination. I'd have been wrong." I rested my forehead against the glass and stared out the window at the library's tiny parking lot, Melanie's unfulfillable need for an answer that wouldn't change things a weight against my back. The truth always changed things. Not always for the better.

"It turned out that Edmund Prewitt, the eldest brother, was all about thinking outside the box. When the mine produced significantly less silver than anticipated, Eddy refused to give up his dreams of wealth in the wilderness. He invited his investors and their families up from Toronto to celebrate how rich he was going to make them, and threw a party in his half-finished house. Just before midnight, he chased the wives, the children, and the servants outside to watch . . . something. Falling stars. Northern lights. The Journals of the Four aren't specific. The important thing to remember is that wives, children, and servants were outside, far enough away from the house to see a clear sky, and the thirteen men stayed inside, taking advantage of this private moment to discuss business.

"Where *business* meant Eddy and his brothers/cousins/friend planned to sacrifice the investors to a dark power." The hair lifted off the back of my neck when I said it, but this was not the time to muddy the narrative waters with s-wording. "We call it the Dark. If it has a name, it's never let us know it. A town referendum in the 1920s put a capital on the word although the Journals . . ." I shook my head, eyes aching at the memory. "The Journals are still all over the place. All caps. No caps. D dash dash K like it was a bad word. Eric actually referred to it, on paper, as Big D. Once."

"Cassie."

My name pulled me around. Melanie's expression hit somewhere between impatience and annoyance. But she was still listening. That was good, right? I'd never done this before, and I wished I'd had time to talk to Alyx, to find out what Bonnie, the Mouth before Simon, had told her. It was always the Mouth, just in case things went wrong. Bonnie barely spoke, and when she had to, she chose her words with the kind of precision I only gave to measuring ingredients. I remembered she'd written about the opening of the bookstore, but drew a blank on what she'd written about Alyx. I felt like this was a test I hadn't studied hard enough for.

If I'd planned the time and place of this explanation, I'm sure Aunt Jean would have told me exactly what to say.

Probably for the best it hadn't been planned.

Melanie cleared her throat.

"Okay. Moving on." I could do this. "In return for sacrificing the investors, the brothers/cousins/friend asked the Dark to make sure there'd always be plenty of silver in the mine and to keep the town free of outside interference. I've never understood how they thought they were going to get away with it, given the investors' families were right outside. Oops, we accidentally murdered your husbands and fathers! Who was going to let that go? Unless by *protect the town* what they actually meant was *protect the six of us*."

"The dark drew the line at messing with the heads of the investors' families?"

Sarcasm, sure, and no caps, but a legitimate question. "Messing with their heads wasn't one of the two points in the original agreement. All the brothers/cousins/friend wanted in return for the sacrifice was the silver and a chance to run the town without interference." I drew in a deep breath and let it out slowly. This was the pivot point. "Fortunately, the investors weren't the only ones to die. The house caught fire, went up like a tinderbox, and killed everyone inside."

"Fortunately?" Melanie's voice had gotten a little shrill.

"Depending on how you look at it. The Dark said, 'Thirteen dead? Thank you very much, more than asked for or expected. We have an Agreement.'"

"Funny how those thirteen dead slot neatly into Western superstition," she muttered.

"Total coincidence," I assured her. Turning a chair around, I sat down facing her, my forearms folded across the back. "The fire was so hot that by dawn, nothing remained of the house but the fieldstone basement. The basement walls were solid, although there was a big, scary crack in the dirt floor."

"How does a dirt floor crack?"

"In order for the planned sacrifice to work, Eddy had his house built over a weak point between this world and the darkness." I raised a hand before she could ask. "I don't know how he found it. I don't know how he knew what it was. I know the crack is still there and that it still leads to a place where existence is . . . different, because while I haven't seen the crack itself, I have seen and heard the result of it being there. So have you. Well, heard, at least."

"I haven't—"

"You knocked. It responded."

"You said that the roof was expanding in the heat."

Yeah, I Said that, didn't I. Shit. "That was . . . not true."

"I don't believe you."

I could Tell her to believe me, canceling out what I'd Told her earlier and add explaining *that* to my morning, or I could continue. I took the coward's way out. I ignored the problem and kept talking. "The only piece of unburned wood remaining was the door at the top of the stairs that led up to where Katherine, Mrs. Eddy Prewitt, had planned on putting her garden. You've seen the door."

"That's not a two hundred-year-old door!"

"How do you know? Park maintenance repainted it this spring. Anyway, my suddenly widowed ancestors took advantage of the Dark's good mood and renegotiated the Agreement, making the safety and comfort of their families as important as the continuing silver."

"So, these wives and mothers watched their husbands burn to death and then just got on with things?"

"According to the Journals, yes. Personally, I've always thought that women willing to travel with their husbands to Northern Ontario in the 1830s were plenty tough. Five of the eight wives of the investors had already been widowed once, and you barely have to read between the lines to get the idea that the brothers, cousins, and friend weren't likely to be nominated for husband of the year. Eddy may have come up with the plan to sacrifice their investors, but the other five had to agree to it."

Melanie nodded reluctantly. "That, at least, makes a certain amount of sense. Go on."

"Worried about cutting off access to the Dark and therefore the Agreement, the widows had the basement roofed over instead of filling it in, closed that one remaining door, and locked it.

"Sometimes, bits of the darkness work their way out. We take care of it."

"With magic?" She uncrossed her arms so she could waggle her fingers at me.

"With arc lights, currently. The weakening of the Agreement is causing a bit of a shadow incursion." I ignored the disbelieving snort. "Anyway, back in the day, the silver returned to the mine, and it's replaced every time it's removed. I don't know where the silver comes from," I answered the silent disbelief on her face. "From places silver hasn't been discovered yet. From the darkness. Doesn't matter. What matters is that when passenger rail lines in Northern Ontario were shut down, the line that ends here in Lake Argen wasn't. We can get teachers for our schools, and doctors and nurses for our hospital."

"How?" she snapped. "There's shortages all over the province, no, all over the country!"

Elbows braced, I spread my hands. "The Dark provides. It's a small hospital," I added after a moment. "We don't usually get sick. It's mostly trauma care and obstetrics."

Melanie ignored the addendum. "You expect me to believe that an evil entity provides teachers and doctors and nurses?"

"No, because the Dark isn't evil. It's different. Not human. You can't judge it by the same criteria."

"You keep telling yourself that."

It was the sort of comment that could have sounded fond. It didn't.

"If it's not evil," she continued, "why do you call it dark?"

"Because it isn't light."

"Do you worship it?"

"What kind of a question is that?"

Her brows went up.

I sighed. "The Acolytes chant to it. But it's not worshipping. It's sort of like the chanting during sports. Not the best example," I admitted a moment later.

"Is this Agreement the reason the Mattagami First Nation doesn't send their kids to your high school or, I assume, use your hospital?"

"Oh, they use the hospital for trauma, injuries that can't wait or wouldn't survive a trip to Timmins. And no one's going to risk the life of a mother and baby over something that happened two hundred years ago."

"Really?"

"The hospital has a helicopter."

"A helicopter?"

"A small one."

"Of course it does." Melanie uncrossed her arms and crossed them again in the other direction. "If the dark provides teachers and doctors and nurses, where do they come from?"

"Sometimes, we go out and come back. Sometimes, people come in—"

"And accept the whole welcome-to-Sunnydale situation?"

"I don't know what that means." I raised a hand before she could respond. "Can we save sidebars for later? Please."

Lips pressed into a thin line, she nodded.

"Lake Argen is a great place to live if you can accept the way we do things. If the people who want to move here can't accept that, they don't stay. The same way people don't stay if they can't accept Toronto. We make sure incomers are in the right place—emotionally, not geographically—before they get the backstory."

"How?"

"How?" I'd expected her to ask what happened if incomers didn't accept the backstory and couldn't make her question fit.

"How do you make sure incomers are in the right place? Do you sleep with them?"

"What? No! Eric can Hear if they—incomers—resonate with the town."

Her eyes narrowed. "So, you slept with me because Eric told you to?"

"No! Also, eww!"

She shrugged, a short, truncated movement that suggested *eww* had occurred to her as well.

"I slept with you because you're amazing, and beautiful, and funny, and interesting, and sexy, and you smell really good!"

At least I got her to stop glaring at me. It's hard to narrow your eyes when your brows are up. "But you're sure of me?"

"I'd like to be," I admitted softly, and decided I should say the important part out loud. "No relationship can be based on a lie." When she didn't respond, I swallowed a sigh, hung on to hope, and made a lateral move away from the personal. "You met Alyx. She's an incomer. She settled here first, then what was left of her coven moved north."

"Her coven? Alyx is what, a witch? Like an actual witch, not a tree-of-life tote-bag carrier? I thought she sold books."

My turn to fold my arms defensively. "Why can't she do both?"

Melanie's shrug seemed to reluctantly allow that she could. If she had to. She shifted on the chair and glanced over her shoulder at the door. Strange that *Alyx* was what had finally unsettled her, although I supposed her world had given her a better reference for witches and books than negotiations with a different reality.

I needed to wrap up the history lesson. "The Agreement gives us great internet access and a clear cell signal all over town. We've never had an OPP station, summer people from Toronto, or interference from government—federal or provincial. Fascinated by the changes the widows had negotiated, the Dark tagged four people to be its Eyes, Ears, Hands, and Mouth, and it uses them to maintain contact between it and the town. That's our best theory, anyway. When one of the Four dies, a new one is chosen, and its only criteria seems to be that all Four are direct descendants of the original thirteen. Eric is the Ears. That's why he could Hear you resonate." Deep breath. Here's where it got personal again. "For the last eighteen months, I've been the Mouth of the Dark."

"And that explains the random capitalization."

"What?"

Melanie shook her head, a strand of honey-blond hair swinging free. My fingers itched to push it back, so in place of willpower, I gripped the chair. "Never mind," she said, and it took me a moment to realize she meant never mind her question. "You're the mouth; that makes you special?"

"No."

She rolled her eyes. "Being one of four people chosen by the dark doesn't make you special?"

"Well, yes."

"Make up your mind."

"It's like . . ." I searched for a metaphor. Or maybe simile. I'd never been able to keep them straight. "It's like being automatically entered into a beauty contest and winning. Everyone knows who you are, and they're kind of proud of you, and everyone knows what you can do, but unless there's a ribbon to cut at a shopping-mall opening, it doesn't really take up much of your time, so, mostly, you just live your life."

She stared at me for a long moment. "Beauty contest?"

"Ish."

"And what does that shopping mall represent, Cassie?"

"If there's an incursion from the darkness, the Four deal with it. Like volunteer firemen who live their lives until their skills are needed."

"Volunteer firemen who won a beauty contest."

Yeah, that had kind of gotten away from me.

"How do the Four *deal with it*?" she asked.

I held up both hands. "Can we get through the basics first?"

"Fine." She folded her arms again. "You said you use arc lights."

"On shadows. They're nothing much." I remembered Blair. "Unless you keep your windows open at night."

"Do you get paid?"

"No."

"Because you're rich."

Okay, I was not defending that. I didn't *need* to defend that. "Yes," I said flatly. "Because we're rich. We also keep the connections between the town and the Dark open. It stays aware of what's going on. We can go to it for help."

"Do you have to sacrifice someone first?"

"No!" I remembered Lillian pushing her brother into the lake. "You don't *have* to," I amended. "Not for the little things."

"But you can."

"Everyone can," I pointed out. "Difference is, we get an answer. Bottom line, if the Dark wants to say something, it uses me to say it."

Her eyes narrowed again. "Like it did earlier, in your kitchen?"

"Sort of like that." I touched my throat. There'd been minimal damage compared to the busy signal in the town hall.

"So, what did your Dark say this morning?"

"No idea."

Foot tapping, jaw tight, she made a noise that didn't sound encouraging. "So, when does Travis Brayden enter this fairy tale?"

"Soon," I said quickly, more than willing to skip right over *What happens when you speak for the Dark?* "Travis Brayden is building the shopping mall."

"Cassie."

"No, really. We think the Dead Ground became a weak spot between Lake Argen and the darkness when Charlie died on it."

"Sacrificed?"

"No, just died. He was very, very old." Explaining about the Guardians seemed like a lateral move away from the story I was trying to tell, so I decided to leave it for later. "Edmund Prewitt found a weak spot that became the crack in the cellar during the sacrifices. Or maybe during the fire. No one knows for sure. The two realities, the darkness and us, are close together in this whole area." I circled my hand to indicate I was talking about more than the library. "Sometimes, bits of the darkness make pinholes"—the spot in the cemetery was bigger than a pinhole but I was trying to hang on to the big picture—"and squeeze a tiny something through."

"But the Four deal with it."

"Yes!" I smiled. Melanie didn't. So, I kept going. "Another crack opened in the lake, but Alice takes care of that."

"Alice?"

Could I explain Alice? Sure. Did I want to? No. And I'd already made a decision about Guardians and lateral moves. "We'll get back to her."

"Fine. Travis?"

"Right. Travis had apparently heard about the weakness—"

"How?"

"No idea."

"So, no one who's gone out and come back ever got drunk or high and blabbed about the wonders of their hometown?"

I hadn't. Chris hadn't. "Uh, maybe?"

"Jesus. Or can't I say that here?"

"There's no rule against it."

"Joy." Her movements sharp and jerky, she picked at the embroidery around the hem of her blouse for a moment, then looked up and said, "Get back to Travis."

"Okay, so, at dawn on midsummer, the weak points are weaker still—"

"Because of course you're using a pagan calendar tied to pagan beliefs created by people from a different part of the world."

"Charles Prewitt's wife was Irish, if that helps."

"Just. Get. Back. To. Travis." She slapped her hands down flat on the table.

Guess it hadn't helped.

Janet peered in the through the glass half of the door. I shook my head and she moved on. "We focus most of our attention on the cellar: actual crack, no Alice. One of the Four is sent to the lookout to keep an eye on the Dead Ground. This year, it was me. Travis, who couldn't get to either crack and so had to settle for the large, easy-to-find weak spot, was there when I arrived, *on time*. He'd set up a barrier so I couldn't get to him."

"What kind of barrier? Chicken wire? Snow fence?"

"Small stones, metaphysically charged. But a different metaphysical than ours. Alyx says it's closer to her lot but not quite."

"Oh, for—"

"As the sun rose, Travis stabbed himself through the foot with that knife"—I pointed at the knife on the table—"and disappeared. The knife didn't."

We stared at the knife together for a minute or two, then Melanie sat back. "So, rather than explain all this to the OPP, you convinced them that he got lost in the woods. Specifically you explained, you as the mouth?"

"Yes, I Explained. It wasn't hard."

"He sacrificed himself?"

"Yes. Exactly!"

"And Janet was studying the knife to figure out how it had allowed Travis to . . . to disappear. Disappear theoretically into the land of the dark."

"The Dark," I corrected. "Or into the darkness. But yes." There'd been a few bumps along the way, but her last comment suggested she'd accepted the whole explanation.

She stared down at the table for a long moment. Or two. Or three. I waited, feeling my heart pound, using the time constructively to memorize the highlights in her braid and wonder if I'd ever get to touch them again. Finally, she looked up and smiled.

It wasn't a happy smile. It didn't say anything about acceptance.

And she said, "Bullshit."

SIXTEEN

Melanie

I couldn't believe Cassie had the nerve to look hurt when I didn't immediately believe her line of bullshit. She stood when I did and held out her hand, but I stepped back. If she thought I was going to believe six impossible things just because I'd slept with her, she could think again. It hadn't been that good.

Except it had.

Better than good.

Deep-emotional-connection-and-multiple-orgasms good.

At least I still had the memory of the latter. I was not going to let her play on any feelings I imagined might have been between us. And I was not going to cry. I was a grown woman.

"What really happened to Travis Brayden?" I demanded. It had to have been something horrific if she thought word vomit about dealing with the devil was her best chance to cover it up.

"I told you—"

"You told me a fairy tale and I'm trying to understand why!" I grabbed the knife off the table and waved it between us. "Did he get mixed up in a cult? Was he sacrificed at midnight while everyone in the town stood around and chanted . . ." The harmonies of the chant

I'd heard two days ago tried to overwrite my rage. Two days ago. Counting today, it had only been three days. I felt like I'd been there for weeks. Months. I felt like I belonged there, and having that snatched away made me angrier. "Was his mutilated body thrown into that locked cellar? If I bring the police back here and they open it up, how many bodies will they find?"

"The police won't—"

"Why won't they? Are they a part of it? Or are you planning to tell the police you don't know how the bodies got there? That they sacrificed themselves?"

"No one was sacrificed!"

"Except for Travis. No, wait, Travis sacrificed himself!"

"Hey!" Janet jerked open the door and leaned in. "Enough! That's thirteen s-words from you two. Thirteen!"

"The original number," Cassie breathed like it was actually relevant.

"Yes, the original number!" Janet snapped. "You're just lucky that the library's protections kept us from being hip-deep in darkness!"

"So, nothing happened?"

"Did I say that? Miss Peggi collapsed! There's a couple of teeth, a bit of spine, and what might be a knucklebone, but mostly there's dust. Am I supposed to add a little water and reconstitute her so she can explain how she arranged the card catalogue? A hundred and fifty-odd years that woman's been dead, a hundred and fifty-odd years she's been volunteering, and she was fine right up until you two decided to have a domestic in my library!" Janet wiped her nose on her sleeve and slammed the door.

I glared across the table at Cassie. "Is everyone in on it?"

"Nothing Janet just said was about you." Cassie held up both hands and took a deep breath. "This is on both of us. Thirteen s-words on top of the weakening Agreement, and Peggi paid the price."

"Miss Peggi who'd been dead for a hundred and fifty years?"

"She really loved the library."

"A love that transcended death?" I sneered.

"It happens." Cassie's mouth trembled as though she'd tried to smile and hadn't been able to manage it.

Seemed like I'd hurt her again.

She wasn't allowed to be hurt. I was the one being lied to.

"Maybe it happens here," I allowed, "where your money allows people to ignore reality."

"Okay, if you believe in the money, how about this: the day you came to town, I was told that silver mines don't keep producing for two hundred years. This one has." Hands flat on the table, she leaned toward me. "Doesn't that tell you something?"

"That there's always an exception proving the rule."

"The mine—"

"Is a fact, Cassie! Silver is taken out and sent south. Money comes back and you lot live the high life." Or what passed for it in a small Northern Ontario town that didn't even have a Timmies. No. That wasn't the point. "I can see the mine!" I told her.

She stared at me like I'd grown a second head. "You heard the crack respond. You saw Uncle Stu's dogs."

"So?"

"They're not dogs!"

"Four legs, ears, wet tongue, pink plastic collar, tag that says Daffodil, tail that wags when you scratch behind her ears?" I leaned into the calm the memory brought. Things had been so simple then. "She certainly seemed like a dog to me."

"Because you wanted her to be a dog. You like dogs, so your brain filled in what you wanted to see in the spaces where the definition of dog didn't fit. Did you notice her size?"

"Some dogs are big."

"Not that big. How about all the teeth, twice as many as necessary?"

I'd noticed the teeth. "Veterinary dentistry—"

"Or retractable claws?"

This part of the conversation was sliding toward the inane. "Dogs have toenails. Cats have retractable claws."

"That wagging tail? Not a tail." Cassie frowned and visibly reconsidered. "Okay, it's a tail, but it's a tail that's also a tentacle."

"A tentacle?"

"The lack of fur didn't give it away?"

"I've seen mange that bad on rescues before." I folded my arms. "Your uncle is taking terrible care of them. I should report him."

"My uncle—" she began, and sighed. "Never mind my uncle."

I'd be perfectly happy to never think of her uncle again. Or this town. Or . . .

Or her.

I pressed my folded arms in against the pain in my chest.

"Melanie, they're not dogs. They're eldritch horrors. Or hellhounds if you want to be flip and Uncle Stu can't hear you."

"Hellhounds? If you hurt those dogs to support your delusions . . ." I began, then let the threat trail off. I didn't, couldn't believe she'd ever hurt a helpless animal. But something had happened to Travis . . .

Cassie leaned back, beat her head lightly against the wall, and finally dragged her hands back through her hair, making no significant difference to the amount of hair sticking up. "Okay," she said straightening. "I can prove it. Not the hellhound part, because like I said, until you accept what's real, you'll see what you want to see."

"More speaking in tongues?" In retrospect, there'd definitely been words amid the choking, back in her kitchen. She'd been laying the groundwork for the fairy tale she planned to tell me. Except she'd only told me because I found the knife. Had she been laying the groundwork in case I found the knife? Who'd think that was a good idea? Someone who had to cover up a murder? There had to be a simpler way.

"Melanie."

I shook it off and focused on her face.

"Do you tr . . ." Closing her eyes, she bit her lip, and took a deep breath, not finishing the question. And it was a good thing, too, because against my better judgment, I might have said yes. Maybe that was proof I'd been taken over by a different reality, since finding the knife and enduring Cassie's non-explanation had destroyed any trust I'd had in her. When she opened her eyes, they were damp with crocodile tears. "Melanie, will you come with me to the Dead Ground? Please."

Was *please* a magic word up here? "So you can prove this whole ridiculous story?"

"So I can prove one part of it, to help you believe the rest."

I should leave the library, get in my car, and drive straight to the nearest OPP station. They needed to reinvestigate what had happened to Travis Brayden. The last thing I should do was play along with what was either a terrifying level of delusion or a cruel joke.

No. The last thing I should do was look at the hope on Cassie's face.

The last thing I could do was destroy the hope on Cassie's face.

"All right," I said. "But just to the Dead Ground."

"Thank you."

"If I still don't believe you . . ."

She swallowed. Hard. "Then I'll Say goodbye."

I'd miss the random capitals when I left. Because I was going to leave. It wouldn't matter what she showed me. "And you don't care about what I tell Mrs. Brayden?"

"No."

"Fine."

"Janet!" She ran out of the room. I followed, holding the knife. "Janet, I need to borrow your car."

Janet looked up from sweeping a pile of dust into a large dustpan. "Why?"

"Mine's at home, and I need to take Melanie to meet Jeffrey."

"Jeffrey," I said before Janet could answer. "Your naked, blueberry-eating buddy?"

"He's a Guardian."

"But still naked and blueberry-eating," Janet added. She sat back on her heels. "Are you sure visual aids are the way to go, Cassie?"

"Evan's up near the north boundary, so it's Jeffrey or Alice."

I don't know what conflicted mess of emotions Janet saw when she studied my face, but she nodded. "Might work. The keys are in the car."

———

Neither of us spoke while Cassie maneuvered the old Honda out of the parking lot.

"So, your deal with the dark prevents car theft?" I asked as we turned toward Argen Street.

"There's no AC, and this thing has shit traction in the winter. No one wants it."

I settled back into the surprisingly comfortable seat and rolled down the window. "No one wants it because you sold your souls, and you have lots of money."

"There's some disagreement about the soul thing. At worst, Edmund Prewitt sold them for us. We just keep the terms of the Agreement." She swallowed. Hard. "Travis is weakening the Agreement."

"By building the shopping mall?"

She glanced over at me and sighed. "Maybe we should let that go."

"He could be trying to set you all free."

"From what? Good cell-phone reception? A lack of government interference? The ability to get a family doctor? Fully funded schools?"

Sunlight and shadow flickered as we passed under the big elms. "All that and your dark is an environmentalist, too."

"It's a what?"

"These elms should all be dead. They're too far north, and they're dead everywhere else."

"I didn't know that."

"Right." The smell of fresh asphalt drifted in through the open window and I could hear the distant chug of the resurfacing machine. "The sidewalks . . ." I felt like I almost had it without asking. ". . . what's that about?"

"Step on a crack, break your mother's back."

I stared at the side of her face. She didn't look like she was kidding. Mind you, she hadn't looked like she was kidding at any point during her story of a perpetual silver mine and a hellhound in a pink plastic collar. "Seriously?"

"Seriously." Cassie drummed her fingers on the steering wheel. "There've been times when a child was tapped to become one of the Four. If that child became the new Mouth and didn't watch what they Said and who they Said it in front of . . ." She shrugged. "Back in 1982, eight people stepped on cracks, six mothers were dead and two paralyzed before the other Three figured it out. Bonnie hardly Spoke as an adult."

"Because her mother was dead?"

"She Said, 'Step on a crack, break *your* mother's back.' Not hers. Hers was fine."

"And the words have lingered in the pavement ever since?"

"What? Oh, the resurfacing. No. It's just . . ." She drew in a deep breath and released it slowly. "It's just we never want it to happen again."

"Oh." I could check the deaths. Although if the people of Lake Argen avoided dealing with the provincial government, there was no telling what would be listed as the cause. Or was death federal? And then I realized the implications. "You're the mouth now."

"I am." She sounded tentative, like she knew what I was going to ask and wished I wouldn't. There'd be a lie prepped, but I asked anyway.

"If whatever you say happens, did you Say anything to me?"

"Did I make you do anything you wouldn't have done?"

"I asked you first."

"You can't ask me that if you don't believe what I've told you. And when you do believe . . ."

I snorted and pointed out the windshield, letting her know she should watch where she was driving.

Reluctantly, she turned her attention to the road. ". . . and you *can* ask, I want you to remember, I'm still me. I'm still the person you ate with and talked to and . . . and asked to go to Toronto with you so we could come back here together."

I'd asked her that, hadn't I? She would have loved my mother. My mother, on the other hand, would have regarded her with suspicion proportional to her bank account. But she'd have come around. Cassie baked, and my mother's affection could be bought with butter tarts. I crushed the seatbelt strap with both hands, remembering the possibility of a happily-ever-after and not wanting to let it go.

How did you get through something like this?

Cassie'd laughed with me, not at me, and I'd laughed with her. She liked potato salad and deviled eggs but didn't like mayonnaise, which was enchantingly strange. Her house was turquoise. Our broken pieces had fit together perfectly. Comfortably. She'd trembled when I trailed kisses up her inner thigh.

"I'm still me."

That person, that wonderful, amazing person was under all this—and I had to keep using the word because nothing else fit so perfectly—under all this bullshit.

Did I want to find her again?

How would I start looking?

We parked by the roofed-over cellar and got out of the car.

"Why not show me the infamous crack?" I asked as she tossed the keys onto the driver's seat. "Wouldn't that convince me?"

"It's not safe. That's why we keep the door locked."

I glanced down at it as we passed. "It's not much of a lock."

"Yeah, that's what Alyx says."

"Because she's a witch?"

Cassie shrugged. "She's very practical."

We walked in silence up the hill, and I asked myself what I thought I was doing here. There was nothing naked, blueberry-eating Jeffrey could say to convince me that every word out of Cassie's mouth hadn't been . . .

. . . bullshit.

How could she expect me to believe her?

Why did she expect me to believe her?

What had really happened to Travis Brayden?

In spite of all the questions, I kept walking up the hill. Beside her. Because that was where I wanted to be for as long as possible.

The Dead Ground and the edge of the cliff and the view of town and lake and trees looked exactly like it had yesterday. I looked at the circle of bare dirt. Did it look different now I knew that Charlie, who-ever he was, had allegedly died there? No. "So, now what?" I asked.

"Wait there." She pointed at the scrubby grass on the far side of the circle. I took two steps sideways to stand on similar scrubby grass over by the end of the path, opposite to where she wanted me. "Yeah, okay. There's good too."

The world felt empty. I was probably imagining the distant sound of chanting. "What if Jeffrey's not around?"

"Then I guess you'll meet Alice."

"What makes you think either of them will be able to convince me?"

"They're very . . . convincing." She rubbed her hands on her shorts and took a deep breath. "Jeffrey, please come to the Dead Ground."

Goosebumps pebbled the skin on my arms. Her summons should have sounded like an airline paging a tardy passenger. It didn't. It res-onated in blood and bone. Cassie hadn't raised her voice, but I knew that no matter how far away he was, Jeffrey had heard her.

The underbrush rustled at the edge of the cut grass.

Seemed like he hadn't been far.

I braced myself for naked. For a naked Guardian. What could a naked man guard against?

Naked didn't really matter because of the thick ginger fur.

The same way naked wouldn't matter on a bear.

He might have been mistaken for a bear . . .

Huge. Humped back. Too-long arms bulging with ropey muscle.

. . . if it was dark . . .

Ivory claws stained purple curled over too many fingers and too many toes.

. . . and you were drunk . . .

Fleshy tentacles in constant movement hid his mouth.

. . . and you'd never seen a bear before. I'd never seen a bear before.

His eyes were blue. Not like husky eyes. Like human eyes.

He moved like his body didn't quite fit, lurching forward like he was still learning how to use the new proportions.

His eyes were human.

And I just . . .

I couldn't.

I screamed and ran.

SEVENTEEN

Cassie

Melanie's scream filled all the available space with terror. It slammed against the trees. It slid over the cliff. It bounced back from the other side of the lake, and it pushed the air aside so that I could barely breathe.

She turned to run.

I had one foot in the air, ready to go after her, when Jeffrey reached me and knocked me on my ass. I felt the ground shake as he landed beside me. Before the dust settled, he yanked me onto his lap, making panicked chuffing noises.

"Shhhh, shhhhh." I laid a hand on his chest, felt the shudders running through the heavy slabs of muscle, and scratched my fingernails through thick, rust-colored fur. "It's all right. I'm here. You're safe. I know it was a loud noise, but it can't hurt you." Later, he'd take the screaming in stride, but he was still young and not entirely used to what he was becoming. I squirmed in his grip and pulled out my phone. "I'm going to text Bridget. She'll come and sit with you. Is that okay?"

"Riiigee. Yesh." The tentacles that had replaced his lips made certain sounds impossible for him, and I had no idea of what was going on inside his mouth. I was ninety-nine percent sure that *Riigee* was as close as he could get to Bridget, and *yesh* was definitely approval.

Unfortunately, although I had three bars, the text didn't go through.

Fucking Travis Brayden.

Wriggling around inside the circle of Jeffrey's arms, I looked out over the cliff, over the lake, and finally over the town. Sure, sound carried a fair distance from up there, but Bridget wasn't Eric. Would she hear me? As far as I could remember from the Journals, the last time a Mouth had tried this was back in 1951, when they had to alert the town to a lightning strike and the resulting fire. I took a deep breath, got a white-knuckled grip on my connection to the Dark, and Called with everything I had, "Bridget! Come to the Dead Ground now! Jeffrey needs you!"

Jeffrey rocked back and forth.

"Hey." I swallowed a mouthful of blood and poked him on what served him for a chin. "Are you going to be okay until she gets here?"

"Yeesh."

"Good, because I've got to . . ."

"Guu afeer heeer." Then he launched me at the path.

Somehow, I managed to both land on my feet and hold on to my phone. I'd spat a mouthful of blood out into the underbrush and taken one step forward when that unholy banjo notification on my phone began to announce the general unhappiness of the other Three. Not literally, but it didn't take a genius to reach that conclusion when it sounded again, and again, and again. I'd Called out Bridget's name first and would have assumed, if I'd thought about it, that no one else would hear me. Obviously, they had. Without breaking stride, I fumbled the notifications off and shoved the phone in my pocket.

Terror had lent Melanie speed, but the soft curves I'd worshipped with hands and mouth wouldn't be doing her any favors, and more importantly, I knew the path. Lengthening my stride, I recklessly used the slope to close the distance. I'd run on a broken ankle if I had to.

She'd almost reached Janet's car when I ran out onto level ground. I couldn't catch her.

And if I Told her to wait, to stay, she'd never trust me again.

Would she have to know? I hadn't told her about what I'd Said at the cellar. If I was already hiding that from her, what was one thing more?

One enormous, coercive thing more.

Crossing the boundary would wipe Jeffrey and Daffodil from her memory, but I had no way of knowing if she'd forget what I'd told her. About the fire. About the Dark. About the town.

There was only one way to keep us safe.

And that's what I did; I kept us safe.

That's what I had to do.

I stumbled to a stop, sucked in a few gasping breaths, and, as she opened the door, Said, "Melanie. Forget everything I told you. Forget me."

My heart stopped. The world stopped. I wished I could believe that it hadn't worked, that I had a chance to do something else, anything else. But I was the Mouth of the Dark, and it always worked.

Always.

She didn't turn toward the sound of my Voice. She threw herself into the car, cranked the engine, slammed her foot down on the gas, and sprayed gravel all the way to the road.

Where she turned right. Toward town.

I nearly choked on a surge of hope, then swallowed it when I realized why. Her car, her things were at the guest house, and Melanie had grown up without things; she couldn't leave them behind. Or it might be as simple as her being too good a person to steal Janet's car. Either way, she had to pass the park to leave, and I'd see her again.

Still breathing heavily, I staggered to the cellar and collapsed onto the door, a red dot almost instantly appearing on my knee. I waved off Security's concerns. I wasn't okay. I might never be okay again. But they couldn't help.

A minute later, I heard the roar of an engine. Bridget fishtailed into the parking lot and skidded to a stop, leaving the door open behind her as she raced over to me.

"Jeffrey?"

My throat had almost stopped bleeding. As this was not the place to spit blood, I swallowed. "Just scared."

"I passed Melanie in Janet's car—"

"Yeah."

"I heard her scream. Are you . . ." She shook her head. "Of course you aren't. Can I help?"

I jerked my head toward the path.

"Cass . . ." She took another step forward, cupped my face, and kissed me on the forehead. Then she turned and ran for the Dead Ground and her little brother.

Bridget had probably reached the top of the hill when Eric, driving only slightly more sedately, pulled in. Before he got the car turned off, Aunt Jean threw open the door. Dust rose up around the four impact points of her cane.

"Cassidy Prewitt! Just what exactly is going on? The whole town heard you Call Bridget, like you were the megaphone of the Dark. That is not how we behave. What were you thinking?"

I shrugged. "I told Melanie the truth about the Dark. She didn't believe me. I brought her to the lookout and introduced her to Jeffrey. She didn't take it well."

Aunt Jean reached for her glasses.

I wasn't sure what she was planning to do beyond Look at me, nor did I care.

"Leave it, Jean," Eric snapped. "I was Listening as we drove up and I Heard Cassie tell Melanie to forget. She's dealt with it."

"There shouldn't have been anything to—"

"Jean." Closing the car door behind her, Amanda put her hand on the older woman's shoulder.

"Most of the town heard the screaming too!" Releasing one hand from its white-knuckled grip on her cane, she lifted a finger. "Then you, Shouting from cliff tops, letting everyone into our business." A second finger. "Telling—"

"Bridget's business," Amanda pointed out. "And if she isn't complaining—"

"She's too simple to realize—"

"Enough! Not one word against Bridget, Jean. Not one. As for Cassie, how about you open your eyes and take a look at what's happening under your nose."

Jean huffed but remained silent.

Lifting T'geyer out of a car seat, Eric carried it toward me.

It had grown to about the size of a three-year-old, and when Eric set it in my lap, it wrapped its arms around my neck, tucked its face up against my throat, and hummed. I rested my cheek against its cool, smooth skin, took a deep breath . . . and cried.

EIGHTEEN

Melanie

I had no clear memory of leaving Lake Argen. I had a vague recollection of the motel flashing by on my right, but that was it except for a blur of trees until the Gogama turn-off on 144. The sign passed so quickly, I glanced down at the speedometer. One-forty. One-forty on one forty-four. I either needed to either go four kilometers faster for the sake of congruency or slow down.

I picked door number two. One-twenty would be fine; I was heading home, not racing for the border. No one was chasing me. The car shook as a transport roared by heading north. And it wasn't like anyone else on the road kept to the speed limit.

About half an hour later, I pulled into the Arctic Watershed Rest Area to pee. Either I hadn't bothered to go before I left or I'd already lost my "teachers don't get to excuse themselves to go to the bathroom" superpower. Returning to the car, I glanced through the back window and saw that I'd tossed everything I'd taken north with me onto the seat in one jumbled mess—clothes, books, luggage.

"*Why bother packing,*" said a voice in my head. "*It's all laundry. No reason to be neat.*"

That made sense.

The empty travel mug made less sense until I remembered the coffee shop in Lake Argen kept irregular hours. Made sense that it hadn't been open when I'd left.

By Dowling, just outside Sudbury, both the car and I were almost out of gas. I filled the tank, hit a drive-through, and since it was about two in the afternoon, managed to get through Sudbury without much trouble. Normally, for an eight to nine hour drive, I'd have left a lot earlier but missing rush hour, such as it was in Sudbury, was much smarter. Go me.

When I approached Toronto after five hours on the 400, say five and a half depending on the length of time it took to get through Barrie, the highway should be relatively empty. Traffic would still suck because traffic always sucked getting into or out of Toronto, but with luck, it would be moving. Some days, movement was all you could hope for.

I really wanted to get home. I could almost feel a push in that direction and hoped I wasn't having a freaky premonition about my mother. Was I sensing a threat? She'd love that. I could have called to check she was okay, but instead, I kept driving.

The two days I'd taken to drive north now seemed like a colossal waste of time. Subconsciously, I must have had doubts about Mrs. Brayden's job, or about Mrs. Brayden, and wanted to spend her money while I had the chance.

Turned out actual moving traffic on the way into the city had been a little more than I could hope for, but I pulled into visitor's parking at Mom's apartment by nine forty-five. Turns out the timing in internet trip prediction is almost accurate if you only stopped at gas stations, and if you were close enough to get by the idiot who changed lanes without turn signals before the emergency vehicles blocked the road. While passing slowly and carefully, I could hear the driver yelling at a pair of OPP officers.

". . . that's bullshit! I always use . . ."

Bullshit. The only word for the situation?

Had I intended to talk to the OPP? I felt like . . .

Nope. It was gone.

Nine forty-five, ten by the time I got inside, was far too late to head out again. I couldn't even text Mrs. Brayden to let her know I'd returned, because my phone was dead.

I never forgot to charge my phone.

My cable was probably buried in the mess left in the back seat. With any luck, I'd go down in the morning and find elves had sorted dirty underwear from clean. I borrowed Mom's charger and headed for the shower.

Cut-rate apartment bathrooms had the kind of lighting that could make anyone look haggard. I looked like death warmed over. Dark circles under puffy eyes, hair escaping a braid I'd clearly put in wet, and an unpleasant shade of sunburn across my nose and the upper curve of my cheeks. And why had I thought driving home in the only decent outfit I'd taken with me was a good idea? The ass of the palazzo pants hung stretched and loose, and what looked like permanent creases had been crushed into the fabric at the hips and knees. My gauze top smelled like I'd been wearing it for days.

Or unending hours in a car with crappy air conditioning.

That made sense.

I turned away from the mirror as I pulled the top over my head, and used a two-finger grip to drop it into the laundry basket. Mom was working the dinner shift this week, so, with no fear of being mocked, I finished undressing, stepped into the shower, and made obscene noises as hot water pounded down on my stiff and aching muscles.

Damp body stuffed into boy shorts and a tank top, I grabbed a piece of leftover pizza I was fairly certain hadn't been in the fridge when I left, and collapsed onto the couch.

When I finish eating, I told myself while picking off the mushrooms for no apparent reason, *I'll make up the sofa bed, get a pillow from Mom's room, and . . .*

———

"So, velociraptors in Northern Ontario is a new one for me." A hard poke to my shoulder punctuated the sentence. "Where did you get this?"

"A raven gave it to me," I muttered into the sofa cushion. "And get out of my purse."

"Purse? Don't you mean your gender-neutral carrying bag?"

"Too many words."

"There's a black feather in there, too. Probably nestled in half a million bird lice by now."

"A couple hundred must've come out on your hand."

"I was careful."

"Mom, get out of my gender-neutral carrying bag."

"It's ten o'clock. If you'd woken up earlier, I wouldn't have been tempted." Another poke.

I sighed and rolled over onto my back.

My mother was sitting on the coffee table, bare knees almost touching the sofa, my messenger bag open beside her, the blueberry-stained claw in her hand. Blueberries. Wasn't there . . . She poked me with it again. "You can't call and tell me you're coming home? What if I'd had company?"

"You were at work."

"What if I'd dragged one of the line cooks home, intending to have him right there, on that sofa?"

"You have a bedroom, Mom."

"Not the point. What are you doing back?"

"I'd found out everything I was going to find out. There didn't seem to be a reason to hang around. And," I added as she opened her mouth, "my phone was dead."

"I assumed, given that you'd stolen my charger."

"It's right where you left it."

"I didn't leave it plugged in to your phone. No thanks for throwing a blanket over your unconscious body when I got home?"

"Thank you."

"You're welcome. I also removed a slice of pizza stuck to your cheek." She cocked her head and frowned slightly. "I thought you were having a nice vacation."

I shrugged as deeply as my position allowed. "A nice, short vacation."

"Meet anyone?"

My brain skittered over a kaleidoscopic of faces, refusing to settle. "Lots of people."

"Uh-huh. The hickey on your shoulder have anything to do with your early departure?"

I twisted around to take a look.

"Nice try. Other shoulder."

Right. Huh. I remembered a pub. Beer. The taste of oatmeal-apple bread.

Mom plowed on without waiting for me to sort through fractured impressions. How much had I had to drink? "Is the person who gave that to you one of the reasons you left early?"

"Yes . . ."

Because that made sense.

Her face folded into a deeper frown. "Do I need to head north and kick butt?"

"No, Mom, it's fine." It wasn't, though, and the not-fine was connected to that claw. The claw I had a solid memory of. But not . . .

Not . . .

I kicked off the incredibly ugly crocheted afghan that always smelled a bit like ass, and sat up. "What about you? Get arrested?"

"Not this time." She grinned. "Heaved a clump of dried mud at a cop's feet, but he didn't know where it came from."

"Mom!"

"Spur of the moment, regretted it instantly. Now"—she slapped my thigh hard enough, flesh jiggled between hip and knee—"shower, dress, and go claim that ten grand so I can get my sofa back before the chef fires my line cook. Or sleeps with my line cook," she added thoughtfully as I stood. "Could go either way."

———

"What are you doing here?" Mrs. Brayden demanded, glaring out at me, her French manicure digging into the edge of her front door.

I spread my hands and squelched the urge to ask about her car insurance. "I've completed the job."

"In five days? When two days were spent traveling?"

Three, I corrected silently, resisting the urge to wipe sweaty palms on my skirt. "Yes."

"You were to be there for seven. Minimum."

"I work fast."

The silence lengthened. I could hear a sprinkler, a lawn mower, the breeze moving through tall, healthy, rich-people trees. Not elms, though. Of course not elms. Most of the elms had died before I was born. Why was I suddenly thinking about elms?

Finally, Mrs. Brayden exhaled, nostrils flaring, and stepped back. "You'd better come in." The three-quarter-sleeved white blouse, the navy linen slacks, the white ballet flats, and the straw purse made her look like every Pinterest page ever on "what to wear over sixty."

A suitcase, slightly larger than carry-on-sized, stood in the front hall, a navy-blue sweater draped over its raised handle.

"I'm sorry. Have I interrupted travel plans?" Or was she running out on paying me?

"I had no reason to expect you back this quickly."

Which didn't quite answer the question, unless she'd planned on joining me there.

She gestured toward the front room, the company room with the cream-and-gold wallpaper. "Go. Sit. I'll make tea."

"None for me, thanks."

Her expression explicitly said that if she was making tea, I was drinking tea. I hadn't yet been paid, so I rolled my eyes at her back as she headed for the rear of the house, then went in and sat in the same place at the end of the sofa where I'd sat before.

The room hadn't changed.

Of course it hadn't. It had only been five days. Felt longer. Did distance traveled affect the perception of time away? Made sense that it would.

The wallpaper made me think of the wallpaper at the guest house, and I decided that should I ever have to choose between slightly tacky and entirely sterile, I'd go with tacky every time. I couldn't remember settling my bill, but it made sense that all they'd needed was the record of Mrs. Brayden's credit card they'd taken when I checked in.

Why did I keep thinking that things made sense?

"It needs to steep." Mrs. Brayden carried in the same tea tray as the last time. Still no accompanying snacks. Impressive willpower kept my stomach from gurgling. "While it's steeping, give me the knife."

"The knife?" The knife . . . Oh, shit. The knife. "I left it in the car."

"Then go and get it."

As her knuckles whitened, I got a little worried about the handle of the teapot. "It's not in my car. I left it in the librarian's car in . . . up north."

"You don't have the knife?" Each word sounded like it had been individually cut from crystal.

"I'm so sorry. It's not an heirloom, though," I continued quickly, doing my best to make that sound like good news. "According to the librarian, it was made recently." I could remember her telling me about the knife, although I couldn't remember her name. "Peter, the blacksmith"—no trouble remembering Peter's name—"said it was forged near Kitchener."

"Kitchener?"

"It's—"

"I know where Kitchener is, Ms. Solvich. I went to school near Kitchener. Was either the librarian or the blacksmith"—the teapot handle creaked—"able to tell you what the runes said?"

"No. She looked." She went down into the basement. "But she couldn't find anything."

Mrs. Brayden released a deep breath that seemed weirdly like relief, and poured the tea. I tried not to look like a hot cup of tea in July was the last thing I wanted. "Drink up," she said, "and we'll talk about what I want you to do now."

———

"You're heading back north?"

"I'm heading back north." I had no safe way into the left lane, so I passed the dipshit doing a hundred in the center lane on the right.

"Just like that?"

"Just like that. Good thing I didn't empty the car."

"You couldn't swing by to tell me?"

"You said you were meeting Lisa before work. I had no idea if you'd be home."

"You could have called!"

"This is me calling!" I slid into the space between two transports.

I heard her take a deep breath. "I don't like old Mrs. Brayden saying jump and you asking how high on the way up. It's only ten grand. Don't sell yourself so cheaply."

"Mom, it's my own fault I'm going back. I found the knife." Although she couldn't see me, I flicked up the first finger on my right hand. "I forgot the knife." Flicked up the second finger. "She won't pay me without the knife." I folded the first finger down.

"Shouldn't that have been established in the original contract?"

"It wasn't exactly a contract. And it was. Sort of." The knife had definitely been part of it.

Since I had the correct finger raised, I flipped off a Tesla. Just because.

"I don't like this." The silence stretched, lengthened, was interrupted by the sound of a siren in the distance, and finally, Mom said, "You're going back to the person who gave you the hickey."

"No, I'm not!" Although I . . . I . . . No, it was gone. Whatever it was, the absence hurt.

She snorted, deliberately loud enough to be heard over the ambient noise. "I should head over to Rosedale and have a word with old Mrs. Brayden."

"She won't be there."

"Where's she going?"

"Why would she tell me?"

"Because you'll need to meet up with her to give her the knife and collect your money."

"She'll be back by then."

"You know when she'll be back, but you don't know where she's going?"

"You're naturally suspicious and I love that about you, but I'm the one who forgot the knife." It just made sense that I'd go back. I assured her I'd be home as soon as possible, and hung up.

Traffic wasn't moving freely until past Vaughan. When I finally hit the speed limit, I did some math, and realized that if I drove straight through, reliving yesterday in reverse, I could be there by 2 AM.

If I broke a few laws, maybe midnight.

NINETEEN

Cassie

T his is Brian Rickford."

I glanced up at Ms. Morton, who nodded, then leaned in toward the landline and Said, "Mr. Rickford, I'm calling about the mine inspection you have planned for next Wednesday at Lake Argen. Cancel it."

"I can't . . ."

We'd been afraid of that, Ms. Morton and I. She'd found a Journal entry by Nedra Prewitt, the Mouth of the Dark in the 1960s, that recorded how she'd called her grandson Robert in Montreal, Ordering him to return home. Apparently, he'd fallen in with a bad crowd. Here and now, the weakening Agreement couldn't force a hundred-and-eighty-degree turn over the phone, so we moved on to the gentler nudge of Plan B. "Mr. Rickford, I want you to postpone the Lake Argen mine inspection until September."

"I have September fifth available."

"Later would be better."

"September ninth, then."

Another glance at Ms. Morton, who sighed and nodded again.

"The ninth will be fine, Mr. Rickford. Lake Argen thanks you. You've been terrific."

"You've been terrific?" Ms. Morton crushed the notice from the ministry as I hung up. "He was barely helpful."

"And now he's in a great mood, and when he thinks of Lake Argen, he'll remember that mood." I swallowed and sucked blood off my teeth. "It can't hurt."

"I suppose not. A month to get on top of this situation with the Dark a is definite improvement on next Wednesday."

"We're not going to have a month." I wiped a smear of blood off my lips with a tissue. "Pressure's building. I can feel it." Melanie's presence had distracted me from it, or Melanie's absence had exposed it—I didn't know.

"How long, then?"

"No idea."

"What do we do?"

"Alice told us to get ready. So, we need to get ready." I had nothing else.

"What does getting ready mean in this context?"

"I don't know. We can't stop Travis from building his shopping mall, so all we can do is wait until he's finished."

"He's building a shopping mall? Did the Dark—"

"No!" I snapped. "The Dark didn't! The Dark has Said nothing that helps!"

I felt her touch my shoulder. "Cassidy?"

If she asked if I was all right, I was going to Say something I'd regret. "If that's all you need me for, I have to get to the bakery."

"I'll drive you."

"No." I stood and moved away from her desk. "I'll walk."

Melanie had probably still been speeding down Gogama Road in her disaster of a car when Ms. Morton called all Four of us, voice a bit shrill as she read a new notice from the Ministry about the mine inspection. She needed me to fix it. Eric had put T'geyer's car seat in the trunk, handed T'geyer to Amanda, and driven me to the mine office before taking the other two home. The ride had been quiet. No one mentioned Melanie, or ugly-crying, or hard choices. Everyone else in the car, except maybe T'geyer, knew the price of Power. And honestly? We knew nothing about T'geyer.

I'd calmed Ms. Morton. I'd rescheduled the inspection. Now I needed to spend some time alone to try and come to terms with the loss of a relationship that could have defined me. I couldn't spend fifteen minutes in a car with Ms. Morton, not sitting in a silence that would demand to be filled. I'd have walked to the bakery in a blizzard had that been my only choice.

Rather than take Argen Street and be painfully visible to anyone driving to or from the mine or the station, I cut in a block and took Queen instead. Trees, houses, laughing children, and except for the pair of cats who followed me for a block, I remained unseen.

This was my town, and I was supposed to keep it safe.

And I had.

And I would.

Life sucked.

Ditch lilies filled the space between lawns and road with orange. Big-white-fluffy-bush-flower things were blooming at a Prewitt house— a fourth cousin married to a second cousin once removed—and next door, Mrs. Morton—Ms. Morton's grandmother—was on her knees, weeding the narrow garden next to the porch. She heaved herself to her feet as I passed, wobbled, and would have fallen had I not raced over the lawn to catch her.

"Thank you, Cassidy, dear." She pulled off a gardening glove and patted my arm with a damp hand. "I have to keep reminding myself I'm not eighty anymore."

"Did you need a hand up onto the porch?"

"Oh, I'm not going in yet. I still have deadheading to do."

"If you're sure." She seemed steady on her feet, so I released her arm. A glance down at the garden as I turned to go catapulted me back to sixth grade and my spring project on poisonous plants. "You're growing oleander."

"I wasn't yesterday. I came out this morning, after my toast and jam, and there it was. Poof. Overnight, surprise oleander."

It seemed that more than just the Agreement was weakening.

Together we watched a bee waddle to the edge of a pinkish-purple blossom and take flight.

"Well," she said thoughtfully, "that's going to make this year's honey a lot more interesting."

"You need to pull it out."

"No, I don't think so. It's pretty." Her smile refolded her face into a challenging pattern of wrinkles.

I was not in the mood to be challenged by a garden gnome. "Remove the oleander from your garden," I Told her. "Dig a hole in the yard and bury it." Shit. Loophole. "Do not poison anyone between digging the oleander out and burying it. Do not dig it up again."

"Nice catch. Although I probably wasn't going to poison anyone, I totally understand why you wouldn't want to take the chance." She rummaged in her apron pocket and pulled out a lint-covered cough drop. "Go ahead and spit."

"Thanks." I spat blood into the grass, popped the cough drop, lint and all, into my mouth, nodded goodbye, and headed for the road.

I had one foot on asphalt when she called, "Oh, and Cassidy, I was sorry to hear that your young lady friend had to leave."

It had only been a few hours. The hand I raised in acknowledgment was just a hand, not the response I wanted to make. Half a block away, I realized I'd forgotten to Say, *Do not have someone else dig the oleander up for you after you've buried it.* If she wanted to poison someone that badly, more power to her. And as she'd said, she probably wouldn't.

A pack of kids ran down one driveway, across the road, and up another. I wondered if Melanie wanted kids. She'd be good at it. Firm but fair. Laughing with them, not at them. There'd be a lot of hugging.

We'd argue over whose turn it was to drive them to the pool or the park or the cemetery. I wasn't as sure about me and kids, but the bloodlines were getting pretty diluted, and I should probably find a distant cousin and do something about it.

In a few years.

When it stopped feeling like my heart was pumping broken glass.

"Cassie? Cassidy Prewitt?" I turned to see Marian Foster running down her front path toward me. "Oh, thank the Dark, I thought it was you. You have to come inside and look at my linen closet."

"I'm the Mouth," I reminded her as she reached me. "If you want someone to Look, you want Aunt Jean."

"Not Look, look. And besides, you're here." She grabbed my arm and dragged me toward the house. "I was sorry to hear that Melanie left. I saw you two in the pub last night; you were cute together."

Just last night. There was so much I wanted to say—to Marian, to the whole town. Starting with: *I did this for you. I ripped out my heart for you. I hope you fucking appreciate it. And don't try and tell me that's what the Four do. The Four didn't. I did. Me. Not them.*

Good thing I'd learned to keep my mouth shut.

Better late than never.

The linen closet occupied the space between the bathroom and the bedroom. I looked at the closed door. I looked at Marian.

"Open it!" she urged.

I touched the wood. It was cool. Too cool? I listened. Nothing. Too quiet? I opened the door.

Smoke that smelled like swamp mud billowed, flames burned with colors I couldn't identify, existential dread froze my blood in my veins. I wet my lips and Squeaked, "Go away."

Laughter from deep within the infinite space cut like flensing knives. "**No**."

"Okay, then." I closed the door and sagged against it, gasping for breath.

"You Spoke—"

"Yes, I did."

"It said no."

"Yes, it did."

"So, what should I do now?" Marian demanded.

"Nail the door shut."

"But my towels!"

"You might want to get some silver nails from the mine office," I added on my way out.

A half-block later.

"Cassie!" Jordan Prewitt, six-year-old third cousin, once removed, leapt out in front of me. "My cat just gave birth to three kittens!"

"Congratulations."

"They're blue. And they have wings. And my cat is a boy."

Around a corner and a block after that.

"Cassandra!" Mrs. Foster, my mother's cousin's great-aunt, thrust a bandaged arm into my face. "That dogwood"—she pointed at a blooming tree-shrub thing in her side yard—"bit me!"

"What were you doing to it?" It's what my dad asked when I got bit by a tourist's dachshund.

Her eyes widened. "Pruning it. But that's not—"

"Stop doing that, then," I Said, dangling from the end of my rope. She began another protest, but I kept walking.

So much for alone time.

———

Before I turned off Carlyle, I took a look at the lake. There was a definite chop out beyond the line of buoys.

"Alice is upset," I muttered sarcastically and very quietly, because I was heartbroken, not stupid. "Join the club, squirmy lady."

In the bakery, Chris took one look at me and pulled me into a hug.

His apron smelled like cinnamon buns. Tori and Lu at the coffee shop had a weekly order—which was stupid in July. Who ate cinnamon buns when it was thirty degrees out? Then I remembered that it had been so important for me to prepare food for Melanie, I'd made oatmeal-apple bread in July because I hadn't gone grocery shopping for a while, and it was all I had the ingredients for. I may have whimpered. Chris tightened his grip.

"That bad?" I asked against the warmth and safety of his chest.

"Worse. You look like shit, and your parents have been in, looking for you. Twice."

I squirmed around until I could free my phone, had a flashback to a similar maneuver in Jeffrey's arms, and stomped down hard on rising emotions. Forty-three messages. "I turned off the notifications. Too many people were . . ." I waved a hand to fill in the missing words. Too many people knew part of what was going on.

"Even if you don't get into the details, you need to let your parents know you're okay."

"Seems I need to do a lot of things."

"Cass . . ."

"I'll text them."

He lifted my chin so he could look into my eyes, nodded, and said, "All right."

"I'm starving. Have you eaten?" The oatmeal-apple bread had been a whole other life ago.

"I'm a big guy. I could eat."

"Can you go get us some lunch? Please. I'll watch the ovens."

"Text first." He leaned in, kissed my forehead, and let me go. "And you'll tell me the details while we eat. BFFs have rights."

I kept the text to my parents short because I knew Chris would reassure them. I couldn't face parental sympathy or, when they'd learned what I'd done to drive Melanie away, a parental attempt to understand motives I considered exceedingly simple. I wanted her to stay, so she had to be told the truth. Her finding the knife just moved up the timeline. My father would say, "Just?" in a tone that suggested I was making excuses.

Just, no.

I told Chris the whole thing over BLTs and barely cooled chocolate macadamia nut cookies.

". . . assumed she'd believe me when faced with fact, but Jeffrey was a little too factual."

"Jeffrey's a little too imaginary." Chris brushed crumbs off his fingers. "You thought love would be strong enough to face the truth."

"I thought what I felt between us would be strong enough to face the truth."

"You don't want to call that love?"

I pushed the cookies away before I made myself sick. "I only knew her for two days—"

"I knew after two minutes with Alan."

"Because you're a romantic, and I'm a Conduit of the Dark."

And we both knew that was an excuse.

When the remainder of the cookies had been arranged out front, and we'd finished icing a special order of birthday cupcakes together, he dropped me at home, and I rode my bike up to the Dead Ground. The path nearly killed me, but thighs aching and dripping with sweat, I felt a lot more alive when I reached the top. Exercise and fresh air might make a minimal difference, but they made enough of a difference, I knew I'd survive this.

The waters of the lake were still rough. Curves too solid to be waves appeared and disappeared out in the center. Alice was finally reacting. To what?

"*Be ready* was not helpful," I told her. Small *t*. I was heartbroken, not stu— "KESH A'SOGATH AKOOM!"

Do not cough up blood on the Dead Ground, I thought mussily from my knees, realized there was only water in sight, and dragged myself in from the edge of the cliff. Pulling out my phone, I flopped over onto my back and began typing in what I could remember.

"T'geyer," Jeffrey said softly from the trees.

Had Jeffrey met T'geyer? Had he been watching while I cuddled it after Melanie left? Did Jeffrey speak the language of darkness? It made a certain amount of sense that he would. "Was it a message for T'geyer, Jeffrey?"

"Nooom, ouurr T'geyer."

"Okay. I'll see that T'geyer gets it."

Wood cracked and I rolled over to see Jeffrey staring at the upper half of a young pine he held in one hand, huge, curving claws dug deep into the wood. "Stuuuuid," he moaned, threw the broken tree over my head and off the cliff, then stomped away.

Should I call Bridget?

No, I decided after a moment's consideration. If Jeffrey was jealous of the attention T'geyer was getting, he didn't need his big sister patting his hand and telling him everything was going to be all right. He needed to break some trees and get it out of his system.

I heard drums as I rode past the cellar. Big, deep ones that made my bones vibrate and my heart try to match the rhythm. I pedaled faster and flipped up the red flag indicating *action at the house* when I left the park.

We'd always believed the drums were nothing more than bits of the darkness, probably younger bits, being annoying. I had a feeling that belief was about to be changed.

═══

No one came to the Friday evening question-and-answer session. Maybe they had too many questions. Maybe they knew I didn't have any answers. Once freed from obligation, Eric and I headed to his place, sending Bridget, who'd been staying with T'geyer, home.

"Four business. Got it." She kissed the top of T'geyer's head and smiled at Eric.

Eric smiled back and watched her leave, little animated hearts floating over his head. Not literally, thank the Dark.

I pulled out my phone and found the words I'd saved. "*Kesh asogath akoom.*"

Head cocked, T'geyer blinked, nictitating membranes momentarily dimming his blazing orange eyes. "Esh."

When I glanced over, Eric shrugged. "Too bad I wasn't Listening when you Said it. It's harder when it's just you repeating it, but I'm Hearing *tell them together.*"

"Tell who together? Jeffrey seemed to think it was a message for T'geyer."

"Yeah, but Jeffrey . . ." He shrugged again. "Bridget says that while his shape has finally settled, he's still settling into it. You can't really count on anything he says."

"Fair," I acknowledged. "So, Bridget and T'geyer?"

He laughed. Not dismissively, like I half-expected, but happily. "I think she feels responsible because the Flock provided all those bags of shadow for them."

Nothing suggestive. No trying to twist the situation into something it wasn't. Personal growth by way of an eldritch horror. Wow.

"So . . ." He took a deep breath and continued. "After we dropped you off, Jean told Amanda and me that she thinks you're doing too much."

And there went the burgeoning warm and fuzzies. "In a *how dare I* way? I thought that was what you lot wanted." I shot a narrowed-eyed glare in the general direction of Aunt Jean's house. "Or is it because I'm broken right now? And are you even allowed to tell me that? Isn't it breaking the rules?"

He perched one butt cheek on the arm of his sofa—and didn't immediately slide off the slick leather. I kind of admired that. "I follow the only rule you do, Cassie. I help keep the town safe. Your heart's broken; you're not. We want you to be everything the Mouth of the Dark can be, but while Jean can say she wants you to take up the mantle, she Sees little Cassidy Prewitt when she Looks at you. And maybe a bit of Simon. His tenure left us with a few trust issues. Give her time."

I frowned. He was almost my father's age, and wearing a Hawaiian shirt printed with 1940s pinup girls. "When did you get wise?"

"Damned if I know."

"Wait . . ."

His brows rose into a sarcastic *was I going somewhere* arch.

". . . you referred to T'geyer as *them*."

"I did." And the subtext said *Aren't you clever for noticing.* That was more like the old Eric. I'd miss the old Eric if he completely disappeared. "T'geyer may be an eldritch horror," he went on as I dealt with that revelation, "but they're living in my house. I can't keep referring to them as *it*." He opened his arms and T'geyer launched themself upward out of the chair, nuzzling into Eric's neck. Launch. Landing. They'd been fast enough, I hadn't seen the middle bit. One arm supporting T'geyer's butt, Eric stretched out the other and snagged a ribbon-covered basket from the table. "You hungry, Tee? Want some shadow?"

"Nice basket."

"I've had twelve-year-olds in and out all afternoon. They think he's adorable. I'm telling you, Cass, I wouldn't want to be a shadow in this town right now. There's a whole lot of skewer-sharpening going on." He scraped off a clump of glitter and settled the piece of shadow inside the curve of T'geyer's claws.

"Esh."

"Food?" I asked as T'geyer began mouthing the edges.

"Or shadow, since that's all they eat. *Esh* is their second favorite word after their name."

"Are they still growing?" They didn't look bigger than they had . . . this morning. It had only been this morning. I'd woken up with Melanie, I'd fed her, I'd Told her to forget me. "Never mind. I can see they're not bigger, you know, than they were. I have to go."

"Cassie."

I paused, one hand on Eric's ever so modern and expensive doorknob, and turned back toward him.

"We'll be ready."

"We don't know what we're to be ready for."

"Yeah, but we're adaptable." T'geyer reached up to pat his cheek, drawing blood.

I touched the scab on mine. "I guess we are."

Safely outside, I wondered if Melanie would have thought T'geyer was adorable.

We'd never know.

━━━

I spent the next day, my first full day without Melanie and the shape of all my days to come, putting out fires. Literally, after Eric Heard shouting and I arrived to find Greg Worth poking at a frightened salamander with a pair of barbecue tongs, his deck smoldering. I Told Greg to back off while Eric coaxed the salamander back into its nest in the briquettes with his shiny new eldritch-wrangling abilities. Before we left, I Suggested Greg read up on the local wildlife.

He had a salamander in his barbecue. He didn't get to opt out.

Later, I cried on my parents. It was both cathartic and embarrassing.

Later still, I stared at the lake, watched the waves get larger, and decided I wouldn't have another non-conversation with Alice, since she'd been so incredibly unhelpful the first time.

And after that, I had dinner with Chris and Alan, and let Natalie climb all over me. It didn't really help, but she'd grown out of chubby toddler to three-year-old with sharp knees and elbows, and the random bruises were distracting.

Then I went back to my empty house.

———

Awakened by a blast of obnoxious music, I fell off the sofa scrambling for my phone. For the second night in a row, I hadn't been able to sleep in the bed. On the one hand, I wanted to bury my face in Melanie's pillow and surround myself with her smell and never come up. On the other hand, it was all I had left of her and it would kill me when it faded, so I stayed downstairs. If I ignored it, maybe it wouldn't hurt as much when it was gone.

I crawled across the living-room floor to the phone charger and managed to find the right icon. "Theresa, it's one in the morning!"

"I know," she whispered, "but she's here!"

"She who?"

"Her. Melanie Solvich."

The world stopped. My heart stopped with it.

"Cassie?"

"I'm on my way."

———

Melanie looked confused about why she was still standing in the lobby, and the staccato rhythm her left foot beat out on the floor told me she was reaching the end of her patience. I stumbled in, rocked to a stop, and she stared at me like I was a total stranger. Which as far as she was concerned, I was.

She stepped back, brows in, chin up. Suddenly wary.

What expression was I wearing? I forced my face into the general vicinity of neutral. "Hi. I'm Cassie. We met briefly when you were here before. I thought you'd . . . left."

"I did." Her frown deepened. I could see questions rising behind her eyes only to be slapped almost instantly down. She brushed at the creases in her green skirt, and I remembered her talking about the clothes she kept for parent/teacher meetings. She was in her parent/teacher meeting clothes. Why?

"Was there a problem with your car?" I asked, tucking my hands into my pockets so I wouldn't reach for her. How far had she managed to get?

"My car's fine," she answered defensively. "It got me to Toronto *and* back."

I waited.

Melanie sighed. "I left a very important item behind, so I had to return for it."

"You forgot something?"

She jerked back at the unexpected reverb, and behind me, Theresa murmured, "Too intense."

I faked a laugh.

A snort from behind me. Daniel that time.

"It must've been important," I said hurriedly. "To have come all this way. You know, when you'd just left."

"It was important to my employer." She threw a silent question past me to Theresa, brushing a bit of wavy hair back off her face. It was wavy because she'd braided it wet. At my house. Before . . .

The knife.

She meant the knife.

Of course she meant the knife.

I hadn't told her to forget the knife.

"Are you all right?" Head cocked, she studied my face.

No. I wasn't. I shrugged, forcing knotted muscles to lift and lower my shoulders. Her presence pulled me one way. Her belief that I was a stranger pulled me another. I was being pulled apart. "It's been a long day."

"Tell me about it." When I blinked at her, she sighed. "Actually, don't. Mrs. Prewitt, is the room ready?"

"Of course, dear. You're in the room you had before."

Melanie's expression suggested there was no *of course* about it. "Then why . . . You know what, never mind."

I wondered what lie Theresa had told to keep her in the lobby. Or maybe Daniel had taken over and told it. He'd happily embraced the whole cranky-old-man persona and never worried about upsetting people.

Melanie had managed to wearily climb half the first flight of stairs when I couldn't stop myself from calling out, "It was good to see you!"

She looked back at me and frowned. She'd forgotten me again.

Getting s-worded with the knife would have hurt less.

———

"Who doesn't love to start their day with revenants?"

I sagged back against the cemetery fence. "Revenant. Just one. Good thing you Heard the flies."

Eric grunted and sagged beside me. "They don't make mausoleum doors like they used to." We watched T'geyer rise up on his hind legs to investigate a rosebush. "If I wanted to get up at dawn," he said after a minute, "I'd have a job. You okay?"

I'd expected him to snark about the inconvenience of being drawn away from whoever he'd had sharing his bed. Or complain that Bridget hadn't been. Here he was, subverting expectations. Go him. And he clearly hadn't been Listening last night. "Melanie came back. Well, she was sent back. For the knife. Theresa called from the guest house about one AM."

"And you went over. Why?"

That was very dad-like. Maybe older brother-like. I'd never had one, so how would I know. "Ask the Dark," I sighed, "because I have no idea."

———

"You went over," Chris said, easing a second tray of choux pastry into the upper oven, "because the pain of seeing her again and her not remembering you was less than the pain of never seeing her again."

"You sound like a Hallmark movie," I grumbled, tying on my apron.

"Am I wrong?"

"No. And unless we're swarmed by an army of darkness, with or without Bruce Campbell, I'm spending the rest of the morning making fruit tarts."

"Because you have to think about the pâte sablée so you won't have the brain space to think about Melanie."

"Enough, Chris." But I bumped against him as I passed so he knew I didn't mean it. He was my emotional anchor in this mess.

I was reaching for the handle on the walk-in fridge when the back door slammed open, the impact of the heavy wood against the wall vibrating through the whole building. Bent over, peering into the lower oven, Chris twisted toward the door without straightening.

Alyx pushed past him without even a glance at his ass. "Cassie! We're about to be swarmed by an army of darkness!"

Seriously? Had she been listening outside the door? I bit back the question about Bruce Campbell. I had a suspicion she wouldn't find it funny. "What are you talking about?"

"I know what Travis Brayden has been up to!"

"Building a shopping mall." Frustration forced it out before I could stop it.

"What? No. Are you . . . Never mind. Should Chris stay for this?"

"For what?"

She took a deep breath and let it out slowly. If looks could kill, I'd definitely have been slapped around a bit. "I know what Travis Brayden has been up to," she repeated, slowly and deliberately.

Okay, then. "Chris, you staying?"

He moved to stand beside me. "I have choux pastry in the oven."

"He's staying," I told Alyx before she put words to her expression. "I should contact the other Three and set up a meeting—"

"How long will that take?"

"No idea."

"Group call?"

"That important?"

"Cassidy," she sighed. "Don't make me say it again."

"Right, that important." I pulled out my phone. Aunt Jean wouldn't stop complaining, so, rather than argue, I muted incoming sound— technology, so much more ethical than Telling people to shut up— and, with the other Three listening in, pointed the microphone at Alyx and said, "Go ahead."

"All right." Another deep breath. "One of my people went on a vision quest last night . . ." She held up her hand as I opened my mouth. "No, I am not going to explain what that involves. First, it's a craft secret, and second, it's not what's important right now. It's not something that we do often, and we never do it without first checking in with the Dark, which is a whole different story," she added hurriedly before I could ask, "but did you honestly think we'd live here if we couldn't check in? It's an entirely different relationship, mostly involves not pissing off a powerful entity, and not really any of your business. May I continue?"

"I didn't say anything," I protested.

Both brows rose above the upper edge of her glasses.

"You didn't get time," Chris pointed out.

"Please," I said, checking the phone to make sure we hadn't lost anyone, "continue."

"We don't do it often," Alyx repeated, "because around here, it's too easy to get pulled into the darkness, but Zara wanted to help, and she's old enough and powerful enough she felt she'd be safe."

Chris sighed. "She got pulled into the darkness, didn't she?"

"She did. But we think the Dark may have nudged her."

Alyx had my full attention. Odds were even between stunned silence and surprised babbling on the other end of the call.

"She saw a light in the distance."

"In the darkness?"

Alyx folded her arms and two tattoos slipped from right to left. She nodded. "In, as you say, the darkness. She went toward it. At what she considered a safe distance, she could see that it radiated out from what was essentially a young human male—and if he wasn't Travis Brayden, we're in more trouble than we thought. Zara says the light was probably some kind of protection, because although she could feel the darkness roiling around him, it couldn't actually touch him."

I raised the hand not holding the phone. "Two questions. *Essentially* a young human male?"

"He's been in the darkness since midsummer. Changes are only to be expected."

Fair. With luck, Travis was becoming more a Jeffrey than an Alice. Or an Evan, for that matter. It was better for all concerned that Evan barely interacted with people. "Okay, and did Zara see what kind of protections? I got the full monty, and there were no visible marks."

"She thought the protection was part of his essence. Is that important?"

I frowned. "I don't know. Sorry. Go on."

"Zara eased in a little closer and heard him shouting that the means of death would be theirs. Then the darkness gathered around him shouted, *Death, death, death!*"

"In English?"

"Zara didn't say, but I assume so."

"Great first word to learn," I muttered, added another *sorry*, and indicated she should continue.

"Then there was a call and response: *Are you ready?* Followed by: *Death! Death! Death!* Apparently, it went on for some time."

"If he's working them up, it's going to happen soon," Chris said thoughtfully. "Really soon. Coach doesn't get the team revved like that until just before they go on the ice."

"Really soon. Great. Then what?" I asked.

"Then nothing." Alyx ran a hand back through her hair, the fuchsia strand flicking in and out of sight. "She was sent home. Woke in her own body with a headache and a nosebleed. Debriefed the coven. I came to you."

"The means of death would be theirs," I said thoughtfully, unmuted the phone, handed it to Alyx, and ignored the shouting. The means of death. There were a lot of those. I ran my finger around the rim of a mixing bowl. The darkness was a whole different reality. How many more means of death would *they* have? I moved the flour scoop back from the edge of the work table. The means of death. I dropped a 1.24 milliliter measuring spoon into the junk drawer—what was wrong with *a pinch*? Why did we even have something that small?— and my attention was caught by a slightly bent kitchen skewer.

"Silver," I said into a pause in the shouting. I closed the drawer and turned. "Silver kills everything that emerges from the darkness. As far as they're concerned, the means of death is silver."

"And they're going to gain the means of death," Eric said. "They're going to break through and take the mine."

"That's a bit of a jump." Aunt Jean snorted.

"Is it?" Amanda asked. "Let me break it down to basics for you." It was her kindergarten-teacher voice. "Silver means death to the darkness. The darkness is going to gain that means of death, which is silver. We have silver. We also have, in the cellar, a crack that leads to the darkness. To and from. If the darkness is going to gain the means of death, aka the silver, it only makes sense they gain it from us."

"I'm not five!" Aunt Jean snapped.

"Then stop acting like it!" Amanda snapped back.

Too bad Eric wasn't physically in the bakery; I had such a look to exchange with him.

"Hang on," Chris protested. "Eldritch horrors can't handle silver. I mean, that's the irony of the Dark protecting a silver mine."

"Travis Brayden can handle silver," I reminded him.

"And the mine is automated," Eric added. "No one has to touch the ore."

"But what are they going to do with it?"

"Nothing good," Amanda said at the same time Alyx asked, "Does it matter?"

"No," Aunt Jean and I answered.

"We wouldn't let them have it even if they were going to make overpriced artisan jewelry," Aunt Jean continued. "Which they aren't."

"Then we need to get ready." I took off my apron, hung it on the hook, and stepped outside. I remembered the scramble to the Dead Ground back when this all began, and knew how quickly I could make it to the top when I had to. Sound carried from up there, so much better than it would blocked in by buildings, but no matter how fast I'd proven I could move, I didn't have that much time to waste. I hoped this worked at street level. Deep breath. Reach deep. *Think about what you're going to Say, Cassie.* "EVERYONE! THOSE WILLING AND ABLE TO DEFEND THE TOWN, MEET IN THE TOWN HALL. NOW."

As I straightened from spitting blood into the gutter, I felt a hand on my arm and turned to see my mother holding out a cup of tea. "This'll help. I found the recipe in your great-grandmother's stuff. Her mother made it for her sister. Her mother, your great-great grandmother's sister. Not your great-grandmother's."

"Okay." The tea was warm, not hot, and tasted of honey and mint, and under that swirled an earthy flavor that coated my tongue.

"Dried mushrooms," Mom said. "Four different kinds. I should have been making it all along, but . . ." *But we haven't been taking this, you, seriously.* She hadn't said it out loud, but I'd heard it. "We'll close up and meet you at the town hall. Your dad and I are here for you, Cassie."

I took the mug back into the bakery with me. Alyx glanced at it and nodded. One of her coven was an herbalist; maybe she recognized the scent. I wasn't sure my throat felt better, but the tea had erased the lingering taste of blood, so I took the win. "You, your people, don't have to be there," I began.

"Brain first, Cassie. Mouth second. This is our town, too. I'll make some calls on my way to the meeting. Besides," she added, pausing with one foot out the door, "my courage always rises at every attempt to intimidate me."

I blinked.

She sighed. "*Pride and Prejudice.*"

Of course it was. "I'm going to read it. I promise. When this is over."

The tattoo on her forearm rolled inked eyes as she left, both thumbs already working her phone. Alyx's thumbs. I wasn't sure the tattoo even had thumbs . . .

While I'd been talking to Alyx, Chris had dragged Kynda into the bakery and settled her in front of the ovens. He pointed at the ticking plastic cupcake on the counter. "When the first timer goes off?"

"I'll be at the town hall with you." She reached out and turned the ovens off. "With all due respect to the importance of baked goods, are you having a stroke?" He scooped her into a hug, and wearing a long-suffering, very teenage expression, even though we both knew Chris gave great hugs, she peered at me over the curve of his shoulder. "Cassie? I'm sorry Melanie left. She was like totally perfect for you."

I hadn't thought of Melanie in . . . minutes. I didn't mention she was back.

The three of us had almost reached the town hall when I realized Chris was carrying a bakery box.

"Cookies," he said in answer to my silent question. "Facing the apocalypse is easier with chocolate chips."

TWENTY

Melanie

Wake up!"

I clung to the tattered remnants of my dream—clever fingers and warm lips against a turquoise background. The shift to a man-bear with tentacle lips was a little confusing, but I could still feel comfort and a sense of belonging that wrapped around me like a microfiber fleece on a cold day.

I heard a hiss. Felt a fine lavender-scented mist on my face. Gasped and inhaled damp air that filled my lungs until it felt like there was no room remaining for me.

"Melanie Solvich, wake and rise!"

I had no choice. I opened my eyes and found myself sitting on the edge of the bed before I realized I wasn't alone. "Mrs. Brayden? What are you doing here?"

"It's Lammas and I'm here to finish the job."

"Lammas?" I sighed. "And here we are, back to a pagan calendar tied to pagan beliefs created by people from a different part of the world. Midsummer. Lammas. My subconscious is appallingly unimaginative." I knew what this was. This was a manifestation of my guilt for having forgotten the knife. I was still dreaming.

She stepped back and gestured to the pile of clothes I'd discarded on the floor. "Get dressed."

As Mrs. Brayden was in natural linen trousers and a navy off-the-shoulder blouse with three-quarter balloon sleeves and looked amazing, I felt that yesterday's clothes, crumpled and sweat-stained and smelling like hours of driving at the end of July with insufficient air conditioning, would put me at a distinct disadvantage. On the other hand, could you smell things in a dream? I didn't think so.

Looking at me like I'd forgotten to sprinkle the cinnamon on her low fat oat-milk chai latte, she lifted the large glass perfume bottle she held in her right hand and spritzed me in the face. "Put them on!"

I put them on. *This is one weird dream,* the me pushed to the back of my head observed.

When I was dressed, Mrs. Brayden grabbed my arm, her fingernails imprinting the skin. It hurt, but it didn't matter. "Now, tell me," she demanded. "Where is the knife?"

"I left it in the librarian's car."

"I don't care where you left it; where is it now?" she snapped.

"I don't know."

"You don't know? How long did it take you to get back here? What have you been doing?"

"Sleeping." That seemed obvious. We were standing next to the bed.

"This would be so much easier if you'd just found the knife and remained here for the length of time you were instructed to," she muttered.

"It was a suggestion," I protested. "You suggested I stay for a week."

"I don't make *suggestions.*" She glanced at a watch that probably cost as much as my car. "Fine. We have time if we move quickly." Another spritz. Yet more lavender. "Walk down the stairs to the lobby."

"Because walking up the stairs to the lobby isn't an option," I pointed out, heading into the hall. "What's with all the misting?"

"This liquid works on the same principle as the tea," Mrs. Brayden said from behind me with the kind of nonchalance that said she'd been desperate for someone to ask. "A few rarer ingredients, of course, and it's significantly more concentrated. The tea left you open to suggestion. The spray makes you compliant to my commands."

"Obedient." *"Remember the tea? You drank the tea and forgot to ask questions. This isn't a dream,"* the me shoved to the back of my head announced. *"It's real. It's happening. Why are you so calm about this?"*

"I beg your pardon?"

Why was I so calm about this? No, that was in my head. What wasn't? Right. *"Obedient* means the same thing as *compliant to commands,* but sounds less like comic-book villainy." I thought I heard her mutter about side effects, but decided not to pursue it. "Why use lavender? I mean, everything's lavender-scented these days. I bought a foam mattress topper a couple of years ago, and it had to be aired out for almost a week before I could use it."

"Lavender relaxes you." Her implication being that only an idiot wouldn't know that.

"But does it, though? Because honestly, at this point, it just makes me annoyed and—"

"Shut up." She sighed. "Just shut up."

I shut up, but I wasn't happy about it. I felt like I had things to say. I had quite a bit more to say about the omnipresence of lavender.

When I reached the lobby, I froze, unable to go any farther. *Go down the stairs to the lobby,* she'd said. Here I was.

Mrs. Brayden descended the final three steps, walked around me, and . . . spritz.

"Hold your breath!" screamed the me in the back of my head.

I didn't.

"How can you be so stupid! She told you what the spray would do!"

"All right, Melanie, let's set a few ground rules or I'm going to strangle you before we retrieve the knife, and won't that just ruin everything. You don't speak unless you're instructed—"

The lower half of the door to the owners' private quarters slammed open, hit the wall with a crash, and cut her off. "What do you think you're doing?" Theresa demanded, charging forward until she was nose to . . . chest with Mrs. Brayden. Theresa wasn't very tall, but she was furious and looked dangerous. The me in the back of my head shrieked her name. And that me had called this me stupid. She should know by now that no one could hear her. "You don't just waltz into my house," Theresa raged, "and you don't—"

Mrs. Brayden spritzed her. "Theresa Prewitt, walk into the lake. Swim past the buoys. Tell Alice I said hello."

Theresa blinked, licked her lips, turned away, and twitched. When she turned back toward us, her body language had changed. Her shoulders had squared, her eyes had narrowed, and her hands had curled into fists. "I don't think so, Cecelia. Now you're dealing with—"

"Really? You're still around?" Mrs. Brayden rolled her eyes, looking put upon. "I haven't the time for this nonsense."

"Stop her!"

My right hand twitched. Interesting. If the spray made me compliant to commands, could I command myself?

"Grab the bottle!"

Apparently not.

Her smile both mocking and triumphant, Mrs. Brayden sprayed Theresa again. "Go away, Daniel."

Theresa coughed. I didn't blame her. The lobby reeked of lavender. Her eyes widened, then rolled up until only the whites showed. When she collapsed, her head hit the tiles with a hollow melon sound.

"No, no, no, no!"

Mrs. Brayden glared down at the body like she'd been personally offended by it falling, took a step closer, and poked Theresa's leg with her foot. "It's not the lake, but I suppose it'll do for now."

For now implied there'd be a later. Theresa wasn't dead, then. That was good. I'd liked Theresa.

"She shook off the command! You saw her! If she can, you can!"

Maybe. But who was Daniel? The only Daniel I knew of, Theresa's husband, the one who used to cook at the guest house, had died.

"Come along, Melanie." Mrs. Brayden headed for the side door, sensible heels clicking against the floor. "Walk with me to my car, then get in. We need to retrieve my knife."

———

Although I could hear quiet voices coming from the nonfiction section, the librarian stood alone at the desk. I recognized her. We'd talked. Someone must have told me her name. Why couldn't I remember it?

She smiled as we approached, happy to see me. "Melanie! What are you doing back?"

"Help me!"

"She forgot my knife in your car." Mrs. Brayden pressed up against the desk and answered for me. "Where is it?"

"Are you Travis Brayden's grandmother? The one who sent Melanie to Lake Argen? I'm sorry for your loss." Glancing between us, the librarian's pale eyes widened. One step back, two, and her shoulder blades hit the reserve shelves. She hadn't gotten far enough away. Mrs. Brayden had long arms.

"Warn her!"

I couldn't.

Flashing a big public-service smile, the librarian stepped sideways. "I'm glad to see you again, Melanie, and it was nice to meet you, Mrs. Brayden, but I've got to—" A double spritz from the perfume bottle hit her in the face. She closed her eyes. Unfortunately, she didn't hold her breath. "I hate lavender."

Right? Way too much of it around.

"Where," demanded Mrs. Brayden, lifting the hinged bit of counter and walking behind it, "is my knife?"

Tiny beads of moisture decorated the librarian's pale eyelashes. She blinked. "It's locked in the Archive."

I thought the runes had upset the books.

Why did I think that?

"I'll need you with me to open the Archive, won't I?"

"Yes."

"You!" Mrs. Brayden glared at me. "Don't move. Don't speak to anyone. You!" A second glare at the librarian. "Take me to the knife."

I couldn't turn my head and watch the librarian lead Mrs. Brayden away. I heard a door open, then two sets of feet on metal treads. As I listened, the sound faded into the distance.

"Don't just stand there!" shrieked the me in the back of my head. *"Move! You have to move!"*

I couldn't. The me in the back of my head could scream all it wanted, and it certainly seemed to want to, but it made no difference.

"This is bullshit!"

The words felt familiar even if the desperation didn't. I couldn't remember saying them, although I knew I had. This is bullshit. What was bullshit?

"This!"

It was the only word that fit—

"Are you waiting for Ms. Janet?" asked a child approaching the desk with a stack of books. "She's busy sometimes when Miss Peggi isn't here, but you don't need to wait for her to come back. You can use the honor system." She walked under my eyeline and all I could see was the top of her head bobbing past. "First, you scan your library card with this green light and then, after it beeps—"

It beeped.

"—you scan your books with it. They have a sticker on the back, see?" The top edge of a book appeared and disappeared. "Then you can keep them for two weeks. But you can bring them here sooner if you read fast. I'm going to read *Black Beauty's Revenge* this afternoon. Unless we're going to the station this afternoon, you know, 'cause of the horde, then I'll take a new book, but I'll probably have to read it out loud because no one else remembered to be prepared. Okay, bye."

A gust of warm air wrapped around me as the outside door opened and closed.

"Why didn't you tell her to go for help?"

I read the titles I could see while I waited, ignoring the sweat I could feel dribbling down my sides.

"Don't just stand there! Do something! Save yourself!"

The me in the back of my head had become annoying.

Eventually, a single set of footsteps returned.

"Things should not have been this difficult, but I think we have certainly proven the adage that if you want something done right, do it yourself." Mrs. Brayden held the perfume bottle in one hand, the knife in the other. I had a bad angle, but it looked as though the angular letters carved into the handle were darker than I remembered.

"It's blood! Oh, my god, it's blood. That crazy old lady killed the librarian!"

Mind you, my memory seemed a little unreliable of late.

"Walk with me to the car." She sounded pleased. Cat-getting-the-cream pleased. "You and I, Melanie Solvich, have an appointment with destiny."

Really? Destiny?

I had so many questions.

TWENTY-ONE

Cassie

This is precisely why the Four are here!" yelled Jim Haven, the mayor, who I hadn't voted for because Chris's mother, one of my favorite people in the world, had been running against him. "It's their duty to face this oncoming horde, not ours!"

"The Dark forbid you should do anything," Amanda sneered.

"Why should I when you can do it all?" he demanded.

I also hadn't voted for him because he was an asshole.

"This has nothing to do with the day-to-day running of the town," Ms. Morton shouted from the other end of the table. "And therefore nothing to do with you, Mr. Mayor! If you're neither willing nor able to defend, why are you here? This is not about garbage pickup! In times of war, politicians give way to generals. Cassidy!"

I choked on a mouthful of cookie. I hadn't wanted to sit behind the table, on the dais, at the front of the room, but that was where the Four sat—with the mayor and the head of the mine's board of directors, facing a capacity crowd containing almost everyone in town over the age of twelve. Or younger. I could see Lillian Prewitt and Hannah Morton.

"Cassidy, you were there when Travis Brayden s-worded himself,"

Ms. Morton continued. "You were the first to acknowledge the danger. You sounded the warning. Tell us what to do."

Yeah, that wasn't happening. Beyond *defend the town and keep an army of darkness from taking the mine*, I had no idea. I mean, I knew what I was going to do. I was going to Yell a lot. The rest of them, however . . .

"Cassidy Prewitt? She's a baker!" Mayor Haven shouted.

"She's the Mouth of the Dark!" Ms. Morton shouted back.

"I am fully aware of that, Nancy! I'm saying she's not a general!"

"Enough," Aunt Jean snapped, from her seat next to the mayor. "The Four will face the horde. We defend the town; it's what we do. It's up to you lot"—her gesture included everyone crammed into the hall—"if we do it alone."

"We've all enjoyed the benefits of the Agreement," Amanda added, crushing her coffee mug into a compacted ball of cheap ceramic. I suspected she wasn't aware she was doing it, but it was a great visual.

"What about the Guardians?" called a voice from the back.

One of a group of teenagers put his hand up, and snatched it back down again when the friends surrounding him burst into laughter. "The, uh, club had drones up this morning. We noticed a lot of movement in the trees on the northeast side of the lake, so, you know, maybe Evan's heading this way."

"Yeah, but he's slow," someone pointed out. "Will he get here in time?"

"Jeffrey's just a baby," Jeffrey's grandmother wailed.

We ignored her. And by *we* I meant *everyone*. The Dark didn't make mistakes when it chose Guardians, which was why there were so few of them. Well, there were probably other reasons, like how noticeable they'd be if there was one around every corner, but as I understood it, the scarcity of people who could do the job was the main reason. Jeffrey, like every other chosen Guardian, had accepted the change. End of argument.

"I say we stop the horde before it emerges!" Uncle Stu heaved himself up onto the edge of the dais. "We get a couple of trucks of ore from the mine, I get my backhoe, and we bury the cellar, the horde, the whole thing."

This suggestion set off a barrage of shouting. Beside me, Eric had his head in his hands because he had to Listen, and that meant he could Hear everything while I could only pick out a few of the louder voices.

"That much silver will destroy the Agreement!"

"You don't know that!"

"We've known that since the beginning! I've read the first Journals!"

"Bullshit!"

I flinched at the painfully familiar expression. With any luck, by the time the horde emerged, Melanie would have retrieved the knife and be on her way to Toronto, to her ten thousand dollars, and to a wonderful life. Without me.

"Why didn't Alice warn us?"

"She told us to be ready!"

"That's not a warning; that's a platitude."

"You wouldn't know a platitude if it bit you on the ass!"

I recognized a couple of teachers from the high school, including Mrs. Boman, who'd been teaching there for so long, she might have taught Miss Peggi. She waved an ancient, duct-taped textbook like a weapon. I was fairly certain the final comment had been hers.

"What if we only bury the door in silver?"

"You're missing the point! We can't use silver at the House!"

"I've been saying for months that tradition is one thing but security is another, and both lock and door needed to be replaced with a layer of concrete." Alyx's matter-of-fact statement cut through the noise. "A thick layer of concrete."

"Cassidy," Aunt Jean murmured.

I sighed, stood up, and Said, "Be quiet."

And they were. Because they had to be. I didn't want to tell people what do to; I wanted to make pie, and hang out with Chris and Alan and Natalie, and remember how whole I felt making love to Melanie— although not at the same time—but I was the Mouth of the Dark, so . . . "We aren't an army." That seemed obvious. "We don't have time to become an army." That too. "We're . . ." in big trouble? "We're resistance fighters, and we each have our own strengths. And we are strong. We are not going to allow Travis Brayden and his army of darkness to take the mine."

No response.

Oh. Right.

"You can talk now," I Said.

"Is that where we make our stand?" someone yelled. "At the mine?"

"No." Duh. "The town is between the cellar and the mine. We stop them as they come out of the cellar, when they're all crowded together."

"Why don't you just Tell them all to drop dead?" a different someone demanded.

"Gee, why didn't I think of that?" Aunt Jean poked me, and I sighed. "Without specifics, everyone who hears me will drop dead. It'll be *step on a crack, break your mother's back* all over again."

"Then face them alone!"

"How loud will I have to be so that the whole horde hears me? How far will away will you have to be? There's too many variables I don't know."

"You don't seem to know a lot!" This someone was standing next to my Uncle Stu. It'd be his last objection of the morning.

But he was right.

"I don't know a lot," I admitted. "But do I, do any of us, need to know any more than that we have to be ready to defend our mine, our town, our lives?"

"We're ready!" Kynda punched her fist into the air.

The crowd of teenagers took it up. "We're ready! We're ready!"

Then the rest of the crowd. Most of them probably because they didn't want to be shown up by teenagers. Didn't matter. As long as they were on side. Acolytes in the crowd added harmonies.

"WE'RE READY! WE'RE READY! WE'RE READY!"

"T'geyer!"

I grinned down at the eldritch horror cuddled up on Eric's lap. "Yeah, dude. You too."

"Cassie!" A woman's voice pierced the chanting. The crowd parted, giving Theresa room to stumble forward. "Melanie . . ."

I had hold of her hands, having gone over the table rather than take the time to go around. "What about Melanie?"

"Daniel's gone!" My knuckles creaked in her grip. "She sent him away!"

"Melanie did?"

"No, Cecelia!"

"Who?"

But Theresa was no longer looking at me; she stared past me at Aunt Jean.

So, we all turned to stare at Aunt Jean.

Who didn't look happy.

She took a deep breath, braced herself on the table, and stood. "Seventy-eight years ago," she began.

Then the crowd parted again and Bridget, sweat plastering her bright pink crop top to her like a second skin, ran up and grabbed my shoulders. "Cassie," she gasped, "I was at the Dead Ground with Jeffrey—who seems to think you're a bit of an idiot, though he won't tell me why. I think he's sulking. But that's not important now." She took a deep breath, glanced around, and said, "The drums have stopped."

"You should've called!" Aunt Jean told her.

"No signal!"

Everyone reached for their phones and the combined, shocked inhalation sucked enough air out of the room that I felt dizzy.

———

There was a car already in the parking lot when our column of overstuffed vehicles—six, seven and eight people crammed in each one, twelve in Vic's truck—raced past the red flag. The horde hadn't yet arrived. We had time to prepare. Build barricades. Dig trenches. Sing *Les Misérables*.

I untangled myself from Aunt Jean and T'geyer, forced myself through the half-open car door, and would have hit the gravel on my knees had Amanda not grabbed my arm and kept me on my feet. She swung me around to face the cellar, and any protest I may have made about being Handled died when I saw Melanie and another older woman on the roof, shuffling forward, toward the edge.

The other woman held a familiar knife at Melanie's throat, and Melanie looked . . . stoned. Like she could barely stay on her feet.

"Get your hands off of her!" I Yelled, struggling against Amanda's grip.

"Your words have no power over me, Cassidy Prewitt." The other woman had positioned Melanie in front of her like a shield. I could see her hand and the knife and little else. "If you try to breach my mystical defenses, I will slit this girl's throat."

"Mystical defenses? Seriously?" asked Amanda behind me.

"Girl?" asked the teen with the drone. "Rude. She's like thirty."

"Let her go!" I Shouted.

"No." I couldn't see her smile, but I could hear it. Who the hell was she? How was I going to save Melanie if the Voice didn't work?

"Save your strength, Cassie." Amanda gave me a shake. "You'll need it. Melanie will need it."

I closed my mouth, sucked blood off my teeth, and locked my eyes on the knife so close, too close, to the pale skin of Melanie's throat. I didn't need the Voice, I decided. Given half a chance, I was going to punch that woman in the face. The crowd of townspeople stood by the cars, silent for the most part, radiating unhappiness about my failure to Talk the older woman around.

"I am so pleased to see you all gathered here to witness my triumph." She shifted her feet but remained shielded behind Melanie. "You'll be able to watch me advance at the head of an army, leading them to domination in first this world and then the next."

"I thought Travis Brayden was leading the army," someone yelled.

Seriously, when this was over, someone was going to get a kick in the ass for all these interruptions.

"He gathered the army," she replied smugly. "I shall lead it!"

"I know that knife!" Peter, the blacksmith, bellowed.

"No, you don't. You may have seen it before, but you don't know it. I found the ancient instructions. I had it made. I carved *I open the way* on this blade to pierce the barrier between this world and the darkness. All it needs is blood. Travis's blood, my descendant's blood, spilled to enter the darkness. This one's blood, an outsider's blood, untainted by the Agreement, to release my army. Blood is always the way."

Smug, sanctimonious, and playing with a deck of jokers. Would she wave the knife triumphantly in the air, giving me a chance to get to Melanie?

No.

Damn.

"Who are you?" I demanded.

"Cecelia Foster," said Aunt Jean beside me, leaning heavily on her cane. "Seventy-eight years ago, she was banished from Lake Argen for attempting to break the Agreement."

"I wanted to make a better one!" Cecelia Foster snarled. "One that would allow us all to rise up and take the place we deserve!" I saw her fingers tighten on the knife, and stopped breathing until they relaxed again.

"You were the only one who wanted that," Aunt Jean scoffed. "And you got what you deserved."

"Seventy-eight years ago?" My fingers flicked as I did the math in my head. "That would make her—"

"Old," Eric said.

"Oool," T'geyer repeated.

Oool. I frowned. A possibility struggled to surface.

"She's a hundred and two," said Aunt Jean.

And it was gone.

"She looks good," Amanda admitted. "Why wasn't she Told to forget?"

"Oh, I was Told to forget; forget my family, my friends, my life, ambition. Unfortunately, all that forgetting resulted in a bit of instability, which led, in time, to electroshock therapy." Cecelia Foster shifted her feet again, but this time, the shift rippled through her whole body. A tiny dribble of blood ran down Melanie's neck. Amanda maintained her hold on me while I tried not to hyperventilate. "Imagine my surprise when my memories sprouted and blossomed, opening up a whole new and amazing world. I felt so much better afterward that—"

"That you took up the study of sorcery." The crowd parted to let Arthur through. He was dressed in his ubiquitous worn cords and ratty sweater, his hair looked amazing, and I had no memory of ever seeing him away from the motel. "According to our agent in the area at the time," he continued, as he joined the Four of us out in front of Eric's car, "you were near the bottom of your class in the University of Guelph's Unnatural Philosophy program." I had a feeling that program wasn't on the university's website. "You barely managed to graduate, your low marks primarily a result of you ignoring the approved curriculum in order to concentrate on creating defenses against the

Four. Although records show you had a certain affinity for potion work."

A sliver of expensively dyed hair appeared from behind Melanie's head. "Who are you?"

"Arthur Nollen." He folded skinny arms. "From MAD."

"Mothers Against Drunk Drivers?" a confused voice called from the crowd.

"An impressively successful organization," said someone else. It might have been Mrs. Boman.

A murmur of agreement followed. The relief of arriving to find no emerging horde had made some of the crowd a little giddy. Not me, though, because I was staring at a knife held against Melanie's throat.

"We're the Metaphysical Abnormalities Division," Arthur snapped, sounding more like himself.

"I've never heard of you." Ms. Morton's tone made it clear that if she'd never heard of it, it didn't exist. "Division of what?"

"It's classified, toots." And there he was.

"They're a myth!" Cecelia Foster called out before Ms. Morton could react. "A bureaucratic bogeyman used for years to control the practice of sorcery. Don't raise an undead army. Don't subvert the will of thousands. Don't experiment with the water supply of a major city. Don't embrace your power at all or MAD will get you! But does MAD ever step in? No!"

"No undead armies. No subverted thousands. No inhabitants of Vancouver turned into dinosaurs." Arthur's lips drew off his teeth in what might have been a smile. "Cecelia Foster married Samuel Brayden for his money. Had a son. Might have lived happily ever after except she came across an ancient text that taught her how to gather an army of darkness with no actual danger to herself. We've been looking for that book for a while, by the way." He directed his non-smile at Cecelia. "MAD has removed it from your library."

Her smile had jagged edges. "Too late."

"True. You'd fallen off our radar until Ms. Solvich told me who was paying her, then we started doing some research. Your son was too old to take the kind of protections that would slip past our notice—full-body tattoos using actual eldritch designs ring alarm bells—so as soon as he produced a child, you murdered your son and his wife. We assume you dosed the wife with eldritch potions while she was pregnant and then kept dosing the child. His protections are internal."

"Hold on for a minute, Arthur." Amanda released me and stepped forward. "If you found out she murdered her son and his wife, why don't you get the police involved?"

"Wasn't a mystical abnormality, was it? And I have my own problems, don't I?"

"You run a motel!"

"Yeah, so I can keep an eye on Lake Argen. Or on people heading into Lake Argen who might take advantage of the situation because you lot are contained, mostly harmless, and so fucking Canadian that half the time, home office doesn't believe my reports."

"Oh, yes," Cecelia hissed, "talk amongst yourselves. Ignore me." Another line of blood ran down Melanie's throat.

"We're not ignoring you," I told her, arms spread, embracing her crazy. I leaned sideways until I could poke Arthur. "Why Melanie?"

"No idea," he grunted. "Ms. Foster?"

"Why not Melanie?" She sighed. "I had to send someone to retrieve the knife, I certainly couldn't do it myself, and I overheard her mother talking about how she needed work. Once I waved that ten thousand dollars in front of her, I barely needed the potion to keep her from asking questions. A little annoying when she returned early, yes, but I dosed her again, sent her and her untainted blood back, and here we are, waiting for noon."

Why noon? Symbolism? So the darkness could destroy the day?

It didn't matter.

And it wouldn't matter, because Jeffrey heaved himself up onto the roof behind her. His claws screeched against the metal that creaked under his weight.

Cecelia turned just enough to be able to see him, the movement shifting her out from behind Melanie—

A red dot showed on her forehead for an instant, and then the top of her skull blew off, blood and brains spraying out over the steel.

"It's like she thought we didn't have any actual security," Aunt Jean sneered.

Jeffrey had scooped Melanie up, burying her screams against his chest. My heart started beating again. She was safe. She was probably the safest of any of us as the first dribble of Cecelia Foster's blood ran off the roof and dripped onto the door.

The door crumpled. The lock, still locked, bounced off into the grass.

"What about blood untainted by the Agreement?" someone yelled. "What about the knife? What about noon?"

"Did I not say that she barely managed to graduate?" Arthur growled.

An army of nightmare creatures began surging up and out of the basement, the darkness itself taking shape. It wasn't that the creatures were individually horrific—we'd all seen things—it was that they were wrong. Wrong in a visceral, emotional, impossible way. And as more creatures emerged snarling and snapping, oozing and flopping, defying reality, the wrongness grew.

They. Didn't. Belong. Here.

My skin crawled. I could feel a greasy patina of wrongness coat my throat and lungs with every breath—hopefully all imagination, but did it matter? I felt it. I had to fight against it.

The wrongness grew to become another creature we had to fight.

"At least they're leaderless," Eric said, as T'geyer growled.

From out of the cellar came a howl of triumph. "I FELT THE DEATH OF GRANNY! MY CHAINS ARE BROKEN! I AM LEADER NOW!"

Travis Brayden. What goes around, comes around.

"ATTACK!"

TWENTY-TWO

Melanie

I screamed when I saw him. Arms too long, too many fingers with raptor claws, tentacled mouth; his proportions were wrong, grotesque. His eyes were blue. His eyes were human.

And they were kind.

Over my screaming I heard a *crack*.

Something hot splashed against my cheek.

I heard a wet thud and the clang of metal on metal.

He held me close, and I stopped screaming. Fingers clutching red-gold fur, I remembered blueberry stains on a claw left by a crow. I remembered sunlight on the water of a lake. I remembered dark hair that stuck out in all directions. I remembered laughing. I remembered feeling like I belonged.

I remembered everything.

"Jeffrey?"

"Elllinee."

And I believed everything.

After Mrs. Brayden's lavender-scented mind control, it wasn't hard. Being forced to stand motionless with a knife held against my throat, knowing I was about to die, made what I thought was unbelievable unimportant. An Agreement with the Dark for cell service? Why not. It made more sense than a Rosedale lady-who-lunched trying to kill me.

I believed Cassie.

But did I believe in Cassie?

Under all the weirdness and the terror, she was still the same person I'd shared meals with. Laughed with. Slept with.

I still wanted her. But I'd wanted her when I'd been furious with her, so not really relevant.

Cassie could have Told me to forget the knife, and we could have gone on like we'd planned. She didn't need to take the risk of me rejecting her history of Lake Argen; she could have Told me to believe her.

She could have Told me to love her.

She didn't.

And now she was facing . . . actually, I had only the vaguest idea of what she was facing, but I wanted to face it with her. I wanted to be a permanent part of the weirdness that was her life.

First, I had to find out what was going on.

When I tried to turn my head toward where memory put Mrs. Brayden, Jeffrey stopped me with a blueberry-stained claw. He was, I remembered, a vegan. Had the crow been giving me a heads-up? Had it known? Did it matter? He was Cassie's naked vegan buddy. I tried to turn my head again, and again Jeffrey blocked me.

"Yoou nooo lookkk."

The *k*s were coughed out, more throat-clearing than the actual sound of a letter, but he wasn't hard to understand. He didn't want me to look.

Another *crack*. Followed by howling, shrieking, and a hundred sounds I couldn't identify.

Jeffrey started to scoop me up, but this time I stopped him. "If there's going to be a fight—"

"I FELT THE DEATH OF GRANNY! MY CHAINS ARE BRO-KEN! I AM LEADER NOW!"

"—I need the knife."

He nodded. "Eee iiight." Holding me in the curve of one arm, he stretched out the other. The steel roof shrieking under his claws, he grabbed the knife. "Eee goo nauw," he declared, and handed it over. Still holding me in just one arm, he stood like I weighed nothing at all, then jumped off the roof into a writhing mass of . . .

Things. *Things*, I decided, was a perfectly fine description. Details were very much not necessary. Slashing out with his free arm, claws dripping black and green and red, Jeffrey forced his way forward. He'd managed ten, maybe twelve steps when a cross between a tentacle and an arm wrapped around my leg, the talons on multi-jointed fingers snagging on my skirt, the points unable to deal with cheap polyester.

I jabbed the knife down into the fleshiest bit I could see, and it slid in like it was going into soft butter. It sliced easily through the tenta-cle/arm until the upper half dangled from the snagged talons. It felt like the greasy debris of a Christmas turkey left four months in a for-gotten roasting pan when I yanked it free. If there'd been anything in my stomach, I'd have thrown it up.

Cassie's voice rose above the noise, above the near-deafening pound-ing of my heart. "Blue creature with six arms and elbow horns, die!"

At the edge of my peripheral vision, a blue creature with six arms and elbow horns died. That was . . . specific. Would a simple *Drop dead* take out anyone who heard it? I'd heard it. Jeffrey had heard it.

When he reached a point where I'd be in no immediate danger, Jeffrey put me down.

"Iiight nauw, tgeeeyer!"

Fight now, together! Why not? I had a dull knife that cut flesh like butter, had it been able to cut butter. "Be careful!"

His entire mouthful of tentacles quivered when he laughed, then he jumped back into the chaos. With both hands free, he cut a wide swath through lesser creatures heading for a huge . . . Yeah, I was going back to *thing*. Off to one side I saw a group of old ladies with cable knitting needles—stab, stab, strangle. I saw Daffodil lock her massive jaws around a bare-bones rib cage, crushing the bones and the throbbing organs they held. Dexter—I assumed the identical dog next to her was Dexter—snapped at a squat toad-like creature and swallowed the upper half. Here and now, it was obvious, even to me, that they weren't exactly dogs.

"Fill your belly when we're done, Dex!" yelled a dark-haired man who had to be Cassie's Uncle Stu. He pulled the trigger on a pump-action shotgun and sprayed an attacking spider/giraffe with a whole lot of tiny pieces . . .

. . . of silver.

All the weapons wielded by the people of Lake Argen had been augmented with silver.

Of course they had.

One of the kids I'd seen in town held a silver lance and yelled directions at the two kids pushing his chair toward a slow-moving purple/black blob. Race in. Puncture. Pull back. Race in. Puncture. Pull back. Avoid the leaking ooze. Drones armed with whirling silver blades flew at any writhing body part that rose above the crowd. Half the time, the drones were knocked to pieces by the impact, but I saw a group of teenagers with remotes getting more into the air. Above the drones, a flock of ravens wheeled and dove and destroyed anything that flew.

"Target to your right, Flight Sergeant!" Standing on the roof of a car, Reggie Morton waved a pair of black triangular flags. "Squadron! Execute maneuver delta omega!"

The ravens separated and re-formed and ripped a pair of enormous wings to shreds. I watched the pieces fall. There appeared to be no body. Just wings.

At the edge of the park, Vic in his truck worked with the sidewalk-resurfacing machine to run over anything that tried to run/lurch/slither away.

I'd almost reached Cassie when a very old woman pulled a slender silver sword from her cane—a four-pronged aluminum cane with tennis balls, not fancy wood—and yelled, "I See you! Can't fool me with a glamour!" She stabbed nothing. Nothing became something dead. Cackling, she shuffled deeper into the fight.

A middle-aged woman in pink capris grabbed a pair of creatures by their heads, one in each hand, and smashed them together like they were raw eggs. I was pretty sure both things she held were heads; they were where heads were supposed to be.

Eric—I'd met Eric; he'd driven me to the motel back in what felt like a previous life—Eric wore noise-canceling headphones and worked another pump-action shotgun, shattering bodies that shouldn't have existed. Memory brought up the voice of the crazy survivalist biology teacher I'd worked with in Saskatoon declaring that a shotgun had more coverage than a rifle. That seemed obvious now. Lines of blood dribbled down Eric's neck from under the headphones.

They didn't seem to be helping much.

I could hear chanting.

I could hear Cassie Speak.

"Travis Brayden, drop dead!"

"CAN'T HEAR YOU. NAH NAH."

She'd been Yelling that intermittently as I moved toward her. Tell a specific creature to drop dead. Tell Travis Brayden to drop dead. I understood the random capitalization now.

Another very old woman used a large textbook wrapped in duct tape as a weapon.

Off to one side, a circle of nine robed women walked widdershins, the enemy vanishing in a flash of light when they charged forward—drawn to the circle and nullified by it. I thought I saw Alyx, from the bookstore, but they were moving too fast for me to be sure. The woman from the secondhand store had tied silver fish knives to the ends of skipping ropes, throwing them like bolos. Given the eyepatch and her choice of weapon, she was surprisingly accurate. Someone in tie-dye held two spray bottles of colloidal silver, using them to finish off any stray pieces still moving or trying to reform. Chris, Cassie's partner from the bakery, used a silver tray as both a shield and a weapon, as if Luke Cage had taken up the mantle of Captain America. Cassie's parents were fighting together, her mother shooting, her father reloading.

I looked toward a flash of color off to my right.

I looked again. "Are those Oompa Loompas?"

"Yes." Cassie closed the final distance between us, wrapped me in her arms, and buried her head in my chest.

"Sweetheart, I can't breathe."

She eased off and lifted her head. "You're not dead."

"I'm not dead," I agreed, wiping away the tears running down her cheeks with my thumb.

"You're hurt." Fingers trembling, she touched my throat. "I couldn't stop her."

"It's okay." It wasn't. We were reuniting in the midst of a battle against eldritch forces that vastly outnumbered us, and nothing in that sentence would have made sense a week ago. But also, it was. "We'll talk later."

"Yeah."

A tentacle whipped out and curled around her neck. I sliced through it and kicked the piece away.

Cassie smiled. "I am so into you right now." Her teeth were streaked with red. Blood had crusted in the corners of her mouth. Black viscous fluid dribbled down her arm. She was beautiful.

"Same."

"You remember?"

"Everything. Seeing Jeffrey brought it back." It had been slightly more complicated, but now was not the time. I jerked back as something about the size of a German shepherd leapt past us and onto the creature about to attack. Almost too fast to see, it disemboweled both halves of the pulsing torso, then hung for a moment, the claws on the end of one long arm hooked in the dying creature's eye socket. It was clearly on our side and weirdly adorable, with little clumps of tentacles for ears.

Holding Cassie's hand, I kept the knife ready as she Shouted. "Travis Brayden, drop dead!"

"STILL CAN'T HEAR YOU, BITCH!"

"Pale green creature that looks like a fifty-kilo three-headed Canada goose, drop dead."

"We could use some Canada geese on our side," I muttered as it fell.

We weren't without our own casualties. At least one raven was down, a spray of black feathers marking the gravel where it had impacted. I couldn't see the old woman with the textbook, although I could see the textbook lying open, half the pages flicking in the wind, half a red-brown mass. Arthur from the motel, who, surprise, surprise, was some kind of government agent, seemed to be running a med tent out by the road, and the teenagers who'd run out of functional drones were carrying people to doctors and nurses who worked on the injured. The shotgun blasts continued, but how much ammunition did they have?

Dexter yelped. Daffodil roared.

Cassie spat blood. "We could win if there weren't so many of them."

I glanced toward the thick of the fighting and through a break in the crowd saw what looked like smoke roiling up from the cellar, solidifying into a bat/pig after it moved through the legs of the vaguely human shape straddling the wreckage. I remembered Cassie saying the darkness was a different reality. It looked like it didn't have a physical shape until it emerged. That explained the spider/giraffe.

Actually, no, it didn't.

"Can we plug the hole?" I wondered.

"With what?" Cassie demanded.

"With a backhoe load of silver ore!" Cassie's Uncle Stu yelled. He pulled his phone from his pocket, had it slapped from his hand by a—still going with *thing*—and dove into the melee to find it.

I pulled a crumpled napkin from my pocket and handed it to Cassie so she could wipe her mouth. "Will that work?"

"If he can get hold of someone at the mine. In the meantime, we have to keep fighting!"

The weirdly adorable thing paused with one long arm thrust deep inside a seeping wound ripped in the side of its opponent's torso. "Tgeyer! Oor t'geyer!"

"T'geyer's their name," Cassie told me. "They yell it every time they hear someone say *fight* or *fighting*. It was the first word we heard them say." She winced as the weirdly adorable thing pulled out a pulsing body part.

A leg with too many knees landed at my feet.

"Ooooreee!" Jeffrey called.

I stomped on the leg until it stopped twitching. Jeffrey had said, *"Iii-ight nauw, tgeeyer."* A little more emphasis on the *e* but the same word from a mouth no longer made for human speech. *Fight now, together.*

The weirdly adorable thing kept calling out, "Oor tgeyer." *Oor together.* It was the first thing Cassie heard them say, and they kept saying it. That meant it was important. What could be that important?

"Creature that looks like a giant slug with grasshopper legs, drop dead!"

The Four.

Oor tgeyer.

Four together.

"Cassie, did T'geyer come out of the cellar?"

"No. There was small crack in the cemetery. It's sealed now. Why?"

"He's a messenger from the Dark. Your Dark."

"Yeah, thanks, we figured that out ourselves."

I crammed the last piece into place. "The Four are supposed to fight together! *Oor. T'geyer.* Together."

"We are fighting together. Eric. Amanda. Aunt Jean." She pointed them out with a hand smeared in red. "We're all fighting!"

"T'geyer!"

There wasn't time to convince her. Darkness kept billowing and re-forming, and silver could only do so much. I grabbed Cassie's wrist and dragged her over to Eric, shouting, "Jeffrey, bring Amanda and Aunt Jean here!" Not my aunt, but not important right now.

"Tgeeeyer!"

"You said it, Jeffrey!" How long had he been saying it? Again, not important right now. Recriminations could happen later.

"What are you doing?" Cassie tried unsuccessfully to dig her heels in, but I had size and inspiration on my side.

"Outsider point of view," I told her. "Do you trust me?"

She stared at me for a long moment, and I remembered I hadn't trusted her when it counted. Shit. How could I ask her to— "Yes. I trust you. What do I need to do?"

"First, get Eric's attention without getting shot."

She poked Eric's shoulder, then when he turned toward her, grabbed his shotgun, yelled "Bridget!" and tossed it to a blonde in a bright pink crop top who'd just run out of ammo. Not quite what I'd intended, but whatever. It worked. Eric looked confused but not as confused as the old woman with the slender sword or the middle-aged woman in the pink capris when Jeffrey dropped them beside us then returned to fight. The weirdly adorable thing joined him, swinging a length of intestine. I gagged, beginning to miss the smell of lavender.

"Now, see here," the old woman began.

"No time for that, Aunt Jean," Cassie Said, gripping my arm. "Trust Melanie."

"The Four are supposed to fight together," I told them, pushing and shoving and nearly getting a sword point through the foot. "Get in close, shoulders touching, and grab hold of each other's wrists."

I peered over Cassie's shoulder to check they'd made as much contact as possible, reached in, and yanked the silver sword out from the old woman's hand and pulled it out of the circle.

"What do you think you're doing, young woman!"

"The Dark is of the darkness!" I couldn't believe I'd just said that. "It's not going to like silver."

Nothing happened.

Why was nothing happening? I checked again. Full contact. Mouth, Eyes, Hands . . .

"I've had about enough of . . ."

Ears! The headphones! While obviously not blocking all sound, they were clearly blocking enough. Sticky with blood, they made a disgusting sucking sound as I yanked them off Eric's head. His shoulders rose to try and block the noise—the yelling, the shrieking, the wet noise the thing with the nozzle face was making.

For them to be Four, he had to be able to Hear.

Still nothing.

Was I wrong?

"STOP! STOP THEM!"

Travis Brayden didn't think I was wrong. Maybe not the best affirmation . . .

The flash of dark, like a flash of light, only dark and with substance, threw me backward. My ass squashed a random lump of oozing flesh. I lost my grip on the sword but clutched the knife like it was the final piece of pizza in the staff room. Arm raised to block debris thrown up by the sudden blast of wind, I blinked red and purple afterimages away and tried to figure out what was going on.

The wind stopped.

The noise stopped.

I lowered my arm.

Where the Four had stood—where Cassie had stood—was a figure so dark it absorbed the light that hit it. It was about six meters tall with arms and legs and a head. A silhouette without features against a surprisingly blue and cloudless sky.

I SEE.

I FEEL.

I HEAR.

I SPEAK.

I peed myself a little.

YOU SEDUCED AWAY WHAT WAS MINE, TRAVIS BRAYDEN.

The thought of Travis Brayden, who was human, seducing anything like what we'd been fighting was just . . . eww.

YOU TOLD THEM LIES OF CONQUEST.

Oh. Not physically seducing. Still, eww.

HERE, YOU HAVE NO PROTECTIONS.

It wasn't shouting; it didn't need to shout. I felt the squashed flesh under me vibrating along with the sound, and lurched up onto my knees.

It . . . walked. *Walked* had to be close enough, because English didn't have a word for how it moved. German might. German had a number of useful words. Unfortunately, I didn't speak German.

It walked toward the cellar, destroying every creature it passed. It smacked one hand down on the cellar entrance, collapsing it, and snatched Travis Brayden up with the other. I had a second to realize that Travis hadn't been able to hear Cassie because he had no ears, and that both his eyeballs jostled against each other in one socket, before the Dark slapped him against its chest and absorbed him.

Travis screamed and kept screaming.

After fifteen or twenty seconds that felt like days, he stopped.

If Arthur and his organization were right, his grandmother had started dosing him with potions in the womb. If they'd included anything like what she'd given to me, he'd had no choice at all in going along with her plans. Her death had released his chains. I felt sorry for him. Not sorry enough to wish he was alive—he had, after all, taken command of Granny's army—but sorry.

In the sudden silence, what had been a battle looked like a group of people playing a particularly ugly game of statues.

The lack of a face didn't keep the Dark from looking down at Jeffrey and T'geyer.

GUARDIAN. MESSENGER. JOIN ME.

It was a slaughter after that.

The people of Lake Argen and I moved back behind a barricade of parked cars and watched. The Dark did most of the work, its limbs extending to capture anything that ran, but Jeffrey and T'geyer looked like they were enjoying themselves. The horde fell to literal pieces in a surprisingly short time.

"Okay," Alyx said softly, having moved up beside me. "Now, how do we get it to go away?"

"Banishing spell?"

"Sure. We can modify the one we use for bedbugs."

"Really?"

"No."

The chanting, a constant, strangely inspiring subtext under the fight, grew louder.

The Dark pointed what wasn't quite a finger at a small clump of people in stained robes. **YES. KEEP MAKING THAT SOUND.**

I couldn't have been the only one who suspected they wouldn't be able to stop.

"By the authority of the Metaphysical Abnormalities Division . . ." Arthur's voice trailed off as the Dark bent over him.

YOU HAVE NO AUTHORITY HERE, BROWNIE.

"That actually makes a certain amount of sense," Alyx muttered.

I assumed he wasn't going to grow up and become a Girl Guide. Good thing; I like Girl Guides, and that fucker had drugged me . . . so I'd answer his questions? He could've tried asking first, but oh, no, straight to mind-altering substances. I didn't care if his basis for violating consent was because he was a sort of cop or because he was a paranormal entity; if we both survived this, we were going to have words.

And I was done accepting tea from strangers.

I MUST HAVE MORE.

Someone in the crowd asked, "More what?"

If the Dark Heard, and it had to have, given Eric, it paid no attention. Grass dying where it walked, it headed for the path to the Dead Ground.

"What can it do up there?" asked a different voice.

"Anything it wants," said Cassie's Uncle Stu. "Same thing as it can do down here. Probably just going for the high ground to get a look at its new territory." He cradled as much of Dexter as possible in his arms. The dog struggled for breath, blood dripping from the end of his hanging tongue, most of his tentacle tail missing.

"Come on." Alyx grabbed my arm. "We can see the top of the cliff from over here."

Everyone still ambulatory followed, and by the time we reached a spot where we could see, the Dark was standing on the stone at the edge of the cliff, arms spread.

THIS WILL ALL BE MINE. THERE WILL BE A NEW AGREEMENT.

Tentacles rose up out of the lake. Fifteen, twenty; they moved too quickly for me to count. And these weren't cute little mouth or ear tentacles but the kind that could pull down a fully rigged ship, all the more terrifying because they moved with purpose.

"Holy shit!" Kynda, the teenager from the bakery, slapped both hands over her mouth. I couldn't argue with her reaction. How did the lake have room for water?

"Alice!" Many voices shouted her name. "Alice can take him!"

"Alice is a squ—" A filthy hand clamped over my mouth and four more grabbed hold of various body parts.

"Not a . . . one of those," Alyx said, waving the others off me. "She's a little sensitive about that word."

Whatever she was, Alice couldn't quite reach the top of the cliff. Those cheering her on might be right, she might be able to take on the Dark, but only if it was stupid enough to go closer to the water.

ENOUGH, GUARDIAN.

Alice didn't like being told what to do, and for all that they were nothing more than giant tubes of muscle, her tentacles were expressive. After making her opinion clear, they eased back to the other side of the lake and snapped forward.

Closer.

Not close enough.

The Dark laughed, and had I anything left in my bladder, I'd have peed a little more.

I heard a rumble, like thunder in the distance.

YOU WILL NOT—

It flew forward, like it had been blasted off the cliff.

Alice caught It.

On the edge of the cliff stood something that looked like a moose the same way Jeffrey looked like a bear.

"Evan!" The group of teenagers jumped up and down and waved.

Evan stomped a clawed hoof, tossed enormous hand-shaped antlers, ripped a bush from the ground with his tail, and ripped it to shreds. I was starting to figure this place out. Had I been close enough to see them, his eyes would be human.

Out over the lake, Alice flexed and ripped the Dark into four pieces. The shock wave knocked most of us off our feet.

Once more, I scrambled up onto my knees.

The Dark was gone. The tentacles were gone. Four bodies were falling toward the water.

"CASSIE!"

TWENTY-THREE

Cassie

I was no longer a part of a greater whole. No longer stretched beyond my limit to hold universes within me. No longer Voice and Voice alone.

I was myself.

And I was falling toward the lake from an uncomfortable distance up.

Well, fuck.

TWENTY-FOUR

Melanie

We found them draped over the line of buoys, chins resting on individual bright yellow floats.

Cassie blinked blearily at me as I reached her.

"Are you hurt?" It was hard to check for injuries underwater, but I tried. Arms and legs seemed to be in one piece. "How?" I asked when I surfaced.

She made a tiny wave with her floating hand and rasped out something that sounded like "Alice."

"Alice caught you?" I hadn't seen the impact. I'd already kicked off my ichor-covered sandals and been racing for the beach.

"Ish." Her voice caught in her throat, sounding like she'd just had her tonsils removed. "Alice is an ass."

The man working on Eric shot her a panicked look.

I checked her pupils, not entirely certain of what I was supposed to see, and kissed the corner of her mouth. She tasted like lake water and the future. "Let's get you to shore before you tempt fate."

The water lapped my chin at the buoys. It would have been eye level or higher on Cassie, so I carried her to shore. I didn't see who carried the other Three. To be honest, I didn't give a rat's ass about the other Three, not when I had Cassie in my arms. I staggered a little when the water dropped to waist height and had to put her down, holding her against my body with an arm around her waist. Alyx waded in, slipped her shoulder under Cassie's arm, and together we got her to dry land.

"Even my hair hurts," she mumbled as we laid her down.

"Anything else?"

"Everything else. But I'm okay."

A bit bruised, a bit battered, but basically okay.

It seemed I needed to start believing in miracles along with everything else.

Voices rose up around me in a comforting babble as people worked together to reclaim the Four. Jean had broken an arm, and Eric had cracked a rib. Possibly two. Amanda seemed in the same shape as Cassie. None of them should have been alive. Not from that height.

The lake had washed the blood off Cassie's teeth and Eric's ears. Given our afternoon, it wasn't a stretch to assume blood had been washed off the other two as well. Washed off into the lake. Given to Alice.

Maybe Mrs. Brayden / Cecelia Foster had been right about the importance of blood.

I touched the knife wound on my throat.

After helping Cassie to sit up, I kissed her gently and stood. "Don't go anywhere," I told her. "There's something I have to do."

Aware of eyes on me and the growing attention of the crowd as I walked out into the water, I could hear voices rising. Questions. Speculation. No one tried to stop me.

Hip-deep, I stopped. "Hey, Alice!"

Someone's voice rose out of the background noise. "What is she—"

"Shhh," Said Cassie.

Waves began to rise and fall on the other side of the buoys.

I pressed the wound on my throat, hard enough to make it bleed, then dipped my hand in the lake and washed the blood off my fingers. "Thank you for catching her. Them."

Something patted my ankle. Once. Twice. It might have been a fish, but with Alice in the lake, I very much doubted it. Apparently, the buoys were more of a guideline, a promise people would be safe inside them, but nothing more.

No one spoke as I walked back to the beach and dropped to my knees by Cassie's side.

She grabbed a fistful of my shirt. "I'm still the Mouth of the Dark."

"I know." I wanted to kiss the doubt off her face. "Mrs. Brayden thought nothing of forcing me to obey, not only today but every time she spoke to me. While it wasn't her intention, she trained me to recognize what happens when power creates a monster that cares only about themselves. Cassie, I can tell the difference between you and Mrs. Brayden, and I am ninety-nine point nine percent sure you'll never abuse your power."

"How can you be that sure?"

"I'm sure of you."

Her eyes widened. "So, you're staying?"

I thought of saying something witty, something clever enough that when the people listening thought of me later, that's what would come to mind. I didn't. I said, "Yes."

They cheered when we kissed. Why not. After the day we'd had, they needed something to cheer about.

After a while, I vaguely heard laughter and voices suggesting people stop staring. A while after that, we separated until only our noses touched.

Cassie smiled.

I smiled back at her.

Then I remembered.

"Mrs. Brayden killed Janet and left her body in the Archive!"

"Are you sure?" She clutched at my clothes. "Did you see the body?"

"No, but I saw the two of them go downstairs and only Mrs. Brayden come up, holding a bloody knife. *The* knife!"

"I'll check." One of the men kneeling around Amanda as she coughed out lake water stood. "I'm on the Library Board."

"Be careful," Cassie warned him.

He nodded and ran off.

"What does being on the Library Board—" I began.

Cassie cut me off. "The locks will recognize him."

Okay. We'd deal with that later. "Be careful of what?"

"Of a bloody librarian left in an archive of powerful books." Cassie patted my cheek with a sandy hand. "Janet might be dead, but she's fine."

And life carried on around us.

TWENTY-FIVE

Cassie

Three months after Travis Brayden's attempt to replace his grandmother in her plan to do whatever it was the crazy lady was planning to do—after *Rah rah, let's capture the silver mine*, things seemed a little undefined—I watched Melanie lay a raven feather on the newly finished monument. She pressed her palm against the stone for a moment before stepping back. It was warm for early November, so instead of a jacket, she wore a cable sweater my mother had knit for my father which had never fit him and looked better on Melanie anyway. We were still working on her money issues; she wouldn't let me just buy her stuff, but gifts from my family, citing the coming winter, now filled her half of the closet. My family loved Melanie, because my family had excellent taste.

I still hadn't said anything about how I'd Told her to believe me back at the cellar. Fortunately for me, it had turned out to be location-specific, since she definitely hadn't felt obligated to believe me later at the library. Would I ever tell her? I didn't see the point.

It had been for her own good at the time.

And it was way past when I could drop it casually into conversation.

You couldn't build a relationship on lies, but I very much doubted one had ever existed without a few stuffed into the superstructure.

Moving away from the abstract sculpture of stone and silver, she stopped to talk to Uncle Stu and the dogs, causing Dexter to thrash his regrown tail in excitement and nearly knock her off her feet. She stumbled and looked up, and I waved. It was worth being apart, even for only a few hours, just to see her reaction. One last pat for the dogs, a return wave to let me know I should stay put, and she started toward me.

Only to be stopped by Alyx and promptly tangled in Mulder and Zod's leads. Melanie got along better with Alyx than I ever did, but then, Melanie had read *Pride and Prejudice*. All the way through. Disregarding the total absence of zombies. The corgis thought she was the greatest thing since liver treats, and even the bookstore ghost liked her better. The current conversation included a fair bit of enthusiastic hand-waving, a peal of laughter, and a hug before separating.

Arthur, who spent more time in the community than he used to, faded back into the crowd as Melanie passed him. I hadn't been with her when she'd confronted him about the drugged tea, but I appreciated the effect.

"You finally got here," she said, close enough for me to take her hand and tug her up against me.

"I'm not late."

"The other Three have been here for about fifteen minutes."

"They were early."

Aunt Jean's arm was back in a cast. She'd removed her first with a sledgehammer to get to an itch and done enough damage she'd needed surgery. I couldn't hear what she was saying, but the Mattagami Elder standing beside her looked like he was about to make a run for it. Amanda looked distracted. Hardly surprising; her daughter had put out an audition call for a Christmas production of *The Grinch*, and she was mere weeks away from wrangling Whos. Eric was talking to

Bridget over the head of a sleeping T'geyer. The Flock had gathered up all the chunks of creature carbonized when Alice disassembled the Dark, packed them into bins, and stored them in Eric's basement. He wasn't thrilled about the sudden influx of preteens into his life but endured them for T'geyer's sake. I'd stopped worrying about them— Eric and Bridget, who were getting closer, not Eric and T'geyer, who were velcroed together. Bridget might not be the sharpest crayon in the box, but she was a grown woman, and if she wanted to attach herself to a single father with issues, it was none of my business. Maybe, just maybe, I'd been wrong about the whole thing.

"What were you and Alyx talking about?" I asked casually, arm around Melanie's waist. Alyx was gorgeous, okay? I was allowed to be a little insecure.

"Book stuff." She nuzzled the top of my head. "Copies of *Moon of the Turning Leaves* are in. Which is great timing, because we're almost finished with *The Sun Sword*."

We'd never found Mrs. Boman's body, so we buried her battered, bloodstained, and ancient copy of *Our Latin Legacy* under the monument. The school board, heavily influenced by Ms. Morton, who held the mine's purse strings, had offered Mrs. Boman's job to Melanie. Having been given permission to juice the curriculum, she now taught Canadian literature to all grades.

"And," she continued, "Alyx got in four copies of the second book: two for the store, two for the library."

Janet had been bloody but alive when Archive was unlocked. If she'd been dead, well, that was between her and the books. Unable to stay away, Miss Peggi, slightly translucent now, read the ghosts of children's books to a circle of kids every Saturday. The kids were enthralled. Not literally. I checked.

"Five-minute warning." Melanie gave me a quick kiss. "You should go join the others."

If I had to. "You should be speaking too."

"I was nearly an unwilling s-word. You were a hero. Go." She gave me a little shove, but it was Aunt Jean's expression that got me moving.

As I reached the monument, I felt my throat grow tight and my Voice Said, "CAN'T BLAME ME FOR TRYING." A few heads turned, but I'd made more random Observations in the last three months than I had in the previous eighteen, and people had grown used to me rasping out non sequiturs. The Dark seemed philosophical about its defeat, and the original Agreement was as strong as it had ever been.

And we couldn't blame it for trying. It wasn't like it was a tame eldritch entity.

Swallowing blood, I acknowledged that the only downside was the wear and tear on my voice. I'd started to sound like Bea Arthur. Melanie was streaming *The Golden Girls* in response.

TWENTY-SIX

Melanie

My mother called during the introductions. I'd let the last two calls go to voicemail, and as I, personally, was not a metaphysically powerful Conduit of the Dark, I wasn't going to risk the repercussions if I did it again.

"I'm a little busy, Mom." I mouthed *sorry* at my nearest neighbor and moved to a bit of a rise at the back of the crowd, where I could see the ceremony and Cassie could see me.

"Obviously, you're busy." Mom snorted. "Or you'd answer your phone. I wanted you to know that I checked, and there are no passenger trains heading anywhere near Lake Argen later this month or next month or any month."

"Just do what it says on the ticket we sent you."

"I'm not walking through a brick wall, Mel."

"Glad to hear it."

"Or sitting on a pile of silver ore in a boxcar."

"The ore goes in the other direction." And it wasn't in a boxcar, but why split hairs.

Another snort. "Is your rich girlfriend subverting the entire rail network just so I can come and visit you?"

"Yes. She wants me to be happy."

"I knew it!"

"I'm kidding, Mom."

I tuned out a short lecture on the distribution of wealth and tuned back in at a familiar name.

"At least old Mrs. Brayden paid you that ten grand before she fucked off into the woods after her grandson."

Devastated, Mrs. Brayden had driven to Lake Argen, staggered into the woods searching for Travis, fallen into a very deep crevasse, and smashed her skull into pieces on impact. I was unsurprisingly all right about Cassie Lying to the police. It was Arthur who'd ensured I got paid. I didn't know how he'd arranged it or who had actually paid me, but I cashed the check because I'd done the work.

"You're sure she wasn't taken out by a bear?" I could hear my mother's fingernails tapping against her phone. "As much as I want to see you both, I'm not entirely happy about the potential for bears."

A fringe of red-gold hair, barely visible behind the monument, flashed in the sunlight.

"I am absolutely positive it wasn't a bear," I said, as it started to snow.

TWENTY-SEVEN

Cassie

Shoving my gloved hands into my pockets, I pressed back against Melanie, sharing her heat as a November wind whipped along the train tracks. The mild weather we'd had at the first of the month for the memorial had turned cold and dismal. November was part of the Canadian identity, and no Agreement with dark, light, or medium-grey powers could improve it. "Why don't we wait in the station?" I whined.

"I want to be on the platform when my mother arrives." Melanie wrapped her arms around me. "It won't be long now."

"Gloria!"

I sighed. "Here we go again." Mr. Foster remained convinced that Melanie was his dead wife. Not content with random meetings, he'd knocked on our door one morning at about 3 AM, announcing he was there to pick Gloria up after work. While we waited for one of his grandkids to retrieve him, the three of us had a perfectly lucid conversation about the upcoming federal election and the shockingly high price of cotton underwear. At this point, we pretty much just rolled with it.

"Are you trying to catch your death?" he demanded as he shuffled up to us, face barely visible between hat and scarf, nose red and dripping slightly. "If you won't come inside, at least stand out of the wind."

"He has a point," I allowed.

Melanie huffed out a quiet laugh and released me, allowing Mr. Foster to tuck her hand into the crook of his elbow and draw her back against the side of the building. "I've warned my mother about you," she said.

"Your mother loves me, Gloria."

Melanie dimpled at him. "I'm sure she will."

"How is he?" I asked, as Mr. Foster's grandson Keith joined me.

"It wasn't pneumonia, but . . ." Keith shrugged. The shrug acknowledged his grandfather was ninety-eight, and even in Lake Argen that was old. "He insisted on meeting the train, and it was easier to bundle him up than to argue. Stephanie and the girls have been gone," he added as though the whole town didn't know that Stephanie and her adult daughters had just spent five days visiting wholesalers in Montreal. I mean, I liked clothes as much as the next person who preferred not to be naked, but I thought the excitement over Foster's—the store, not the family—getting new stock had gone a bit over the top.

"Melanie's mother's coming in on this train too," I told him.

"Yeah." He smiled, flashing his own set of dimples. "I heard."

The whole town knew that too.

A distant whistle turned my attention south, and when I turned back, Keith had shifted his attention to the open book in his hand. Janet had told me that one of the reasons she'd been thrilled when Alyx had opened the store was that Keith loved taking books out and hated returning them.

Still, there were worse things you could say about someone. Unless you were a librarian.

Another whistle, much closer, and when I leaned out, I could see green lights to the north and an approaching headlight to the south. A minute later, I grabbed a handful of Keith's jacket and tugged him away from the platform edge as the train rattled into the station. No point in Telling him to move; he wouldn't have heard me.

"Boy'd lose his head if it wasn't attached," Mr. Foster muttered as he joined us.

Boy was my father's age, but sure.

Melanie held my hand a little too tightly. "Ready to meet my mother?"

"I think the question should be is your mother ready to meet your husband."

"Don't worry, Gloria." Mr. Foster reached past me to pat Melanie's arm. "Like I said, your mother loves me."

The train sighed . . .

"Air brakes," Melanie said, aware of what I was thinking.

"I can show you a universe in a linen closet. Who's to say the train isn't sighing?"

"Fair."

. . . and the doors opened. There was a bit of a scrum as Keith's sister and nieces emerged first, the platform suddenly seething with tall blonde women. Liz and Meg were friends of mine, not super close but we'd shared classrooms for twelve years, so I got pulled into the greetings, and I pulled in Melanie while old Mr. Foster declared they'd sell polyester socks over his dead body.

Then things calmed and I heard Melanie say, "Hey, Mom."

We'd FaceTimed—Melanie, me, and Dorothy Solvich—but live, she was so much more . . . alive. She bounced off the train, a backpack in one hand, a patched duffle bag in the other, eyes shining, smile wonderfully familiar. First she hugged Melanie, said something I couldn't hear, then she turned to me.

She hugged with her whole body. We were the same height, although I'd have been taller if not for the thick soles on her boots. "Cassie, Cassie, Cassie! What do you know about the surprisingly tasty food and actually drinkable coffee they served on the train?"

"Dorothy, Dorothy, Dorothy!" I pulled back and grinned. "Try to remember, I'm rich."

"Rich off the back of the working classes."

"Eat me."

We hugged again. I could hear Melanie laughing.

Then I heard Stephanie snap, "You could carry a suitcase if you'd put the book down!"

The three of us turned to see her glaring at her brother, attempting to pull the book out of his hands.

"This is a first-edition Marrowvale!" Keith yanked it back, but Stephanie hung on.

"And this is a suitcase no one's carrying!"

Dorothy released us and walked, head cocked, toward the argument. She stopped an arm's length away and stared. "Keith?"

Keith's eyes widened. He released his grip on the book and Stephanie staggered backward. "Dot?"

Turning to face us, Dorothy held out her hand. "Mel, come here. I want you to meet your father."

ACKNOWLEDGMENTS

Change is difficult after so many comfortable years without it and I'd like to thank the people at Astra, most especially Navah Wolfe and Joshua Starr, for making it a positive experience.

And thanks to Joshua Bilmes, my agent, who reminded me that times have changed and my pitch needed adjusting if I wanted to get it over the plate. He was absolutely right—as he has been innumerable times in the past.

I'd also like to acknowledge that *Direct Descendant* owes a certain amount to Jordan L. Hawk's *Widdershins* series, my comfort read throughout the pandemic. Except book two. Book two is not comforting. Book two is terrifying. But it's supposed to be, so that's okay.